W9-CUZ-485

BGSU LIBRARY
DISCARD

HARD-BOILED DAMES

HARD-BOILED DAMES

Stories Featuring Women Detectives,
Reporters, Adventurers, and Criminals
From the Pulp Fiction Magazines of the
1930s

Edited and with an introduction by
BERNARD A. DREW

Preface by
MARCIA MULLER

St. Martin's Press
New York

JEROME LIBRARY-BOWLING GREEN STATE UNIVERSITY

Introduction copyright © 1986 Bernard A. Drew

Preface copyright © 1986 Marcia Muller

"Riddle in Silk" by Theodore Tinsley, *Crime Busters,* December 1938. Copyright © 1938 Street & Smith Publications Inc., renewed 1966 The Condé Nast Publications Inc. Used with permission Condé Nast and Mary White Tinsley.

"Cash or Credit" by D. B. McCandless, *Detective Fiction Weekly,* September 18, 1937. Copyright © 1937 Blazing Publications Inc. (*) All rights reserved. Reprinted by special arrangement with Mystery Writers of America Inc.

"The Deadly Orchid" by T. T. Flynn, *Detective Fiction Weekly,* April 15, 1933. Copyright © 1933 Blazing Publications Inc. (*) All rights reserved. Reprinted by special arrangement with Mystery Writers of America Inc.

"Hit the Baby" by Roswell Brown, *The Shadow Magazine,* February 15, 1936. Copyright © 1936 Street & Smith Publications Inc., renewed 1964 The Condé Nast Publications Inc. Used with permission Condé Nast and Jean Francis Webb.

"Flowers for Violet" by Cleve F. Adams, *Clues Detective Stories,* May 1936. Copyright © 1936 Street & Smith Publications Inc., renewed 1964 The Condé Nast Publications Inc. Used with permission Condé Nast.

Permissions continued on page 331

HARD-BOILED DAMES. Copyright © 1986 by Bernard A. Drew. All rights reserved. Printed in the United States of America. No part of this book may be used or reproduced in any manner whatsoever without written permission except in the case of brief quotations embodied in critical articles or reviews. For information, address St. Martin's Press, 175 Fifth Avenue, New York, N.Y. 10010.

Library of Congress Cataloging in Publication Data

Hard-boiled dames.

1. Detective and mystery stories, American.
2. Women—Fiction. 3. American fiction—20th century.
I. Drew, Bernard A. (Bernard Alger), 1950–
PS648.D4H37   1986   813'.0872'08352042   86-3671
ISBN 0-312-36188-2

First Edition

10 9 8 7 6 5 4 3 2 1

CONTENTS

ACKNOWLEDGMENTS

The following people in various ways helped in the compilation of this anthology. Thanks. Judson Philips, Walter B. Gibson, William R. Cox, Harry Steeger, Robert Weinberg, Will Murray, Robert Sampson, Bill Blackbeard, Daniel Gobbett, Albert Melle, Joel Frieman, William P. Rayner, George Witte, Marcia Muller, Leonard and Clara Archambault, Warren and Jennie Drew, Donna and Jessie Drew.

PREFACE
by Marcia Muller

During the past couple of years, the popular press has re-
peatedly brought us the happy news that the mystery novel
is alive and well. Moreover, these bearers of glad tidings tell
us, the mystery featuring the strong contemporary woman is
in particularly robust health. The media treat this revelation
as if it were something astonishing and unprecedented—
rather on the order of having a woman candidate for Vice
President.

Is it true that the proliferation of these supposed super-
women in suspense fiction is a startling modern-day phe-
nomenon? In part it is—but only in part.

The abundance in contemporary mystery novels of tal-
ented, gutsy, and often charmingly idiosyncratic female
sleuths is a fact that can't be denied. Many of them work in
official capacities, such as Lillian O'Donnell's Norah
Mulcahaney of the New York Police Department and, on the
other coast, Lesley Egan's Delia Riordan of the Glendale, California, P.D. In a semi-official capacity, private investigators
Kinsey Millhone (Sue Grafton's Southern California sleuth),
V. I. Warshawski (Sara Paretsky's Chicago-based operator),
and Sharon McCone (my own character, who lives in San
Francisco) prowl the mean streets as fearlessly as their male
counterparts. Walter Wager's former CIA-agent-turned-pri-
vate detective, Alison Gordon, is featured in three high-tech
thrillers.

Amateur detectives in no way take a back seat to these professionals—and their callings when they're not caught up in crime are varied indeed. Amanda Cross's erudite mysteries feature a college professor, Kate Fansler; Charlotte McLeod's Sarah Kelling is a former Boston society matron who now takes in boarders; Vejay Haskell, Susan Dunlap's creation, is a Pacific Gas & Electric Company meter reader; Julie Smith's Rebecca Schwartz is an attorney whose clients have an unusually high mortality rate; and Clarissa Watson's Persis Willum runs an art gallery. Even the traditional old-lady sleuth has been updated for the 1980s: Richard Barth's Margaret Binton is an urban dweller with interests far more significant than knitting.

Such a lineup (and there are many more) would tend to prove the claim that the contemporary female sleuth is enjoying her Golden Age. But is this really something *new?*

When one considers the stories presented in this anthology, the answer to that question is a resounding "no." Although the courageous, independent female sleuth may have, for whatever reasons, gone somewhat out of fashion in the suspense fiction of the 1950s and '60s, she was very much in evidence in the pulp magazines of the '30s and '40s. No mere male's sidekick, she often ran her own investigative firm, such as Carrie Cashin's Cash and Carry Detective Agency, where Theodore Tinsley's heroine employed a male "front" because "most clients had no faith in the ability of girl detectives." (Shades of *Remington Steele.*) My own personal favorite, Cleve F. Adams's elephantine Violet McDade, preferred to employ other females—and bullied them in the same manner as would an equally tough-talking male. Hard molls with soft hearts—such as Perry Paul's Dizzy Malone and C. B. Yorke's Queen Sue—often graced the pages of the pulps. The Domino Lady, created by Lars Anderson, was a Robin Hood in silken sheath. And even though the women in Frederick Nebel's Cardigan stories were mere employees of the Cosmos

Agency, they were able to help out the boss in forthright and startling ways.

What this diverse group of women had in common—and the heritage they have left their present-day sisters—is the ability to stand alone and face the world on terms that they themselves defined. Whatever their callings, however they became embroiled in crime, they confronted adversity with grit and determination—and (no pun intended) they always got their man. These "hard-boiled dames," we contemporary writers have found, are an inspiring act to follow. And it's a delight to finally have these entertaining stories collected in one volume.

INTRODUCTION
by Bernard A. Drew

Tough, gun-toting fictional private eyes abound in the 1980s, and a modest number of them wear lipstick. Sara Paretsky's V. I. Warshawski has tracked down sabotage in the Great Lakes shipping industry. Marcia Muller's Sharon McCone has uncovered huge fencing operations. Walter Wager's Alison B. Gordon has tangled with Las Vegas hit men, while Sue Grafton's Kinsey Millhone has solved eight-year-old murders.

This wave of women P. I.'s has evolved naturally in the flourishing mystery-novel genre, but it is rooted in an earlier generation of "hard-boiled dames" who appeared in story series in the pulp fiction magazines of the 1930s. Theodore Tinsley's Carrie Cashin headed her own agency, fifty years ago. Cleve F. Adams's Violet McDade tossed gangsters around left and right, and Whitman Chambers's Katie Blayne used her strong news nose to solve arson and other crimes, in the old pulp stories.

In the adventure fiction category today, Peter O'Donnell's dynamic Modesty Blaise is involved in escapades all over the globe; decades earlier, Hulbert Footner's elegant Rosita Storey flirted with international intrigue in the pages of pulp magazines.

Yet to be duplicated by contemporary writers are the pulp magazine series that spotlighted the darker activities of gun molls and crooks, such as C. B. Yorke's Queen Sue Carlton or Perry Paul's Dizzy Malone. But it may only be a matter of time.

The pulps were enormously popular in this country in the early half of the century. Evolving from the slim dime-novel format, they were printed on cheap, untrimmed pulpwood paper. As many as 200 titles were on sale at a time during their heyday. Selling for ten to twenty-five cents, they were eagerly purchased by an estimated 30 million readers.

The pulps packed 128 pages or so of excitement inside colorful, often garish painted covers. These thrills-and-action magazines offered an array of yarns about cowboys, quarterbacks and air aces, space explorers and bug-eyed creatures, ugly villains, cooing heroines, and daring heroes. There was something for everyone.

Pulp readers came from all walks of life. "Harry S. Truman and Al Capone were each on the subscription list at Popular (Publications) at about the same time," claims Henry Steeger, a former pulp magazine publisher, "because I remember we remarked to some advertisers that we covered the entire gamut from Presidents to gangsters."

"The pulps in a way are a misnomer," says the dean of the old-time storytellers, Walter B. Gibson. As "Maxwell Grant," he churned out the incredible adventures of The Shadow. "It was really the writers who called them pulps, to separate them from the slicks, the quality magazines such as *The Saturday Evening Post* and *Colliers.* I don't think the public ever thought of them that way . . . sometimes they just referred to *Fight Story, War Aces,* and everything of that sort as trash."

While the magazines had an early reputation for printing stories with melodramatic plots and purple prose, they in fact produced a number of fine craftsmen, many of whom went on to write for hardcover book publishers. Among these were Tennessee Williams, MacKinley Kantor, Rex Stout, John D. McDonald, Erle Stanley Gardner, Raymond

Chandler, Dashiell Hammett, Louis L'Amour, Max Brand, and Edgar Rice Burroughs.

The pulps were a breaking-in point for young writers, and if they were prolific enough, it could become a steady occupation. "The basic pay rate was a penny a word," recalls Judson Philips, who now writes mysteries under his own name and as "Hugh Pentecost." "But I got up to five or six cents. I did an awful lot of work. My average output was forty thousand to fifty thousand words a month. We were living in clover, for the economic times."

The hard-boiled school of detective fiction originated in the pulps, in the pages of *Black Mask* magazine. The publication was established by H. L. Mencken and George Jean Nathan in 1920 to stave off the debt incurred by their more genteel publication, *The Smart Set.* After they sold *Black Mask,* and during George Sutton Jr.'s tenure as editor, from 1922 to '34, it began to carry Carroll John Daly's smashing Race Williams yarns—the first hard-boiled mysteries. Soon Hammett's Continental Op cases appeared. These and other stories were a sharp contrast to the tamer, English school of crime puzzle fiction then dominant, and they caught the fancy of Prohibition-era readers.

Under editor Joseph T. Shaw, from 1929 to '36, *Black Mask* became a showcase for city-oriented, tough-guy fiction with such authors as Gardner, Chandler, Frank Gruber, George Harmon Coxe, Raoul Whitfield, and Cornell Woolrich.

Black Mask was a male stronghold. E. R. Hagemann's *A Comprehensive Index to Black Mask, 1920–1952* shows it had no women series characters in its thirty-one-year history. And this is despite having a woman editor in its later years (Fanny Elsworth from 1936 to '40) and occasional women writers (such as Katherine Brocklebank and Agatha Christie). *Black Mask* is not represented in this anthology, though many of its writers are; their women series characters appeared in the competitors and imitators of the day.

A trio of magazines nipped at *Black Mask*'s heels during the 1930s. *Detective Story Magazine* favored the classical clued detective tale and dandy rogues. *Dime Detective Magazine* took the private op theme into dark, menacing realms. And *Detective Fiction Weekly* carried dozens of series, some serious, some nutsy, all lively.

Series characters were the prime meat of the marketplace. "Of course we all had running characters, series characters," says William R. Cox, a mystery, Western, and sports novelist today. "They assured us of work. I had as many as three running in *Blue Book* at one time, The Neighborhood stories of Murphy the Cop, the Willie Boulders, the Lucky Youngs. In pulp, I had so many I can't remember them all. . . ."

What might be labeled the "companion tradition" in American literature dates from James Fenimore Cooper's Leatherstocking Tales of the 1820s, in which the hero Hawkeye is accompanied on his adventures by Chingachgook, a staunch male of another race. Similarly, Mark Twain's Huckleberry Finn had his black friend Jim, and Herman Melville's Ishmael found companionship in the savage Queequeg.

Stretching the archetype slightly, companions came to include a male of another sex.

Women were regularly featured as secondary characters in popular fiction printed in the American dime novels. As Robert Sampson observes in *Yesterday's Faces*, "It was in the dime novel that really competent feminine characters appeared. Calamity Jane and Annie Oakley (freely romanticized from the originals) appeared as self-sufficient women holding their own in a tough country. Stella Fosdick and Arietta Murdock continued the trend in the post-1900 Western dime novels. At about the same time, as the detective action story focused on the city, additional, strongly characterized, secondary feminine characters were appearing—

particularly in the Nick Carter series, which was replete with competent women on both sides of the law."

Marie LaSalle stands out as an energetic secondary character in Frank L. Packard's Jimmy Dale series, which appeared in *The People's Magazine* beginning in 1914. Dale fought crime disguised as The Grey Seal. Not to be outdone, Marie also adopted a persona, two in fact. She was both the wizened Silver Mag and the deadly Tocsin.

Arabia Marston was typical of the lady criminals of the 1910s era. A smuggler, she matched wits with Jack Kelly of the Secret Service in Victor Maxwell's stories in *The Popular Magazine.*

When the pulp magazines proliferated in the 1920s, and the hero titles such as *Doc Savage* and *The Spider* began in the 1930s, there were invariably women companions.

This female sidekick in the pulp mysteries and hero adventures was often a patient girlfriend waiting for the hero to get over his crime-fighting kick and settle down to raise a family. Typical are Sue McEwen in the Moon Man series in *10 Detective Aces*, Dolores Colquitt in the Jim Anthony tales in *Super Detective*, and Muriel Havens in *The Phantom Detective* yarns.

Or she was a full-fledged member of the hero's band, a secretary or operative. Notable examples are Nellie Grey in *The Avenger*, Patricia Seaward in the Cardigan stories in *Dime Detective*, and Trixie Meehan in the Mike Harris cases in *Detective Fiction Weekly.*

"A female leading character did have as large an audience as a male," says Steeger, "provided the activities in which she was engaged would appeal to a male reader. When we first began to add females to the cast of characters, we found out, much to our surprise, that the circulation did not diminish any. If anything, it went up higher.

"The pulp editors did not do much to regulate the appearance of women characters," he continues. "Quite frequently they did ask an author to put female characters in the story, but generally speaking, the habit of having only male characters was too ingrained in the writing habits of the authors to make them change their accustomed ways. In other words, we didn't pay too much attention to women characters except to ask now and then that they be put into stories."

Readers weren't always tolerant. "Women weren't particularly popular in *The Shadow*," says Gibson. "The Shadow was knocking down so much crime, cleaning up the crooks and so forth, that women were comparatively subsidiary. I would bring them into the stories as needed. . . . When I put Margo Lane into the stories (she was first a character on the popular radio program), a lot of readers began to scream. In fact, a lot of them said she was a troublemaker. That's true, that was the comic relief. . . ."

The sheer volume of material printed in the mystery pulps favored the use of women characters in much the way Westerns would throw in a Canadian Mountie story to relieve the sameness of its cowboy-and-Indian tales; readers numbed to a steady diet of hard-hitting male detectives and thug-thumping male cops could thus take refuge in a lead-spitting feminine story.

Strong women characters are to be found in all the pulp genres: Señorita Scorpion in the Westerns, Barbe Pivet in the aviation titles, Sheena in the jungle pulps, Jirel of Joiry in science fiction magazines.

One of the first female sleuths in mainstream mystery fiction was W. S. Hayward's Mrs. Pascal, who appeared in a novel in 1861, according to Patricia Craig and Mary Cadogan in *The Lady Investigates.* Wilkie Collins, Hal Hurst, and other writers produced Victorian mysteries with women protagonists.

Women in detective fiction at the turn of the century, observes Howard Haycraft in *Murder for Pleasure,* were frequently nosy spinsters, "women who gum up the plot" and "heroines who wander around attics alone."

Some of the dowagers turned up in the pulps. Miss

Rachel, D. B. Olson's (Dolores Hitchens's) series character, could be found in *Detective Story Magazine,* and Miss Marple, Christie's sleuth, appeared in the same publication.

"In the succeeding years," says Michele B. Slung in *Crime on Her Mind,* "women detectives became a regular and accepted part of the genre. . . . Besides the plethora of elderly and middle-aged snoops mentioned earlier as coming to the forefront in the Thirties, a number of younger women also found themselves involved with crime during this period."

The most dramatic change came in the pulps, where women detectives were given star billing in their own series.

And this leads us to the contents of this anthology: eleven stories featuring robust women detectives, reporters, and crooks, and four stories in which women characters play second fiddle, but with great dexterity, to male series characters. They represent the best of the pulps.

Theodore Tinsley's Carrie Cashin leads these intelligent, physical, female private eyes. Appearing in thirty-eight stories in *Crime Busters* and, later, *Mystery Magazine,* she owns her own agency but employs a rugged male named Aleck to front for her. How many clients, after all, would put their trust in a woman?

Two less glamorous women—the truth is, they're overweight and often grouchy—also head agencies. They are D. B. McCandless's Sarah Watson and Cleve F. Adams's Violet McDade. Watson employs Ben Todd to do legwork in the series published in *Detective Fiction Weekly.* McDade has pretty Nevada Alvarado as an operative in her stories in *Clues Detective Magazine.*

Roswell Brown's Grace Culver is an able member of Big Tim Noonan's detective agency in a series of twenty stories in *The Shadow* magazine. "Redsie," as she is known, packs a pistol in her garter holster.

Two women characters are included here who don't have their own series, but deserve them. Trixie Meehan frequently saves the bacon for detective Mike Harris in the stories written by T. T. Flynn, while Patricia Seaward provides support for Frederick Nebel's ace private eye, Cardigan. A third series, not represented in this anthology, is reminiscent of Stout's Nero Wolfe. In it, professorial I. V. Frost is a cerebral puzzle solver who employs leggy Jean Moray to do his running. Donald Wandrei penned the tales for *Clues Detective Magazine.*

Reporters are a vigorous subcategory of tough-guy crime fiction. The best of the lot is Coxe's "Flashgun" Casey from *Black Mask.* On the distaff side, and included in this book, are Katie Blayne, who works the police beat for *The Sun* in Whitman Chambers's series for *Detective Fiction Weekly,* and Dinah Mason, both love interest and working companion in the Daffy Dill tales Richard Sale wrote for the same magazine.

Ellen Patrick is the ultimate crime fighter, molded after The Shadow. As The Domino Lady, Lars Anderson's heroine from *Saucy Romantic Adventures* has confronted society blackmailers, horse-race fixers, and even the dreaded Black Legion.

Many female characters worked the darker side of the law. Judson P. Philips's Ivy Trask is a popular stage actress and skilled thief in the *Detective Fiction Weekly* series.

At the height of the gangster era, pulp titles capitalized on the nation's headlines. C. B. Yorke created a daring female hoodlum in the Queen Sue Carlton series for *Gangster Stories,* while Perry Paul came up with Dizzy Malone, a denizen of Hell's Kitchen, for *Gun Molls Magazine.*

Eugene Thomas's Vivian Legrand, The Lady from Hell, was fond of foreign intrigue. She was first featured in what was said to be a series of true stories in *Detective Fiction Weekly.* She proved so popular that her adventures were continued without pretense to truthfulness.

Another world adventurer is Rosita Storey, one of the best known of the pulp fiction women in this volume. Hulbert

Footner's character appeared in *Argosy* and also in six books.

The pulps disappeared in the late 1940s, victims of wartime paper shortages and the advent of the paperback novel and television.

The hard-boiled school of detective fiction has survived the pulps and is thriving today. The "hard-boiled dames" who flew from the creative typewriters of male writers in the 1930s have found new strength in series often coming—appropriately enough—from women writers.

Here's a taste of the past, to enable a greater appreciation of the present.

CARRIE CASHIN

The huge magazine publisher Street & Smith, enjoying great success with its single-character titles *The Shadow* and *Doc Savage,* in 1937 launched *Crime Busters.* It was intended as a breeder for new hero titles and featured an array of series characters by its regular stable of writers: Maxwell Grant's Norgil the Magician, W. T. Ballard's Red Drake, Lester Dent's Gadget Man, and Theodore Tinsley's Carrie Cashin.

Crime Busters, retitled *Mystery Magazine* in 1943, ran for fifty issues, and Carrie appeared in all but twelve. As pulp historian Will Murray observes in an article in the fan publication *Xenophile,* Carrie "might have had a chance in a magazine of her own, but Street & Smith never went ahead with that idea."

The magazine's editors remained cautious about women. Says an editorial in the December 1938 *Crime Busters:* "Usually women detectives are not favorites with men readers; that's why you see so few women detectives featured in mystery stories. We have been fortunate in the character of Carrie Cashin, probably the most popular woman detective in fiction today. Originally used as a test as to whether our men readers would like the character, we find that they do—very much so! Of course, the manner in which Theodore Tinsley describes the adventures of shapely Carrie probably has a lot to do with this great popularity. . . ."

Tinsley (1894–1979) left teaching and insurance sales to

pursue writing as a career. He sold to *Action Stories* and *Wings* and had twenty-six stories in *Black Mask,* many featuring Broadway columnist Jerry Tracy. He wrote hundreds of stories for Street & Smith, including twenty-eight Shadow adventures under the "Maxwell Grant" pseudonym. He later moved on to radio scripting and worked for the Office of War Information. He was a speechwriter for General Omar Bradley.

Carrie Cashin appears in this anthology in the story "Riddle in Silk," from *Crime Busters'* December 1938 issue.

RIDDLE IN SILK

A new Carrie Cashin Novelette

By Theodore Tinsley

CHAPTER I.

DEAD ON ARRIVAL.

THE girl parted the blue velvet drapes of the doorway and tiptoed silently into an empty living room.

She looked very pretty and very French. A maid's lacy cap was perched atop her dark hair. Her lips were vivid scarlet. But her face was dead-white—chalky with terror.

Except for the maid's frightened breathing and the beat of rain against the curtained windows, the house was deathly quiet. There was a telephone on a desk near the wall. The maid unhooked it gently. Her whisper was barely audible.

"Queeeck! Important! I want a policeman!"

There was no answer. All she could hear was the pulse of blood in her listening ear. Her rigid glance peered at the wall beneath the desk.

The telephone wire was cut!

The maid had barely realized it, when a faint click sounded behind the velvet drapes of the doorway. The room was plunged into total darkness. Through that darkness came the swift thuds of unshod feet.

The maid's mouth flew open to emit a scream.

Her cry was never uttered. A hand tightened murderously on her throat. The pale glimmer of a knife lifted in the darkness. The blade was long and thin. It plunged into the maid's body, and the point pierced her heart.

For a moment, there was silence. Then the dangling telephone clicked back on its empty cradle. A chair moved. A gasp of exertion indicated that the killer had picked up the crumpled victim. The slow thud of stockinged feet retreated behind the velvet doorway drapes.

Then ceiling lights glowed into sudden brilliance.

The room was empty. There were no ugly hints of struggle or death. An overturned chair had been set neatly back on its legs. The telephone was in its accustomed place. A handkerchief pressed over the maid's wound had stanched the drip of her blood.

Rain pelted against the window-panes with a dreary, wet sound. The hands of a carved mantel clock pointed to the time. It was 6:25 in the evening.

FIFTY minutes later—at exactly 7:15—Carrie Cashin and her broad-shouldered assistant, Aleck, stood in the same living room, listening to a man and a woman dressed in formal evening clothes.

"Thank God you've come!" the man said.

Gray-haired, deep-voiced, the man radiated wealth and distinction. His name was Ralph Vallon. He was the president of the Seacoast Air Line,

The maid's mouth flew open to emit a scream. . . .

and uncle of the girl who stood tremulously beside him.

Carrie Cashin thought that Dora Vallon was one of the most attractive blondes she had ever seen. The girl's excitement merely intensified her beauty. Her evening gown could have come from no place but Paris. It clung like a smooth sheath of metallic silver over slim hips and a full, rounded bosom.

Neither Dora nor her uncle paid much attention to Carrie Cashin. She looked like a demure, brown-eyed stenographer in a tailored jacket and tweed skirt. She helped out the illusion by producing a pencil and a notebook. She was used to big, broad-shouldered Aleck posing as the head of the Cash and Carry Detective Agency. It was her own idea. Most clients had no faith in the ability of girl detectives. They had no idea that "Cash and Carry" was an amusing reversal of Carrie Cashin's own name.

"You've got to find that thieving French maid—and recover the silk stockings she stole," Vallon told

Aleck jerkily. "They may mean the difference between peace and war in Europe—if they're sold to a certain air power on the Continent."

It was a strange statement; but Vallon had already disclosed matters even stranger. The silk stockings had come to him from a trusted pilot of the Seacoast Air Line. The pilot's name was Traynor. He had been engaged in secret experimentation for Vallon with long-range television photography in the lonely air lanes above the Caribbean.

The idea, Vallon explained hurriedly, was to take pictures from the air and transmit them by television. The feat was already possible over short distances—but Traynor was seeking a technique to send picture images a thousand miles!

"You mean," Aleck said slowly, "that a robot plane, flying over enemy territory, could map their locations from the air and reproduce the photos simultaneously in our own army headquarters?"

"Exactly. And Traynor did it! What his new method is, God only knows. The televised pictures came over the air to my New York office from a location somewhere off the coast of Cuba. Then—they stopped abruptly! That was all I knew until I got the pair of silk stockings from Havana."

His voice trembled.

"There was a note with the package in Traynor's handwriting. He said to guard the stockings with my life until he could explain by registered letter. His plane was seen leaving Havana harbor that night. It was never seen again. Traynor perished somewhere in the ocean —killed, I believe, by agents of a certain warlike power."

"Why didn't you test the stockings while you had them?" Aleck asked.

"They were gossamer silk. I was afraid a test might destroy them, ruin any message they contained. And I still hoped to receive the registered letter Traynor's note said he had mailed. Two swift burglary attempts have since been made at my home. So I took the stockings to my niece, figuring no one would suspect her. I told her to wear them whenever she left the house. That's why tonight, when I learned she had been drugged and the stockings stolen——"

"Suppose you tell me about the theft, Miss Vallon," Aleck interrupted.

DORA'S story was brief. She had dressed for dinner without the help of her maid, Marie. Marie had pleaded illness and was upstairs. Having finished dressing, Dora Vallon took a drink of iced water from her thermos jug on the bedroom table. Almost instantly, she became faint. She tried to call for help, staggered toward her bed, fell unconscious. When she recovered her senses she found that her feet were bare! Some one had removed her evening slippers and peeled off the silk stockings.

RIDDLE IN SILK

The maid was the first person Dora thought of. Frantic, she searched the house; but Marie was gone. The telephone wire was cut. It was then that Dora heard the front bell. It was her uncle, arriving promptly at seven for his dinner engagement.

Carrie Cashin's pencil began to tap idly against the cover of her steno's notebook. The tapping was in Morse Code. Hearing it, Aleck flushed. Dora's silver evening gown was short enough to expose her ankle and instep. Her legs were smoothly stockinged.

"I thought you said you were barefooted?"

"I was," she said, "when uncle arrived." There was a faint edge to her voice. "Naturally, I put on another pair while uncle went out to telephone your agency."

"*All* of your stockings weren't stolen?"

"No. Just the pair I was wearing when I collapsed."

Carrie's brown eyes were glancing unobtrusively about the room. She saw massive furniture, an imported rug, tasteful drapes. Rain was still pelting the curtained windows.

Suddenly, Carrie's hand rose sleepily to her mouth as if to cover a yawn. It was instinctive camouflage on the part of a girl trained to hide her emotions. The mouth that gaped behind her polite palm was wide with astonishment.

She had seen a human eye peering at her.

It vanished instantly. The lower corner of the window drape no longer bulged slightly where the eye had been. But Carrie knew that a watchful prowler was lurking in the rain outside the ground-floor living room.

Aleck was the only one in the room who saw Carrie deliberately

break the point of her pencil. He was surprised, but he took the signal at once. He murmured something that gave Carrie an excuse to leave the room.

The moment she was out of sight, her lazy indifference vanished. Darting across the hall, she entered a dark sitting room on the other side of the house. The window lifted without noise. Carrie's slippers made no sound as she dropped to the wet turf below.

THE house was an old-fashioned dwelling, set back from the sidewalk behind a grilled fence. Shrubbery dotted the dark lawn that surrounded the house. With noiseless haste, Carrie glided swiftly toward the rear.

A tug at her tweed skirt disclosed the gleam of an automatic pistol in a special garter holster. The weapon looked almost like a toy. But its stub-nosed barrel was a deadly bullet mill—especially at close quarters.

Taking advantage of the cover afforded by rain and darkness, Carrie was able to spy on the intruder outside the partly opened window of the living room.

It was a man. He had dropped to his haunches in the dark shadow beneath the outer sill. He was unexpectedly good-looking, with wide shoulders and a young, clean-shaven face.

His eyes, however, were furtive. He was holding close to his bent body a weapon that looked like a nickel-plated revolver.

Carrie crept silently across the dark rain-swept turf. The noise of the storm blotted out the faint squishy sounds of Carrie's creeping knees. The prowler heard nothing. He was warned of danger by some nervous sixth sense.

His whirl was lightning swift. The gun pointed toward Carrie, But before he could squeeze the trigger, Carrie was plunging forward. Her head rammed into the man's stomach with a force that blew a gasping "Ooof!" from him.

They crashed against the house and rebounded in a staggering embrace. Breathless, the man tried to smash his gun against Carrie's temple. He was off balance. The blow thudded against her thick mop of chestnut curls.

It gave Carrie an opportunity to wriggle desperately behind her assailant. Both arms circled his ribs. One hand tightened on his gun wrist; the other slid to the hollow of his elbow, with Carrie's thumb digging like an anchor opposite her four clamped fingers.

She was an adept at jujitsu. The most famous Japanese instructor in New York had spent many patient hours teaching Carrie the art of applying leverage against brute strength.

The man's body doubled as his arm was relentlessly stiffened. He tried to turn to ease the agonized pressure. but Carrie's hooked leg held him motionless. It was more than a human being could stand. He uttered a scream of agony and the revolver dropped from his fingers.

"Drag him inside, Aleck!" Carrie panted. "He's lost his gun!"

Aleck had heard that shrill scream from outside the window. He was leaning out, his face grim with astonishment. He grabbed the prisoner by the armpits and hauled him athwart the window sill. A swift clutch at a shoulder and the seat of his pants, and Aleck tossed him to the living-room floor like a butcher handling a quarter of beef.

CHAPTER II.
SLEUTH MEETS MAN.

BY the time the prisoner swayed to his feet, Aleck had a gun on him. Carrie Cashin squirmed through the window with a blur of silken legs.

"Who the devil is he?" Aleck asked her.

"I don't know."

"I'll make him talk," Aleck growled.

"I want to talk!" the young man said eagerly. "You're a detective, aren't you?"

There was a sudden cry of excitement from Dora Vallon as she stared at the captive. Her quickly indrawn breath tightened her silver evening gown over the rounded fullness of her bosom.

"I know him now! He's been here several times to visit my maid. His name is John Cooney. He helped Marie steal those silk stockings! He's her boy-friend—her accomplice!"

"Accomplice, my eye!" Cooney said. "Marie and I are engaged to be married. She's on the level and so am I. If this blond hophead says that Marie stole something, she's lying. She's trying to cover up something."

"Hophead?" Aleck snapped.

"That's what she is. Marie was scared to death of her. She used to grab Marie by the hair and bat her around when she was hungry for drugs. Marie said this Vallon woman kept a jug of water in her bedroom to dissolve the white tablets when she——"

"That's a contemptible lie!" Dora Vallon choked. "The—the tablets I take are for high blood pressure. This lying thug and his crooked French——"

Cooney leaped wrathfully forward at the insulting epithet, but Aleck's gun halted him.

"Take it easy, Cooney! You were caught with a loaded gun. You tried to shoot when you were cornered and——"

"I thought your partner was the Vallon woman."

"What were you doing out there?"

"I was trying to find out what had happened to Marie. She was supposed to meet me tonight. She never showed up. I think Dora Vallon killed her."

"Why?"

"Astrology, for one thing. Marie and I both believe in it. She had her horoscope cast last week. It warned her that her life was in danger unless she changed the locality where she was living. Her birth sign is Pisces, you understand, and she——"

Aleck interrupted Cooney's eager astrology lore with a faint smile.

"Any other reason for accusing Miss Vallon of murder?"

"Plenty. Marie found out Dora was taking dope. She threatened to expose her to her uncle if there was any more hair-pulling stuff. Honest, the woman was like a tigress! She told Marie that if she squealed to her uncle and caused him to cut off her allowance, she'd stick a knife into her! I told Marie to pack her bag; that I'd meet her tonight at the back door. I was going to take her to my aunt's house to live until we could get married. She never came out."

"Lies, all lies," Dora Vallon said harshly.

She looked like a golden-haired statue in her gleaming evening gown. Her face was drained of color. Her hands were clenched tightly at her sides. Ralph Vallon patted her bare shoulder.

"Don't worry," he told her. "I'm not impressed by the clumsy falsehoods of a trapped gunman. We'll hold him here in custody until we can find out more fully——"

"You'll hold nobody!" Cooney growled. "You're not going to shut my mouth while you and your niece cover up a murder! If I'm guilty of a crime, I'll take jail. Call in the cops! Is that fair—or not?"

He turned pleadingly toward Aleck. Puzzled by the queer turn the case was taking, Aleck looked at Carrie. But her pretty face was inscrutable. She was apparently taking no part in the grim discussion. She was moving about the room in a sort of aimless scrutiny of the furniture.

"You want the police, Mr. Vallon?" Aleck asked.

"No! I hired you as a confidential agent to recover a pair of silk stockings. I want neither police nor publicity."

CARRIE CASHIN could hear the angry rumble of his voice as she continued her personal investigation of the room. She dropped to her knees at the spot where the telephone wire had been cut. She crawled under the desk and examined the rug. There were no marks on the rug or wall. But the tiny dot of light from Carrie's lead-pencil flashlight showed her something that brought a quick glint to her eyes.

She was staring at a brownish smear on the insulating wrapping of the telephone wire. It looked like dried blood.

Carrie's lips tightened. Suppose the frightened Marie had really been attacked! She'd have rushed to the phone to call for help. A slash at the telephone wire—a quick thrust with the same knife, might have dropped the maid in a dead huddle before the desk. If the knife was a thin-bladed one, there would not be much hemorrhage; perhaps barely enough blood to be soaked up in a handkerchief. But if a nervous killer had brushed the wet handkerchief against the phone wire beneath the desk——

Carrie rose to her feet. She stared at the dark velvet curtain that screened the doorway of the living room. A few quick strides, and she was examining the heavy material at a spot somewhat higher than the level of her own shoulders. It was a spot more nearly approximating the height of Ralph Vallon—or his tall, full-bosomed niece in the silver evening gown.

There was another dried smear on the outer side of the curtain, close to the edge.

Carrie was convinced that the blood had come from a dangling body slung across the shoulder of a killer. She was certain now that the missing maid had been stabbed to death!

Her voice, however, betrayed no tension as she turned to face the four people in the room. Aleck's gun was still pointed warily toward John Cooney. Vallon was at Aleck's elbow, glowering at the maid's captured boy-friend. Dora's lovely blue eyes were studying Carrie with a kind of frozen, bewildered expression.

"Keep those three people right where they are, Aleck," Carrie ordered calmly. "Don't let any of them leave the room until I come back. I've got a slant on this case."

"Okay," Aleck said.

"Look here," Vallon fumed, "if you think you can treat a respectable client in this high-handed——"

He winced as Aleck's gun jabbed him briefly. A quick wave of the weapon halted Dora's sly movement toward the opposite door.

"You try a sneak like that, lady," Aleck warned, "and I'll have to give you the foot-twist. I wouldn't want to trip a lady, but you can take your choice. You can either sit quietly down in that chair over there, the one away from the door, or you can sit down hard on the floor—with a thump!"

She didn't say anything. Her only reply was the scornful sway of her tightly sheathed hips as she glided past him. But she took the chair his gun barrel indicated.

Cooney said pleadingly, "Call the cops! Why don't you call in the cops?"

CARRIE CASHIN dropped the doorway drape behind her. She hurried along a corridor that led to the rear of the house.

A servants' staircase gave access to the upper floors. Carrie climbed to the top floor, looking for Marie's room. She found it in a shedlike extension that overlooked the rear grounds. Nothing seemed to have been disturbed. There was a leather suitcase on a chair, but it was empty. A few garments were piled neatly on the bed, as if the vanished Marie had intended to pack and had changed her mind.

Carrie hurried to the front of the

house and descended the main staircase to the second floor. Dora Vallon's ornate bedroom was on the left of the corridor.

Unlike the maid's room, it looked messy. The coverlet on the bed was rumpled. The pillow lay on the floor. But it was the bureau that attracted Carrie's gaze. The middle drawer was partly open. Someone had attempted to close it hurriedly and had pushed unevenly, jamming the drawer in its grooves.

Carrie pulled it open. Nothing seemed to have been disturbed except the contents of a wooden stocking box in one corner. The box was empty.

Carrie remembered Dora Vallon's statement to Aleck in the living room. Dora had said no stockings were stolen except the pair she wore when she had fallen unconscious across the bed. Why had she lied?

The rumpled edge of the carpet in front of the bureau brought Carrie swiftly to her knees. Her slim fingers explored under the bureau. She touched something and pulled it out. A silk stocking! There were more of them, shoved farther back. Had Dora deliberately hidden them?

The foot of the bed looked the neatest. That was why Carrie examined it. She found nothing until she lifted the mattress. Then she uttered a grim exclamation. Jammed between the spring and the underside of the mattress was a blood-soaked handkerchief. The stained initials in the corner were "D. V."

Carrie's mind considered calmly the tall, full-bosomed blonde downstairs in the gorgeous cloth-of-silver evening gown. Had Dora deliberately received her uncle into searching the house for a vanished French maid—whom Dora knew was a corpse?

The bedroom window was open at the bottom. Rain was slanting inward on the soaked carpet. Carrie leaned over the sill and peered downward. As she did, she uttered a gasp of dismay. She was staring into the wet, upturned face of a man barely two feet below her eyes!

THE man was crouched on a narrow stone balcony outside the window. He rose with a snarl and his uplifted hands looped something thin and snaky around Carrie's neck. It was a strangulation cord!

It choked off Carrie's scream as the man who held the tight cord squirmed over the sill. He fell to the floor with his victim. Carrie got a thumb under the noose, but she was unable to tear it loose.

She could see the grim face of the killer through waves of pain. She recognized his wet, frightened face. A picture of him was in Carrie's international crime files at the agency. He was Jean Despard, a crook who had fled from Paris to avoid arrest by the Sureté. The New York police had been unable to locate him.

He straightened as Carrie's body went limp. Hurdling her, he raced to the bureau. He pulled it aside and fumbled underneath. Then he darted from the room and sneaked noiselessly along the hall to the front staircase. A Luger pistol gleamed in his hand. He began to descend cautiously.

On the floor of Dora's bedroom, Carrie Cashin writhed dizzily to her knees. Her thumb was still jammed under the tightly knotted garrote cord, but she was unable to ease the pressure on her windpipe. Her lungs were like raw flame.

She sensed, rather than saw, the open door of Dora Vallon's private bathroom. She fell through on her face. The cool tiled floor revived her slightly. She pushed herself upward with one hand and reeled toward a medicine cabinet above the white porcelain sheen of a lavatory basin.

Through waves of sick agony she peered blindly for a discarded razor blade—and found one lying on the lower shelf of the cabinet.

Its quick slash at the knotted cord brought blood spurting from Carrie's throat; but it sliced through the noose.

The bathroom was whirling about her like a white-tiled cyclone. Round and round. Faster, faster! Carrie took a feeble step forward, like a toppling child trying to learn to walk.

Then she fainted.

CHAPTER III.
CRIME'S RIDDLE.

ALECK was completely unaware of events upstairs. He had trouble enough in the living room with three unwilling prisoners. John Cooney was edging toward the door, in spite of the threat of Aleck's gun.

His good-looking face was pale, but his words were quietly stubborn. "You have no legal right to hold me here. You're playing into Vallon's hands. He and his niece have done something to Marie. I'm going for the police!"

"You're going to do as I tell you," Aleck snapped, "or I'll——"

Cooney sprang at him. His fist rammed hysterically at Aleck's jaw. But Aleck, alert and ready, sidestepped and swung his clubbed gun. The young man ducked wildly and took the blow on his upraised shoulder. He was wrestling fiercely, trying to snatch Aleck's weapon, when there was a shrill scream of terror from Dora Vallon.

Dora had leaped from her chair and was cringing backward, staring at the doorway of the living room. Her uncle was staring, too. Vallon's ruddy face was the color of clay. He shouted in a hoarse, strangled voice: "Don't shoot! For God's sake, don't kill me!"

Jean Despard was standing in the doorway. The black muzzle of his gun menaced every person in the room. There was a cruel flick of a smile on Despard's thin lips. Not a sound had betrayed him as he descended the stairs from Dora's bedroom. The surprise of his victims was complete.

"Drop that gun!" he snarled at Aleck in a nasal, heavily accented voice.

Aleck had jerked away from the struggling Cooney. He was still holding the weapon that Cooney had tried to seize, but its barrel was slanted toward the floor. A single twist of Aleck's wrist could have snapped it level. But Aleck knew that any attempt to shoot would spell suicide. Despard's trigger finger was white with tension. There was death in his cold, wrinkled eyes.

He laughed as Aleck's gun dropped to the carpet with a dull thump.

"*Bien!* Back up—all of you!"

Aleck and Cooney retreated slowly, unwillingly. But Vallon and his niece obeyed the command with alacrity. They seemed eager to please this snarling French gunman.

Despard kicked Aleck's fallen weapon into a far corner. The side pockets of his coat were jammed with a queer cargo. Every pair of silken hose that Carrie Cashin had seen hidden beneath Dora Vallon's bureau was now in possession of the smirking Despard.

"Per'aps I've got the right pair, and per'aps I haven't," he growled. "I'm not taking any chances on miss-

The black muzzle of his gun menaced every person in the room.

ing what I came for. You with the blond curls—walk over to that chair, mademoiselle, and sit down!"

Dora hesitated. Her blue eyes jerked tensely toward her uncle.

Vallon nodded slightly. He seemed to have recovered his lost composure.

"Do as you're told," he said evenly. "It's foolish to try to argue with a loaded gun."

With a swish of her silver evening gown, Dora walked to the chair and sat down. Her pose was one of scornful indifference. But Despard's curt command brought a gasp of alarm from her.

"I desire those stockings of yours, mademoiselle. Remove them!"

Again there was a split second of hesitation, a swift glance between the blond niece and her gray-haired uncle.

"Let him have the stockings, Dora," Vallon said.

He looked frightened, but his voice was calm. Aleck wondered what his real game was. Was he trying to kid the man with the gun? If Dora's story to Aleck were correct, the stockings she was now wearing were valueless, donned after the real ones had been stolen. Yet she had hesitated. Was it merely because she was jittery?

SLOWLY, with her face flushing red, Dora unstrapped her fragile slippers. She lifted the hem of her silver evening gown to her knees. She held the gown bunched like silver froth, while one hand vanished from sight and nervously unhooked a garter. She drew a sagging left stocking downward and peeled it from her bare toes.

Despard bent cautiously and snatched it as she flung it fluttering near his shoe. His agile gun prevented any interference.

"*Bien*—very good! The other stocking, please!"

Aleck swayed imperceptibly forward on his toes. A sudden quick pressure against his ribs restrained him. Cooney, standing alongside, had dug him gently with an elbow.

The brief flick of Cooney's eyelid was interpreted instantly by Aleck. He was being signaled to wait, to let Cooney try something.

As modestly as she had unhooked the first stocking, Dora Vallon's hand vanished tremulously to loosen the second garter.

"Don't do it!" Cooney shouted suddenly in a cracked, dry voice. "Don't be a fool!"

The girl hesitated. Despard uttered an oath and swung his gun muzzle sideways. Cooney skipped suddenly away from Aleck and darted behind the protection of Vallon's back.

"Don't give him that stocking!" he screamed. "The stars in the heavens forbid it! It means disaster—death!"

He was clutching tightly to Vallon's shoulders, preventing him from escaping from his dangerous position as a shield against a gunman's bullets.

Cooney's eyes were bright and staring. He peered straight at Despard over the shoulder of Vallon. His talk was a strange gibberish of astrology. It sounded like the ravings of a man gone mad from the strain of facing a gun.

"If you give him that stocking—you're lost! I've written your horoscope and cast your fate. You were born under Gemini! Gemini—that's the sign of the twins. You and Marie! Don't you understand your danger? He's got one already—he wants the other. Defy him! He has to have both—or he'll fail!"

As the whirling nonsense about

astrology was shrieked at her by Cooney, Dora stiffened in frightened rigidity. But Aleck tensed his muscles for a forward leap. Cooney was pulling a shrewd act to attract the gun and the gaze of the puzzled Despard.

"You can't harm me!" Cooney cried. He had stepped from behind Vallon. His arms were flung upward over his head, as if inviting a bullet into his exposed body.

"I was born under Scorpio. The moon was in conjunction with Mercury, the black star of thieves! If you cut the Gemini twins in half, you've got only one—not two! But the moon is mine! It's over the 96th water parallel. You daren't kill me unless you join the split Gemini twins on the moon. Astrology proves it!"

"That's very marvelous," Despard breathed. "Tell me some more."

His taut lips flicked in a cruel grin. The muzzle of his gun dropped slightly, so that it pointed toward the center of Cooney's stomach. His turned profile offered the brief opportunity Aleck wanted. He took it with a swift leap and a swing of his clubbed fist.

He reckoned without the catlike agility of Despard. The gunman had heard the slight creak of Aleck's shoes as he set himself for attack.

Aleck's fist missed the ducking head of Despard. His momentum carried him past the crook's twisting shoulder, almost into the lap of Dora Vallon. She writhed from her chair, and Aleck tripped over her bare leg.

The thump of his body on the floor and the crack of Despard's pistol butt against his skull were almost simultaneous.

A shrill cry from Cooney was followed by a deep groan. It faded into the whirling inferno of flame that spouted in Aleck's skull. The flame vanished into darkness. The darkness became cold nothingness that——

CARRIE CASHIN could hear a monotonous rattling sound like someone shaking loose sand in a sifter. She was lying flat on her face with her eyes closed, listening dully. *Swish, swish, swish!* It was like the measured rhythm of a gourd-shaker in a rhumba orchestra.

Slowly, the sharp pain in Carrie's throat cleared her brain of cloudiness. Her eyes opened. She struggled dizzily to her knees. The sound that had roused her was rain beating in torrents against a closed window.

The coolness under her cheek was the tiled floor of Dora Vallon's bathroom.

As she swayed to her feet, her palm instinctively jerked to her aching throat. It came away smeared with blood. A wall mirror reflected Carrie's pale, drawn face and the oozing cut on her throat where she had desperately wielded a safety-razor blade.

She remembered now! Despard had circled her neck with a thin noose of catgut. He had left her to choke to death. But Carrie, staggering blindly toward the bathroom medicine cabinet, had managed to slash the garrote cord loose before she had collapsed.

Her knees trembled as she leaned against the lavatory basin. The crimson razor blade lay in the porcelain sink where it had fallen from her fingers. She filled a glass with cold water and gulped it eagerly. It eased the burn of her thirst and whipped away the last remnant of her dazed helplessness.

She tiptoed swiftly through the

connecting doorway into Dora's bedroom.

The window was still lifted from the bottom. Rain slanted in on the floor. There was a spreading puddle on the polished wood. A wet, soggy stain was ruining the rich Burgundy-red of the carpet. Carrie ignored the pelt of the rain except for one quick glance outward into the darkness. She could see no sign of a moving, human figure below. The grounds that surrounded the house lay empty and wet under the lash of the storm.

The blood-stained handkerchief with its D. V. monogram was still tucked between the spring and the mattress of Dora's bed, where Carrie had last seen it. But the bureau had been moved. The stockings that had been under it were gone.

Carrie understood clearly what had happened. Her arrival had interrupted Despard in a hasty search. He must have hardly opened the bureau drawer and grabbed for the stocking box, when he had heard Carrie's approaching steps. Shoving the stockings under the bureau, Despard had squirmed silently out the window to the stone ledge below the sill—and had grimly waited for her with his strangle cord.

Her cheeks burned with disgust at her own lack of caution. Despard had come within an ace of choking her to death from an ambush that should have been obvious to Carrie.

But if she had momentarily blundered—she had triumphed, too! The theft of *all* of Dora's stockings by Despard was a clue that verified a bold theory which had already taken shape in Carrie's shrewd mind. She had framed the theory before she had climbed the servants' stairs to search the house. It fitted in with the cut telephone wire in the living room, and the blood smear on the

drape in the doorway.

It also sealed the doom of the missing maid, Marie.

Marie had been killed, as Cooney had charged—murdered as she raced to the telephone to give the alarm. Marie's corpse had been kidnaped from the house by a cunning killer.

Carrie Cashin's pretty face was pale as she tiptoed cautiously along the hallway to the head of the stairs. The house was as quiet as a tomb. Reaching swiftly beneath her short tweed skirt, Carrie grabbed her businesslike little garter gun, which the cocksure Despard had overlooked in his hasty flight with the silk stocking loot.

Carrie descended the stairs and slipped noiselessly along the lower corridor. She paused behind the draped entrance of the living room. She was gently moving a fold of the curtain aside when she heard a faint groan. A quick stare, and Carrie was over the threshold.

ALECK was sitting in a dazed, spread-legged huddle on the floor. His battered head was held tightly in his hands. He looked pale and sick.

But he roused from his stupor when he saw Carrie bending over him. He listened to the quick lash of her questions:

"What happened to Vallon and his niece? Where's John Cooney? Did Despard kill him?"

"I—I don't know," Aleck admitted.

He explained jerkily what had happened. He told of his vain effort to slug Despard under cover of Cooney's rambling nonsense about astrology—only to be knocked senseless by a blow of Despard's gun.

"I think that Dora deliberately tripped me," Aleck growled as he felt painfully of his bleeding scalp.

"My guess is that the uncle and niece are in cahoots with Despard. Anyway, she handed him her stockings."

Carrie's eyes flashed with a quick inner blaze.

"You mean Despard stole the pair that Dora was wearing? The second pair she put on?"

"Yes. It doesn't make sense."

"It sure does!" Carrie cried triumphantly. "It's exactly what I expected to happen. It proves something, Aleck!"

"Proves what?"

She didn't reply. Her whole expression was one of grim understanding. She made Aleck repeat in detail everything that had happened from the moment she had left him to search the room upstairs. Then she nodded, her slim jaw line tense.

"How's your head feel? Still dazed?"

"No. I'm all right," Aleck said.

"It's pouring rain outside. Think you can stand a swift auto ride—maybe a cold swim in the rain and a tough battle afterward?"

"Will it solve this mess about astrology and silk stockings?"

"You're damn tootin'," Carrie said.

It was very seldom that Carrie uttered a profane word. That crisp "damn" of hers was proof to Aleck that she was profoundly stirred, completely sure of her course. In her own intuitive way, she had sensed the true answer to a tangled riddle of crime. She was ready to pounce on a cunning foe with the lightning swiftness of a veteran crime buster.

Aleck sprang toward the corner of the room where Despard had kicked his gun after disarming him. He examined the weapon and found it fully loaded. Characteristically, he asked no further questions that might waste precious time. His broad, loyal face was like granite.

"All set? Let's go."

CHAPTER IV.
THEFT AND MURDER.

CARRIE'S trim little coupé was parked at a dark curbstone a half block away from the home of Dora Vallon. Rain slashed at it in wind-blown sheets, dappled the windshield with bouncing drops. But once inside, the two crime busters were snug and dry.

Carrie took the wheel. The windshield wiper began to swing back and forth across the fogged glass. The coupé darted onward through the darkness with a quick *whoosh* of its spinning tires on the wet pavement.

Carrie kept her glance ahead to watch for the green or red glow of traffic lights. She dodged the red ones by cutting west or north with skillful speed. West and north—that was the route she took through Manhattan's storm-drenched streets. Aleck leaned closer to catch the explanatory murmur of her voice.

"Theft and murder, Aleck. Murder first! I mean, the unfortunate maid, Marie. She was honest, as Cooney said. She was killed as she ran to the telephone to call for help. But—and I'm as positive of this as I am that it's pouring rain tonight—Marie was clever enough to do something that completely upset the plans of a cunning thief. She made a brave attempt to trade stockings!"

"Huh?" Aleck sounded puzzled. "I don't get you?"

"Marie realized what was going on when she found her mistress lying unconscious on the bed. The thief hadn't yet appeared. So the courageous Marie started swiftly to peel off Dora Vallon's silk hose. She meant *to exchange stockings with her* in order to foil a murderous crook. But before she——"

"Look out!" Aleck gasped.

His hand clutched at the rim of the steering wheel. But Carrie, aware of the danger ahead, had already skipped it by an eyelash. The electric-light post on the corner whizzed past the skidding coupé by a margin so close that it scraped the running board with an ugly rasp. There was a bump as the car bounced off the sidewalk and hit the gutter. It headed west.

It raced swiftly down a long inclined street that bored through a tunnel beneath Riverside Drive. Beyond, like a flat blackness in the rain, was the Hudson River, barely visible past the expanse of the new West Side Highway.

The route Carrie took curved the coupé past the highway and led onto the bumpy surface of a timbered wharf. Carrie snapped off her lights. The car halted in utter blackness, and Carrie twisted about and reached for the door handle.

"Marie's corpse is on one of those anchored motor cruisers out in the river. So is the true solution of this case!"

"A boat?" Aleck muttered. "Which boat? Anchored where? How in the name of Heaven do you know all this?"

"You told me," Carrie answered with a strange smile. "Come on! We're going to have to make a quick swim."

THERE was a municipal anchorage for pleasure craft about two hundred yards beyond the wharf. Motor boats and small cruisers swung at their moorings like dark blobs against the rain-pelted blackness of the Hudson. All of them seemed deserted. But there was a faint glow of hazy light visible above the deck of one. It seemed to come from a glassed cabin skylight.

Kicking off her slippers, Carrie Cashin squirmed swiftly over the dripping stringpiece of the deserted wharf. She lowered herself to a jutting timber. Then she dropped feet-first into the water.

Aleck followed her. His teeth chattered as he felt the icy coldness of the river. Carrie's head ducked and her body doubled suddenly under water. When her dripping hands emerged they were holding her soaked tweed skirt. She squirmed out of her jacket and made a bundle of the two garments, knotting the jacket arms loosely about her neck. Aleck did the same with his coat.

Both were excellent swimmers. The slight splashing they made was covered by the hiss and bubble of rain on the dark river. They swam straight for the motor cruiser where the hazy glow of light was visible. Carrie rounded the stern of the craft and reached for the rungs of a short accommodation ladder on the port side.

Aleck was no longer completely mystified by Carrie's behavior. He had read the name of the boat as he swam past the stern! The name didn't explain everything; but it was enough for Aleck to realize how shrewdly intuitive the mind of a clever woman could be.

When he reached the deck of the motor cruiser, Carrie had already donned her soaked tweed skirt. She glided like a dripping patch of blackness to the edge of the cabin skylight. Rain pelted noisily on the glass. The film of water made everything below the glass seem distorted. But the figure of the man was one Aleck instantly recognized.

It was Despard! He was crouched

near the body of a woman in a cabin berth. The dead woman was Marie, the missing maid of Dora Vallon. Despard was coolly stripping a pair of silk stockings from the limp corpse!

Aleck had barely time to utter a gasp of horror when there was a startling interruption. A man reeled into sight from the hidden side of the cabin. He made a grim leap for the snarling Despard and locked him in a desperate embrace.

The man was John Cooney!

Aleck slid the glassed skylight cover aside. Grasping his gun, he swung his dripping legs over the edge. But before he could leap downward, the pelt of the rain warned the struggling combatants below that the skylight was open.

Despard's pale face lifted. So did Cooney's. The fighting men reeled backward. A hand shot out toward the electric-light switch on the wall.

THE cabin plunged into blackness before Aleck's dropping body hit the floor with a thump. He heard a shrill scream—the high-pitched yell of a man mortally hurt. Then an unseen assailant came thudding across the dark cabin.

Aleck's left hand had whipped out his tiny flashlight. With his gun level, he clicked the button of the torch. Nothing happened. The soaked flashlight was dead.

The next instant the point of a knife slashed across the wrist of Aleck's gun hand. The gun fell from his grasp as he was hurled backward by the impact of an attacking foe. But he was able to clutch at the hand with the knife—and to hold on!

The two men fell in a twisted huddle. Aleck was underneath. A bony kneecap jammed with agonizing force against his abdomen. The

killer's breath was fiercely audible as he strove to free his knife and plunge its point into Aleck's heart.

Aleck felt his fingers slipping. With a desperate effort, he managed to topple his kneeling foe and yank him headlong forward.

The effort cost Aleck his grip on the knife.

Then a dripping shadow catapulted itself from the cabin doorway. A tweed skirt flapped like a wet sail against the faces of the struggling men as Carrie Cashin dived into the invisible battle on the floor.

Aleck yelled. Carrie's clubbed gun swung past his head at the formless figure with the knife. There was a soggy impact and a howl of pain. An elbow dug into Aleck's glaring eyes, blinding him. By the time he could struggle to his feet, he heard a sharp snap like the crack of a dry branch. The doglike squeal of a man was followed by a dull impact and a deep groan.

Aleck's outstretched palms touched the soaked jacket of Carrie Cashin. She was standing erect and alone in the darkness.

"I—I think we're safe enough now," she said unsteadily. "He had the knife point at my throat when I broke his arm. I think my gun butt knocked him cold."

"Let's have a look at this sly Mr. Despard," Aleck growled.

Carrie's laughter was tremulous.

"I'm afraid you've got your people mixed. Despard is dead. He was stabbed before the killer tried to finish you."

"Good Lord! Then the killer must be——"

"Cooney would be a good guess," Carrie said shakily. "Turn on the lights."

John Cooney lay flat on his face,

with one broken arm twisted grotesquely beneath his numbed body. A few feet away lay the body of Despard, a long-bladed knife buried to the hilt in his back.

"It's probably the same knife that killed Marie," Carrie said tonelessly. "Her treacherous boy-friend, Cooney, murdered her when she ran to the phone in the Vallon house."

Carrie turned suddenly and darted toward a locked cupboard in the forepeak space just beyond the cabin. When the door swung open, the bound-and-gagged figures of Ralph Vallon and his niece toppled out on their faces.

IT was Aleck who freed them. Carrie was finishing the grisly task Despard had begun. Gently, she removed the stockings from the corpse of Marie. Searching Cooney, she found another silk stocking rolled tightly in his inside coat pocket.

"Two of these three stockings are the pair we're after," Carrie said. "We'll use Cooney's own lamp."

There was a shielded lamp clamped on the cabin wall, above a small desk. Aleck knew what it was the moment he gazed at it. There was one just like it in the agency headquarters. In was in infra-red lamp.

Under its ghastly glow, the stocking that Carrie spread out smoothly for examination leaped into vivid light. Every inequality of the silken threads was emphasized by the searching glow. But the dyed threads were uniform. There was no trace of secret writing.

"It proves what I suspected," Carrie said calmly. "Marie had only time to don one of Dora's hose when she switched with her drugged mistress."

She placed under the lamp the second stocking Marie had worn to her death. Ralph Vallon uttered a gasp. Two columns of livid writing leaped into brilliance on the gossamer texture of the silk. They had been painted with an exceedingly tiny brush. The lamp exposed the secret writing that had marked the threads without breaking them.

"It's a code, of course?" Carrie asked.

"Yes," Vallon said faintly. There was infinite joy in his tired voice. "The left column is the code; the right is the key. Traynor developed it to record the results of our aerial television experiments. He, alone, had the key."

Carrie nodded. She examined the third stocking she had taken from Cooney's pocket. It contained the complete message that Traynor had intended for Vallon. Written in code, it had baffled Cooney. Unable to understand it, he realized at once that his perfect crime was only half perfect.

He had made a bad blunder. He thought the vitally important code-key stocking was still at the Vallon home. That was why he had returned, posing as the innocent friend of the maid he had killed. Not until it was too late, did he realize that the prize he was after was on a cold limb of the maid he had slain and kidnaped aboard his boat—to sink her in the mud of the river before he fled.

"And the name of his boat was the *Moon*," Aleck said grimly. "You suspected Cooney when I told you about all his astrology gibberish?"

"Yes. I knew the maid was dead. I knew some other thief had beaten Despard to the loot because of his clumsy attempt to steal every stocking in the house. Dora Vallon's stained handkerchief shoved beneath her mattress by Cooney, was too obvious to be a real clue. I was more certain of Cooney's guilt after Despard jumped me upstairs. I figured both were international spies, with Despard after something Cooney had already stolen."

"But what about coming to the Hudson River?" Aleck muttered. "How did you know that——"

"Both spies recognized each other when Despard made his stick-up in the living room. He knew Cooney had been ahead of him. Cooney's gibberish about astrology was a veiled tip-off to Despard that he had one of the missing television stockings, and was ready to make a deal. Remember what he said?"

ALECK nodded eagerly. He repeated some of it, filling in with some of his deductions:

"*'If you kill me—you've cut the Gemini twins in half. You've got only one—not two.'*"

Carrie said: "Exactly. And remember the rest? *'But the moon is mine. It's over the water tonight. It's over the 96th parallel.'*"

Carrie smiled grimly.

"Naturally, it couldn't be a real moon in a pouring rainstorm. It was a boat anchored on the water off 96th Street. I eliminated the East River, because I knew there was a municipal anchorage on the Hudson at 96th."

Dora Vallon shuddered. Her uncle's face was still pale at the thought of his narrow escape from death at the hands of two ruthless spies.

"Cooney knocked me over the head as soon as Despard slugged you," Vallon told Aleck faintly. "They joined forces and kidnaped Dora and me to the boat. Despard planned to kill Cooney on the boat and take a hundred percent profit when he sold the television invention to a foreign government. But Cooney's knife was too fast for him."

"If I were you," Carrie said quietly, "I'd grab a plane and fly with that formula to the War Department in Washington—tonight! With a secret like that, the United States can dictate peace in Europe for a generation."

There was a queer smile on Aleck's lips as he laid his big hand gently on Carrie's.

"Peace?" he said huskily. "You're a fine one to talk about that. I feel as if we just finished the World War!"

He sneezed.

"Aleck!" Carrie gasped. "You're wet—you're shivering! Come on—let's hunt up a cup of hot coffee."

Be a DIESEL ENGINEER

Send the coupon NOW

Learn the thrill that comes to the engineer of a powerful Diesel engine . . . the satisfaction of supplying POWER—energy—and comfort to people and industry, for cities, for ships, farms, mines, for all transportation and commerce. Get into this industry that is GOING PLACES—and go with it.

HEMPHILL DIESEL SCHOOLS — COMPLETE DIESEL AND DIESEL ELECTRIC – TRAINING

Start your training now, no matter where you live, in the combination Home and later Shop Course, or in either the day or night resident courses.

HEMPHILL DIESEL SCHOOLS LOCATED IN THESE CITIES:
BOSTON 134 Brookline Avenue
NEW YORK 31-40 Queens Boulevard, L.I.C. - DETROIT 2355 West Lafayette Boulevard - CHICAGO 2038 Larrabee Street
MEMPHIS 457 Monroe Avenue
LOS ANGELES 2129 San Fernando Road - SEATTLE 517 Westlake No. - VANCOUVER B. C. 1369 Granville Street

HEMPHILL DIESEL SCHOOLS
Please rush booklet, and information on training which will qualify me for Diesel.
NAME_____ AGE____
STREET_____
CITY_____ STATE____ m-32-ts

SARAH WATSON

Detective Fiction Weekly was called simply *Flynn's* when it began publication in 1924. It was named for the first editor, Edward J. Flynn, who had served "twenty-five years in the U.S. Secret Service." The magazine went through several name changes: to *Flynn's Weekly* in 1926; to *Flynn's Detective Fiction Weekly* in 1927; to *Detective Fiction Weekly* (formerly *Flynn's*) in 1928; and to *Detective Fiction Magazine* in 1943. It combined with *Dime Detective Magazine* in 1944, but in its last days was known as *Detective Fiction* (1951).

Stoutly built Sarah Watson was a magazine regular in a series written by D. B. McCandless. She employs an assistant, Ben Todd, but seldom lets him in on her theories. Sarah is a tough bird and emerges "from any given fracas with somebody's goat and a substantial amount of dollars and cents."

The Watson-Todd duo anticipated by several years Erle Stanley Gardner's Bertha Cool and Donald Lam hardcover series, written under his A. A. Fair pseudonym beginning in 1939.

"Cash or Credit" originally appeared in the September 18, 1937, issue of *Detective Fiction Weekly.*

By D. B. McCandless

Author of "Crime Begins at Home," etc.

"You're going out, Mrs. Watson," said Jessup, drawing a gun from his pocket

Cash or Credit

*Sarah Watson Never Heard of Omar But She Accepted
His Advice: Ah, Take the Cash and Let the Credit Go*

THE office was square and dusty. Everything in it was battered and worn, even the woman sitting bolt upright behind the rolltop desk beside the smeared window.

The woman herself was square and dusty. She was made up of angles, from the jut of her square chin to the square toes of her commonsense shoes, and her nondescript garments had worn from black to dusty gray.

The woman was engaged in eating a bun. She took man-sized bites. She masticated with a masterful movement of jaws. Her gray eyes, fixed on the door to the hall, were contemplative under bristling gray brows as she ate.

Abruptly, the door swung in, sending a current of air into the office. As though blown in on the air, a long-legged young man plunged through the door, kicked it shut behind him and charged across the dusty floor.

"Sarah!" he said, breathlessly. "Dish the bun! Customer coming up!"

"Ben Todd," said the woman, grimly, rising and shaking the bun under the young man's nose. "This bun is my lunch and I dish it for no man. Who is this customer coming up?"

Ben Todd yanked off his derby and ran long, thin fingers through a thatch of red hair.

"Sarah Watson," he said, "listen. I

overheard this guy phoning in a booth downstairs. He was asking somebody for the name of the dame who runs a detective agency in this dump. So, I grabbed an elevator up, and, for hell's sake, dish that bun, old girl, because the guy coming up is Jack Jessup, and Jack Jessup is right-hand and left-hand man to the famous, the powerful and the wealthy Mose Wesser. . . ."

Ben Todd's voice trailed off. Sarah Watson looked down at the remnants of bun in her hand. She turned her broad back, strode to the trash basket and dropped the bun.

"Ben Todd," she said, sitting down heavily in her swivel chair and scrubbing sugar from the faint mustache which shadowed her upper lip. "Ben Todd, I'm surprised at you—surprised and ashamed that you, young feller, should be so impressed by a prospective customer, because he represents big cash."

Ben Todd glanced at the discarded bun and grinned, widely.

"I ain't the only one," he said, "and neither are you. Mose Wesser is a power in this town, a real power. He has all ten of his fingers in every political and financial pie that's baked."

"Humph," said Sarah. "I've heard talk that some of the pies are nasty pies."

"That's over," said Ben Todd, glancing over his shoulder at the door to the hall. "Mose Wesser's fingers are clean now, Sarah, washed white by charities and public benefits. There's still some talk about his past, old girl, but the talk's done in whispers."

"Shss," warned Sarah. "Somebody at the door."

The door swung in. Ben Todd was seated at his desk, rustling papers that a close inspection would have proved were yellowed with age. Sarah Watson was motionless in her chair, square hands in fists upon her spread knees.

"Mrs. Sarah Watson?" said the man who had stepped through the door.

Sarah nodded, briskly. Her keen eyes roved over the man. He was a small man, soft, with a soft, small paunch, and vague blue eyes magnified by spectacles. The vague eyes wandered from Sarah to Ben Todd and focussed.

"The young man is Ben Todd," said Sarah. "My assistant—when needed."

"If you'll pardon my suggestion," said the man with the spectacles, "he's not needed now."

"Ben Todd," said Sarah, "step into the next room," and she jerked a thumb toward a door at the side.

Ben Todd rose, slowly. Sarah jerked the thumb again. She said, "Git!" Ben Todd disappeared through the side door.

BEN TODD stood in the "next room." Ben Todd's right elbow rested against one wall, his left against another. One foot behind him, another wall rose, a wall half hidden by musty garments hanging from hooks. An old-fashioned, box phone was affixed to the fourth wall, near the door through which Ben Todd had come.

Sarah's voice rasped through the thin boards of that door.

"Tell me what I can do for you, Mr. Jessup," she said, "and I'll do it—for a consideration, of course."

"The consideration," said Jessup's mild voice, "will be ample."

"How ample?" inquired Sarah, crisply.

"Ample," repeated Jessup, gently. "My superior in this matter feels—"

"Who is your superior?"

She wasn't reverent.

"My superior, Mrs. Watson, is a man whose name you must have heard spoken many times. My superior, Mrs. Watson, is Mr. Mose Wesser."

"Wesser, eh? I've heard the name somewheres. Go on."

"Mr. Wesser," said Jessup, mildly, "feels that the matter in hand is one which calls for the tact and discretion which only a woman can display. . . ."

"My!" interrupted Sarah. "Mr. Wesser must be an unusual man. What *is* the matter in hand?"

There was a silence. Ben Todd, peering through a crack in the panel of the closet door, saw that Jessup had risen and was padding softly up and down the dusty floor.

"Mrs. Watson," said Jessup, suddenly. "My superior is a misunderstood man. He has given largely of time, money and service to this town, yet there are still whispers . . ."

Jessup's voice trailed off. Sarah said nothing. Jessup coughed, deprecatingly.

"You will pardon the heat with which I speak," he said. "I feel very strongly on this matter. So does Mr. Wesser. Mr. Wesser is growing weary of lying, malicious whispers, which seek to tear down his reputation as a rising statesman and a great public benefactor—"

"Mr. Jessup," Sarah broke in hoarsely, "you talk fine. Fine! But I like less trimmings and more meat. What does Mr. Wesser want done—and how much do I get to do it?"

"Mrs. Watson," said Jessup, "certain information has come to Mr. Wesser, information which will enable him to perform this town a greater service than any he has heretofore performed. Owing to the nature of the matter, Mr. Wesser cannot perform this service without the help of an intermediary and that intermediary must be a detective— a courageous and clever detective, Mrs. Watson, like you. Through you, Mrs.

Watson, Mr. Wesser proposes to remove from this town's fair name a stain which will soon be apparent to all the world, a hideous stain."

"What stain?"

"The stain of a crime, Mrs. Watson, a heinous crime."

"What crime?"

Jessup paused his pacing at the roll-top desk. He leaned over the desk and lowered his voice so that Ben Todd was forced to inch open the closet door to catch the words.

"Mrs. Watson," whispered Jessup, "something happened last night to a baby known all over the civilized world as the world's richest child, a baby known in this fair town as the only son of the town's first family. Mrs. Watson, the child known as the Millen Billionaire Baby was kidnapped last night."

"Kidnapped!" Sarah Watson rose from her chair and sat down again, hard. Jessup began again to pace the floor. Ben Todd moved the closet door open another inch.

"Kidnapped," said Jessup. "Yes. I am glad to see, Mrs. Watson, that you are intelligent enough to recognize the enormity of the thing, far-seeing enough to realize the blot which this crime will be upon this town's fair name when it becomes known, as it will become known at any minute, if the news is not already on the streets."

"To say nothing," remarked Sarah, grimly, "of the agony to the child's parents, and the suffering of the child itself."

"Yes. Yes, of course," Jessup paused again at Sarah's desk. "Naturally, being a woman, Mrs. Watson, you would think of that angle."

"Mr. Jessup," said Sarah, briskly. "How much do I get paid for this job?"

Jessup cleared his throat, began to teeter back and forth upon his heels. The telephone on Sarah's desk began to ring. Sarah reached for it, listened a moment, and put the instrument into Jessup's hands. Swiftly, Ben Todd drew the door of the closet shut and eased off the receiver of the phone which hung on the wall beside him.

Three minutes later, Ben Todd had his eye back at the crack in the closet door, and the receiver of the old box phone was dangling against the plaster wall of the closet.

In the office, Jack Jessup had replaced the telephone on the top of Sarah's rolltop desk and was leaning over that desk, with his back toward Ben Todd. There was something about the pose of Jessup's small, soft body which Ben Todd didn't like.

"Mrs. Watson," said Jessup, softly, "get your hat."

"My hat?" barked Sarah. "Why?"

"You're going out," said Jessup, gently, and drew a snub-nosed gun from the pocket of his coat.

TWO minutes after that, Ben Todd stood in the empty office, beside an open window, peering down, as he frantically jiggled the hook on the telephone he had dragged from the rolltop desk.

"Pine Street Station?" snapped Ben Todd into the phone. "Gimme O'Reilly, Sergeant O'Reilly. Quick! O'Reilly? Ben Todd. Sarah Watson's in a mess. She's in danger. She—Wait. . . ."

Ben Todd clutched the telephone to his chest and leaned far out the window.

"O'Reilly?" he said, drawing in his head and concentrating on the phone. "Listen. Sarah just stepped out the door of the building here. She's with a man and the man has a gun in her side.

I'd be after her myself, but I locked myself in a damn closet and just broke out.

"The man she's with, O'Reilly, is Jack Jessup, Mose Wesser's man. The car he's leading her to is a brown sedan, probably one of Wesser's fleet. Of course I know Wesser's okay. I'm not talking about Wesser. I'm talking about Jessup. Jessup is mixed up in something screwy. He came here, using Wesser's name, and tried to ring Sarah in on it, because he thought she was a dumb dame. Some tough guy rang Jessup up while he was here and warned him that Sarah was plenty smart. Jessup's scared to the killing point now because he's told Sarah too much. No, I can't tell you what it's about now, but it's damn big and it's damn dangerous. The old girl didn't hear the side of the telephone conversation that I heard, O'Reilly, and she don't know what a tough spot she's in—Wait. . . ."

Ben Todd leaned out the window again.

"The brown sedan's heading north toward the river," he yelled into the phone. "O'Reilly, you put a watch out for that sedan but do it quiet. What's that? You think maybe it's heading for the Joy Boat? Is that the floating night club anchored in the river? Does Jack Jessup hang out there? He owns it? Okay. Don't have any cops butting in on this thing, O'Reilly, unless I yell for help. There's a kid's life at stake in this, maybe, and money for Sarah, and you know how the old girl is. She's damn sure she can take care of herself and she don't like interference when there's cash in the kitty . . . By."

SARAH WATSON leaned over the wheel of the brown sedan, her eyes rapt as she nosed the long radiator in and out of traffic toward the river-front.

"Jessup," she said, "where we bound? I hope it's a damn long ways. I like this car."

The man sitting beside her dropped his vague eyes from her craggy profile to the shining bit of metal which he held against her rigidly corseted side.

"A damn long ways is right, Mrs. Watson," he said softly. "A damn long ways."

"Good," said Sarah, cheerfully, and slowed the car suddenly.

"Mrs. Watson," said Jessup, quietly, "if you stop . . ."

"Fiddlesticks," said Sarah, hoarsely. "You're not going to shoot me in the middle of town. I want to see what extra that newsboy's yelling. Lower the window, Jessup, on your side."

The newsboy sprang on the slowly moving running board of the brown sedan. Sarah leaned suddenly across the small, soft body of Jessup and screwed down the window.

"Millen Billionaire Babe stole!" shrilled the newsboy.

"Gimme," said Sarah, hoarsely, thrusting her right hand through the open window as she steered the car slowly with her left. "Thanks, little boy. The gentleman will pay."

Sarah fell back. She let the spread newspaper fall half over the wheel and half over her wide lap. The car crawled on, close to the curb. Beside her, Jessup cursed luridly in his gentle voice and coins jingled into the newsboy's dirty palm. Sarah shot the car away from the curb and into a clear traffic lane. She drove with one hand, the hand nearest Jessup and his gun. Her other hand was in her lap, under the newspaper, twitching at the voluminous folds of her black skirt.

"Mrs. Watson," said Jessup in a stifled voice. "You got away with that but you'll get away with no more. I'm perfectly aware of the fact that if I shoot now, I'll probably die myself in a wrecked car, but—"

"Nonsense," said Sarah, hoarsely, putting on speed. "Neither one of us is going to die 'til I see that the Millen baby is back with his mamma, Jessup, and I'm not planning to die even then."

A BATTERED, antiquated black car shot away from the curb in front of Sarah Watson's office. In the driver's seat, Ben Todd sat high on the tattered leather cushions, the rattle of loose joints in his ears. The old car headed north, toward the river and began to make extremely audible speed.

Ben Todd's mouth was grimly set, but there was doubt and vacillation in his eyes. Twice, he slowed at the blue sign of a telephone. Twice, he speeded up again, abandoning whatever purpose was in his mind.

The ancient vehicle chugged noisily on toward the river and the white blur of a large houseboat, floating on the gleam of water ahead. That would be the Joy Boat, the floating night club which O'Reilly had said was owned by Jack Jessup.

The long pier to which the gaily painted Joy Boat was moored came into view at the end of the highway. There were three cars parked on the pier. One was shiny silver, one dark blue. The third was a brown sedan.

SARAH WATSON, her hands hanging limply against the voluminous folds of her black skirt, stalked down the dim corridor which bisected the superstructure of the houseboat. She stalked with Jack Jessup's gun pressed against the small of her stiff back, and Jack Jessup still held the gun.

At the end of the long corridor, a single square window revealed a vista of the pier and the waterfront street beyond. To Sarah's searching eyes that vista seemed to be changing—swinging, so that the pier and the waterfront street disappeared, and the window revealed only water, and, far away, a small, white sail.

"Next door," said Jessup, quietly. "On the left."

Sarah obediently opened the next door. She stepped through it into semi-darkness. A lock clicked as Jessup closed the door behind them. Jack Jessup said, mildly:

"This room is soundproof, Mrs. Watson, and steel shuttered, as you will note. It's impregnable, one might say."

BEN TODD braked Sarah's antique car at the very end of the pier to which the Joy Boat was tied. He made no move to descend. He sat, gnawing at his last whole fingernail, his eyes on the gaily painted boat.

Only one hawser secured that boat to the pier. Tide was slowly swinging the boat itself out into the river, so that it lay almost at right angles to the dock, and the one thick rope which held it to dry land was stretched taut.

Just one connection.

Ben Todd's anxious eyes contemplated that rope. It was thick, and it was fairly short. A man could squirm up its slant and crawl from it to the houseboat's deck. A man could do that easily, if it were not that another man were waiting at the boat-end of that rope, a huge man, clad in waiter's garb, a man who seemed to be loitering idly over the rail, studying the water below, a man who played carelessly, as he loitered, with a white napkin which might be just a white napkin and might be a white napkin covering a gun.

Ben Todd tore off the last fingernail and spat.

"Damn," he muttered. "There's only one thing to do. If the old gal lives through this, she'll fire me for good, but . . ."

Ben Todd turned the old car's battered nose and chugged down the pier toward the street.

IN the small soundproof room on the houseboat, a light clicked on. Jack Jessup's voice said, gently:

"Turn around, Mrs. Watson."

Sarah wheeled, looked down into Jessup's face. Jessup was smiling. There was no sign of a gun in his hand.

"Mrs. Watson," said Jessup, smoothly. "My instructions from my superior were to ascertain before sending you out on this job—this very important and vital job—whether or not you were a woman of courage. You are a brave woman, Mrs. Watson. You have—er—passed the test."

"Test?" said Sarah, grimly. "That gun you held in my ribs, Mr. Jessup, didn't feel like a test."

Jessup gave a cackling laugh. He drew a gun from his pocket and flourished it. It was a shiny gun, and small.

"Just a toy, Mrs. Watson," said Jessup. "Just a toy. My superior—"

Sarah reached stubby fingers and closed her left hand over the shiny gun.

"It is against the principles of my superior to carry firearms," said Jessup.

"How fortunate!" said Sarah, hoarsely, and drew her right hand from the folds of her skirt to aim a business-like revolver at Jessup's chest.

"Mr. Jessup," she said, briskly. "This gun is no toy. And it ain't against my principles to do anything, even to shoot. I know you've got a real firearm in your hip pocket. Don't reach. I can't figger yet, Jessup, just why you began trying to lull my suspicions after you got me here. Maybe your nerve failed you—you ain't got much nerve, I've observed."

"Mrs. Watson, my dear woman! I assure you . . . You're making a ridiculous mistake. Everything is as I've explained."

"Don't shake so, Mr. Jessup. It ain't becoming. Maybe everything is as you explained and maybe it ain't. I've got no time to find out. The only thing I've got time for now is to find that Millen child. Keep your hands high, Mr. Jessup, and talk."

"Talk?" stuttered Jessup, his vague eyes rolling. "How can I talk? I know nothing. I—Mrs. Watson, don't—be careful of that gun, Mrs. Watson!"

Sarah Watson took a long, purposeful stride toward Jessup. Jessup shrank closer to the wall.

"Talk!" said Sarah. "Talk!"

Jessup's vague eyes ceased rolling and fixed on Sarah's grim face. He straightened a little. He began to talk—fast.

"Listen," he said. "Listen, Mrs. Watson. Look here. Mose Wesser is in this thing for glory. He's a hog for glory. He'd do anything for glory. Some of his former underworld friends passed him these clues to the whereabouts of the Millen baby and he's willing to use 'em, through you, and willing to take good money out of his own pocket and pay you, just for glory—the glory it will bring him after the baby's returned, and it gets out that he was instrumental in returning it. See?"

"Um," said Sarah, eyeing Jessup. "Yes, I see. Glory, of course, means votes to Mr. Wesser, and votes mean cash."

"Listen," said Jessup, urgently. "Listen. What do we care for glory,

huh? What do you and I care for, Mrs. Watson, if it ain't cash? That extra you made me pay for, Mrs. Watson—it advertised a reward for the return of the baby, a cash reward, Mrs. Watson—fifty thousand dollars cash."

"Jessup," said Sarah, hoarsely, "I'd do anything for fifty thousand dollars. I'd even shoot a man. Not dead, you understand, Jessup. Not right away. Now, you tell me these clues that Mr. Wesser has, and tell 'em to me quick. Talk!"

"But—I—Listen! How do I know you won't double-cross me on this if I—"

"You don't know anything, Jessup, except that I'm going to make mincemeat of you if you don't talk. Talk!"

Sarah took another grim stride toward Jessup. Jessup's legs buckled. Sarah said:

"For fifty thousand, I'd even beat a man up. I'd like to beat a man up proper, for once. I'd begin on the nose, Jessup. The nose is a nice, tender place to begin. Maybe I'd break it—after a while. Talk, Mr. Jessup. Talk!"

"All right," said Jessup, his eyes leaving Sarah's face and traveling to the window where streaks of sunlight showed through the steel shutters. "I'll talk. . . ."

ON the long pier to which the Joy Boat was moored, Ben Todd once again braked Sarah Watson's wreck-on-wheels, and peered up at the boat's deck. The waiter who had lolled over the boat's railing was no longer lolling. His back was to the pier. He was crouching at one of the long line of little windows in the boat's superstructure. He was peering through shutters that held a metallic gleam under the late afternoon sun. He was lifting his right arm slowly, wedging something through one of the interstices of those shutters.

"I'LL talk," said Jessup, his eyes wandering back from the steel-shuttered window to Sarah's bleak face. "The Millen baby is in a white farmhouse, about fifteen and a half miles out from the center of town, a white farmhouse with three poplar trees in front. The house is on one of the main highways."

"Which highway?" demanded Sarah, trying to fix the eyes which Jack Jessup seemed unable to keep on hers.

Jessup swallowed. He said:

"The—" and fell forward as a shot flamed through a slit in the steel shutters and echoed dully against the walls of the room.

BEN TODD was out of the car. He was down on his knees on the pier, reaching for the rope which held the Joy Boat to the shore.

The waiter who had shot through the steel-shuttered window was dashing down the deck, and disappearing through a door that broke the long line of little windows.

Ben Todd was gripping the mooring rope with both hand, swinging himself over the oily water, beginning to go hand over hand up the slant of that rope, toward the houseboat's deck.

Another shot rang out, muffled, from somewhere inside the houseboat's superstructure.

Ben Todd's long legs jack-knifed. His knees scraped the boat's edge, stayed there precariously. He took one hand off the mooring rope, gripped an upright of the boat's railing.

He almost fell.

A figure charged out of the door which the man in waiter's garb had left swinging open behind him, the stocky figure of a woman, clad in dusty, voluminous black.

"Sarah!" yelled Ben Todd. "Sarah!"

The woman turned a blood-smeared face. She said, hoarsely:

"How'd you get here, whippersnapper?" She transferred her glinting eyes from Ben Todd to the rope by which he had come, and made for the rope.

Three seconds later, Sarah Watson, in a welter of black cloth skirts, was astride that taut, thick rope, sliding downward toward the pier.

Ben Todd scrambled up on the railing, gauged the distance between it and the pier. He leaped.

"Idiot!" said Sarah, hoarsely, gripping his arm as he landed and teetered perilously on the dock's edge. "Suppose I'd had to waste time fishing you out of that water! Move, young feller. Move into that car and take the wheel."

Ben Todd slid into the car. Sarah charged after him, banged the door shut.

"Sarah," said Ben Todd. "You hurt? There's blood on your face."

"My face ain't hurt," said Sarah, hoarsely. "It's my legs. That damn rope ruined 'em!"

"But you've got blood—"

"Not mine," barked Sarah. "Jack Jessup's. Get this car moving, whippersnapper. Who's that coming down the waterfront street, do you suppose, in the swell black limousine?"

"That," said Ben Todd, peering as he reached for the clutch, "that would be Mr. Mose Wesser. I telephoned him to come."

"You telephoned Mose Wesser? Ben Todd, you're fired!"

"Why?"

"Listen. There's a fifty thousand dollar reward out for the return of the Millen child. Jack Jessup and me had a little chat on the houseboat, before

Jessup got shot. Jessup didn't see why Mose Wesser should use his information to return that child just for glory. Jessup didn't see why somebody shouldn't get that fifty thousand reward."

"Jeepers! Then you mean— So Jessup was really telling the truth in the office! Mose Wesser really has information?"

"Mose Wesser has. So have I— now."

"Sarah! For hell's sake! What double-crossing game are you working now? . . . I've got it now. You're double-crossing Jessup, of course, and I'll bet you're double-crossing Wesser!"

"Slow up and honk your horn at that black limousine," ordered Sarah. "I'm going to speak with Mr. Wesser."

THE shiny black limousine and the rusty black antique scraped fenders at the entrance to the pier. Sarah thrust her head out of the window, ignoring the muttered curses of the man in chauffeur's uniform at the wheel of the limousine, and making violent motions at the large, heavy-jowled and elegant gentleman who sat in the interior of the limousine.

The gentleman leaned forward, smiling with a tinge of patronage, at Sarah.

"Mr. Wesser?" said Sarah, hoarsely. "I'm Sarah Watson, detective. This is my assistant, Ben Todd. You'll find your man, Jessup, in the soundproof room on the houseboat, Mr. Wesser. He's got a bullet in the fleshy part of his left arm. He ain't dead, but he thinks he is. A man dressed up as a waiter shot the bullet through those steel shutters. I don't know whether the bullet was meant for Jessup or me but Jessup got it."

Sarah paused for breath. Mr. Wesser had his head through his own window,

and his large face was blank with bewilderment. Sarah began to talk again. She said:

"Jessup ain't what you think he is, Mr. Wesser. He actually proposed to me that I work with him instead of for you, on this Millen kidnapping. He actually proposed that he and I should share that fifty thousand reward, Mr. Wesser."

Mr. Wesser's mouth moved. Nothing came forth but a weak splutter. Sarah said:

"Of course, the man in the waiter's suit was one of the Millen kidnapping gang, Mr. Wesser. He's quite safe in the soundproof room with Jessup, and he has an Easter egg on his skull where I hit him. Keep him safe, Mr. Wesser, for the police. Now, Mr. Wesser, if you'll just give me the name of the highway on which that white farmhouse with the poplars stands—the one where the Millen child was taken last night. Jessup was just about to give it to me when the bullet knocked him flat."

"Ah," said Mr. Wesser. "Of course. I know who you are, madam, and I know I can trust you. The name of the highway, Mrs. Watson, is the Prospect Highway, running south from the center of town."

"Start the car, Bennie," said Sarah, giving Ben Todd a vigorous dig in the ribs. "We're on our way."

And so they were.

The battered wreck which was Sarah's lurched forward. The shiny black limousine moved silently and majestically down the pier. Sarah, still hanging out of her window, waved energetically at the large face of Mr. Wesser, peering back now through the rear window of his elegant car. Mr. Wesser nodded solemnly, and tipped his hat.

SARAH'S car, guided by Ben Todd, bounced over the cobbles of the waterfront road and slid on to the asphalt of the road which led back to the center of town. Ben Todd said, sheepishly:

"Old girl, I apologize."

"What for?"

"For thinking you'd sided in with Jessup to double-cross Mose Wesser."

Sarah said nothing. She rose up in her seat, bent and peered through the back window of the car. Ben Todd suddenly stepped on the gas, and cursed softly.

"By hell," he said. "I see it all now. You didn't plan to double-cross Wesser, because you couldn't double-cross Wesser, because Jessup got knocked out before he could tell you the name of that highway. . . ."

"Bennie," said Sarah, quietly, "you wrong me. Jack Jessup did tell me the name of that highway—at least, he told me the name of a highway, after he was shot. But, of course, Bennie, I don't trust any man, even a man that thinks he's dying, as Jessup thought."

"Oh, damn!" said Ben Todd. "The whole thing's beyond me. I can't figure it."

"You don't need to figger it," said Sarah, hoarsely. "You just need to do what you're told. Now listen. A blue car that was parked on that pier is coming up after us. I can't see who's in it, but I've got a feeling the driver is wearing a waiter's suit and a lump on his head."

"Jeepers!" breathed Ben Todd, stepping on the gas. "So Wesser muffed it, and let that guy get away!"

"Well," said Sarah, briskly, "you can't blame Mr. Wesser. He's not used to handling situations like this. Fortunately, we are. Now, Bennie, here's your orders. Slow up. We're hitting traffic now. When you see an empty taxi, slide up alongside it. I'm transferring. You're riding on to the center of town and when you get there, you're going to start off south, on the Prospect Highway . . ."

"But, Sarah— Listen, that's the road Wesser said the white farmhouse was on."

"Exactly. A white farmhouse, with three poplars in front, about fifteen miles from the center of town."

"But, good Lord, Sarah! That's where the Millen kid is, ain't it?"

"That's where the Millen child was taken last night, Bennie. Your job is to find that house."

"But, jeepers, Sarah! You ain't going to leave me in the lurch? You ain't going to leave me to handle this thing alone?"

"You scared?"

"You know damn well I'm not, you moth-eaten old war horse!"

Sarah exhaled noisily.

"Good. Here's a taxi, that red and white one. Slow up."

Ben Todd slowed. Sarah put her hand on the door. She said:

"By the way, that blue car is still on our tail, Bennie. You got a gun?"

"You know damn well I got two. Sarah, what's the idea of leaving me in the lurch like this, with that car after me, and maybe a bunch of the kidnappers hidden in the back?"

"Don't get the jitters, Bennie," admonished Sarah, opening the door at her side. "And if by any chance the blue car should stop following you after you turn into Prospect Highway, you just turn back, young feller, and phone O'Reilly. Tell him to get a car full of cops and guns and drive the car himself lickety split along the Northern Boulevard, 'til he spots a red and white taxi . . ."

Sarah's voice trailed, as a red and white taxi drew abreast. She swung open the door and she hopped. A moment later, there was a shrill cry of protest from the interior of the taxi, as the rear door of that vehicle slammed shut on Sarah's broad back. Two seconds later, a very much flustered spinster found herself forced out of the interior of that taxi and on the street.

Sarah leaned back against the cushions of the red and white taxi and said:

"Drive to the center of town, cab driver, and let the blue car that's coming up behind get ahead. Keep your mouth shut, and remember, I'm good for a much larger tip than the old maid I just shoved out of your cab."

SERGEANT O'REILLY tightened his red, hairy fingers on the wheel of a car full of cops and guns. He curved around a lumbering truck and put on speed. He said:

"We've come twelve miles from the center of town and nothing yet. Sounds like a wild goose chase, but Ben Todd said Sarah Watson gave the instructions and Sarah don't chase wild geese."

Nobody in the crowded car said anything. O'Reilly put on more speed. He passed another swaying truck. Far ahead, a red and white speck rolled in the gathering dusk. O'Reilly stepped on the gas.

"By dom," he said, "there's the red and white cab," and bent over the wheel.

The red and white cab loomed larger. O'Reilly said:

"That's the cab Ben Todd said to watch for, and, by dom, it's actin' crazy. Looka that, will you! Ploughin' through that fence! By dom, it's headin' straight across that field for that white house with the three poplars. . . ."

O'Reilly's headlights went on. They picked out the gap in the fence where the red and white cab had splintered through rickety pickets. They picked out the tire marks in the field, and the police car wheels followed those tracks.

Ahead, the red and white cab ploughed on, lurched, and stopped suddenly, at the side of the white house. A figure descended from it, ran toward the deepening shadows at the rear. O'Reilly shouted:

"Sarah Watson! I might have known!" and stopped his car.

FOR a few moments, nothing moved, except the whispering branches of the three poplars in front of the white house. The windows of the house were dark. The blue car which stood beside the front steps of the house looked as though it had stood there a long time.

Three shots split the stillness. Glass crashed. A voice cried out from inside the dark house. It might have been a woman's voice. It might have been the voice of a man, raised high in terror.

O'Reilly flung himself out of the car. Cops, bristling with guns, piled after.

Feet pounded on boards. A man ran out of the front door of the house and down the front steps—a huge man, garbed in a waiter's suit. Two of O'Reilly's cops went into action, fast action. The man in waiter's clothes tripped over a cop's large foot, and went down.

The front door of the house flew open a second time. A shadowy figure bulked against the shadows behind it, a shadowy figure holding something white.

"Don't shoot, O'Reilly," said Sarah Watson's hoarse voice. "If you do, you'll wake the Millen Billionaire Babe."

SARAH WATSON stalked down the front steps of the white farmhouse with the white bundle in her arms. She said, briskly:

"O'Reilly, if you'll hustle upstairs and talk to Jack Jessup, he'll confess. I had to shoot him and he thinks he's dying. He always seems to tell the truth when he thinks he's dying."

Sarah broke off and shaded her eyes with one stubby hand. She said, complacently:

"It's getting dark, but the old eyes are still good. That's a black limousine coming along the highway, or I'm— Listen, O'Reilly. You get upstairs and get that confession, quick! Jack Jessup did the actual kidnapping of this baby I've got in my arms. The feller in the waiter's suit helped. Get it down. Take these cops with you for witnesses. When you've got it signed, whistle out the window. . . ."

SARAH WATSON leaned negligently against the trunk of one of the poplar trees, the sleeping Millen baby cradled in her left arm, her right arm hanging limply against the folds of her black skirt.

The black limousine swung off the highway, purred to a stop under the trees. The chauffeur jumped out, opened the rear door. Mr. Mose Wesser descended and stood peering at Sarah through the gloom.

"Oh, Mr. Wesser," said Sarah, exuberantly. "I've found the Millen child, just as you said I would. Your name will be famous, Mr. Wesser, all over the world, and you owe me five thousand dollars fee for the job."

A shrill whistle sounded from somewhere above. Sarah shifted her weight on her feet slightly and lifted her right arm. She said:

"Put up your hands, chauffeur, and Mr. Wesser, put yours up, too. There'll be a cop here in a minute to arrest you, Mr. Wesser, for planning the kidnapping of the Millen child. Jack Jessup has confessed."

A POLICE car sped along the Northern Boulevard, headed back to town. O'Reilly sat hunched over the car's wheel. Sarah Watson sat beside him, a complacent smile upon her grim lips, a blanketed bundle on her spread knees.

Behind them, a black limousine rolled. The limousine was driven by a cop, and its elegant interior was filled with cops, entirely obscuring one tall, thin man in chauffeur's uniform, one small, soft man with a bandaged arm and a bleeding leg, and one large, elegantly garbed gentleman who answered to the name of Mose Wesser.

"Sarah," said O'Reilly, "this is going to be a sensation. The great Mose Wesser mixed up in a snatch. Praise be that Jessup spilled his brains with six cops standin' by! Otherwise, by dom, Wesser would have wriggled out. By dom, woman, how in the name of all the saints did you suspect Mose Wesser?"

"I'd suspect any man," said Sarah, grimly. "I'd suspect any man of anything at any time. When Wesser told me the kidnap hideout was on Prospect Boulevard after Jack Jessup had told me it was on Northern Boulevard—"

"But, by dom, woman, Jessup might have lied."

"O'Reilly," said Sarah. "When Jessup told me the Northern Boulevard, Jessup had just been shot. Jessup, as I've remarked before, always tells the truth when he thinks he's dying. . . . Slow up, O'Reilly, there's a car in trouble ahead."

"To hell with that," said O'Reilly.

"This is police business, and I want to get things straight. Why in the name of purgatory, Sarah, do you suppose a man like Mose Wesser engineered a thing like this snatch?"

"Well," said Sarah, "according to you, Jessup said in his confession that Mose Wesser planned the whole thing simply so the credit would go to Mose Wesser, after the baby was returned. Maybe you believe that, O'Reilly. I'll be damned if I do. Mose Wesser likes cash as well as credit, like any man."

"But, woman, where would the cash come in? There was no ransom demanded, and Jessup swore none was going to be asked."

"Wesser was smarter than that, O'Reilly. He wasn't counting on ransom. He was counting on a reward. A new angle in the kidnapping racket, O'Reilly. Keep it in mind. Slow down."

"You kidnap somebody and then act like a saint. You ain't interested in ransom. Oh, no. You're much too holy for that. It's a despicable racket, kidnapping. Most crooks, even, won't stoop to it. Just a few punks with delusions of grandeur. But rewards!—now that's a different matter. If you're in a position to effect the return of some snatch victim and cop a big take and be a hero at the same time, now that's something!

"Keep it in mind. Slow down, you dumb cop, will you? That cart at the side of the road looks like my car. That feller bending over the car's innards looks like . . ."

Sarah leaned across O'Reilly as the car slowed. She lifted her voice and shouted through the open window.

"Bennie," she said, "the Millen baby's going back to his ma!"

Ben Todd straightened, turned, and stared.

On his face was an expression of great perplexity. He regarded Sarah with a mixture of disgust and bewildered admiration. He could never understand what she was up to until everything was over, but he knew enough about her to suspect, almost invariably, that she would emerge from any given fracas with somebody's goat and a substantial amount of dollars and cents. She had a certain genius that way, and once she got started all hell and high water couldn't stop her.

Sarah said:

"What have you done to my car, young squirt? Well, well, let it go. I'm glad to see you had brains enough, anyway, to follow O'Reilly down this road. Wipe the sweat off your face, young feller, and hop in with us. We're going to have fifty thousand dollars reward money in our fists tomorrow—you and me and O'Reilly—and maybe we can afford to have the old car towed back to town, and fixed up a bit."

If You Suffer Itching Burning Torture of

CRACKED BLISTERING TOES SORE BURNING FEET

NORMAL COMFORTABLE FREE OF DISCOMFORT

ATHLETE'S FOOT

MAIL POSTAL FOR **FREE** VALUABLE BOOKLET OF INFORMATION

MERCIREX MILFORD DELAWARE DEPT. A-1

YOUR DRUGGIST STOCKS OR CAN PROMPTLY GET MERCIREX FOR YOU. IF NOT WRITE US.

TRIXIE MEEHAN

Detective Fiction Weekly offered more series characters than any other mystery magazine. One reason was that it came out more often and had a huge appetite for material.

Erle Stanley Gardner wrote about Lester Leith, the gentleman crook, for *Detective Fiction Weekly,* and he wrote about Señor Lobo, the soldier of fortune, and about The Patent Leather Kid. Carroll John Daly's rogue cop, Satan Hall, who also appeared in *Black Mask,* turned up in *DFW,* along with J. Allen Dunn's The Griffin and Milo Ray Phelps's Fluffy McGoff, a slow-thinking young thief. H. Bedford Jones's series character Riley Dillon was a jewel thief. Anthony M. Rud's Jigger Masters solved bizarre murders. H. H. Matteson's Hoh Hoh Stevens grappled with crime in the Aleutians. Two book characters, Frank C. Packard's Jimmy Dale and "Sapper's" Bulldog Drummond, appeared in the magazine.

And T. T. Flynn chronicled the cases of rugged, redheaded Mike Harris and his pert sidekick Trixie Meehan for *DFW.*

Flynn, born in 1902, was profiled in the October 28, 1933, *DFW:* "T.T. stands for Thomas Theodore, which is too much for any chap to hook on the front of his name. I wasn't born in Cork, Ireland. I'll admit to the Irish strain, though—proud of it. Born and raised in Indianapolis, Indiana, decided to be a writer all my life, and set out to see how much

experience I could gather. I have done a little bit of everything, including hitting the grit, or hoboing, if one must be
literary; ship yard, steel mills, house to house selling, traveling salesman; carpenter, clerk, followed the sea on deck and
the engine and fire room; worked in a railroad shop and as a
locomotive inspector. Was a partner in a wholesale candy
marketing business, and a string of other things that would
be boresome to relate. I believe a fiction writer deals with
life as a whole and he or she should know it from all angles.

"At present I am living in the Southwest; where I will be
six months from now, I don't know myself. I have only one
envy—to loll back in an easy editor's chair for a month and
dispense gloom and terror to the poor authors of the land
and good fiction to the deserving readers."

The story "Deadly Orchid" is from *Detective Fiction
Weekly*'s April 15, 1933, number.

The Deadly Orchid

By T. T. Flynn

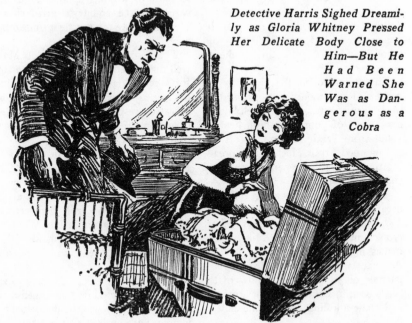

Detective Harris Sighed Dreamily as Gloria Whitney Pressed Her Delicate Body Close to Him—But He Had Been Warned She Was as Dangerous as a Cobra

"They're gone! Every stone and setting; while you played the fool and I played bridge"

THOMPSON, eastern manager of the Blaine Agency, said to me in the hotel room in Jacksonville, " Do dames fall for towheads like you, Mike?"

" Dames fall for anyone with a good line," I said, and waited. Six years' sleuthing with the Blaine agency had taught me that a fellow never knew what was coming next.

" You'll need a good line," Thompson grinned, fishing an old cigar stub out of his vest pocket. " There's a dame in Palm Beach who's responsible for the deaths of two men that we know of. And she's about ready to put a third scalp in her belt. I want you to meet her."

" Says you," I told him. " Figuring me for the third corpse, I suppose?"

" You never can tell." Thompson scraped a match under the edge of his chair and sucked on the cigar, rolling an eye at me as sober as a deacon.

" Who is this female execution squad—and where do I come in?" I asked him.

" She was baptized Gloria Whitney and has a string of aliases. Her nickname is the Orchid. Her specialty is blackmail. When she hooks a man he may as well pay up, take it on the front page, or write his own ticket. They fished one of her boy friends out of the river below New Orleans, and found another in his Park Avenue apartment with a bullet through his head. Not a bit of proof to connect the Orchid with either, of course. But there's no law against guessing."

"They should call her Aconite, the poison flower," I wisecracked. "And what do I do with this hothouse assassin?"

Thompson rolled the cigar to the corner of his mouth and grinned at me. "I'm counting on that well known sex appeal of yours I've been hearing about from Trixie Meehan."

I damned Trixie Meehan for spreading those yarns. She panned me every chance she got.

Thompson grinned again, and then became serious.

"The Orchid is one of the smoothest crooks in the country, Mike. She makes big money and makes it easy. As near as we can find out, she's got a partner or so who don't show often. She's been in Palm Beach for a month, and made a killing—all but the collecting."

"Or the suicide," I suggested.

"Exactly!" Thompson snapped. "I talked to the poor devil this morning. It won't take much to make him reach for a gun. He's Waldo Maxwell of the State Trust."

"Not *the* Waldo Maxwell?"

"None other," Thompson assured me. "No fool like an old widower, and he took it hook, line and sinker, and put it on paper. He won't stand a chance in court. And it will cost him a cool quarter of a million to buy back the evidence."

"Holy catfish!" I gasped. "What a haul! Why doesn't he take the publicity and save the dough?"

"Be yourself!" Thompson said. "He'd be the laughing stock of the country. Men who formerly trusted his judgment would think him doddering and senile. No telling what it would do to his financial strength. Not to speak of winding up a distinguished career as the country's prize clown. He'll pay if we can't settle it some other way."

Thompson was right. Waldo Maxwell had been a national figure for forty years. His bank was a Gibraltar of finance; he was the ultimate in conservative respectability. He'd be finished, out, if the scandal sheets got a thing like this.

"Maxwell retained the B l a i n e Agency," Thompson continued. "The sky is the limit on expense. And we're giving it to you. The Orchid is at the Palm Beach Palo Verde, registered as Miss Gloria Dean and maid. We don't know anything about the maid. It's a cinch she's crooked too. Got any ideas?"

"Plenty," I said, thinking fast. "First, make good on that expense account. And I'll want a good looking woman with brains. Got one this side of New York?"

"Trixie Meehan is due here in the morning from Chicago. She'll work with you."

I groaned, knowing Trixie.

Next morning I bought luggage, evening clothes, dress shirts, shoes, hats, all the clutter an oil millionaire from west Texas would be likely to have.

Trixie Meehan blew in, had a conference with Thompson before he left town, did some whirlwind shopping herself. We made the train together with enough luggage to do a theatrical troupe.

AN hour before dinner that evening we rolled into Palm Beach in two taxis, one packed with luggage. The Palo Verde was four stories high, with sprawling wings, acres of velvet lawns and a golf course; shrubbery, flower beds, palms, and the blue surf of the open Atlantic creaming in on the white sand beach before it. We wheeled up a wide shell driveway and stopped before a long marquee. Four uniformed bellboys ran out to meet us.

Trixie kicked me on the ankle.

"Out, ape!" she hissed under her breath. "Husbands always help the little woman tenderly."

"There you go!" I snarled. "Trying to start something right off the bat!"

"Yes, darling," cooed Trixie for the driver's benefit as I helped her out to the sidewalk.

Trixie Meehan was a little frail slip of a thing with forget-me-not eyes, a knock 'em dead face, and a clinging vine manner that covered concentrated hell. She had a razor tongue, muscles like steel springs, a brain that made me dizzy at times, and absolutely no fear. And here she was cuddling close and cooing up into my face while the taxi driver eyed me like a sap.

I paid him and left the baggage for the bellhops.

"Lay off that googoo talk when you don't have to use it," I growled as we went into the lobby. "You get my goat."

Trixie grabbed my arm and snuggled close. "You big strong he-man!" she sighed.

I couldn't shove her there in the lobby, so I took it out on the clerk. "A suite. Two bedrooms. Best you have. Ocean exposure, on the third floor, if possible."

"A quiet suite, dear," Trixie trilled.

"A quiet suite!" I snapped to the clerk.

"I think we have one that will be entirely satisfactory," he beamed at me. "And I can give it to you for only eighty dollars a day, since this is late in the season."

"Eighty a what?" I gagged.

"Eighty dollars a day," the clerk repeated firmly, and managed to chill me with one eye while he eyed our mountainous luggage, just coming in, with the other.

Trixie pinched my arm, and smiled brightly. "Eighty dollars a day is quite satisfactory, darli, ,' she cooed. "Can't you remember that we have oil wells now?"

The clerk caught it. His face cleared instantly. He handed me a registry card and a fountain pen. I registered Mr. and Mrs. Blain , San Antonio, Texas.

We looked like wealthy young globe trotters, for our old luggage was plastered with labels from everywhere. Undercover work for the Blaine Agency means travel. When the bellhops got their toll and left us alone in the suite, I went to the connecting door of the bedrooms and moved the key to my side.

"Verboten," I grunted at Trixie. "None of your blasted tricks now. I want some peace on this case."

Trixie threw her hat on the bed and made a face at me. "Be yourself, ape. Nobody's pursuing you. What has your massive brain planned for this evening?"

"The Orchid and her maid have three rooms at the end of the hall," I snapped. "I meet her, I make her, and then we take her."

"Just as easy as that," Trixie marveled. "Well, here's hoping. But don't forget we're married, darling, and I get some of this Palm Beach whoopee."

"Nix," I grinned. "That's for me and the Orchid. You're the neglected wife who mopes in her room."

"You'll have whiskers to your

ankles when I do that," Trixie said through her teeth.

THE idle rich! The wisecracker who said that never had more than a week's pay on hand in his life. Golf, tennis, swimming, riding, dancing—and bridge thrown in whenever Trixie could scare up a game. Three days of that to put us in the public eye and get our lines out.

The unlimited expense account made it possible; oil millionaires from Texas, hicks from the sticks, lathery with money. Trixie shopped at those exclusive little Fifth Avenue branch shops. They came to the hotel collect, and we had war the first night.

"Whose little gold digger are you?" I yelped. "Look at these bills I settled today! I knew you were a tough case, but I didn't know you had mucilage fingers. Any dumbwit you drag to the altar will be going for a cleaning instead of a honeymoon. Sixty-seven berries for a hat, and I could wear it for a felt thumb protector!"

"So!" said Trixie with a glitter in her eye. "You were snooping in my packages like a second story mug, Michael Harris?"

"When I pay sixty-seven crackers for a cardboard box and four yards of tissue paper and ribbon, I want to see what I'm stung with!" I gave her.

And Trixie moved in close for battle. "Listen to me, you sack of wind! Nobody ever dragged you to the altar and they never will. Pull those pop-eyes in and get this straight! I'll send the beach up here collect if I feel like it, and you'll pay and thank me. Whose bank account is getting nicked? Not yours! Hand you a five dollar bill and you'd start jawing J. P. Morgan. Gold digger, am I, for providing a little atmosphere? Next time I hear a—"

I slammed the door on the rest. That acid tongue of Trixie's could lift the skin off a cigar store Indian.

We buried the subject of clothes. After all it wasn't my money. I took a flier or so in the market those three days. And the tips I ladled out everywhere disturbed my sleep nights. But they were good advertising. By the second day every flunkey in sight was bowing and scraping when I appeared. Funny how oil millions can spread. We were the gossip of the hotel. Some turned up their noses, and some fell over themselves to gladhand us.

The Orchid did neither.

I spotted her the first evening in the dining room, and the waiter cinched it. "That is Miss Dean, sir."

"Pretty girl to be dining alone."

"Miss Dean seldom has anyone at her table, sir. She is, if I may be so free, a retiring woman." And the waiter rolled an expectant eye at Trixie.

"Perhaps, dear," says Trixie sweetly, "you would like to leave me and join her?"

And the waiter went off satisfied.

The Orchid had everything Thompson had outlined. I didn't try to guess her age. She was like an orchid, slender, graceful, dainty, fragile. She was a natural blonde—Trixie admitted that reluctantly—with a shell pink complexion and ripe red lips. Her eyelashes were long and dreamy, her makeup a bit of art, her expression tender and demure.

One look at her there in dainty solitude and I was willing to swear Thompson was a liar and Waldo Maxwell a lecherous old reprobate. A second look and I was hardboiled again. I've seen enough crooks to have an extra sense about them. Her eyes wandered over and caught my grin. She took me in from hair to second button on my dinner coat, and then went on eating without a change of expression. But my neck hairs stiffened. She was like a beautiful leopard, lazily lapping 'cream. Claws were sheathed behind that fragile daintiness.

Trixie was on tap as usual. "All right, cave man, go into your act," she said under her breath.

"Rats to you," I said. "This is going to take technique."

The waiter returned and Trixie cooed: "Yes, dear." And we had honeymoon the rest of the dinner.

I didn't make a move for three days. But now and then when the Orchid was on the horizon I caught her studying me. The wild and woolly west, with a wagon load of money, and extra luggage in the wife, had come to Palm Beach. I spent as little time with Trixie as possible. I ogled the women when the Orchid was around. I flashed the bankroll and made a fool of myself. Anyone with half an eye could see I was ripe picking for a smart dame.

But it was Palmer, a natty customers' man for Trenholme and Edwards' branch brokerage office, who gave me my break. A little about oil wells and flyers in the market made him my man. He was a good looking young chap, a little too soft and polite; but he knew his Palm Beach, and the Orchid by sight when I pointed her out on the hotel veranda.

"Corker, isn't she?" Palmer sighed. "Haven't met her, but I hope to. See her all the time at Corey's. Say, that's a place you might like. Been there yet?"

"A big gambling joint, isn't it?"

"Yes."

"I'll be glad to take you and Mrs. Blaine there any time."

"Tonight," I said. "Mrs. Blaine will be busy. We'll go alone."

I'D heard about Corey's place; to gambling what Palm Beach was to society. With its clientele a Broadway gambler would have retired in six months. Strict cards of admission were required, and your name almost had to be in the social register to get one. Formal evening dress, of course, and once inside the old lavishly furnished frame building, set back in a tangle of trees and tropical growth, the sky was the limit. Private rooms upstairs for really high play. The drinks and food were on the house. The service was in keeping with the crowd who went there.

Palmer got a card some way. Things like that were his business. I went with a fat billfold, a boiled shirt, tails and everything—and tried to forget that in a few weeks I might be impersonating a longshoreman around the East river docks.

It was a joy to lose the first three hundred, of someone else's money. We shifted from game to game for an hour and a half. Cool, perfumed air, beautiful women — some of them — men whose names made the newspapers, the hum and chatter of conversation, the quiet voices of the house men, now and then a black dressed automaton moving about with a tray. But no Orchid.

And then she came in, wrapped in a black coat with a roll of white around the collar. Stunning? I skipped a breath. "Palmer," I said, "I'm going to need the rest of the evening to myself. Would you mind ordering a Rolls outside in case I need it?"

And I went to the roulette table where the Orchid had drifted. For a few minutes I watched her lose five dollar chips, and then I slipped into an empty place at her side and slapped down five hundred. I lost and raised it to a thousand. And won, and won the next time, and the next. By that time I had the Orchid and everyone else at the table with me.

A fifty dollar bill was slipped into my palm, and I met a cool smile. "Will you play it?" the Orchid asked. "I think you are lucky tonight."

We won together.

Since it wasn't my money I didn't get the cold chills as I pushed my luck. I played the Blaine oil wells in public that night, and had the customers hanging on the edge of the table and standing three deep behind us. No, I didn't break the bank. They tell me no one ever does that at Corey's. But I put on a good show, won six thousand when the plays were evened up, and broke the ice with the Orchid.

I stuffed the winnings in my pocket and grinned at the Orchid. "I always quit while I'm cool, ma'am. Would a little drive along the ocean front cap your luck?"

"It might," the Orchid agreed as she folded her cut. "Shall we try it?"

The motor of that big Rolls purred, and so did the Orchid. Her technique would have made Delilah quit. "You were so calm over those big stakes," she sighed.

"Shucks, ma'am, back in Texas, our stud games would make that piker play tonight."

"You're from Texas?"

"West Texas," I gave her breezily. "Out in the oil country."

"How fascinating! Have you an oil well?"

"A dozen," I grinned. "An' two more spudding-in this week on proved ground. I always told Susan that when I passed my first million I was coming to Palm Beach. And here I am. But

I never thought I'd be riding around with a beautiful woman like you."

"You flatter me," said the Orchid absently. "Your wife—does she like it? I've noticed her. She's a beautiful little thing."

"Susan's pretty enough," I agreed without enthusiasm. "But she says she'd rather be back home where she can be a big frog in a little puddle instead of a little frog in a big puddle like she is here."

The Orchid laughed softly.

"Perhaps she is right at that. A woman has to be used to this life before she can get the most out of it. I owe you more thanks than I can repay for making it possible for me to stay here a little longer."

"I don't understand," I mumbled, and waited for her line.

"The money you won for me," she explained. "That was almost my last fifty dollars I gave you."

"I thought you were—"

"—rich?" She laughed shortly. What an actress! "One thinks that about everyone here. A little insurance money can create quite an effect. But when it's gone—" She broke off on a quaver.

I put a hand over hers. "I understand."

"I thought you would," the Orchid murmured. "Now forget about me and tell me about Texas."

So I spun her a few yarns about how I started as a poor kid in the oil fields and finally got in the money. When I spoke about oil field life she looked out the window, and when I mentioned big money she was all ears again.

"I want you to meet Susan," I said finally.

"No, I don't think I'd better," the Orchid said sadly. "Wives don't seem to like me. They get jealous. We'll keep this to ourselves."

" Perhaps we'd better," I agreed— and wondered what her game was.

Trixie saw the powder on my coat lapel when I came in the sitting room, and said acidly, "Necking?"

" With the Orchid. I wanted her to meet my dear little wife, Susan, but she begged off. Wives don't usually like her."

" Susan?" Trixie had fire in her eye. " I could skin you for that, Mike Harris! Why not Abigail to that hussy?"

" Why not? Susan Abigail it is."

I got the door locked just in time.

THOMPSON long distanced from Washington in the morning.

" She's putting the screws on Maxwell," he crabbed over the wire. " Wants her dough quick, or else. The old man's frantic. He thought he'd have a couple of weeks yet anyway. Haven't you done anything?"

" It looks like I've done too much," I decided. " She wants Maxwell cleaned up before she cleans me."

" Well, get some action!" Thompson yelled. " If this thing goes sour on you, you're washed up with the Blaine Agency. It's that important."

" Button your lip," I advised. " They can hear you across the hall here. Tell Maxwell to put another padlock on his checkbook. No dame's going to toss a quarter of a million away by getting rash. He's safe enough as long as he stalls."

Thompson's groan traveled clear down from Washington. " I hope for your sake that's right," he warned.

And so did I. The Blaine Agency had a little trick of loading all the responsibility on the ones who drew a

case, and then if they didn't come through, heads began to fall. It worked nine times out of ten. But Waldo Maxwell's quarter of a million and the Orchid were a big bite.

She was a wise one, dangerous as dynamite.

Trixie heard me out.

" You can't stall any longer, loud mouth," she decided. "Necking parties may be your forte, but you'll have to cut them short. I've been watching that hussy. She never speaks to anyone who might be in the racket with her. And a dime to a promise that those letters are not in her hotel room here. She wouldn't dare keep them so close."

" She has a maid."

" I've seen the maid!" Trixie snapped.

And so had I. A beauty, and a crook, if I knew my way around. "We've got to pull a fast one," I decided.

" He thinks," Trixie marveled. " Well, produce before we both get fired."

" I'm going swimming," I told her.

I met the Orchid on the beach, where she had said the night before she'd be. She wore black beach pajamas trimmed with white, and against her creamy skin they were enough to stop the breath and scuttle good resolutions. She gave me a smile to go with them. " Where is your wife?"

" Reading. No sunburn wanted."

" You poor neglected boy. It must be lonesome at times."

I held my breath until my face got red, and stuttered, " N-not when I'm with you." And we got along famously.

All the time I was wondering where

she kept those letters of Maxwell's. Trixie was right. Not in her room. That would be the first place private dicks would look. And despite the fact that Trixie had seen no one with her, Thompson's hint that she did not work alone kept pricking at my mind.

So I admired the big diamond ring on her finger and told her about the jewels I had bought the little woman since the oil wells came in. Three hundred grand worth, diamonds, pearls, emeralds and what not.

The Orchid swallowed the hook. "What a fortunate woman your wife is," she sighed. "I haven't seen her wearing any."

I grinned. "She's afraid to. Jewel thieves. So she keeps them in the bottom of her trunk."

The Orchid lay there on the sand like a lazy cat. Her pink finger nails dug in gently when I said that. I saw her leg muscles stiffen slightly. But she didn't bat an eye.

"How dangerous," she warned abruptly. "She should keep them in a safety deposit box."

"Susan doesn't think so," I yawned. "She likes to take them out and play with them. She's like a kid. Always wanted a diamond ring—and then got a lapful. And she's convinced no one would ever think of looking in the false bottom she had built into her trunk."

"I suppose she's right," the Orchid nodded lazily. ". But just the same if they were mine I wouldn't take chances."

"Not you," I thought. Aloud I said: "Let's forget 'em. If she is robbed, I'll buy her some more. And how about taking a ride with me this evening? The wife is going to be downstairs playing bridge until late. I may have to leave tomorrow. Got a wire from my partner."

She looked at me through her lashes, smiling, mysterious, inscrutable. "Do you really want to?" she murmured.

"Try me," I dared.

"At eight," she said.

And I wondered whether I was being a fool after all. She looked soft and inviting as honey—and I knew she was dangerous as a cobra.

WALDO MAXWELL said harshly, "You are a fool!"

"I know I am," I agreed. "We all act the fool now and then."

He winced, said something savagely under his breath and prowled back and forth. I had run him down in one of those fantastic villas that huddled up little narrow drives just off the beach. Simplicity by the hundred thousand dollars' worth. Handkerchief sized lawns, tile roofs, and luxury inside that would dim the Arabian nights.

It was indiscreet, I knew. I shouldn't have gone near him. But I needed action quick, and he was the only one who could give it to me. And there he prowled around the room like an enraged old bear, his dewlaps shaking, his white hair mussed where he had shoved his fingers through it, a scowl deepening the wrinkles over his rimless eyeglasses.

Waldo Maxwell might have been able to tame a multimillionaire board of directors, but he had never tried Michael Harris of the Blaine Agency before. "Do I get it?" I demanded.

"It is an insane request!" he blurted violently.

"I know. I've thought it all over. If something isn't done quick, you're going to be splashed on the front pages, or out a quarter of a million," I reminded. "You haven't a thing on that dame. She's got you by your reputation and you can't even yip. Unless

I'm wrong about the contents of those letters."

"No—no! I was out of my mind when I wrote them. Don't mention them! Are you certain you can control this insane—this plan of yours?"

I would have felt sorry for him, if I hadn't remembered he could sign his name to a check for five millions, and still have plenty left in the sock. "What would you give to have her come begging for mercy?" I asked.

Waldo Maxwell showed his teeth in a smile, gentle as a wolf's. "It would be some consolation for the humiliation I have been put to," he confessed.

"Then come through with what I need."

He glanced at a platinum cased watch and made up his mind abruptly. "They will be delivered to your hotel some time before six," he promised.

"Can I count on that?"

"Young man, you heard me. Sometime before six."

So I left, satisfied.

And he came through.

I opened the sealed brown paper package and poured the contents on the sitting room table. Trixie took one look and squealed: "Mike, where did you get these?"

"Kris Kringle," I grinned. "Now do you believe in fairies?"

"I've never seen such good looking imitations."

"I'll bet you never have," I agreed. "Not a phony among them. Every stone and setting is the real McCoy."

And I didn't blame Trixie for going pale and sick when she looked at me. That mess of diamond rings, bracelets, necklaces and whatnots needed a lot of explaining. Trixie picked up a pearl necklace and ran it through her fingers. "Tell me, Mike," she commanded.

"Waldo Maxwell," I admitted. "It was like pulling eye teeth, but I got him to buy the lot on consignment. If they're returned, he gets his money back. If not—he'll probably have a heart seizure."

Trixie put her little hands on her little hips and looked me up and down with her lips pressed tightly together. "Have you gone insane, Mike Harris?"

"That has a familiar ring," I recalled. "Maxwell wanted to know the same thing."

"I think you have! What are you going to do with all this jewelry? Why, it—it must be worth a fortune."

"It is," I agreed. "And we're going to put it all in that little false bottom in your trunk, and you're going downstairs this evening and play bridge, and I'm sneaking off for an automobile ride with the Orchid."

"And leave all this up here?"

"Exactly."

Trixie bristled. "Now I know you're out of your mind! We'll do nothing of the sort! You can waste another evening making sheep's eyes at that cat if you care to, but I'm staying in and sit on this jewelry, or take it down to the hotel safe."

"Jealous?"

Trixie tossed her head. "Of you, big mouth?"

"We'll do as I say."

"If we do," Trixie snapped, "something tells me we are in for grief. I think that massive brain of yours is cracking under the strain."

"Don't think," I advised. "It's dangerous."

IF I had stopped to think I would have gone shaky myself. For I knew what Waldo Maxwell and Trixie did not—that lot of jewelry was in greater danger than if I had tossed it on the lobby floor and walked off. It might have been returned from there. And I didn't dare use phonies. A slick crook would have spotted them the first look. So I shut my eyes and walked into the manager's office and asked for four young bellhops who could ride bicycles, keep their mouths shut and stay honest for a twenty dollar bill.

He looked at me as if I were addled. "Of course, Mr. Blaine—I mean to say, we strive to furnish every service, but—"

"Then service me," I cut him off. "I'm serious and in a hurry."

Grant the Palm Beach Palo Verde service. They delivered. I chased the manager out of his office, talked turkey to those bellhops, and hung a hundred dollar prize up to sweeten their twenties. All four of them could out-think the average guest they roomed. In five minutes I drilled them letter perfect, and they scattered with expense money.

The Orchid sighed dreamily. "Isn't the surf lovely?"

"Great," I agreed, and held her hand tighter while I looked over to the beach.

Sure enough, there was a surf frothing in through the moonlight. Pretty, too, if a fellow had time to look at it. I didn't. My mind was on Trixie back there in the hotel playing bridge. And on my five bellhops, and the Orchid beside me on the front seat of the big rented sedan. No chauffeur this time. I didn't want to be bothered in case quick action was needed.

But for the time being we had no action as we loafed south in the moonlight with the open sea on the left. Some night. Some scenery. Some girl. I forgot the times I had called myself a fool for throwing in with the Blaine Agency. Nights when the rain ran down my neck, and guns barked out of the blackness. Days when nerves were worn to a frazzle matching wits with the smartest crooks in the country. A dog's life, until I met the moon and the sea, and the Orchid went limp inside my arms as we loafed along through the miles. She was concentrated forgetfulness in a gorgeous shell.

Only I didn't forget. When I wrap my arm around a snake I watch it. I tested her out. "We'd better be getting back, beautiful."

"Not yet," she sighed, and came over another inch. "It's so lovely out here tonight. I could drive until morning."

"You won't, sister," I thought—and gave her three miles more before I turned and stepped on the gas.

"You are driving too fast," the Orchid protested.

I patted her knee. "I'm a fast chap."

"You're a fresh one," she said, and tried to steer me over to Lake Worth and down through West Palm Beach, stalling for time.

"Little girls shouldn't be out so late," I stalled back. "I have a headache, and I'm going to turn in. I'll stay over another day and we'll take this up tomorrow night."

"But I will not be free tomorrow night."

"My loss," I mourned, and rolled her back to the hotel far faster than she had gone away from it.

The Orchid said good night without much graciousness and went in the front entrance. When I parked the car one of the four bellhops popped out of the night. His eyes were wide with suppressed excitement.

"Your room was entered, Mr. Blaine!" he said breathlessly. "A thin man with a black mustache. About twenty minutes ago."

"Any trouble? Where are the others?"

"They haven't come back yet. I've been waiting here for you."

"Be back in a few minutes," I told him, and hurried inside, lifted Trixie from her bridge game and took her up to the suite.

"Powder on your coat again," Trixie sniffed while I unlocked the door. "I'm getting sick of a half baked Romeo underfoot all the time."

"It's my charm," I grinned.

"It's your oil wells!" Trixie snapped as she marched into the room.

She beat me to the trunk while I was closing the door. And a moment later pulled her hand out of the hidden compartment in the bottom and whirled on me.

"They're gone! Every stone and setting; while you played the fool and I play bridge like you ordered! Oh, why did Thompson ever put an idiot like you on this?" She stamped her foot, grabbed my arm and shook it. "Say something! Don't stand there grinning like an idiot! They're gone, I tell you!"

"That's great," I said heartily. And Trixie almost swooned.

While she was getting her breath back I came out of my room sliding a clip into my automatic. "Hat and coat," I directed. "We're going out."

"Where?"

"Ask me something I know. It's a great night."

AND Trixie almost swooned again. But she was ready in sixty seconds, slipping a small edition of my automatic in her purse. Tucked away somewhere, too, was a fountain pen gas gun. Trixie never went without it.

A second bellhop was waiting when we got outside, his bicycle tipped on the grass. "What luck?" I asked him, and held my breath for the answer. It might mean the end of Waldo Maxwell's diamonds and pearls. If it did, it was my finish.

"Over in West Palm Beach," he said quickly. "Two of the boys are watching."

"Get in the back," I ordered. "We'll talk as we drive."

"Who are they?" Trixie demanded as we all tumbled in.

"Bellhops."

"It doesn't make sense."

"Nothing does." And as I drove, the boys in the back seat talked fast. One of them had been in an empty room where he could watch the door of our suite; another outside covering the windows; and the other two had been downstairs near a telephone.

There had been no second story work. A well dressed man had walked down the hall, fitted a key into the door of our suite, stepped inside, remained a few minutes, and stepped out again, natural and easy. He had walked out of the hotel into a waiting car—and three bellhops had jumped on waiting bicycles and followed. Simple as that.

"And you didn't tell them to call the house detective?" Trixie asked thinly.

"Think of the publicity, my dear."

"I think you are a reckless idiot!" Trixie flared.

"You've called me that before," I reminded. "He who steals and runs away will surely pay some other day."

"Mad!" Trixie muttered despairingly. "Stark, raving mad!"

Cross west on the brightly lighted

bridge over Lake Worth and you come into another world. The coast highway runs through West Palm Beach, and now and then a tourist stops off and settles. Apartment buildings, cottages, cozy houses—it was like getting home from phantasy land. We found the other two bellhops beside their bikes at a corner in the residential section.

Their dope was short and sweet. The car they had followed had turned into a driveway in the middle of the block, and was still in there.

"Stay here with the car," I said to Trixie.

And she said: "Never again. You need someone with sense to watch you."

"Meaning a woman," I said sarcastically. "Nevertheless, you stay here. This isn't a tea party."

So she stayed, and two of the bellhops walked down one side of the street and the other guided me to the one story stucco cottage where Waldo Maxwell's jewels had flitted. One side room was lighted. The window shades were down.

I sent the kid across the street and walked to the back of the house. A big car was standing in the driveway, heading toward the street.

No one was worried inside—and why should they be, after strolling out of the Palo Verde so easily? A radio was playing jazz. The screen door on the back porch was unlocked, and so was the kitchen door. I pulled my automatic as I stepped inside.

A swinging door opened out of the kitchen, a hall beyond that, and to the left was an archway into a dining room. A voice said: "God, Harry, this bracelet ought to be worth five grand anyway. The emerald is good for two, and most of the diamonds will bulge a carat and a half."

And a second voice, "Shall we split this necklace and peddle the pearls separate?"

"I wouldn't," I advised as I stepped in. "That's a sucker trick."

There were two of them, sleek, good looking young fellows. One knocked over a chair as he jumped back and reached under his coat. When he saw my gun he stood still.

Waldo Maxwell's bait was spread over the table. They hadn't been able to keep their hands off it. Harry had a little black mustache that jerked as he got out: "What are you doing here?"

"Don't be so formal," I said. "This is a pinch."

And Harry gasped, "It's a frame! He talks like a dick!"

"You mind reader," I said. "He is a dick. Turn around while I collect your rods, suckers."

Harry took a chance, dodged and grabbed for his gun. I shot him through the shoulder. The next instant the light went out as his sidekick reached the wall switch. They both cut loose as I dropped to the floor behind the table. Four shots that were almost one—and a door slammed. . . .

I was alone with my ears ringing and the radio blaring away in the next room.

That was what slowed me up! My ears and the radio. I couldn't hear their movements, had to go slow for fear they were waiting for me. The motor in the driveway suddenly spun. Gears whined as it rushed toward the street.

And just as I opened the front door there was a terrific crash at the street. They had run into another car in front of the driveway as they turned sharp to avoid it.

I ran out.

Two groping, stumbling figures

reeled on the sidewalk, fighting at their eyes. I backed away quick from the thin drifting vapor they were trying to escape.

It was my rented car they had run into. Trixie joined me, and said coolly: "I drove up when I heard the shots, and blocked them. I let them have the gas through the open window of their car."

"Good girl!" I yelled. "Tell those bellhops to collar 'em until the cops get here!" And I ran back into the house while the neighbors poured out into the street.

I reached the street again just as the police car slid up. We settled the rest in the station house. It took the jewels on the dining room table, the testimony of the bellhops, our credentials and a telephone call to Waldo Maxwell to clear Trixie and me enough so we could leave for the evening.

\nd at that we were told it was damn queer business, and there was going to be a lot of explaining before the matter was settled.

"There will be," I promised.

Trixie was wild as a taxi took us back to the Palo Verde.

"See what you've done with that idiotic jewelry!" she stormed. "A man shot, two cars wrecked, serious charges plastered everywhere—with all the publicity it will bring—and Maxwell is as bad off as ever!"

"We'll ask the Orchid about that," I said.

TRIXIE was still breathing hard when I knocked on the Orchid's door. The maid, almost as good looking as the Orchid, answered it. She took one look at Trixie and informed us that Miss Dean had retired.

"Too bad," I regretted. "Get her up." And I pushed on in.

The Orchid met us in a frothy negligee that was enough to stop the breath. "What does this mean?" Her voice was knife-edged.

"Harry and his sidekick are in the West Palm Beach police station," I told her. "They were caught with the jewelry. It belonged to Waldo Maxwell."

I saw the maid, standing in the doorway, turn pale and press a hand against her throat. But the Orchid's eyes began to blaze past her long lashes.

"So you tricked me!" she said through her teeth.

"Gloria," I sighed, "it broke my heart to do it. But you've been loose long enough."

"Waldo Maxwell is behind this!"

"Sad—but so."

I've seen a furious tigress behind the bars. But never have I been so close to one. The Orchid's face turned marble white. Her eyes narrowed to points.

"Maxwell won't get away with this!" she blazed. "I'll spread his name over every paper in the country! Tell him he'd better run here and settle it quick! If those men aren't out by tomorrow, I'll call the reporters in and give them the story of their lives!"

"Can you back it up?"

"Certainly! I have letters!"

"You had," I corrected. "What do you think I planted that jewelry for? I wanted to uncover your boy friends who were probably holding Maxwell's letters. I found them in the bottom of a suitcase in their house. You might call Maxwell from the police station tonight and ask him for a little mercy. He's got an answer all ready."

She spat at me like a cat.

Trixie said later that gave her hope for me.

GRACE CULVER

Week after week, the dime novels sported continuing characters such as Old King Brady and Nick Carter. Their successors, the pulp magazines, preferred an anthology format until the early 1930s, when Street & Smith launched *The Shadow.*

The Shadow became a very popular magazine. It featured the resourceful Master of Darkness in a novel-length tale in each issue. Back-of-the-book series were about Danny Garrett, the Shoeshine Boy Detective; Sheridan Doome, the Navy investigator; The Whisperer; and Hook McGuire, the bowling detective.

Grace "Redsie" Culver appeared in twenty stories in the magazine from 1934 to '37. They were written under the "Roswell Brown" house name by Jean Francis Webb (b. 1910), who also contributed stories under his own name in the categories of mystery, romance, history, and adventure. He wrote the daily radio stories for "Chick Carter, Boy Detective" from 1944–45.

"Hit the Baby" is from the February 15, 1936, issue of *The Shadow.*

Grace "Redsie" Culver didn't know much about the movie business—but when a director cried

HIT THE BABY!

she knew it was time to go for a gun!

"BLUE Monday?" The redhead yawned, stretched, looked up from her desk in the quiet office of the Noonan Detective Agency. "Who started that whoop-de-da about Mondays being blue? You got a whole new week's work ahead of you on a Monday morning. Saturdays, it's all over. Nothing but a picnic in the country or washing out your stockings to look forward to."

Young, good-looking Jerry Riker straightened from the filing cabinet where he was culling routine entries. He grinned at the girl who sat scowl- ing on the other side of the desk sign reading: "Miss Culver, secretary."

"Bored, huh?"

"Alongside of me," said Grace Culver, drearily, "a guy in the last stages of sleeping sickness feels as spry as a kangaroo. Saturdays! Whoever invented 'em?"

Jerry saw an opening and dove into it. They came few and far between with a fast-action girl like "Big Tim" Noonan's red-headed aider-and-abetter. But from long habit, young Riker kept on trying.

By Roswell Brown

"Saturday nights are Heaven's gift to the movie business, Redsie. Every right-minded citizen goes to a show then with her Big Moment." He reached a morning newspaper from his own desk, flicking it open to the amusement page as he laid it down before her. "There's the ads. Take your pick. And a free feed with Jerome A. Riker goes with it."

"Why bother with a show, then? Watching you eat spaghetti is funnier than any comedy."

Grace glanced down at the printed spread propped against her typewriter. Gossipy columns of news from Moviedom separated other columns of advertising on "epic features" and "colossal superspectacles."

"How's about it, lady?"

The redhead smiled at him absent-mindedly. "I see Moe Eisman opened up his Long Island studio again. Shooting a picture with Lulu Doré," she said, dreamily.

"Very interesting. But what about my date for——"

"Listen to this," Grace commanded. "The headline reads, 'Eisman Defies Witch Jinx To Film Doré Extravaganza.' Then it goes this way."

She continued to read aloud, oblivious to the dark looks she was getting from Jerry's corner. The article stated:

Suddenly opening the Eastern studio of Dictator Pictures Corp. for the first time in seven years, Moe Eisman yesterday began surprise production on "Love Locked Out" at his Maysville lot. The elaborate screen spectacle features Lulu Doré, famous French song star now appearing personally on Broadway in "Errors of 1936."

Interesting to the show world in this connection is the producer's disregard of the jinx popularly attributed to Dictator's Long Island plant at the time of its closing in 1929. Folks who are afraid of black cats are asking if Ik-la-Duk still haunts the Maysville stages.

It will be remembered that salary difficulties with the Haitian witch doctor—imported to lend authentic zombie atmosphere to "The Voodoo Vow," the company's last Eastern production—resulted in a complete break between executives and magician. A series of strange and tragic mishaps following the rumpus gave rise to a then-popular superstition that Ik-la-Duk's demons were holding his curse over the studio.

"The Voodoo Vow" was Dictator's most expensive and drastic box office failure.

"So what?" Jerry Riker demanded, as the redhead stopped reading. Zombies and voodoo were so much banana grease to Jerry. But Grace Culver was the kind of girl any young man likes to have hanging on his arm of a Saturday night. "How about our stepping out?"

Big Tim's secretary folded the newspaper slowly.

"Well, it won't be as much fun as tracking down a witch doctor. But it's better than catching up on my back mending. Suppose we——"

WHAT she had been going to say then, was something Jerry Riker never knew. The shrill whine of the telephone on her desk sliced imperiously across the redhead's idle banter. She uncradled the little black instrument and clipped into its mouthpiece the traditional, "Good afternoon. The Noonan Agency."

The voice at the other end was shrill and excited, making the earpiece click so fast that Jerry could catch nothing of what was being said. But he could see Grace's keen sherry-brown eyes going wider and wider.

It was three full minutes before the voice stopped, waiting for an answer. Then all Grace said was, "Right away, Mr. Eisman"—and she hung up.

"Eisman?" Jerry blurted. "That couldn't be——"

"The great Moe Eisman of Dictator. In person. And a pretty excited person, too!"

"What——"

"Tim's visiting at his sister's over the weekend. He said not to bother him unless something hot came up. What's her number?"

Jerry tossed her the Brooklyn telephone directory. "What's Eisman want? Another of his hot-shot movie stars being blackmailed?"

The redhead was spinning her dial with fingers that trembled visibly.

"Blackmail could wait. Murder can't!"

Jerry's jaw dropped.

"Mur—— Say, somebody hasn't gone and gotten bumped off over at that jinxed studio?"

"Somebody's gone and done just that!" She jerked her bright head back to the telephone. "Hello? Tim? . . . Listen, it's Grace. There's a voodoo curse running wild out at Moe Eisman's studio. A guy named Dinty Boyd was killed this morning. Shall we stop by for you?"

THERE was significant rust on the open gates of the old Dictator lot. Seven years is a long time in the movie game, but according to the papers those grilles had been shut since the last "take" on Eisman's ill-fated production of "The Voodoo Vow."

Just outside them, a little caretaker's bungalow looked newer than the rest of the plant. Grace had only a glimpse of its white clapboards and green shutters, as the agency's black sedan roared past it.

At the gates, a uniformed attendant was waiting with hand lifted to stop them. The sedan slowed as Jerry pressured the brakes. Big Tim, on the other side of the redhead, glared like an outraged lion full into the scarred face of the watchman.

"We're expected," he growled.

"Orders not to let anybody in but police and the company," the studio employee answered firmly. "There's been trouble here."

"Yeah. Trouble about a stiff named Boyd." Tim flashed the identification badge cupped in the palm of his hand. "Eisman sent for me."

Instantly the man's manner changed. He stood aside.

"Beg pardon, Mr. Noonan. I took you for reporters. Only expected one of you." His voice was deep and resonant, like a radio announcer's.

The disapproving word "reporters" rang out good and clear. Jerry nudged the redhead in high glee. Time was when the *Evening Banner* had known no better "sob sister" than Grace Culver.

"Mr. Eisman's in his office, Mr. Noonan," the guard informed. "First bungalow on your left inside the lot. He's waiting for you."

Big Tim signaled and his young assistant drove on. When the brakes squealed again, it was before the painted front of the building the guard had indicated. A placard above the entrance further identified it with the name:

M. E. EISMAN.

The agency trio tramped up the steps, with the grizzled chief a step in the lead. He jabbed a rusty button. Inside, a bell warned metallically. The door opened. A thin, horse-faced young man with the look of a secretary stood inside, nervously inquiring.

"Timothy Noonan to see Mr. Eisman!" The giant ex-police inspector's boom seemed to blast the little fellow back into the bungalow's cool interior. Moe Eisman's callers followed.

At a desk between the two windows of the office's far wall, the producer himself was turning toward them. Bald, flabby, the Hollywood tycoon lumbered forward eagerly. His florid face was marked by worry. Purple patches rimmed his glazed eyes.

"Thank heavens you have come, yet! For eight hours already, the village police tear up my studio! They find nothing. Now I send for you. My company gets maybe in such a panic I should have a walk-out, unless your agency finds me who killed poor Boyd."

Big Tim took the floor.

"This Dinty Boyd—who was he? Work here?"

Eisman nodded. "Sure, sure! Nobody, only they got business in 'Love Locked Out,' has set a foot on the lot. Dinty was my gaffer. He——"

"Gaffer?"

"Our chief electrician, Mr. Eisman means," interpreted the secretary's timid voice, somewhere in the background. "It's studio slang, sir."

"I get it. Go on. What happened to him?"

"Must be it early this morning. Six o'clock, maybe. Dinty was alone on the sound stage, working on wires. We got people called for to-morrow. Sunday work on account of Doré is in this Broadway show and only got mornings and Sundays to give me. It must 've shot from behind of him, up on the grid where we got overhead lights banked."

Noonen jerked forward.

"Boyd was shot, then?"

Eisman nodded until his fat jowls shook. Then the movement checked. He had thought of something else.

"But not by a bullet, no! It was a blow-gun arrow, poisoned like—like sometimes they use in voodoo tribes! Mr. Noonan, I ain't a superstitious man —but——"

"Never mind the zombie stuff. Miss Culver here told me that witch-curse yarn the papers dug up. Blow-guns take a pair of real lungs, like an automatic takes a real trigger finger. Let's see the sound stage."

Eisman led the way out of the bungalow. But as his squatty bulk plodded forward, miserable words piped over a thickset shoulder to his followers' ears.

"Only that Doré wouldn't budge a step from Broadway, never had I come back to this place! A square mile of safe million-dollar stages in Hollywood, and why should I? But no! I had to have Lulu Doré in my picture! I had to mess into them same jinx breaks like seven years ago! Ten times the salary I was paying that black devil, and it would have been cheap!"

STAGE 5, the faded paint above its dingy entrance indicated. But it was the only one in the long row that had even been unpadlocked. It was Stage 1, as far as the "Love Locked Out" company was concerned.

The atmosphere of desertion hung heavily over Dictator's Maysville lot. Overgrown weeds had replaced its one-time grass. Windows of locked buildings were screened with dusty cobwebs. Late afternoon sunlight and the little knot of shirt-sleeved workers and uniformed police guards on Stage 5 did little to liven up the barnlike enclosure.

"Where'd you find Boyd?" Big Tim queried.

Eisman led him around a section of erected canvas scenery that seemed to represent one end of a banquet hall. Dead ahead, the blank brick wall of the enclosed stage was pocked with doors that stood like a row of shadows on guard.

"Right—here!"

The movie mogul stopped on a spot not a dozen feet from one closed door. Instinctively, the trio from the agency glanced down. There was a blue chalk mark on the hard, bare floor to show where the murdered "gaffer" had fallen.

Big Tim turned. Behind the painted

canvas set, and a good two yards nearer the rafters, a skeleton iron runway like a fire escape flanked the heavy pipes from which large, unlighted multiple-arc lamps of the type known as "ash cans" were swung.

"That's where the blow-gun artist stood? Up there on the catwalk?"

"Must have, the angle the arrow hit," Eisman nodded, his froggy eyes blinking.

"Tim."

The interruption came from the red-head at the grizzled agency chief's elbow.

"Tim, Boyd was shot in the back, according to Mr. Eisman. Doesn't that add up?"

Noonan frowned.

"Huh? Sure it adds. The guy on the catwalk was no-spook and couldn't risk being seen. So he waited till Boyd was headed away from him before—— Hey! Now I get you!"

He lunged forward eagerly, gray eyes ablaze. Four scant yards lay between that blue-chalked X and a door in the thick brick wall. And on the steel panel, in painted letters that had been white six years ago, were the words: ELECTRICAL SUPPLIES—SUPPLEMENTARY STOREROOM.

"He was heading for that door!" the big detective bellowed. "You're right, Redsie! Whoever dropped him—didn't want him to get there. It's locked. Where're your keys, Eisman?"

Panting after him, the flabby mogul looked blank.

"Boyd—he had the caretaker's set. They—they wasn't found on him this morning, though."

"No duplicates?"

Eisman's head shook.

"Too long it's been locked up. By to-morrow, maybe, I could get——"

"To-morrow's too late. If those keys were worth lifting, I want to see what's inside that store room, right now!"

FROM a shoulder holster, the brawny ex-inspector drew a revolver that seemed dwarfed in his big hand.

Tim stood back a pace from the storeroom door, leveled the gun and pressed the trigger.

An explosion, just loud enough to attract every worker on the big stage, shivered the metal panel.

Noonan snatched for the doorknob, twisted it. As the door jerked forward, halves of its shattered lock clattered to the cement floor.

"Now we'll get at whatever your zombie didn't want Boyd to find!"

They went over the threshold, Grace and Jerry at Big Tim's heels, with the studio employees and their stuttering boss crowding behind. The redhead and her seasoned chief caught at the same eloquent detail with the same soft breath.

"Footprints!"

The supply room was a windowless brick cell, illuminated from a glass skylight and the open door. Rolls of insulated wire were stacked along its walls, covered with the grime of long disuse. Nothing else, except two empty crates for plugs, was visible. The dust lay thick over everything, including the floor—and it was there that the footprints showed.

Two sets of recent male tracks, an average size shoe, were easily traceable. One trail led from the door to an open, empty crate in the far right corner. The other led back again to the door.

Jerry Riker grunted in disgust.

"Shucks! Boyd was in here once, after all. Took away some plugs. There goes your theory, Redsie. It was cute while it lasted."

The redhead smiled thinly.

"It's still cute."

"But——"

"Mr. Eisman, it's true, isn't it, that every technician who works on a sound set in movie-making wears rubber soles to kill any noise the sound tracks aren't supposed to record?"

Moe Eisman blinked.

"Sure! You bet! Nothing but rubber."

Grace met Jerry's puzzled glance. "Leather soles with hard heels made those marks, Bright Eyes. Which means that it wasn't Boyd but our murdering voodoo zombie pal who used those missing keys to get in here, and then——"

Faint but sharp, a distant sound cut across her excited explanation. There was a quality of stark horror in it that jerked every one of the scant dozen in the group erect.

The cry trembled from outside, in through the foul air of the supply room like a scream from hell.

"Help!"

BIG TIM'S feet were pounding the hard floor of the sound stage before his red-headed assistant shook off the freezing terror of that shout enough to dive into action.

Hard on her chief's heels, she raced across the big barn in the direction where daylight showed beyond the huge sliding doors. She was abreast of him when they reached the relative brilliance of the open lot.

That eerie yell had come from somewhere near Stage 1, at the end of the row. Noonan and Grace plowed toward it, trained instinct guiding them through the weedy lawn that once had been a carefully kept-up picture plant.

The late light slanted from behind the last stage, throwing a blotchy purple shadow toward the oncoming detectives. And huddled at the rim of the unobstructed radiance lay what they were racing toward.

A crumpled shape—a man scarcely more than a boy—sprawled limply among the weeds. His face, turned skyward, was distorted with terror, jaw rigid, eyes bulging. Like a giant grinning mouth, a gash clear across his throat was spewing blood in a terrible, swift tide. From the brutal wound, where it had been sunk almost to its hilt, a queer, primitive dagger protruded.

As Grace went down on her knees at the boy's side, she could hear their racing followers thrash to a horror-choked standstill in the undergrowth at her back. Moe Eisman's breathless whimper panted words of recognition.

"Oh! Bill Daley, it is! Is—is it that he——"

"Dead," the girl from Noonan's pronounced quietly. She had seen death strike often enough before in her private detective career. But there was something so wantonly savage in the attack on this good-looking kid, that it left her silent.

"Daley? Who's Daley?" Tim rapped.

"My camera punk. Assistant camera man, that means," one of the shirt-sleeved workers spoke up. "I'm Ziegler, the camera chief. I sent Bill over here to look over the stock, maybe half an hour ago."

"Stock?" Tim cut in. "What stock?"

"All the photographic stuff Dictator didn't ship west when they shut down here is stored on Stage 1. Maybe some things we could fix up, instead of buying new. Bill is—was—good at that kind of tinkering."

Looking up from the dead boy's side, Grace saw her employer's grizzled brows draw together. He queried:

"The kid was alone?"

"Sure. We got only a small crew. All the rest were on Stage 5, working with me, when you blew that supply room door."

TIM bent slowly, squinting down at the knife plunged into its ghastly crimson sheath. He had made no move to enter Stage 1; seemingly because the two local police in the crowd had juris-

diction and had gotten on the job already.

But Grace realized, from intimate knowledge of the older man's methods, that he had taken in the whole layout and figured search to be a waste of time.

"Funny kind of a knife. Looks like one of those native machetes from—from some place like Haiti."

He straightened decisively.

"There's a print of that voodoo movie you made, somewheres around the studio, Eisman?"

The paste-colored face of the terrified executive twitched in stuttering acknowledgment.

"Like all white elephants—sure!"

"And a projection room, of course?"

Again Eisman nodded.

"I want you to have it run through for my two assistants. Right away." He turned to Grace. "There is a tie-up some place. I don't know what you'd best look for. But give that Ik-la-Whoosit a good once-over, anyways."

He strode off purposefully, on some errand of his own. Neither of his helpers followed. They had their orders.

The redhead met Jerry Riker's eyes unsmilingly.

"Well—here's your chance to take me to a Saturday movie," she said.

THE VOODOO VOW

The darkness of the tiny, unadorned cubbyhole flickered as that out-dated picture's title flashed on the screen. Tinny and hard, the voices of the early "talkie" rasped from the screen as the opening sequence slid on.

A native dive in Omoa. Villainous-looking extra people crowded the bar, lounged at tables, chanted with the weird native orchestra. The scene narrowed down to one table.

Two white men, in spotless linen, were talking. An elderly English character actor and a young, almost too handsome chap Grace remembered vaguely as Barit Tyson. He had been a promising second lead, once. Since the coming of talkies, she couldn't remember having seen him.

The Englishman, sardonically amused, said, "So you don't believe in our voodoo magic, eh? Well, Bob, if you'd been here long enough to see the things I have——"

Tyson, interrupting, said, "Magic? Mumbo Jumbo, you mean."

Just four words. But Grace straightened quickly in her hard chair. Ugly voice? It was deep and appealing, even in those first crude days of recording. Barit Tyson had been a talkie natural!

The Englishman's line, emphasized by a curt nod of the head, was, "Yes? Glance over there, then, my friend. See that man near the door?"

The camera trucked across the noisy, vicious crowd, once more to show the dive's battered entrance. A black man, tall but emaciated, crouched there.

He looked like a black skeleton draped in tattered rags. Sunk deep in their sockets, burning eyes stared out from the screen with a fanatic madness that was no act. Ik-la-Duk, the antagonized witch doctor!

"Golly!" Grace breathed in Jerry Riker's ear. "If that face was haunting me with any curse, I'd give up quick! Eisman picked the wrong baby to fight with about salary."

"The first big mistake was ever letting him get out of Haiti."

Reel by reel, "The Voodoo Vow" went on with its story of love under the dark menace of zombies and demon visitations. Tyson, as the unbeliever, was tortured and driven mad himself amid the tropical jungles that once had bloomed artificially in the Maysville studio.

Jerry grunted suddenly.

"That knife there! See it in the zombie's hand? It's a dead ringer for the one the throat-ripper used on that poor Daley kid!"

Grace nodded grimly. Fifty minutes

of sitting in the dark and watching this witch stuff, and you began to wonder.

Could some dark spirit actually be hovering malignantly over this long-closed movie lot? Could that legendary curse of Ik-la-Duk be anything more than tommy-rot to fill the gossip columns?

The terrified producer, she knew, really believed in it. Two men had already been butchered, in the same day and for no sane reason, as soon as the "haunted" lot was reopened. Both weapons used were native devices. And why would any human murderer have picked them; and how come into possession of them?

"I wonder," she muttered in the darkness, under cover of the wailing voodoo death chant that emanated from the screen, "whatever became of Barit Tyson?"

MOE EISMAN was getting ready to leave his office for the day when the little redhead from Noonan's agency appeared on the office bungalow's doorstep. The mogul's car was waiting, and in his eyes lurked something that said he didn't at all like to be in this particular spot after dark.

But the girl detained him with a grin.

"Well, Miss—Miss Culver?"

"I won't keep you a minute, Mr. Eisman. But 'The Voodoo Vow' got me to remembering Barit Tyson. I thought maybe you'd know why he dropped out of pictures? Where he is now?"

The seemingly unimportant question had hounded her, for some reason, to the extent of bringing her here. Yet, despite its insistance, she was unprepared for the way Eisman took it, for the popping of his frightened eyes and the visible chill that racked him.

"Oh! You should ask me now about poor Tyson! It was that no-good of a monkey devil that did it! Just like now he kills off good workers like Boyd and Daley and——"

"Did what?" Grace gasped. "Did Barit Tyson *die* here, before you closed the lot seven years ago?"

"Better he should 've! Such a box office! Such a draw with the women! Only two days and we'd have finished shooting the picture. And it had to happen to Tyson!"

The redhead's brown eyes glinted.

"But *what* happened, Mr. Eisman?"

"A charge of powder is supposed to blow up the witch doctor's hut, for the fadeout."

"Yes?"

"Gives it a defective fuse, gives it voodoo monkeyshines, I don't know. She goes up two minutes too soon. Like a beefsteak, Tyson's face turned out. Scars! Burns!"

"So *that's* why he had to leave the screen?" Grace exclaimed softly. "Poor devil. Where is he now?"

Eisman shrugged.

"To fire him is a crime. He's no more good in pictures. So I give a job as watchman here. I build him a nice bungalow. Still he stays on. It was Tyson let you onto the lot, this afternoon."

Barit Tyson, the scarred gateman? But it was true. That deep voice of his was what she had been remembering all through the voodoo picture. Grace's heart began to pound.

Eisman, turning away, was scurrying into his limousine. She caught at his elbow.

"Mr. Eisman, shooting on 'Love Locked Out' begins in the morning, doesn't it?"

"Heaven help me—yes!—if we have no troubles."

Grace smiled.

"Fine. I'll be on deck. I'm working for you, Mr. Eisman. I'm an actress."

The producer's face registered despair.

"Listen. Actresses I've got. Sure, you're pretty! Sure, you got personality. But now you're in steady work. The movies is no place for a nice, sweet——"

"I'm an actress—for one day only." Grace's voice was firm. "My name's Olga—Olga Egloff. What clothes do I wear? Oh, and you don't know me. Catch wise?"

Mr. Eisman blinked down at her stupidly. Then, slowly, he caught wise.

THE Sunday morning sun was cut off from Stage 5 when the heavy doors rolled shut against it. But the big barn was bathed in a dozen-fold better job of lighting than nature had provided the previous afternoon. Arc lights and "ash cans" glared whitely overhead. Small spots—"pickles"—played from the sides.

The "herder," one of a mess of assistant directors, was collecting his costumed extra people on the set. Ziegler, head cameraman, standing on a box, was training the camera on the pretty blonde who was "standing in" for Lulu Doré.

"Hit the baby!" somebody shouted.

A little Russian actress, with coalblack hair twisted in a heavy braid around her head, turned curious sherrycolored eyes on a girl who had shared her make-up mirror an hour before.

"What do they mean, 'Hit the baby'?"

The girl laughed.

"It's studio for 'Turn on the spotlight.' They're ready for Doré now."

Before Grace could make further conversation, the costumed mob fringing the lighted set fell back. It was Doré, the French prima donna, sweeping in with a blaze of emeralds.

At her heels trotted a stunted man —almost a dwarf, but with bull-like shoulders. He carried a littered tray.

"That's Waxy Lubin with her," the girl at Gracie's side confided. "Greatest make-up man in the show business! But he'd never leave New York. He retired when Dictator's Eastern studio was closed, until now Eisman hires him back.

"They call him 'Waxy'—because he can wax in wrinkles and lines till the oldest living citizen looks like an infant! Why, one time Waxy——"

But Gracie's new-found friend was talking to thin air—for the redhead had disappeared into the crowd.

GRACE waited, crouching low in the tall weeds, until the doors to Stage 5 had rolled shut for the last time. They were ready for the first "take" now. The whole studio would be busy inside.

Slowly she approached the open gate, where a thinning line of hopefuls still wheedled Barit Tyson for admission. Her costume and grease paint made her conspicuous in the bright sunlight. Her knees were unsteady. She'd never tried to fool an actor before.

"Hey! What are you doing off the set?"

A step inside the gates, she gave Tyson's scar-ugly face the full voltage of her big eyes. She was no scared greenhorn now. She was Egloff, the great Russian dancer; and regal enough to make Lulu Doré look humble.

"I am Egloff. I do not dance until ze dinnair scene ees fini."

Tyson stared down at her. His brooding eyes seemed to spark to life, cruel and still handsome in their ruined frame. She flicked an addressed, stamped envelope between careless fingers.

"I take ze walk to ze vil-lage and post my lettaire. You let me in again, yes, no? Bien!"

She swept past him, conscious of the boring of bright orbs into her retreating back. Heart pounding, she passed the caretaker's white cottage and rounded a bend in the road that led down a short hill and so into rural Maysville.

Then, leaping like a cat, she was across a shallow ditch and screened by roadside underbrush.

Slowly, moving with infinite care, she wormed back undercover toward the rear corner of that unimpressive bungalow in the shadow of the studio fence. Its windows, dead ahead of her, looked blank. But if her hunch wasn't a million miles off, that dwelling wasn't empty.

Voodoo? Curse-devils, killing for a witch-doctor's vengeance? Not by a long shot! Not after what Dixie had spilled about Waxy Lubin!

So a one-time star had been content for six years with a gatekeeper's job, had he?—and no suits for damages against Dictator, either. And at the same time, the East's ace make-up man had retired, refusing to go to Hollywood?

Hadn't the "voodoo devils" left the Dictator lot unhaunted, as long as nobody tried to make a picture there? And hadn't Barit Tyson been in possession of the only set of keys to the buildings inside, until by Eisman's order they were turned over to unlucky Dinty Boyd?

Grace flashed across the narrow strip of lawn that separated the rear of Tyson's bungalow from the tangled thicket overgrowing the slope below. Flat against the white wall, she edged toward the screen door that marked the kitchen entrance.

Inside, as the knob of the wire panel materialized under her groping fingers, she heard the guttural mutter of voices. Two men were talking.

THEY hunched over the kitchen table, like ghouls dabbling in gore as they ran their fingers through the little pile that glittered between them atop a square black box. Face pressed to the wire, the girl from Noonan's waited.

Both of the thugs were gang-stamped. One, she recognized as a gun named "Butch" Pember, with his face on file at police headquarters. The other was a stranger, with the shrewd look of a fence about him.

That pile on the box -which, Grace saw now, was a collapsed camera— sparkled like a haul from a jeweler's vault. Stolen jewels! So that was what Tyson had been hiding away, unmolested, in various safe places around the old studio!

This looked like the end of a good many trails of unsolved Manhattan gem thefts.

"Gee, but that young punk came near to settin' us in the hogpen yesterday!" Butch confided. "Seems he got sent down to Stage 1 to rubber over the old equipment. First thing his eye lands on is this old color camera Tyson had the Chinese stones put away in."

"Yeh? That's maybe why I got the hurry-up call to come out here and move the stuff?"

"Sure! Tyson just spotted this Daley goin' into the stage, Jake. Time he got there with a knife from the prop room, the kid was streakin' back to Ziegler with his find as happy as a pup with a bone. Boy, oh, boy, if they'd ever got that box opened up they'd 'a' seen plenty of color, all right!"

Grimly, the girl from Noonan's remembered young Bill Daley's dead eyes staring with horror. And the native knife. She should have had that figured long ago.

Tyson was the only studio employee with a key to the building where props used in "The Voodoo Vow" had been stacked away. Nobody else *could* have gotten at the bizarre weapons the killer had used—the machete and the blowgun.

Inside, the men were beginning to shovel the stones back into their square black nest. Grace groped in the deep pocket of her Russian smock, fingers closing over the steely coldness of the midget automatic she carried there.

"That's two narrow squeaks since this

cursed picture crowd showed," Butch growled. "First was Boyd, all but walkin' in on the gold plate Ty had stacked in a crate of plugs. And him with Tyson's only keys, too!"

Jake, the fence, kept on pushing away the "hot ice."

"Seven years of breaks, you can't expect everything. With Tyson actin' any part from a pushcart guy to a visiting duke, and Waxy fixin' up his pan according, things ain't been too tough."

Butch started a reply, then his voice broke into a startled grunt. Grace, automatic leveled to cover them, had eased the screen door open and started forward with stern purpose in her eyes.

But that wasn't what warned Butch Pember. Behind the girl from Noonan's, a voice yelled sharply.

"The dame! Watch her, boys!"

Arms flung about the agency detective's slim shoulders, knocking down her gun hand with brute force. The automatic, springing from stunned fingers, leaped away like a jackrabbit. Before she could twist to meet the unexpected rear attack, she was pinioned helplessly in a grip of terrific power.

Waxy Lubin's distorted face leered over her shoulder as she tried to turn.

PANTING, fighting like a hellcat, using sharp heels and writhing body, Grace battled to break that grip.

But the malformed make-up man only croaked with malignant laughter. His long, apelike arms imprisoned her as relentlessly as steel bands.

His subnormal height was the only weapon nature had handed her for a fight that left every other trick in the monster's stack. They stood eye to eye. Eeling in that wicked grip, Grace had twisted to partly face him. His hot breath blasted in her face.

Her head thrust forward suddenly, like that of a striking snake. Small, strong teeth pinioned Lubin's bulbous nose between white rows—and clamped. They clamped hard.

With a shriek of anguished astonishment, the ape-man let his powerful hands fly from their old grip to a belated defense. Grace whirled away from him.

Like a catapulted bullet, she dove across the room toward the little automatic that glittered where it had fallen almost at Butch Pember's feet.

A huge paw smacked flat across her chin with the power of a driven pistol. Butch had awakened from his amazement at Grace's attack.

Off balance, Grace struggled to ward off a second descending clout from Pember's rock-ribbed fist. It landed just where he'd planned it to. Her jaw snapped back inches. Then she crumpled against him.

Vaguely, she knew that she was being carried across the room. Sudden darkness enveloped her, and she heard a latch click. She was held erect by a strength not in her battered body—by the narrow walls of the closet, so close together that she couldn't fall.

Far away, Lubin's voice said: "She can't get out of that. I'll get Tyson, see what he wants us to do."

FIVE minutes must have passed, but Grace's jaw hadn't stopped throbbing any. Propping her pounding forehead against the wooden panel in front of her, she listened to the heavy thud of feet tramping into the kitchen outside. Tyson had arrived with Waxy.

"Waxy says you caught a dame snooping." The deep, actorish voice paused significantly. "A dame with a rod."

"Dame, hell! Didn't you pipe Waxy's schnozzle? That's a wild panther, that frill is!"

Tyson chuckled, a sound as cold as the click of ice cubes.

"Well, she's caged now. What she look like?"

Butch Pember growled. "Russian, kind of. Black hair done up in a braid. It felt like a wig, though, maybe."

"Wig?" There was a murderous new throb to the scarred actor's exclamation. "Say! She passed me. Dancer, she said. But I got her figured now! That's the dame from the Noonan Agency, the bonfire skirt."

Grace, upright in her narrow prison, heard him pace up to the door, wheel and stride away again. There was scarcely space to shudder in the broom closet. She'd seen coffins that were roomier.

"The studio's getting too hot. Too many cops, along with the dicks." Tyson paused only an instant. "The zombie's going to pull his last curse—right now!"

"Huh?"

"The poor, faithful watchman is going to lose his bungalow. By fire! Too bad that pretty little cutie has to burn. But that's how it is with a voodoo hex."

He went on swiftly, his cold, deliberate voice outlining the steps of his hellish plan to cover all tracks.

"Jake, you'll stay here. Stack rags, papers, wood from around the place against the broom closet. Douse 'em with gasoline and start a good blaze. Then grab the ice and the camera and scram. Later, when the crowd collects, you're a news photographer here after pictures. Hitch back to Maysville with the fire company or the cops, camera in the open. You won't be tracked that way."

"O. K., chief." Jake sounded pleased.

"You, Butch—you and Waxy and I are leaving, too. But not without that Doré's emeralds. On Stage 5, in about three minutes, the hex is going to show up plenty! Good luck, Jake."

The heavy footfalls receded—three pairs of them. Then the screen door slammed. In the kitchen, Jake began to whistle softly.

The noise of a table being dragged

toward the broom closet door scraped menacingly across the scrubbed planks.

Three minutes!

Twisting frantically in the narrow space, the girl from Noonan's worked her arms aloft. When they were level with the heavy Russian braid atop her head, supple fingers went to work.

They found what they were seeking quickly, settled down to the swift business of unplaiting the false black hair.

"Here's where that Culver gal's last chance to stay uncooked takes the spotlight for fair!" she whispered grimly.

In her eager fingers now was a little green pellet. It was one of Gracie's many crime-solving gadgets. A single wisp of string, protruding from it, unwound slowly out of the loosened braid. Gracie pressed the green "pill" into the keyhole of the closet door. A match, from a pocket of her smock, was lighted and the flame applied to the dangling string.

"Well, redhead: Hit the baby!"

THE muffled *boom*, like a single drum beat, jerked Jake from the pile of rags he was gathering from a far corner of the kitchen.

Spinning, he was in time to see the narrow door of the broom closet splinter open as if a mule had kicked it from inside. And right behind the door came a small, leaping figure made up of shredded clothing and a powder-blackened face.

Jake let out one yell. Then he dove. And the dive was in the direction of a corner cabinet, where two guns—a businesslike army pistol and a midget automatic—lay cuddled together like sleeping lovers.

That instinctive move was just what the girl from Noonan's was figuring on; just what her keen, brown eyes had been watching for. It located the weapons for her.

Swerving, she bore down on the cabinet.

Still dazed, Jake swung to attack her. He balanced hastily; and, as she flung herself abreast, leaped with a sprawling forward lunge. His fists flayed murderously.

Spinning like a leaf on a whirlpool, Grace slid past the driving knuckles so close that they contacted her swaying braid. Back slammed to the corner cabinet, she thrust a lightning-swift arm behind her.

Twisting, Jake lunged again. His eyes glittered wickedly. He left his feet in a direct dive, thrusting forward with all his weight and with telling speed. The space between him and the cornered girl closed like——

Cra-ack!

Scant inches from his prey, Jake jerked back as if a rope had caught him. A tiny black hole appeared between his eyes. Surprise, then terror, flickered over his pasty face.

Sobbing softly, he buckled to his knees and slumped against an old black camera lying unheeded on the floor.

Palmed gun still smoking, the girl from Noonan's leaped across him and sprinted for the kitchen screen.

STAGE 5 loomed ahead of her in the glaring noon light as she sped across the empty lot. The open gate had been unguarded. Barit Tyson was through playing watchman.

The heavy roller doors were shut and locked for the "take" supposedly going on inside. But what must really be happening on that set was something Big Tim's helper flinched to think about.

Panting, she drew up before the big barn. Directly in front of her, set into the huge roller door, was the regulation small hinged one for the necessary passage of technicians during a "take." Had they thought to lock that on the inside? But she was praying Tyson had left it ready for a quick get-away.

Automatic steady despite her jerky breathing, she thrust out for the latch left-handed. It moved under her clammy fingers! Sobbing with relief, Grace flung her whole weight against it. The panel gave. She hurtled forward —into inky darkness.

The blaze of lights she had left on the busy Stage 5 had been blotted out. Blackness blanked the walls, the cameras, the catwalk and light grid. Dead ahead of her, one white spot gleamed from above like a devil's eye. Undiffused, it hit the gay canvas of the backdrop. And against the canvas, arms above heads, the "Love Locked Out" company huddled like sheep.

The direct glare from above, pointed full into their eyes, blinded them. Staring into it, with various expressions of fear or baffled rage, Grace could glimpse Ziegler, Lulu Doré, Big Tim, Jerry, Eisman. And it was hands up high for every one. Tyson's masterly surprise, depending only on blanked lights and fiendish speed, had caught them all!

From the utter darkness behind the light, a deep, cold voice—the scarred killer's voice—was speaking:

"All right, Miss Doré. Off with the emeralds. All of 'em! Hold them in front of you at arm's length. Now walk forward, toward my voice. You can't see me. I won't shoot unless——"

Grace ducked. An inch or so to her left, where the brief flash of light had shown as she whipped through the door, something whizzed past with the silken sigh a hurled knife makes. Butch Pember's shout followed it.

"Boss! Somebody just came through the door——"

Up snapped the automatic in Grace's cold fingers. The trigger kicked daintily at her expert touch, and a little orange eye of flame winked once. It didn't wink in Pember's direction, though.

There was a tinkle of shattering glass. The girl from Noonan's whirled back against the roller door and dropped to her knees, as the bullet-riddled spotlight sputtered out.

Instant lead, pumped from two angles at once, snarled in the place where she had stood a split-second before.

SOMEBODY shouted: "Cops!" Feet thudded across the stage, running frantically. Women screamed. Tim's warning yell split the tumult: "It might be Redsie, Jerry! Don't shoot unless——" The hammer of racing feet drew nearer, nearer, nearer——

Still crouching, Grace swung to face the spot where the small hinged door would offer the crooks their only out. Nothing to do but wait. Her jaw was set.

Suddenly, light appeared. A square of garish high noon showed, against which three backs in seething, crowded motion were outlined sharply. They had closed in on the exit together. Now Tyson was shoving back Butch Pember. Waxy Lubin was crowding into Tyson.

"Stop! Right there!"

They didn't stop. Butch bellowed frantically. Waxy went down on one knee, flung backward by Tyson's shoulder. Grace clipped a single shot above their heads.

"You get the next ones! I mean that!"

She did, and they knew she did. The fact that she was there at their backs, instead of locked in a burning closet, argued coldly for her feeling about them. Up crept their arms. Rage, impotent hatred, showed in the set of their backs; but not one of them tried out that move they had been warned against.

Grace lifted her voice.

"Lights, please! There are your zombies, Mr. Eisman; and you'll find the real curse in a camera over at the watchman's bungalow. Let's have a look at 'em. There's plenty of arcs and whatnot for somebody to turn on around the place, even if one of my slugs did have to—er—hit the baby!"

VIOLET McDADE

Clayton Publications launched *Clues* in 1926. The title was broadened to *Clues Detective Stories* when Street & Smith acquired it in 1933 and ran it for another decade. The title offered a number of series, including Oscar Shisgall's Barron Ixell and Earl W. Scott's Hammerlock Wilson, the Fighting Dick. Johnston McCulley's Thubway Tham also lisped his way through adventures in the magazine.

Another regular contributor was Chicago-born Cleve F. Adams (1895–1949). Adams worked as a detective as a young man. He wrote reams of detective stories in the 1930s for *Black Mask* (the Canavan and Kleinschmidt series) and for *Detective Fiction Weekly.*

He created chunky, no-nonsense Violet McDade for *Clues Detective Stories.* Violet and her pard, Nevada Alvarado, are unusual both as a team of women and because of the latter's Hispanic ancestry.

"Flowers for Violet" is reprinted from *Clues Detective Stories'* May 1936 issue.

FLOWERS for VIOLET

A Violet McDade Story

"Drop the rod; you're covered!"

by
Cleve
F.
Adams

VIOLET McDADE in a night club is as conspicuous as an elephant in an aquarium. It isn't altogether her prodigious size, nor is it her atrocious taste in clothes. Rather, it is a combination of these things added to the manner of a precocious child bent on attracting attention. She was attracting it, beyond a doubt.

The floor show at the Green Kitten was pretty good; exceptional, in fact. The crowded supper room didn't even know it was there. All eyes were centered on that great lummox who is my partner. Or, at least, that's the way I felt. I was never so embarrassed in my life.

I said, "Violet McDade, if you ask another man to dance with me I'll —I'll scream!"

"Go ahead," she said. "People will just think you're drunk." She waved a pudgy, beringed fist at the second drink I'd had in the last hour, her fat nose crinkled in disgust. "There you go, soppin' up liquor, spoilin' the effect of all the swell contacts I'm makin'."

"Contacts!" I said. "All the contacts we've made to-night have been on my feet. I've danced with fat men, lean men, in fact every man in the room who has been unfortunate enough to pass our table. I'm sick of it. I'm going home!"

"Trouble with you"—she sniffed —"trouble with you, Nevada, is you don't realize what contacts mean to a couple of female dicks like you and me. Look, here comes Stephen Wright, the assistant district attorney. I'm going to hornswoggle him into dancin' with you and after that —well, after that mebbe I'll go home, too."

Wright seemed in a great hurry to get back to his table. His cold eyes missed her smirk of recognition and she calmly stuck out a foot, tripped him. He stopped then. Square, granite face aflame with wrath, he righted himself, muttered an ungracious apology.

She beamed. "Think nothin' of it,

Stevie. Meet my partner, Nevada Alvarado. Senator Hymes will wait for you. Fact is, it looks like you're both waitin' for somethin'. Couldn't be your new boss, the district attorney, could it?"

He glared at her, made as if to pass on, thought better of it and pulled out a chair. "Why should you think Alvin Foss is coming here to-night?"

"A little birdie told me," she said easily. "Or maybe it was a stool pigeon. Tell you the truth, that's the real reason I'm here myself. I'm kind of keepin' an eye on Rose Donelli in case her husband gets into trouble."

Something flamed in the depths of those cold eyes opposite. He said, "Why should Mike Donelli have any trouble with Alvin Foss? The Green Kitten is a licensed club."

"There's things upstairs that the license don't cover, Stevie. Mike's real business is gamblin'. He's in the rackets up to his ears, and I got a idea"—she winked owlishly—"I got a idea that a certain state senator's dough is behind him."

Wright said, "You're talking wildly, woman. Perhaps too wildly." He let that sink in, rose. His eyes on a distant table, where sat State Senator Hymes, he bowed absently. "I'll bid you ladies a very good evening." He went away.

MIKE DONELLI, very genial, very hearty, came in through the arch which led to the stairs, paused beside us just as Rosita was announced. Rosita was Rose Donelli. She did a whirlwind number, clad mostly in brilliants, and was the big drawing card of the Green Kitten— the supper room part of it, I mean. I hadn't known about the other diversions upstairs until just now.

Violet, eyes on Rose, addressed Donelli. "Why don't you get out o' the rackets, Mike? Rose is too nice a kid to be mixed up in—well, in things that'll likely make her a widow before she's twenty."

He was watching his wife. His smooth, round face was a little troubled. "You think a lot of Rose, don't you, Violet?"

"No, you ape, I don't. I think she's an empty-headed little tramp. I think she was a sap for marrying a guy like you. But"—Violet's little greenish eyes got that far-away look which somehow always brought a lump to my throat—"but Rose's mother was damn white to me back in the old days when she was tops and I was doin' the fat lady in the same circus. I—I kind of owe Rose somethin' for that."

Mike looked at her then. The lines about his mouth softened. "You're a good egg, Violet McDade. And for your information I'll tell you that I'm trying to get out. It—isn't easy." Dark eyes swept the great, crowded room, dwelt on Rosita's exit, caught sight of something which made his lips tighten suddenly. He left us hurriedly. Turning, I saw District Attorney Alvin Foss enter the lobby, go directly to Senator Hymes' table and, ignoring the senator, speak crisply to Stephen Wright.

Violet said, "I better have a word with Rose. Pay the check and I'll meet you out in the lobby." She waddled away toward the rear of the orchestra platform.

It was raining outside, not heavily, just enough to freshen the air and I breathed it gratefully after the smoke fog I'd been inhaling for what had seemed ages. The doorman signaled Sweeney, Violet's diminutive chauffeur, and presently the great limousine rolled up to the curb.

We got in. The door slammed, and I prepared to unburden my mind of several things I'd been meaning to tell the great gooph. I might as well have saved my breath. She was asleep. It was, I think, a little after one when we reached home. I kicked off my mistreated slippers, donned mules and started to mix myself a nightcap before getting ready for bed, had got as far as the ice cubes when the doorbell rang.

Violet, plumped down on the chaise longue, opened an eye sleepily. "See who it is, Mex."

"See who it is, yourself!" I snapped. The bell rang again, insistently. Violet grunted, got up and waddled into the hall. Surprise, then dismay, registered in the rumble of her voice. The front door slammed, the chain rattled. The elephant returned, ushering in Rose Donelli.

I set my glass down, prepared for anything. Or so I thought at the time.

"Mike Donelli," announced Violet cheerfully, "has just shot a guy." She went to the windows, eased one of the drapes aside and peered out into the night. And I? Well, I just stood staring at the girl. Still in her spangles with nothing but a sheer negligee to cover her, feet bare, face pale and hair disordered, she essayed a wan smile in my direction, failed miserably and tumbled in a heap at my feet.

THERE WAS the rasp of gears from the street, sound of a car getting under way. There followed an instant of silence, then the roar of a second motor, coming up very fast. Tires shrieked down the block. And Violet said, "Douse the lights!" She dropped the drape, swiveled, to see me rooted above the prone figure of Rose Donelli.

"Well, for cryin' out loud, don't stand there gawking like she was a ghost or something! I said, douse the lights!"

As if in a daze, I moved to the wall switch, clicked it. The dim glow from my bedroom door showed me Violet stooping, lifting the girl as she would a feather. Breathing imprecations against some unknown, the creature strode into my room. I followed.

Violet laid the girl on the bed, said, "O. K., revive her." Just like that. Busy with smelling salts and a wet towel I watched the lummox pawing through my wardrobe and inquired with exaggerated calm what she was looking for.

"Something for Rose to wear!" she snarled. "You can't take her to a hotel lookin' like that!"

"Oh, so I'm taking her to a hotel?"

"Of course. She can't go back to the Green Kitten 'cause she's scared Mike'll kill her, too. She accidentally busted in on this party just after the guy got the one-way ticket. Mike and a couple other bums locked her up, but she got away."

"And came here. Thoughtful of her. Very. But now she's here, why can't she stay here?"

Violet glared at me over a piece of my very best lingerie. "Because, you nit-wit, she didn't get away as clean as she thought she did. A couple of mugs just went by in a car and likely they're havin' a talk with her taxi driver. I'm kind of expecting them back."

I started to shiver. Since becoming Violet McDade's partner I'd been led into practically everything except a gang war. It looked as if my education was about to be completed. Rose Donelli chose this moment to sit up.

Violet said, "O. K., kid, everything's going to be all right. Nevada will rustle you some duds and then we'll find you a place to sleep." She left us, went out into the living room again. She didn't turn on the lights.

I helped the girl as best I could. She said, "Sorry to be such a nuisance, Miss Alvarado. Murders are pretty horrible things, aren't they? Especially when your own husband commits them." Her teeth started to chatter. "Mike's been so darned good to me that I guess I've sort of shut my eyes to a lot of things. But to-night, when I actually saw him with that gun in his hands, with that awful look on his face, I—I lost my head. I'm still scared silly."

"Did you," I asked, "recognize the dead man? Or the other two who were with your husband? There is no doubt, I suppose, that the man was really dead?"

"He was dead right enough! No one could live with his face shot away, could he?" She got the jitters at that, communicated them to me. After a little: "No, I don't know who he was, but the other two I've seen around with Mike. One had very white hair, I remember."

"You're still crazy about Mike, aren't you?"

Her "yes" was smothered in a sob. And right after that the whole world exploded. The floor rocked, buckled beneath my feet. Numbed, I stood there, watching with a sort of dispassionate interest as window glass shattered, slashed through sheer hangings. The lights went out, blinked on again just long enough for me to catch a glimpse of Rose's terror-stricken face, then something very heavy—probably the ceiling—crashed down upon us both.

II.

I AWOKE with a terrible roaring in my ears, a hissing, crackling roar that could be but one thing: fire! I opened my eyes, discovered that I was hanging over some one's shoulder. Fire was licking up at the skirts of the some one, and the stench of smoke was thick in my nostrils. Those skirts could belong to no one but Violet McDade. She was carrying me somewhere. I passed out again.

Fresh air brought me around the second time—fresh air tainted with smoke, but that terrible heat was gone, and the flames. No, the flames were still there, gnawing greedily at the base of a door through which we'd evidently just come. I was lying on the floor in almost pitch darkness, and Violet, cursing under her breath, was tugging at something heavy.

I sat up. The room reeled dizzily, steadied. My eyes picked out Violet's bulk heaving at a fallen ceiling joist. Lath and plaster littered the floor, what was left of the furniture. And I discovered another form beneath that massive beam. Bridget, our housekeeper!

"Violet, is—is Bridget dead?"

"Nope. Give me a lift with this damn timber, will you?" Our combined strength managed to raise one end and Violet wedged it with something. She said, "Bridget, can you hear me?"

"Who couldn't?" The voice was very weak, husky, but it was the sweetest sound I ever expect to hear. "Am I dyin', Mac?"

"Hell, no," said Violet grumpily. "Nothin' wrong with you except a couple of broken ribs and a crack on the dome. Now, look, Bridget, I've turned in the alarm and the fire boys'll be here 'most any minute.

In case it gets too hot for you, we've raised the timber so you can crawl out. But stick if you can."

"She'll do no such thing, Violet McDade!"

"I will too," said Bridget. "If Mac wants me to stick, I'll stick. I'd go to hell for her and she knows it!"

"Sure I do," said Violet. "But this time you don't have to. All you do is let 'em drag you out and act kind of hysterical, 'cause Nevada and me is buried up ahead in the ruins. Get it?"

I said, "I'll be no party to it!"

And Violet's great arms infolded me, lifted me, carried me, struggling and kicking, through a rear door. The flames, mounting skyward, cast a lurid glow over the back yard and the limousine waiting in the alley behind the garage, but there was no sign of the neighbors. They must have all been out in front. I opened my mouth to scream and Violet clapped a hand over it.

"Shut up, you sap! Shut up and quit kickin'. You want to catch the lice that done this to us, or you want to give 'em a bigger and better chance? Bridget's all right!"

SIRENS wailed around the corner behind us. I was suddenly assured of Bridget's safety; and the promise of vengeance was sweet. I stopped struggling. Little Sweeney opened the car door for us; I got a flash of a huddled figure on the floor of the tonneau; then we were inside and the great car was rolling down the alley, into a cross street.

"Is—is Rose all right, too?"

"Sure." Violet leaned over, tucked the robe clumsily about the still form. "Still out, but O. K."

"By the way," I demanded, "where were you when the bomb landed? I thought you were in the living room."

"Me, I was out in the garage waking Sweeney, so you and him could take Rose and park her somewhere. Lucky for you I was, too. You and the kid would have been a couple of roasts by this time if anything had happened to me. Just like I'm always tellin' you—without Vi McDade you wouldn't be worth the powder to blow you to hell."

"I guess you're right," I said, and suddenly found myself crying on her shoulder. She patted my knee awkwardly, stopped that as if embarrassed, and began her ominous sleeve-gun practice. Her left arm, flexing up and down, kept digging in my ribs. It hurt like the very devil but I didn't have the heart to tell her so. Rose Donelli heaved a tremulous sigh, sat up.

"Violet?" she queried. "Violet, is that you?"

"In the flesh."

"What—what happened?"

"Friends of your dear husband tossed a pineapple through our front window. I told you not to marry that guy."

Rose covered her face with her hands. Then, with a sudden fierce little gesture said: "Mike never ordered that. Mike wouldn't—couldn't do such a cowardly thing! But there, I've been enough trouble to you. Let me out here." She struggled to rise. "Let me out and forget that you ever saw me!"

Violet lifted her to the seat. "Look," she said, "look, Rosie, Mike gunned somebody out. You happened to bust in at the wrong time and stumbled into him and his two friends. Naturally, your runnin' away would make 'em all kind of nervous. Far as I'm concerned it's dead open and shut. You can believe Mike's the curly-haired boy who wouldn't rub us all out to save his own skin. Me, I'm for not lettin'

you stick your neck out. Not till I've paid off a couple of debts I owe, anyway." She clamped her jaws shut on this last, lapsed into a brooding silence.

Sweeney tooled the car into Wilshire Boulevard, pulled up before the Lancaster. And it wasn't till we'd actually entered the lobby that I fully realized the enormity of our position. Violet—well, I've seen her look worse though her eyes were red-rimmed, her moon face grimed with smoke and soot.

But Rose and I resembled nothing so much as a couple of plasterers after a hard day. There was a bluish welt on my forehead; blood from a nasty cut in my cheek had streaked down, dried in a pool at the base of my neck. Rose's face and arms were scarred with deep scratches; her dress—my dress, rather—was positively charred all down one side of her.

A full-length mirror in one of the great pillars told me all this—and more. My shoes were not mates. I cursed Violet under my breath for this added indignity, remembered suddenly that she had done exceedingly well to find me any shoes at all, remembered that but for her I'd be beyond the need of shoes.

SHE, the pachyderm, was at the desk, trying to convince the clerks we were respectable. Beside her, the tiny Sweeney in his outrageous uniform looked a solemn, wizened midget. It was no go with the clerks. Even the sight of the enormous roll Violet always carries had no effect. The Lancaster, you see, was our newest, smartest hostelry.

One of the desk men beckoned a house detective, evidently with the purpose of having us ejected. Mortified? I was petrified. And then, wonder of wonders, the dick recognized Violet. They fell on each other's necks like long-lost buddies.

"Hi, Mac!" he cried.

"Hello, yourself," she said. Then: "Look, Elmer, tell these dumb apes at the counter who I am, will you? Our house just burned down and we got to get a roof over our heads."

Elmer addressed the chief clerk in an undertone. The fellow eyed Violet with a new respect. Still a little doubtful he finally capitulated.

"How many rooms will you need?"

Violet said, "Four of your best, all in a row."

He raised an eyebrow, stared hard at Sweeney's uniform. "Four, madam? Did you say four of our best? We have a servant's annex, you know."

Violet bridled. "Sweeney ain't no servant! Sweeney's as good as I am and probably a damn sight better. So we want four rooms just like I told you. Servant's annex!" She snorted.

And I thought of poor Bridget lying back there in the wreckage. A servant undoubtedly. An Irish cook who called her employer "Mac" and was not always civil to me. But a servant ready to risk her very life for Violet McDade. I resolutely put Bridget from my mind and trailed rather forlornly after the others as they were escorted to the elevators.

One thing I'll say for the Lancaster. They may be snobbish; they may rob you of your eyeteeth when it comes to charges, but you can get almost anything you want, night or day. In half an hour's time we were all fairly presentable, and Violet was just finishing with her hair when I entered her room.

"What do you intend doing, Violet?"

"Doing?" she snarled. "I'm going to get the two guys that tossed that pineapple and tear 'em limb from limb. Now, of course, don't mind—now—petty annoyances like having your cook half murdered and your house burned down around your ears, so you can stay here and play nurse to Rose until I get back."

"Oh, I can, can I? Well, if you think I've got any love for Rose Donelli you're crazy. She's the one that caused all the trouble. Sweeney can stay here if she has to be nursed. And I've got a gun that's aching for a target as much as yours are!" I bethought myself to feel for the little .32 I carry just above my right knee. It wasn't there. I'd noticed its absence before but had forgotten it.

Violet opened her purse, produced the gun. "I kind of thought you might be wantin' it," she said. "After you got the shock out of your system. O. K. then, me proud señorita, we'll let Sweeney guard Rose while we go gunnin' for her husband."

Sweeney demurred. "Gosh, Mac, I ain't no hand with women. Besides, I'd like to take a cut at them bozos, myself."

ROSE DONELLI must have heard the argument. She came through the adjoining bath, stared from one to the other of us with suspicion.

"You're intending to pin that bombing on Mike? You're—you're going to hurt him?"

"Not much," said Violet grimly. "I'm going to put about six slugs in his middle is all."

Rose was upon her like a raging cat. "You're not! You're not! You're not!" Small fists beat against Violet. "You've other enemies! I tell you Mike wouldn't do such a thing!" Her wild eyes sought the telephone. "I'll warn him, that's what I'll do. Let me go!"

Violet calmly slapped her down, nodded to Sweeney. "Take care of her, runt. Don't let any one get to her or I'll skin you."

We went down to the lobby. The after-theater supper crowd was just breaking up and I realized with a start that it was only a little after two—scarcely an hour since we'd left the Green Kitten. In that short hour our home had been demolished and Bridget, poor old soul, had sustained injuries that might well keep her in the hospital for months.

My heart crawled up into my throat, jiggled there uncertainly, and then dropped like a plummet at sight of a familiar figure between us and the doors—Lieutenant Belarski! Belarski whom Violet didn't like and who certainly didn't like Violet. She'd bested him too many times.

She saw him at the same instant. "Well, for cryin' out loud! Of all the dicks in the city we would have to run into that rat, Belarski!"

He spotted us, advanced unhurriedly, a sardonic grin on his lean, dark face. "Well, well, well!" he said. "Fancy meeting you here!" His grin vanished. Clutching Violet's cloak in his two hands, he snarled: "Who did it?"

"Who did what?" she inquired innocently.

"Don't stall!" he grated. "You know damn well what I'm talking about. Who bombed your house? Why did you run out on your cook, carefully coaching her in a pack of lies before you left? I'll tell you why, you fat imitation of a female shamus! You were trying to give the law a run around till you could find the mugs that did the job."

"That's what you think," said Violet. "Take your hands off me

before I flatten you!" Her voice suddenly lost its belligerence, her shoulders sagged. "O. K., Belarski, you're a smart dick. I figured we'd got away clean." She eyed him appraisingly. "Anybody else know we're still alive?"

He grinned again, wolfishly. "No," he said. "The cook put it over for the rest of the boys, even for the reporters. They're still waiting for the embers to cool so they can look for your remains. But it happens that I know you, know that any job you're interested in smells to high heaven. So I found a neighbor who thought she'd seen you leave the back way, and put a quick check on the hotels. Who tossed that pineapple?"

"O. K.," she said. "I admit I was goin' after the mugs, myself. Nobody, I says, is going to do my work for me. I figured that bein' dead would maybe give us a little edge, see what I mean?"

Belarski's dark eyes got cunning. "Yes, I see what you mean. With half an eye I could see you've got a damned good idea of who you're looking for. So open up and maybe I won't take you down to headquarters yet. Maybe I'll just leave you in your rooms under guard until I make the collar."

Violet looked relieved. "Now you're talkin'. That's what I call bein' a pal, Belarski. One of the men in the blue sedan that passed our house just before the blow-off— one of them guys looked like Broken-nose Murphy. You 'member? I helped put him away a few years back."

"So that's it!" Belarski positively beamed. "Well, I think I can locate Broken-nose!" He swiveled, signaled to a detective lounging against a pillar. The fellow came up. "Hammel, escort these two—ah—

It seemed as if the whole world had exploded.

ladies to their rooms. See that they stay there until I get back."

Violet winked broadly, linked her arm in that of the fat detective. "Sarge, you look like you're going to be interestin' company. Come on, Nevada, let's show the sarge our suite." We entered an elevator, leaving Belarski staring after us with a look of indecision on his hatchet face.

III.

THE DOOR to my room was locked. So, too, were all the others. Sweeney evidently was taking no chances. And wrangling voices from within told me that Rose Donelli wasn't being too docile. Violet knocked, and after a moment Sweeney's wizened face appeared in a cautious crack.

Violet said, "Open up, you lug, we've got company." She stepped back politely, let the burly sergeant enter first. And the moment the man's eyes rested on the bound figure of Rose Donelli he knew something was wrong.

"Rosita! Rose Donelli!" He turned accusing eyes on Violet. "So you crossed Belarski, huh? Ten to one Mike Donelli is behind all this, and you sent the lieut kiting after poor old Broken-nose Murphy. Lemme at that phone!"

Violet hit him with a hamlike fist —once. He went down like a poled ox. Violet said, "There, Sweeney, is another charge for you. You ought to be able to take care of two as easy as one." And as Sweeney looked doubtful, she added: "Well, be seein' you," and waddled to the door.

Rose Donelli screamed. Sweeney, a look of long-suffering patience on his face, clapped a hand over her mouth. And Violet came back to stare down gloomily at the figure on the bed.

"Look, Rose, you came to me 'cause you was scared to death of your own husband. Now, like all women, you've changed your mind and think he's a curly-haired angel or somethin'. You want to help him, huh? Well, neither you nor all the Belarskis in the world is going to keep me from gettin' to Mike Donelli!" She strode to the door.

Under a full head of steam she sailed through the lobby below only to halt before the news stand as if she'd run into something solid. It wasn't solid, but it was startling. A boy had just deposited a stack of extras on the case. Other boys screamed: "District Attorney Foss Murdered!" A boxed-in account gave the place as an alley near Pico and Central; the time of death as approximately one o'clock, and the cause as a large-caliber bullet which had entered the back of his head and, emerging, practically obliterated his face. I thought of Rose's description. It fitted. But Pico and Central was a long, long way from the Green Kitten.

WE WENT out into the night and I climbed under the wheel of the limousine. "Violet," I said, "Alvin Foss was at the Green Kitten at one o'clock. We saw him. Do you suppose he is the one——"

"That Mike shot? Why not? Alvin Foss has been threatenin' to raise hell with places like Mike's ever since he was elected. Maybe he got tired waitin' for Steve Wright, his assistant, to do something. Maybe he decided to do it himself and Mike had to plug him. The only thing is—well, in the back of the head don't sound like Mike's way of doing things. And in his own office, too."

"They could have carried the body away easily enough; planted it in that alley where the rain would obliterate any traces. I mean, the police could never prove that Foss wasn't killed right where he was found." I remembered something Rose had said. "Violet, I believe Senator Hymes was there when it happened! Rose said there was a man with white hair."

"Yeah, and she said there was another guy, too, maybe with green hair. Maybe the two of 'em left Mike Donelli to get rid of the body while they tailed Rose and bombed our house. Which reminds me, I want to find a phone."

I obediently parked before the first all-night café we came to, and she got out, went inside. She emerged presently with a curious look on her moon face. "I located Rose's taxi driver," she said.

"You did! What did he say?"

"He didn't say nothin', Mex. 'Cause why? 'Cause he's deader'n a mackerel. Them bozos caught up with him, found out where he'd dumped Rose, and slugged him—for keeps. Why do you reckon they'd do that?"

"I—I don't know," I said faintly. "Unless he knew them, would be able to identify them."

"Or the car they was drivin', huh?"

"You told Belarski it was a blue sedan!"

She stared at me in disgust. "I must be improving," she said. "Or you're dumber than I thought. You think I'd tell that guy the truth about anything?"

We drove on. It was raining again and the street lamps made pale blobs of reflected light against the glistening pavement. The clock on the dash said 2:15 as we approached the neon sign of the Green Kitten. A car was pulling into the curb ahead of us, a tan touring car with

a khaki-colored top. It looked like one of the county cars, and as we passed it I saw the familiar insignia on the front door.

Two men got out, nodded to the doorman, pushed on through into the foyer. I parked a little way down the block. Violet, with a prodigious grunt, heaved her bulk to the sidewalk.

"Don't lock the car," she said. "We may need it in a hurry." She strode away down the curb like a man going to a fire; and, despite her clothes, despite her ridiculous, tent-like opera cloak, she looked like a man, a veritable mountain of a man, masquerading in woman's garb. I followed as best I could, caught up with her for the sole reason that she'd stopped beside the county car and was deliberately removing her cloak.

The doorman stepped forward. "May I help you?"

"Yeah," she grunted. "Yeah, you can help me by minding your own business." She had the cape off by this time and seemed bent on arranging its folds so that they draped over the car's right door. Satisfied, apparently, by the effect thus obtained she once more donned the garment. Peeling a bill from her roll she tendered it to the man.

"Look, general, the two dicks that just went inside. Were they here before—say, around one o'clock?"

He shook his head.

"Well, then, is Mike Donelli still here?"

"No ma'am," he said. "Mike came out and got in his car at ten after one. I ain't seen him since, but he's sure to be back before closing time."

"Swell," said Violet, "my partner will wait for him. Me, I got business down the street a ways." She gave me an encouraging shove toward the entrance, hunched over against the driving rain, and disappeared in the darkness.

WELL, I managed to get past the check girl with a casual nod, flashed a glance into the main supper room as I passed. State Senator Hymes was still at his table. There were two girls there now. And over against the far wall, partially obscured by the crowd on the dance floor, I saw Assistant District Attorney Stephen Wright. With him were the two men who had gotten out of the tan car.

Wright, I thought, looked worried, but there was no sign of excitement such as should have attended a shooting in the club. And apparently news of the district attorney's death hadn't spread this far. Possibly the two detectives had come to notify Wright.

The colored orchestra was blaring away as if nothing had changed. Perhaps it hadn't—for them. I thought of our house, of Bridget, went up the broad, carpeted stairs hoping, yes, praying that the doorman had lied, that Mike Donelli was in and that I'd get to him before Violet did.

People passed me on the stairs, in the hall above. I was barely conscious of them. The door to the gambling salon stood wide, inviting. I paused there a moment, didn't see Donelli, and went on to his private suite. As I touched the knob a man stepped from the shadows. "Mr. Donelli isn't in just now."

"I know. He's down below. I'm to wait for him." He looked at me searchingly, evidently was of two minds. I decided for him and with an assurance I certainly didn't feel twisted the knob, went in. The great room was empty. I waited, heart pounding, to see if the man would follow me. He didn't. I went

on through into Mike's bedroom and, beyond that, into what must have been Rose's. No one there, either.

Back in the combination office and living room, I looked around for signs of the shooting. There were none—or so I thought till I noticed from the impressions in the thick carpeting that the desk had been moved. The thing was very ornate, heavy as the devil. I couldn't budge it.

Dropping to my knees I crawled about, searching for something, I hardly knew what. And then, just inside the knee hole I found it. A little smear that the left-hand pedestal didn't quite cover. Unmistakably blood. Not much, but the spot was still moist, sticky and gave me a pretty good idea that there was a lot more under that pedestal. Well, that was that. Rose Donelli had actually seen something.

I HEARD the door open, stood up confusedly. A man came in, his face shadowed by a pulled-down hat brim. It wasn't the fellow I'd left in the hall. It wasn't Donelli. It was—yes, it was one of the men from downstairs, from that tan car outside, a county dick.

"I thought this was a private office!" I said. "What happened to the man outside?"

"Why—uh—he was called away on business, ma'am. I just thought I'd" —his eyes, studiously avoiding mine, roamed over the entire room—"that is, I wanted to see Mr. Donelli."

"Well," I said, "he isn't here. And when he gets here he's going to be very busy, so perhaps——" I let the suggestion hang in mid-air. It didn't hang long. Or maybe it's hanging yet. I wouldn't know, because at that moment the door opened again, and in walked Lieutenant Belarski. I nearly passed out.

He closed the door behind him quietly enough, passed the county dick with barely a flicker of recognition, planted himself squarely in front of me. His dark, narrowed eyes were hot and his jaws were clamped so tightly that the skin at the corners of his mouth showed gray. He said nothing for a moment, just stared at me with a glare so baleful, so ominous, that I sagged against the desk, weak with fright.

At last he said, "Well, Miss Alvarado, we meet again."

I said, "How true." And even though my voice was quivery I managed a flippant, "And how is Mrs. Belarski?"

His control broke then. "By Heaven!" he rasped. "By Heaven, where is that she-devil partner of yours?" His hands snaked out, clutched my shoulders, dug in hard. "I found Broken-nose Murphy. And you know where I found him? In jail! Right where the McDade woman knew he was all the time. You tell me where that fat fool is or I'll break every bone in your body!"

"I'm lookin' at you, Belarski," said a hoarse voice from the bedroom door. And there was Violet, very composed, very dirty, rust streaks all down the front of her, but her two .45s held unwaveringly on the irate lieutenant. "Yep," she went on, "I'm here, so mebbe you better unhand the señorita, huh?"

He took his hands away, made a half-hearted movement toward his gun, thought better of it. The county dick, over by the door, was staring at Violet as if she were a ghost.

"You—you mean to tell me, lieutenant, that these two dames are the private dicks, McDade and Alvarado?"

"Not only telling you," said Belarski. "I'm telling the whole cock-eyed world! But they won't be private dicks much longer. They'll be occupying cells next to that runty chauffeur of theirs!"

Violet grunted. "You got Sweeney?"

"I've got Sweeney! I've got him booked for kidnaping an officer. And that's what you two will be booked for."

"What happened to Rose Donelli?"

Belarski cursed luridly. "I had her, too, but the little spitfire got away. Oh, don't worry, we'll pick her up! And with what we can wring out of the three of you we'll find out what this case is all about."

VIOLET SAID, "The guy behind you could mebbe give you the lowdown, Belarski, if he would." The lights clicked out as Belarski whirled. There was a sudden burst of flame, another. I heard a body fall to the floor, the soft thud of hurried feet on the thick carpet.

By the time I had my own gun out, the lights were on again. Violet was at the switch. The county dick was gone. And Lieutenant Belarski lay on the floor, almost at my feet, a thin trickle of blood oozing from under his hat brim.

Violet knelt beside him, lifted the hat. With a vast sigh she replaced it, stood up. "Just a crease, Mex. And that's about the first lucky thing that's happened to me tonight. If Belarski had got it for keeps I wouldn't have a damn thing left to live for."

I stared. "I thought you hated him!"

"I do, you sap! But a enemy like him keeps you on your toes, keeps you from stagnatin'.'" She tilted her head, poised in a listening attitude. There was no sound from without. How had the county dick got away? How, for that matter, had Violet got in? The three-room suite was a solid unit, no other door but the one from the office into the hall.

She read my mind. "The fire escape in Rose's bedroom, ninny. He knew about it, too, which proves somethin' or other." She brushed rather aimlessly at the rust streaks on her cloak, looked down at the prone Belarski. Rose escaped by the fire ladder, so did the dick. More'n likely the corpse went down that way, too, the hall and stairs bein' full of people most of the time. Point is, who helped him?"

"Couldn't we," I demanded, "do our wondering in some other place? Belarski isn't going to stay put all night."

She nodded absently, took pencil and paper from the desk and scribbled a note. This she fastened with a paper clip to Belarski's coat lapel. The scrawl said:

Honest, Belarski, I never done it. I never fired a single shot in this room and neither did the Mex. Be seeing you.

IV

SHE tiptoed to the door, opened it cautiously. The man who had accosted me was still missing. We negotiated the corridor, noting no sign whatsoever that the shot had been heard, descended the stairs. The crowd in the supper room was thinning out and a hurried glance through the great archway told me that Senator Hymes had gone; so, too, had the assistant district attorney.

Violet halted, caught the eye of the head waiter. He came over and she whispered to him for a moment. I saw a bill change hands. Impatiently I waited as she was led away, back toward what must have been the kitchens. And then the lummox was waving at me from out on the sidewalk. She'd gone clear around the building!

I went out vowing I'd give her a piece of my mind. But I didn't. Not then, anyway, for she had again buttonholed the doorman.

"So Senator Hymes and Steve Wright ain't been out of the club all night till just now, huh?"

"That's right, miss."

"Thanks a lot, fella. If you ever get into trouble just look me up."

I said, "Yes, Miss McDade could give you a lot of new ideas. If we're not at home, try the county jail." I departed hastily for our car, fully intending to leave her, but Violet moves rather swiftly at times. She was beside me when I meshed the gears.

"What do you mean, if we're not at home? We ain't got no home—nor no housekeeper if we did have a home. We can't go back to the hotel because Belarski will have that sewed up. Where the hell can we go?"

"You just mentioned one place. I think that's where we're pointing!" I found myself weeping. The tears ran down my nose, dripped off onto my hands at the wheel. "Have—have you forgotten that little Sweeney's in jail?"

"How could I?" she grumbled. "You never let me have a minute's peace, you cry baby. Like I'm always tellin' you, when the going gets tough you lay down on me."

I stopped crying then. I was so furious I could have killed her. "Listen to me, you hippopotamus, you're everything Belarski ever called you! You're a menace to society. I'm darned sick of being played for a sucker to help out some of your so-called friends. What did Rose Donelli ever do for you? Why should I take the rap for helping her? Did I ever ask you to help one of my friends?" I shook a fist under her fat nose. "Did I?"

She reached over, steadied the wheel. "Come to think of it, you never did, Nevada. I—I guess maybe I've been expectin' too much of you. But if you didn't have such damn high-class friends, if ever any one of 'em did get in a jam I expect maybe I'd be around, huh?"

Never a word about going into that flaming room after me to-night; not a hint that she'd saved my life a dozen times in the past. Violet McDade is—well, just Violet McDade. I suddenly felt very small.

"I'm sorry, Violet. I'm a—a cat."

"'Course you are," she acknowledged comfortably. "A regular hell-cat. So let's forget it and concentrate on our problem. You see, Mex, we're in what they laughingly call a predicament. Havin' lied to Belarski so I'd get first shot at Mike Donelli; havin' bopped his helper, the sarge; havin' left Belarski with a bullet crease in his head; all them things is—now—mere details. The real facts of the matter is that poor Sweeney's in jail, we've lost Rose, and we ain't yet met up with Mike Donelli. Our results, to date, is null and void."

"And apt to remain so." But I was feeling more cheerful for some unknown reason. The tears may have helped. "You've stated our position with admirable clarity. Is there supposed to be a solution?"

"They's always an answer," she affirmed. "An answer to everything. Maybe you ain't got it, maybe I ain't. But it's there, Mex. 'Member that

time we got Sweeney out of jail down in San Juan Batista?"

"Violet McDade, you're not thinking of trying that trick again! No, you couldn't be—not even you!"

"Nope," she said, "nope, I'm afraid it wouldn't work in the United States of America. 'Fraid we'll have to use a little—now—finesse in Sweeney's case. Meantime, let's forget him and think of Rose. Thinking of Rose reminds me that we'd better turn around and go back to the Green Kitten."

"Belarski," I reminded her, "is at the Green Kitten."

"I hope so," she said. "I hope he's still there and that Rose runs right into his arms. I'd a lot rather Belarski had her than some others I know." She cursed the girl under her breath.

I TURNED RIGHT at the next cross street, headed back in the general direction of the Green Kitten. I wasn't pushing the car too hard. It was still raining, but the rain had nothing to do with my caution. Personally, I was hoping that Belarski had collared Rose and her husband, too. I only got half my wish.

We were just in time to see Belarski escorting Rose out the front door and into his car. I cut the lights, skidded into the nearest alley, halted with my heart in my throat. Belarski's car passed the alley doing fifty.

Violet grunted, "Well, that's a relief. Back out and let's buzz the doorman again."

The doorman was indignant. "You again! Mike's been raising merry hell with me about you and one thing and another!"

"Mike's been here, huh?"

He spat disgustedly. "Yeah, and gone again. He comes busting in, goes upstairs, and right after that here comes Rosita. She goes upstairs, too. Couple of minutes later he comes tearing down, cussing somebody about a pineapple job. He's got a rod in his fist, this time, and he offers to slap me down if I don't tell him all I know. Which is practically nothin'. but——"

"Save it," Violet advised. "Mike was plenty mad, huh? You know where he was goin' this time?"

"So help me," said the fellow earnestly, "if you was to give me another fifty bucks I couldn't tell you."

We got back in the car and rode aimlessly for a while, Violet apparently sunk in a stupor. I should have known better. Presently she straightened. "Why," she demanded, "why would the bombing of our house make Mike Donelli mad? Because it failed? Why'd he leave Rose to the—now—tender mercies of Belarski, when all the time his main idea must have been to shut her up?"

"You tell me," I suggested wearily.

"All right, I will!" But she didn't. For just at that moment I discovered that we were being tailed. My cry of dismay brought a snort from Violet.

"Hell, I've known it for fifteen minutes. The only reason we went back to the Green Kitten this last time is because they missed us before. I wanted to give 'em another chance."

"Who?"

"The mugs that tossed the pineapple, I'm hopin'. This damn rain has rubbed out what little chance I had of pinning the job on anybody. And all the actors are hopping around like fleas. I'm going to let 'em light on me for a change."

The car was about two blocks behind us. It showed no lights, which is probably why I hadn't noticed it before.

Violet said, "Give 'em a few whirls around the block and let's make sure." So I did. I turned corners till I was dizzy, wove in and out of dark streets, decided finally that we'd lost our shadow. And was proved wrong the minute we turned into the boulevard again. The car was still there and coming up fast. There were no other machines in sight either way. At this hour in the morning the thoroughfare was as deserted as a county road in the sticks.

"What do we do now, run for it?"

"For a ways," said Violet, peering back. "Just enough to get 'em going good. When I give you the word, slam on your brakes."

I fed gas for all I was worth. We might as well have been standing still. That car behind certainly had something under its hood that we didn't have. In less time than it takes to tell it were were doing seventy, our limit. And the other car crept up on us steadily. I could make out its color now and the fact that it held two men. It was less than fifty yards behind us when Violet said, "O. K."

WELL, we did have brakes—and good tires. We stopped right now. The shock threw me hard against the wheel; I heard Violet go "Oo-o-m-ph!" The other car slid by us, rocking crazily, brakes grinding. A double burst of orange flame cut across our hood; there was a rattling, tearing sound as metal ricocheted off metal and into glass. The windshield developed a sudden case of smallpox, but held. And the open car righted itself, whirled on two wheels, started back.

Violet grunted, "I expect we'll be safer outside, Mex. Not that I want

He went down like a poled ox.
"Here, Sweeney, is another charge for you. We'll be seein' you."

to be safe. This is the first sign of action I've seen to-night." Which would have struck me as extremely funny at any other time. She opened the door on the curb side, floundered out. I followed, reaching for my gun. I got it, came up behind the hood just as the touring car slid to a halt.

The driver opened his door. "We must have got 'em, Logan, but we've got to make sure this time. Darker than hell, ain't it?"

I shot him. Shot again and again at that vague blur which was his face. Shot until the hammer of my gun clicked on an empty chamber. I saw him slump, slide into the street. And Violet's voice, quite calm, said: "Drop the rod, fella. You're covered."

She was evidently talking to the man on the off side. I couldn't see him. I couldn't see her, either. But he could. Or thought he could for he didn't drop his gun. He used it. The darkness suddenly became a bedlam of sound, of stabbing tongues of flame that looked two feet long from where I crouched. As swiftly as it had all begun, it was over. Silence descended like a pall, broken by Violet, slightly petulant.

"Where the hell are you, Nevada? I can't make out what this guy's sayin'. Must be a Greek or something."

I rounded the two cars, saw her on her knees beside a huddled form. The man wasn't a Greek. His voice just sounded that way because of the blood welling from his graying lips. He was one of the two county detectives I'd seen talking to Stephen Wright; not the one who had shot Belarski in the office, but the other.

Violet McDade isn't much good as a nurse. She can shoot people but after she's done it she's rather helpless when it comes to patching them up. Not that any one could have done much for this chap; he was about through. I found my handkerchief, wiped some of the blood away, lifted his head. His eyes opened a little and he coughed, horribly.

Violet said, "You're the guys that tossed that pineapple. Who gave you your orders?"

He just looked at her. Thick lips curled in a mirthless smile and he said—his words, too, were thick, mushy: "Wouldn't you like to know?" He died in my arms.

In the near distance now there was the crescendo of sirens; in the other direction headlights were coming up, too close for comfort. Violet said, "Let's be on our way, Mex."

A swift look at the driver told us that for once my shooting had been excellent. He was dead. We were on our way. Where, I didn't know, nor did I care. I was content to go anywhere away from there, grateful for the cool freshness of the rain, for—yes, for being alive instead of lying as were those two behind us. Did I feel badly for having just killed a man? Not then. Perhaps I would later, but now I was pleasantly numb.

V.

VIOLET'S VOICE, seeming to come from a long way off, impinged on my consciousness. "I got to make a couple of phone calls, Nevada, if you can tear yourself away from your meditations."

I sat up straight. "I'm not meditating, you elephant, I'm resting."

"Rest to-morrow, or next week. If you think we're through because we rubbed out a couple of blots on the county's—now escutcheon, you're silly. Let's find a phone."

We found the phone—in a bar that was still doing business. The place reeked, and there were a couple of drunks. I ordered a drink, downed it and immediately felt better. Violet emerged from the phone booth as I was lighting my first cigarette in hours.

"There you go," she complained. "There you go, carousin' again. No wonder I can't get nowhere with drunkards and cigarette fiends for partners." She led the way outside, climbed under the wheel herself. "Can't afford to let you drive with the taint of liquor on your breath."

I actually giggled. "No," I said, "imagine being arrested for drunken driving with our spotless record. Belarski undoubtedly has forgotten all about the other minor crimes you've committed to-night—this morning, rather. Poor Sweeney."

She said, "Shut up!" and clamped down hard on the accelerator. Fifteen minutes of silence after that, and we wheeled into Gramercy Park Lane. The Lane is pretty exclusive, great stone arches at either end of the block-long street frowning on anything less than a millionaire—or a state senator. I remembered that this was where Senator Hymes lived.

As we whirled through one arch I saw headlights bearing down on the other. Violet, seemingly bent on destruction, hurled the limousine straight into their path. Brakes squealed, not ours, at first.

A thickset figure detached itself from the coupé, crossed the sidewalk on the run and disappeared into a tree-lined drive. Violet took the turn on two wheels, rocked into the drive and applied the brakes just back of the running man. The front bumper caught him, staggered him, but he didn't fall. One up-flung arm ended in a gun. He swiveled, cat-like, and I recognized his face in the headlights' glare. He was Mike Donelli.

"Drop the rod, Mike," said Violet, and as he hesitated, "Drop it," she urged, very low, almost as if she were afraid of being overheard. "A guy we both know is plenty dead because he didn't drop his when I told him." He dropped the gun.

"Come over here, Mike. Over by the left-hand door. You can let your hands down."

He let his half-raised hands fall to his sides, came slowly around the left front fender. His broad face, always ruddy, genial, looked positively haggard now.

"What is this, a gag, Violet Mc-Dade?"

"In a way," she said. And crowned him with one of her guns. The movement was so swift, so utterly unexpected that even I was stunned. I barely caught the flash of her down-swooping arm before the blow landed. Mike's eyes crossed, he started to sag. Violet leaned out the window and supported him.

"Get out the other side, stupid!" she hissed. "If I let him fall he'll get all mussed up."

"You've just mussed him considerably," I said. "And anyway, I thought that was what you intended to do all along. You were, I believe, going to put six slugs in his middle or some such a matter."

"Don't argue!" she snarled. "Can't a lady change her mind?"

I got out, sighing a little, and between us we managed to get him into the tonneau, fixed him nice and comfy. "Do you mind, sweet Violet, explaining your unwonted solicitude?"

"I'm savin' him," she said. And led the way majestically up the drive.

SENATOR HYMES answered the bell in person. I thought he was going to faint when he saw Violet. His long face, bleak as a winter's day, under waving white hair, turned a sickly yellow; myriad tiny lines appeared in the skin as if the flesh beneath had suddenly shrunk.

He said, "I—I don't believe I can see you. I'm—uh—in conference."

"Right ungrateful, I calls it," said Violet. "Here I just saved your life —yours and Stevie Wright's—by stopping Mike Donelli."

"You—you stopped Donelli! You mean you—killed him?"

"Nope," said Violet, "just stopped him from becoming a murderer." She shouldered her way past the agitated Solon, held the door wide.

A voice from down the hall said, "Bring them in, senator, bring the ladies right in. I'm sure we're both very glad to see them." Stephen Wright, the assistant district attorney stood in the shadows beside an open door. There was a gun in his hand. He gestured with it impatiently. "This way, ladies. Hurry please. My nerves are not at their best and this gun might go off."

"Like it did once before to-night, huh? Or did Senator Hymes bump Alvin Foss?"

I felt Hymes sag against me, tremble violently. He said, as Wright lifted the gun, "No, Stephen, not here! Don't do—don't do anything you'd be sorry for."

"My sentiments, exactly," Violet approved, and waddled toward the man with the gun. "We're all friends, ain't we?" She leered at Wright. "You know us private dicks can always be fixed—if the price is right. So let's talk it over and forget our past mistakes, huh?"

"Mistakes?" said Wright. He stood there, gun poised steadily

until we'd entered the room, then followed us in and closed the door.

I rubbed one knee surreptitiously against the other, felt my gun in its holster, realized with a terrible sinking in the pit of my stomach that I'd emptied the weapon into the county detective. I wondered if Violet's .45s was empty, too.

She was saying: "Yep, it was a mistake to have your two dicks bomb our house tryin' to get Rose Donelli."

"My two dicks?"

"Yours. In a way you was smarter than Mike Donelli when Rose got away. You knew she was a friend of mine 'cause I told you so myself. You knew I was a dick and you put two and two together, figured she might run to me. Now Mike, of course, knew of other places she might run and wasted a lot of time lookin' there first. You, bein' a very efficient guy, just phoned your office and gave Logan and the other guy their instructions."

"She knows!" moaned Senator Hymes. "She knows, Stephen! She's got to Logan!"

"Shut up!" said Wright. "I've heard about this she-devil. She'll talk you into hell if you let her." His eyes rested with cold malice on Violet. "Why do you think this— ah—Logan was connected with me?"

"Well," she said, "I'll tell you. Just after Rose broke the news to me I took a peek out our front window. I thought I recognized one of the county's cars, but couldn't be sure because it was travelin' dark and somebody had, thoughtfullike, tossed a coat over the door insignia. It was just an idea of mine. I couldn't prove it because again the boys was very thoughtful. They took care of the taxi driver, too, so

FLOWERS FOR VIOLET

he'd never mention taking Rose out to our neighborhood.

"Later on one of the lugs stumbled into me and Nevada in Mike's office, knew the pineapple had failed, reports that sad fact to you, and you tell him to try again. Which he done with a sawed-off shotgun. I called the sheriff's office later and he says that car was assigned to the district attorney's office. And that reminds me, Stevie, the death of Foss makes you the new district attorney."

"I'm the new district attorney," said Wright grimly. "And I intend to remain in office if I have to kill a dozen, including you."

"Pshaw!" said Violet. "I never realized how much it meant to you, Stevie. Not until I got to thinkin' that a guy must be pretty desperate to shoot a man in the back of the head. And only a fella that would do that would resort to bombin' helpless women without givin' 'em a chance. Didn't sound like Mike Donelli, but still you can't ever tell, I says. Wasn't really until I find out how surprised Mike is about the pineapple business that I figure him for a—now—innocent bystander. Did he take the gun away from you, or from the senator here?"

"Not from me!" screamed Hymes.

WRIGHT SHOT HIM. Even as the old man started to sag Wright turned the gun on Violet. And Violet just stood there; stood perfectly still without lifting her arms. Her guns must be empty!

"Fortunately," said Wright, "the family is away. I think that I shall enjoy sending you flowers, Violet

McDade." His finger whitened on the trigger; his lips grew taut. I made a dive for my gun intending to throw it. And Violet, wrist flicking like a striking rattler, shot him just as the door burst open.

Belarski snarled, "You promised, you she-devil! You promised not to kill him!"

"And I didn't," said Violet calmly. "He'll live to hang, but, hell, I couldn't wait any longer for you. His remark about sending me flowers kind of got me nervous."

"You mean," I gasped, "you mean that you sent for Belarski?"

"She phoned me," Belarski snapped, "phoned me and guaranteed a pinch if I'd forget about Sweeney and Rose and Mike and Heaven knows who else!"

Stephen Wright sat up, stared about the room uncertainly. Then: "I—I guess I won't be sending you flowers, after all, Violet McDade."

"You wouldn't have, anyway," said Violet gloomily. "You send pineapples. I'm sorry I made the deal with Belarski, sorry I promised not to hurt you—much. There's a little old lady down in the receiving hospital, an old lady I'm kind of crazy about. The killin' of Alvin Foss and"—an overlarge foot stirred the limp form of State Senator Hymes—"and this guy don't mean a thing to me. My family does." She scowled at Belarski as he clipped the cuffs on Wright. "You sure got the best of the bargain this time, you mug!"

"I suppose," Belarski said, "that I should send you flowers!"

She brightened. "Now that," she said, "that would be kind of sweet of you, Belarski!"

TURN OUT THE LIGHTS, by Arthur J. Burks, an Eddie Kelly story in the June issue of Clues-Detective.

PATRICIA SEAWARD

Popular Publications' *Dime Detective Magazine* was one of the leading mystery pulps. Running from 1931 to '53, it printed fiction by Raymond Chandler, Erle Stanley Gardner, and Carroll John Daly, with the emphasis on crisp action. In 1944, it absorbed its rival, *Detective Fiction Weekly.*

Frederick Nebel (1903–1967) began selling stories to pulps as a teenager. Roaming Canada, he absorbed background for his Corporal Tyson of the Mounties stories for *Northwest Stories.* He penned a series about police Captain Steve McBride and his chum, reporter Kennedy, for *Black Mask,* and another about the Driftin' Kid for *Lariat.*

Nebel's Jack Cardigan, an operative for the Cosmos Agency, appeared in forty-three novelettes in *Dime Detective.* In the tale "Murder by Mail," he not only has a gal companion, Patricia Seaward, but also a very capable secretary, Miss Elfoot. The story first appeared in *Dime Detective*'s June 1936 number.

MURDER BY MAIL

Cardigan didn't even know Talbott was a client of the Cosmos Agency till a man with a gun walked in and demanded the correspondence on the case. That just got in the big op's hair, and it wasn't till they began bumping off his office force and kidnaping his staff as prelude to the murder of the unknown client that he really got hot, determined to bust the racket wide and collect his fee with blue steel.

. . . A CARDIGAN STORY . . .

by Frederick Nebel

Author of "Lead Poison," etc.

CHAPTER ONE

Death in the T-File

CARDIGAN stood at the window of the Cosmos Agency's St. Louis office and stared biliously down **into** the noontime traffic of Olive Street.

In his left hand he held a half-smoked cigarette, in his right a ten-ounce glass of tomato juice seasoned to fiery strength with tobasco sauce. His shaggy hair looked more rumpled than usual; a black bow tie was askew against the soft white collar of his shirt. His head ached and he felt pretty mean. It was the worst hangover in years. Draining the glass of tomato juice, he rasped his throat, blew out a hot breath and turned away from the window.

His office staff was out to lunch, but standing in the doorway between his inner office and the reception-room was a very well dressed slender man who dipped his head and said: "Good-day. Are you Mr. Cardigan?"

"*Uhn,*" grunted Cardigan and carried the empty glass across to the washbasin behind a screen. Rinsing the glass, he said, "Yeah, I'm Cardigan," and came from behind the screen drying his hands on a towel.

THE stranger came all the way into the office, placed his dark blue Homburg, his gray suede gloves, on the desk. "I am John Strawn," he said. He was tall and his dark blue overcoat, his light blue shirt complemented each other. He had long, white, smooth hands. His face was long, well shaved, a little wolfish, and his hair was black, crisp. He had brown, level, almost mocking eyes.

Cardigan was too concerned with his hangover to pay much attention to him. "Sit down, sit down," he muttered, and sitting down himself, said: "What can I do for you?"

Strawn remained standing, smiling slightly. He gave a small, amused laugh. "I'm afraid I'm disturbing you."

"Well, we can skip that, Mr. Strawn. I got tangled up in a drinking marathon last night, and maybe I ain't the man I used to be."

Strawn's eyes drooped, slid round the office, came back again to rest on Cardigan's wrinkled, unhappy face. He said: "Do you recall any correspondence you had with a man named S. N. Talbott?"

"Talbott? *Uh-uhn.* No. Why?"

"I am representing Mr. Talbott. I as-

sumed you'd recognize the name and the circumstances surrounding it."

Cardigan shrugged. "We have a lot of correspondence and you can't expect me to remember everything. Hang around. My secretary ought to blow in soon and she'll hunt it up."

Strawn looked a little pained. "Unfortunately, I've an appointment at one. Would it be asking too much if I asked you to look in your files? The name is Talbott—S. N. Talbott. The circumstances were so thoroughly outlined in his letter—"

Cardigan pushed himself up to his feet, scratched his head and said, "O. K., O. K." He slouched into the outer office and crossed it to a high, green, steel filing-cabinet. Strawn came in with him, saying in an apologetic voice: "I'm sorry to disturb you but—"

"Think nothing of it," Cardigan rumbled. "If I can see yet, I'll find the correspondence. Guy that invents hangover-less liquor is going to make a fortune. Talbott . . . . that's in the T's," he said, pulling out a drawer marked *T—U—V.* "Let's see, now." He began thumbing through the T-file, came to a thin sheaf marked *Talbott, S. N.* "Yup—here it is," he muttered, and pulled out the sheaf. "Dated—hell—a month ago—"

"That will do," Strawn said quietly.

Cardigan felt a sudden hard firm pressure against the small of his back. He twisted his head and looked into the cold, mocking eyes of the man—bent his gaze down over his shoulder and saw part of the gun that was pressed against his back.

"I'll take the correspondence," said Strawn gently. "Don't be foolish about anything. Raise both hands high."

Cardigan's face began to look very sour. He raised his hands and Strawn with his left hand reached up and took the sheaf of correspondence, thrust it into his left overcoat pocket. He said: "Now in the other office."

"You know, now that I get a good look at you, I don't like you already."

"In the other office."

Cardigan moved backward slowly, his hands dropping inch by inch until they were level with his shoulders. His eyes were heavy, dull, and anger was beginning to stir slowly in their depths. He backed through the doorway, kept backing up until the desk stopped him.

"Sober, I'd resent this," he growled. "With a hangover, I resent it twice as much. What kind of a chin have you got?"

Strawn, smiling coolly, picked up his hat and gloves. "I noticed there's a key in the connecting door. I'm afraid I'll have to lock you in here. I'll leave the key on the desk in the other office."

"That's nice."

"I'm very considerate, Mr. Cardigan."

"With a gun in your mitt, you can afford to be. I'm still wondering what kind of a chin you've got."

Strawn's smile was razor-thin. "I'd hate to have to shoot you."

Cardigan, giving him a contemptuous look, reached over and removed the telephone receiver from its hook, placed it on the desk.

Strawn's hand tightened on his gun. "Hang that up!" he said.

"Hang it up yourself, Mr. Strawn, if you—"

THE man took three strides, picked up the telephone receiver and slapped it into the hook. Cardigan swung at the same time. His big fist caught Strawn on the side of the jaw, sent him revolving wildly across the office. The screen crashed down, the gun was knocked from his hand and sent arcing across the desk, and Strawn landed on the floor with his heels kicking.

Cardigan growled: "That telephone trick was to get you near enough, honey-bunch." He reached across the desk, yanked open a top drawer and was reaching for the gun inside when Strawn said: "Hold it!"

Cardigan looked at him.

Strawn, holding another gun, this time in his left hand, said: "I'm always prepared for an emergency." He jumped to his feet, his chin red where Cardigan had smacked it. He moved fast; kicked shut the desk drawer, went around and recovered his first gun and put the other back in his left-hand overcoat pocket.

His cool bloodless smile had returned. "The trouble with your telephone trick, Mr. Cardigan, is that it doesn't work twice." He walked swiftly to the connecting door, drew the key from the inside, thrust it into the outside keyhole.

The front-office door opened and young Buddy Miller, the tow-headed office boy, came breezing in. He took one look and stopped in his tracks. His blue eyes popped wide, his little chin shot forward.

Cardigan bawled out: "Buddy, keep clear!"

"Get in this office, son," Strawn clipped. "Quick!"

"Get in here, Buddy," Cardigan said, his voice heavy, anxious.

The boy's eyes were flashing, his lips were shaking but beneath them his chin was trying to be very stiff. He moved across the outer office, walking on his toes. He stopped in front of Strawn and demanded: "What you tryin' to do here?"

"Get in, brat."

Buddy yelled, "You can't do this!" and leaped at him.

"Buddy!" shouted Cardigan, starting forward.

Strawn's gun exploded as he leaped

backward and Buddy turned and fell through the doorway into Cardigan's arms. He fell heavily, a little grimace on his mouth. Strawn flashed out of the office, banging the outer door.

Buddy choked: "Go—get him, chief."

But he was heavier now in Cardigan's arms and somehow Cardigan, despite his fierce desire to follow Strawn, could not let the boy go. He knew Buddy was hit; how seriously, he didn't know. And then the boy fainted. Cardigan lifted him clear of the floor. "You fool kid!" he muttered. "You poor kid!"

He carried him out into the corridor and half walked, half ran with him to the elevator. But he saw by the indicator that the car was up at the top floor. He turned and ran down the stairway—two flights to the lobby. People were streaming back from lunch. Suddenly Patricia Seaward was in front of him.

"Chief, what's wrong with Buddy?" she cried.

"Plenty. Go up to the office. Don't touch the phone in my office. Get that? Don't touch the—"

"I get it. But—Buddy—" She stopped short, put her hand to her lips, when she saw blood. For an instant she seemed to wilt. "Good God, what happened?"

But Cardigan was on his way to the street. "Taxi!" he bawled. "Taxi! Taxi!"

A fat man was just about to step into one parked at the curb. Cardigan rushed up and said: "Out of the way!"

"Look here! I saw this first—I engaged—"

"You get out of the way, mister, before I step on you!"

The driver said: "Now looka here, buddy, this gentleman—"

"And you drive this wagon, brother, or I'll poke your face in and drive it myself! I got a sick kid here!"

CHAPTER TWO

Enter the Law

PAT SEAWARD entered the office, paused and looked carefully around. Her heart was pounding and the red color in her face had not come entirely from the cold out of doors. She moved slowly across to the connecting doorway, looked into the rear office, saw the overturned screen. She crossed to the desk, pulled out the drawer, and saw Cardigan's gun lying in it, beside a flask of rye. She looked at the telephone, remembered that he had told her not to touch it. She sat down because her legs were shaking and she remembered the blood on Buddy Miller. Her body shook as though a chill had struck it and she got up again, went to the window. Restless, upset, she walked aimlessly into the outer office.

Miss Elfoot, the secretary, came in puffing a cork-tipped cigarette and reading a folded newspaper. She was a flat-heeled woman, thin as a rail, who wore huge horn-rimmed glasses and a long, belted overcoat.

Pat said: "Did you see the chief?"

"See him? I saw him when he rolled in at about eleven but I doubt if he saw me. He was fried."

"Elvina—Buddy was shot."

Miss Elfoot looked up crisply. "Who says so?"

"I saw him. Downstairs in the lobby. Jack was carrying him—taking him to the hospital. I don't know how it happened. Jack was in a hurry. He didn't have time to say."

Miss Elfoot sat down, took off her hat and scaled it on the desk. "I know I should have remained in social-service work. This is a screwy business. It does nothing but go round and round—like the music. The poor little kid—"

The door swung open and Lieutenant Bozeman Shadd strolled in, knocked an

Inch of white cigar ash to the floor and said: "There was some shooting up here, sisters."

Miss Elfoot slid an ashtray across the desk. "I don't know who you are, mister, but I'm not your sister—and use an ashtray next time."

"He's Lieutenant Shadd," Pat said, "from the police. This is Miss Elfoot, Lieutenant, the new secretary. She's only been here three weeks."

Shadd said dryly: "And getting tough like Cardigan already." He was a wide-shouldered gaunt man in a hard white collar that at no point touched his brown, long neck. His eyebrows were black, bushy, forebidding. He had high reddish cheekbones and a deep furrow ran from each one, downward to his bladelike jaw. His eyes were deep-set, sultry, and his mouth was a sardonic slash beneath his big nose. Looking hard at Miss Elfoot, he said: "Don't get off on the wrong foot with me, lady."

Miss Elfoot slid an ashtray across the only next time you've got ashes to dump, dump them in the tray. The floor is to walk on. I met hundreds of cops when I was in social-service work, so don't think you impress me." She removed her glasses, polished them, added: "Now what's on your mind?"

Shadd eyed her stonily. "There was a shot up here, lady. You're smart. Now what would be on my mind?"

Pat said: "As I was coming in from lunch, I ran into Jack downstairs in the lobby. He was taking Buddy Miller, our office boy, to the hospital. Buddy'd been shot."

"How'd it happen?"

"I don't know. Jack didn't have time to stop. He was carrying Buddy."

Shadd looked at Miss Elfoot. "What do you know about it?"

"Nothing. I came in just a minute or

so ago. I didn't even know there'd been any shooting until Pat told me."

Shadd put his cigar carefully between his teeth, dug his hands into his overcoat pockets and strolled into the inner office. He walked around the office, toed the overturned screen, stopped before the desk and picked Cardigan's gun out of the drawer. He broke it, saw that it was fully loaded, and replaced it.

"What hospital?" he asked.

"I don't know," Pat said.

Shadd sat on the desk and laid his hand on the telephone.

"Don't use that," Pat said.

"Why not?"

"Jack told me not to."

Shadd chuckled dryly. "Told you not to. That's just the kind of a mugg he is —always trying to hide things from the police."

"No—it wasn't that—"

"Don't tell me, sister!" he said, and picked up the instrument, called headquarters. "Gus, I'm over at the Cosmos Agency. This is Boze talking. There was a shooting here, nobody knows about what. I'll hang around till I find out . . . No, he ain't. The kid in the office was shot, the gals say—but they weren't here. Cardigan took the kid to a hospital . . . . Yup, later—I'll let you know." He hung up and chuckled again. "Just like Cardigan—telling you not to phone!"

She flashed back at him: "He didn't say not to phone—he said not to use *that* phone!"

"Just take it easy, sister. Sit down and take it easy. Get in a sweat and you'll catch cold." He pulled out a dirty deck of playing cards and said: "I'll kill time at a little solitaire till your boss gets back."

With an impatient gesture Pat whirled and went into the other office.

WHEN Cardigan blew in, bare-headed, his hands and face red with the cold, he said to Pat: "He got it low on the right side. We won't know for hours if he'll pull through." His face was grave, his forehead ribbed with wrinkles. "If ever I lay hands on the lug that pulled that trigger—"

"Who was the lug?" Shadd called out from the inner office.

Cardigan started. Through the doorway he saw Shadd sitting at the desk and playing cards. He said: "Who let that guy in?"

Shadd scooped up his cards, fanned them once and stuck them back into his pocket. He leaned back in the chair and said: "Now don't tell me the kid was playing with a gun and it went off."

Cardigan strode in, lifted the flask of rye out of the drawer to see if any had been drunk, replaced it and said: "A guy came in and asked me to check up on some correspondence with a guy named S. N. Talbott. I hardly got the stuff out of the file when he stuck a gun in my ribs and took it away. Buddy came in, tried to block the guy and the guy let him have it. Get out of my chair."

Shadd, his eyes narrowed and glinting, got up and slouched back on his heels. "Who was the guy?"

"He said his name was John Strawn. Sometimes they say John Smith or Bob Brown. Tall. About thirty-five. Blue overcoat and blue hat and blue shirt. Brown eyes. Long, dark, good-looking mugg. I pick him for a con man. He can sling the English."

"What about this S. N. Talbott?"

"You got me. The file was thin, maybe two or three letters, and I don't connect the name with anything important. My secretary's new—this correspondence was dated a month ago and the secretary I had then went to China. Do you remember anything, Pat?"

"No, I don't," said Pat Seaward. "I was in Toledo then."

"Well," said Cardigan, pulling the telephone over. "I got the lug's fingerprints on this telephone receiver, anyhow."

Pat chuckled. "Ten'll get you twenty you haven't."

Cardigan jabbed her with a look.

Miss Elfoot said: "Mr. Know-it-all had to call headquarters."

"I told him," Pat said, "not to use it but he just laughed and said you were trying to put something over on him."

Cardigan pushed the phone away, threw up his hands and said: "Well, I always wondered what happened to cops when they became lieutenants, and now I know: they put their brains away in mothballs."

One of Shadd's eyes bulged while the other narrowed down very tightly. He barked out: "I'm sick and tired of being insulted around here—first by the dames and then by you! It looks damned funny to me that this here S. N. Talbott'd be important enough for a guy to pull a stick-up over and you don't even remember what about Talbott." He shook his finger at Cardigan. "I ain't no fool!"

"Don't be too sure about that," Cardigan said. "You've been wrong before."

Miss Elfoot said, "Crazy people never think they're crazy, either," and went into the front office.

Cardigan stood up, said: "Suppose you blow, Boze. You get in my hair like dandruff."

"Listen," grated Shadd, red-faced, "what hospital's the kid at, huh?"

"The South Side Emergency."

Shadd took off his hat and slapped it back on again. "O. K.," he bit off, his jaw determined.

"Now you listen!" Cardigan yelled. "You leave that kid alone. He's undergoing an operation and when he comes out, if he does come out, you leave him alone. He don't know anything. He just happened to walk into something."

Shadd, on his way, said over his shoulder: "I wouldn't trust you no further than I can throw a horse, and I can't throw a horse."

"You sure can throw the bull, though," Miss Elfoot said.

"If you were a man, sister, I'd slap you down."

"If I were a man, pickle puss, you wouldn't dare."

Shadd snorted, *"Mayhn!"* and banged out. They could hear his heels slamming hard on the way down the corridor.

AT midnight the hospital waiting-room was deserted except for Cardigan. He lay slumped in an armchair, dozing, with his big feet propped on another. The boy had been through the operation but was in a coma and Cardigan had been in the hospital for the past three hours.

Presently the clicking of heels on the cement floor stirred him, did not rouse him completely. A nurse came round a corner of the corridor and reaching him stopped and said: "Mr. Cardigan."

"Hahn? Huhn?" he muttered, blinking.

"On the telephone."

He yawned and heaved out of the chair and started down the corridor.

"This way," the nurse said.

He turned around and followed her to a switchboard set in an alcove. She picked up a phone and handed it to him and he said: "Yowss? . . . . Yup . . . . Why? . . . . Well, why didn't you say so? I'll be over in a shake."

He hung up and turning, said: "Nothing new about the kid?"

The nurse shook her head.

He went back to where he had been sitting, put on his shabby old ulster, pulled his hat down over his shaggy hair and left the hospital. The wind was sluggish and laden with a damp cold. Mist sheathed the street lights and the sound of a distant trolley car slapping over a switch was sharp, distinct. He coughed and the sound echoed round his head. When he had walked two blocks he found a cab standing outside an all-night lunchroom. The cab was empty and he reached in and punched the horn button. The lunchroom door opened, the smell of frying hamburger sailed out, and with it came the driver.

"Y' wish a cab sir?"

"Yeah. Hit for Sixth Street," Cardigan said and climbed in, sprawling in the back seat as the cab shot away from the curb. He could hear the tires sucking at the wet pavement, the driver humming cheerfully to himself.

When they reached Sixth Street Cardigan said: "Turn right and keep going till I tell you to stop."

Beyond a wide parking-space and hard by the flat dull side of a brick warehouse, a cluster of lights glowed wetly in the cold mist. Figures moved. One came out into the street and held up his hand. Metal buttons and a shield gleamed.

"Pull up," Cardigan said, and stepping out, as the cop came up, "I'm Cardigan. Where's Shadd?"

A voice brayed from the mottled darkness: "You, Cardigan?"

"Yeah."

"I thought so by the loud mouth."

There was an ambulance among the parked cars. The mist had beaded on the wires and was dripping like rain. Other uniformed cops moved among the crossed beams of the various headlights. There was a cleared space alongside the warehouse and lying in the short bleached grass between it and the sidewalk was the body of a man.

The red end of a cigar moved from Shadd's mouth down to his side and he said: "Well, here's S. N. Talbott."

A COP sprayed a flashlight down upon the dead man. Cardigan bent over, bracing his arm straight against the cold wet wall of the warehouse. The face of the dead man was white, it was a middle-aged face, small, kindly even in death. White-gray hair bushed around the head. Overcoat, suit-coat, vest and shirt had been opened and the wound was darkly visible—beneath the heart and a little to the left.

Cardigan straightened. He said in a low voice: "How do you know it's Talbott?"

Shadd held out a gold watch, its back cover open. "I opened the back of it. It's engraved inside. *Samuel Naylor Talbott, with great affection from his staff.* It was in the watch pocket of his pants. The guys that knocked him off must have missed it, because all the labels are ripped out of his clothes. They figured he'd be pigeon-holed as an unidentified man."

"Who found him?"

"Schwartzhaus, on the beat. About half an hour ago. Offhand, the doc says he's been dead about a couple of hours. Now I suppose you're going to stand there in all your bare face and tell me that you know nothing about S. N. Talbott."

"Did you get me down here to start that over again?"

"Listen, Cardigan—"

"I suppose with the kid in the hospital, still unconscious, and maybe dying, that I'd try to fox you. Don't be as dumb as you look, Boze. I tell you I don't know anything about Talbott. He wrote us—all right, he wrote us, because we had a file on him. But what it was about, I don't know. Am I a memory expert? This lug that swiped that file—he knew Talbott wrote us, he came in and swiped the file, to get his hands clean. He knew I didn't remember about Talbott. So with the bridges burned, it was safe to kill Talbott—but why he was killed I don't know."

A plainclothesman came up and said: "Lieutenant, I phoned all the hotels and there ain't no S. N. Talbott registered at any of them."

"Did you look in the local phone directory?"

"Yes. No soap there, either."

"Well, if he ain't registered at any hotel, he must live here anyhow, and no phone."

Cardigan said: "If he lived here and wanted to consult us about anything, ten to one he'd have phoned or dropped by the office, instead of writing."

The ambulance doctor said: "How about it, Lieutenant—can we load up and shove off?"

Shadd was biting his lip. "Yeah," he grunted. "Yeah, go ahead. To the morgue. I'll want the bullet." He turned and strode off; then swiveled and came back again and said to Cardigan in a hard, rasping voice: "By cripes, if you're horsing around with me!"

Cardigan started to say something, but he spat disgustedly and stamped over to the taxicab.

Shadd came after him, grinding out: "I said if you're—"

Cardigan whirled on him, his mouth savage. "If you think I am, damn you, pinch me! Toss me in the can! But cut out airing your dirty mind around me! By cripes, I think they stuck you in plainclothes because they ran out of uniforms! Nuts to you—especially big ones, like walnuts!"

He slammed into the cab and said: "Hotel Romany." As he drove off he caught a glimpse of Shadd's bitter, anger-ridden face.

When he reached his hotel room, he was still boiling. He uncorked a bottle, slopped liquor into a glass and threw it down his throat. Undressing, he walked

up and down the room and left his clothes
strewn about; climbed into a pair of
wrinkled blue pajamas and had another
drink and then picked his clothes up and
hung them in the closet. He scrubbed his
teeth, gargled loud and long, and then
piled into bed.

The telephone woke him up an hour
later and he said into the transmitter:
"Yeah, this is Cardigan." His eyebrows
snapped together and his hands tightened
on the instrument. Now his voice came
very thickly: "Sure, we'll take care of
things . . . . Nope, he didn't have any
parents. . . . *Uhn*—thanks."

As he put the telephone down his big
hands shook a little and the cordlike muscles in his neck stiffened, bulged. His
face got dark as a thundercloud and his
lips flattened so hard that his teeth appeared, clenched.

"Died . . . . poor kid," he muttered.

CHAPTER THREE

The Empty House

WIND blew the mists away and by
morning the streets were dry. But
the wind was strong, heavy-handed; it
whistled on the boulevards, cracked and
boomed in the alleys, tore the smoke from
chimneys. Cardigan cut through it across
Twelfth and dug down into Olive Street,
his ulster ballooning at his knees, the
brim of his weather-beaten fedora clap-
ping against the crown. Auto horns and
trolley bells crackled and bonged around
him. He turned into the Edge Building,
pounded his feet up two flights and strode
into the Cosmos office.

Miss Elfoot was grave. "I'm sorry
about Buddy—"

"H'm."

He had been over all that with Pat.
Pat said: "Every time I think of
it . . . ." and grimaced.

"HOLD YOUR HARPOON ...I GIVE UP!"

A CLAMMY pipe full of seaweed tobacco is a
weapon that will overpower any innocent
whale. But if you're fishing the stream of life for
pleasure and companionship, here's bait worth
two of that: Sir Walter Raleigh in a pipe kept dry
and shipshape. Sir Walter is a cleaner, cooler,
milder smoke that raises no dark clouds anywhere.
Instead, this sunny blend of well-aged Kentucky
Burleys spreads only a winning fragrance that
gains respect for all who puff it. In a modest way
it's become the sensation of the smoking world.
So try a tin; follow it with another—and you'll
be the catch of the season!

SWITCH TO THE BRAND OF GRAND AROMA

SIR WALTER RALEIGH

15

UNION MADE

SMOKING TOBACCO FOR PIPE AND CIGARETTES

"Sooner or Later—Your Favorite Tobacco"

FREE booklet tells
how to make your old
pipe taste better,
sweeter; how to break
in a new pipe. Write
for copy today. Brown
& Williamson To-
bacco Corporation,
Louisville, Kentucky.
Dept. PP-66.

How to TAKE CARE *of* your PIPE

"*Sh, sh,*" Cardigan said, giving her a slap on the shoulder. "It's tough, Patsy. It's done and it can't be undone—though I'd give my right arm to have that kid alive. But"—he scowled—"some things can be done. Miss Elfoot—"

"Yep?"

"Call the motor-vehicle bureau—long distance. Ask 'em if a man by the name of S. N. Talbott ever took out a license. If he did, get the address." He swiveled. "You, Pat—you hike over to headquarters. If I go over, there'll be a fight. Turn on the personality and find out if the bullet they took out of Buddy matches with the bullet they took out of Talbott. Go right to Corniff, the ballistics man. Step on it, kid."

H E WENT into his office, sat at his desk and ran through the morning's mail. It took him twenty minutes to do this and he was taking time out to light a cigarette when Miss Elfoot appeared in the doorway and said: "I've got them on the wire. Samuel Naylor Talbott—"

"That's it!"

"Operates a dark blue Farman five-passenger sedan. License number KX-22101. Motor number 1324659—"

"Address."

"Just Dryden Hill, Missouri."

"Oke."

"That all?"

"That's all from them. Hang up and get Dryden Hill on the phone pronto. It's a little town out in the Ozarks."

Five minutes later the Dryden Hill operator was on the wire and Cardigan said: "This is the Cosmos Detective Agency, St. Louis. Has Mr. S. N. Talbott got a phone? . . . . Ring him." He waited until another voice, a woman's voice answered. He said: "Are you Mrs. Talbott? . . . . Oh, his housekeeper. Is Mrs. Talbott there? . . . . Oh, I didn't know. Well, do you know who Mr. Tal-

bott went to see in St. Louis? . . . . Do you know who would know? . . . . I get it. And thanks."

He hung up and said to Miss Elfoot: "Dryden Hill again. This time Oscar Hedvig at the Dryden *Sentinel.* Talbott runs it."

When he was connected with Oscar Hedvig, he said: "This is Cardigan, the Cosmos Detective Agency, St. Louis. Mr. Talbott left there for this city and I wonder if you know who he was going to see? . . . . Oh, me, eh? Well, he never got to see me. He must have seen somebody else first. D'you know who it might be? . . . . I see . . . . No, go ahead." He began writing on a piece of paper. He asked: "Do you know why? . . . . Oh, he was, was he? . . . . Well, Mr. Hedvig, it's bad news—bad as bad. Mr. Talbott was found dead last night in Sixth Street, here. Shot . . . . I don't know. Nobody knows . . . . The police department, of course . . . . I'm sorry as hell, Mr. Hedvig."

Miss Elfoot stood watchfully in the doorway. "Soap?" she said, as Cardigan hung up.

He nodded. "Maybe. Talbott left Dryden Hill, driving, three days ago. He was coming to see the agency—and, Hedvig thinks, some automobile club called the Coast-to-Coast Auto Tourist Society. Ever hear of it?"

"No."

"Look it up in the telephone directory."

She looked it up, shook her head. "Nope."

"O. K. Call the post office, ask for McAlmon, tell him who you are and ask if they've got an address."

Five minutes later she reported: "Out on Washington, number—"

He wrote the number down, stood up and said: "Now go through the storage garages listed in the classified directory. Call the garages and see if Talbott's car is stored in any of them. Mention his name and the license number." He was getting into his overcoat. "I'll be back."

"If Shadd turns up, what should I do?"

"Spit in his eye."

"I can't spit, chief. Every time I try, I whistle."

"Well, whistle."

He sloped out of the office, caught a downbound elevator and crashed into Shadd in the lobby. Shadd reeled back, almost lost his hat, recovered it with one hand and pointed with the other.

"Hey, you!" he barked.

Cardigan went sweeping out to the sidewalk and found a cab waiting at the curb. He said: "Go to—"

But Shadd was there, spinning him around. "Cardigan—"

Cardigan shoved him away, turned back to the cab-driver and started again: "Go to—"

Shadd pushed in between Cardigan and the cab and clamped an iron hand on Cardigan's arm. "No, you don't!" he grunted, his eyes hard and angry, his face a deep scarlet. "So you tell me everything. You don't hold nothing from the police department. Ha!"

"All right. Ha! What do I know now? Maybe I've been going around—"

"Listen, you big loud-mouthed Irish bum! A guy out in Dryden Hill just calls up and asks what about Talbott, his boss? I say, 'Who is this and what do you know about Talbott?' He says, oh, Mr. Cardigan phoned him and said Talbott was dead—"

"Well?"

"Well!" yelled Shadd. "How the hell did you know Talbott came from Dryden Hill? I thought you said you didn't know nothing about him! I thought—"

"You thought! Any time you'd think, Boze, the experience'd give you a brainclot! Leggo my arm!"

Shadd's eyes were wild and dangerous. "You know more about this than—"

"Listen, you mud-turtle. I found out where he came from simply by calling the motor-vehicle bureau and finding out if he owned a car."

Shadd held on. He grated: "Why didn't you tell me? Why didn't you tell the police department?"

"Am I your errand boy? No! And, I tell you, sweetheart, leggo that arm or I'll stand you on your head."

Shadd snarled: "The kid's dead. O. K., he's dead. If you'd had any guts he'd be alive—you'd have taken that shot—"

Shadd said "Ooo!" and closed his eyes tight as Cardigan struck him. Shadd hit the pavement hard, his legs sprawling, his hat flying off and rolling away.

Cardigan got into the cab, slammed shut the door and said: "Head out Washington—quick, before that animated cartoon goes into his dance again."

THE house on Washington was two-storied, with a dirty yellow brick front, and with ten stone steps leading up to a gloomy vestibule. It looked deserted. There was a single bell-button inside the lobby and Cardigan punched it, heard a bell ring somewhere far in the house. He flipped the metal cover of a mail-slot in the door. No one came. He rang the bell again, keeping his thumb pressed against the button. The sound of the ringing bell seemed only to accentuate the emptiness of the house. He turned and went down the steps, looked up at the building, noticed a sign in an upper window—*For Sale*. The name of a real-estate agency was appended.

He walked to the next corner, counting off houses, then turned right, walked half a block, turned right again into an alley that paralleled Washington. Again counting off the houses, he stopped when he came to the rear of the eighth. There was a small back yard, littered; a ramshackle stable. He stepped down into an areaway, peered through a dirty window and saw what looked like a basement kitchen. There were three windows and all were bolted. There was a door. Using one of his master keys, it took him five minutes to get the door open.

The kitchen was bare of furniture and he could tell that the gas stove had not been used for a long time. Dust was thick. He tried a light-switch but no light came on. A closed-in stairway led him to the first floor and he entered another room bare of any furniture. Dust on a mantel was thick and fuzzy. All the rooms on the first floor were empty and he climbed to the second floor and found the rooms there empty also. He scowled, puzzled.

Returning to the first floor, he went to the hall door and saw on the floor beneath the mail-slot half a dozen letters. He picked them up. Each was addressed to the Coast-to-Coast Auto Tourist Society. He tossed them back to the floor. Moving to the rear of the hall, he descended to the basement, let himself out the back door and locked it.

He went around to a telephone booth in a cigar store and called his friend McAlmon at the post office, talked with him for three minutes. Then he took a cab to an address on Locust Street. An automobile salesroom occupied the street-level floor of the five-storied building and there was a side lobby leading to the offices upstairs. From the directory board Cardigan got the location of the real-estate agency and climbed two flights of stairs.

H E WALKED into an office where a curly-haired blonde sat at a desk reading a newspaper and smoking a cigarette. It was a one-room suite and there were two desks.

Cardigan said: "The boss around?"

She sat back and crushed out her cigarette. "No. He stepped out a couple of minutes ago. Can I do something?"

He mentioned the address of the empty house on Washington and asked: "Who's renting it?"

The girl got up, sauntered across to a filing-cabinet and took out a card-index, which she thumbed leisurely. She shrugged. "Nobody. It's for sale."

"When was it last rented?"

"No record here that it was ever rented. The owner moved out a year ago and went to California. Why, would you like to rent it?"

He shook his head, said: "No. Who was the owner?"

She put back the card-index, closed the filing-cabinet and came sauntering back to the desk. "Gustav Wohlman. He used to be in the dairy business." She sat down and took a pat at the curls above her left ear.

Cardigan was eyeing her steadily. "Ever hear of the Coast-to-Coast Auto Tourist Society?"

"*Uh-uhn,*" she said, shaking her head. "If you're trying to sell me something, you're wasting your time."

"Ever hear of a man named S. N. Talbott?"

She squinted up at him. "What is this, an intelligence test?"

"Did you?"

"No, I didn't."

"Did you ever hear of a man named John Strawn?"

"Listen, mister, are you trying to be funny?"

He said: "I'm trying to get some information."

She tossed her curls, gave him an exasperated look. "Well, this doesn't happen to be an information bureau. It's a real-estate agency. Ansel Bundy owns it. I work for him. My name is Agnes

Mahoney and I get twenty bucks a week and I don't like wiseacres that walk in here and horse around. If it's real estate you're interested in, this is the place. Anything else, you're up the wrong tree. Is that clear or do you want it under a magnifying glass?"

"Agnes," he said, "I could use you. If you ever get out of a job, try the Cosmos Agency and ask for Jack Cardigan. That's me."

"Oh, so you sell real estate too, huh? Trying to horn in on that property, huh?"

He shook his head. "When your boss comes in, tell him to phone me—right away." He scaled a card onto the desk.

She glanced at it, then frowned and picked it up. Her blue eyes lifted and for an instant lay curiously on his face. The she shrugged, put the card under a glass paperweight. "O. K., I'll tell him."

Cardigan turned to go out but at that instant the door opened and a small, fat, rosy-cheeked man breezed in, grinned from ear to ear, said: "Well, well—how do you do! Looking for me, sir?"

"If you're the boss here, yes."

"I'm the boss. Have a seat. By all means, have a seat. What was the name?"

"Cardigan. Cosmos Detective Agency."

Bundy took off his derby, scratched his bald head in thought. Then, "Of course, of course! You have an office here in town. Well, sir, I'm at your service."

"Swell," said Cardigan. "You handle a house over on Washington Boulevard. Vacant now. Gustav Wohlman—"

"Yes. Yes, of course. The old Wohlman house."

Cardigan nodded. "The post office has been delivering mail there for quite some time."

Bundy laughed, his stomach bouncing. "Ridiculous! The place has been vacant for a year."

"That's what's funny about it," Cardi-

gan said. "It's vacant, but mail's being delivered there—to the Coast-to-Coast Auto Tourist Society."

Bundy shook his head. "There must be some mistake. I never heard of the people. I ought to know, because I'm the only agent handling the property. You must be in error. You or the post-office department."

"Suppose," said Cardigan, "you and I take a run over there."

Bundy looked at his watch. "Really, I've got an appointment—"

"This is important. We can run over in five minutes."

Bundy looked at Agnes Mahoney. He shrugged and said: "All right, just to convince you, Mr. Cardigan." He put on his derby and said: "Phone for me, Miss Mahoney—and say I'll be a little late."

"O. K.," she said.

Cardigan went out into the hall and walked with Bundy to the head of the staircase. Then he said, "Just a minute —I forgot something," and headed back for the office. As he opened the office, door, Agnes Mahoney clapped her right hand over the telephone mouthpiece, moved the receiver from her ear down to her cheek. Her eyes were wide, level, her lips pursed.

"Don't let me disturb you," Cardigan said, picking up the packet of cigarettes he had left behind.

"I'm waiting for my call," she said dully.

He winked and left, joined Bundy, who had come halfway up the corridor, and went with him down to the street. Bundy hailed a cab and they rode off.

"It's really very curious," Bundy said, putting his round fat head on one side, peering down his short nose. "Are you—er—investigating for the post-office department?"

CARDIGAN shook his head. "No. I'm just trying to locate this so-called tourist society. Somebody apparently once tried to locate 'em—and got knocked off."

"*Mmmmmm,*" hummed Bundy, rolling his eyes in surprise. "That is something, isn't it? Who was it?"

"It's in today's papers. A man by the name of Talbott." He added: "His name ain't in the papers. He was that unidentified man—"

"Oh, I read that. In Sixth Street, you mean. But I didn't read anything about this tourist society being connected—"

"Nobody knew—until I found out this morning."

"Ah, yes. Then I suppose you're working for Talbott's family?"

Cardigan frowned, shook his head, said grimly: "No. There was a young kid killed too. You read about that—"

Bundy struck his knee. "By George, sir, you're right. That's where I saw your agency's name. I'd been trying to recall—Yes, yes, of course." He dropped his voice, shook his head slowly. "Awful, about that poor young boy!"

The cab pulled up in front of the Washington Boulevard house and Bundy bounced out. Cardigan paid and Bundy said: "I've only the back-door key along. We'll have to go around back. Let's do it quietly—so that if anyone's inside—"

"I catch." Cardigan nodded.

Bundy led the way around to the back door, walked on his toes down into the areaway and was careful about making no noise when he inserted the key in the keyhole. He put a finger to his lips, opened the door quietly, inch by inch. Then he entered, still walking on his toes, and Cardigan followed. Cardigan followed him through the basement rooms, then up to the first floor.

Bundy paused at the head of the staircase and whispered: "You see, the place is empty."

"You take this floor. I'll go upstairs."

They moved from the deep gloom of the hallway and then Cardigan climbed to the top floor, walked through the rooms, came out to the top of the staircase noisily. Bundy called up: "Nothing down here."

"Here, either," Cardigan said and rattled his big feet down the stairs. He walked to the hall door, peered through the dirty window into the dim vestibule. His eyes slid first to one side, then to the other.

Bundy struck his hands together. "You see, Mr. Cardigan, there must be some mistake. The place is entirely empty. You can tell by the dust that no one's lived here in months."

Cardigan turned away from the door, went past him and entered a large room where the light was better. Bundy came in, beaming, rubbing his hands together.

"If you don't mind, sir, I'd like for us to get going. I have an appointment—"

"With me," Cardigan said, pulling his gun and turning.

Bundy's features seemed to shoot upward as his eyes popped.

Cardigan said: "Raise your hands."

"But look here, now—"

"Up, up, Mr. Bundy," Cardigan grunted, coming slowly toward him.

Bundy backed up, his short fat arms rising, a look of pain and indignation on his face. "You can't do this!" he bleated. "You can't hold me up!"

"Keep the hands high, Mr. Bundy, and stop backing up."

A spasm of terror raced across the man's fat face and he turned and bolted through the doorway into the corridor, plunged into its gloom. Cardigan jumped after him, heard him stumble frantically down the stairway to the basement. The big Cosmos op bowled down the corridor tunneled down the dark, closed-in stair-case. His feet hammered on the way through the basement and, reaching the kitchen, he took a terrific jump and land-ed on Bundy as the latter yanked open the rear door. The door was slammed shut so hard that its glass panel fell out, crashed on the cement areaway.

"Oh—ah—*uhn*—" gulped Bundy.

Cardigan gripped him by the throat and bounced him off the wall beside the door; caught hold of him again, held him with his left hand while he used his right hand to press his gun against the fat man's stomach. "Now," he said, "what about those letters?"

Bundy choked. "Letters! What let-ters?"

"You picked up some letters that were on the floor inside the front door."

Bundy spluttered: "I beg your pardon, I did not! What the devil are you talking about?"

"Put up your hands!"

BUNDY raised his hands and Cardigan went through his pockets. There were no letters. Cardigan began to get very red in the face and Bundy, pouting indignantly, began to smooth down his rumpled clothing. He panted: "I am be-ginning to think, sir, that you're a mad-man. I've a good idea to have you ar-rested."

"That," said Bozeman Shadd, framed in the broken panel, "would be a very good idea indeed." He opened the door, his face lined with a tight, malicious grin. "Just say the word, mister."

Cardigan scowled. "How did you get here?"

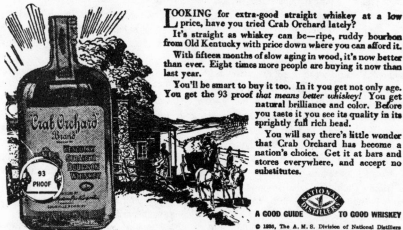

From its
OLD KENTUCKY HOME
it rose to be the nation's choice

LOOKING for extra-good straight whiskey at a low price, have you tried Crab Orchard lately?

It's straight as whiskey can be—ripe, ruddy bourbon from Old Kentucky with price down where you can afford it.

With fifteen months of slow aging in wood, it's now better than ever. Eight times more people are buying it now than last year.

You'll be smart to buy it too. In it you get not only age. You get the 93 proof *that means better whiskey!* You get natural brilliance and color. Before you taste it you see its quality in its sprightly full rich bead.

You will say there's little wonder that Crab Orchard has become a nation's choice. Get it at bars and stores everywhere, and accept no substitutes.

A GOOD GUIDE   TO GOOD WHISKEY

© 1936, The A. M. S. Division of National Distillers Products Corporation, Louisville, Ky.

This advertisement is not intended to offer alcoholic beverages for sale or delivery in any state or community where the advertising, sale, or use thereof, is unlawful.

"Dummy, I asked that taxi-driver where he took you."

Bundy began to look very puzzled.

Shadd said: "I'm Lieutenant Shadd, mister. I just arrive in time to hear you say you ought to have this big bum arrested. What's the charge? Any charge, mister, just so long as I can toss him in the can."

"Listen," broke in Cardigan. "Not so fast. This was all a mistake. I thought I heard someone down here and in the darkness I grabbed hold of Mr. Bundy by mistake, manhandled him a bit, and he got sore."

Shadd grunted. "Suppose you let Mr. Bundy do the talking."

Bundy shrugged. "Well, let's forget it. Fact is, I was sore at being manhandled—even though it was a mistake."

Shadd scowled. "Yeah?" He looked at Cardigan. "And what are you doing in here any way?"

"Well, you see," said Cardigan, "I got a phone call—and I guess it was a crank phone call. Some guy called me up and said that if I wanted to find the man who killed my office boy I should come to this address. Well, I came out and the place looked empty, nobody answered the bell. So I saw Mr. Bundy's real-estate sign in the window and went over and told him. We came over here and he opened up."

Bundy still looked injured, and complained: "He accused me of possessing some letters, even. Why, I don't know. He's a most unreasonable man—but, as I said, we'll drop it. He's doubtless upset over the death of that boy."

Shadd looked angry. "That's no excuse for him to slam you around. You make a charge against him and I'll—"

Bundy shook his head impatiently. "I can't be bothered. I'm much too busy to be running to court. Besides, you two men seem to have a personal grudge, and I want no part in that. I must go. I have

an appointment and I'm late as it is. But," he said to Cardigan, "if you try any of your barroom tactics again, sir, I'll take advantage of the law. And now I'll thank you both to get out."

Cardigan gave him a sour frown and heaved out into the areaway. Shadd followed. Bundy came last, saying: "And I'll have to have this window repaired."

"Send me the bill," Cardigan muttered, climbing up the areaway steps and walking off through the littered yard.

CHAPTER FOUR

Hide-out

ON Washington, Bundy got in a cab and rode off. Cardigan walked and Shadd walked beside him, though Cardigan was so wound up in bitter thoughts that he was hardly aware of the lieutenant.

They came to a corner where two uniformed policemen stood. One of the policemen said: "Hi, Lieutenant."

"Hi, boys," Shadd said; and then, "Grab this guy."

Cardigan stopped and looked at Shadd in dark amazement.

"Grab him!" Shadd snapped.

The two cops closed in on Cardigan. They were big men and they locked him between them. Shadd put on the manacles.

"What's this for?" Cardigan muttered somberly.

"For striking an officer," Shadd said. "Or did you forget?" He whistled for a cab, saying: "Come along, boys, in case he gets ideas."

Cardigan's face grew dull red, his mouth warped savagely. "Some day, Shadd, I'm really going to strike an officer. I'm going to whittle you down to a hoarse whisper."

"Get in the cab, loud-mouth. You're on the wrong wave-length."

At headquarters, Shadd took off the manacles, sat on the desk in his bare office and said: "Are you going to talk or am I going to toss you in the can?"

Cardigan turned around, strode out of the office, down the corridor, and into another office. Shadd came pounding at his heels. Inspector Fisk was sitting behind his desk plunking a typewriter; he was a beetle-browed man with a heavy preoccupied look.

Cardigan said: "Inspector, I want to know what I have to do to keep this guy from getting under my feet all the time."

"Now look here!" Shadd exploded, getting between Cardigan and the desk. "You cut out pestering the inspector."

"Yeah, cut out pestering me—I'm busy," sighed Fisk.

Cardigan rapped out: "I won't be shoved around by Shadd here!"

"I'll shove you around, boy!" Shadd roared; and to Fisk, "He took a sock at me—right in Olive Street! Me—an officer!"

Cardigan said very close to Shadd's face: "You had no right to make that crack about me—about the kid."

"Now, now," said Fisk, "I'm busy. Will you lads please get the hell out of my office?"

Shadd leveled an arm toward the door. "Get out, Cardigan."

"I won't get out! I came in here to get justice!" Cardigan whirled on Fisk. "Because this onion didn't have brains enough to see if Talbott owned a car, he got sore because I happened to find out where Talbott came from. Now I can't shake him. He thinks I know everything about the case. I don't know a thing. I'm trying to find out, but every step I take, he's under my feet."

Fisk pondered. Then he said: "Boze, go downstairs and get what dope you got on the case. Bring it up here."

"Right!" clipped Shadd, and stomped out.

Fisk got up, patted himself on the stomach and said: "Excuse me while I go out and get a drink of water." He marched out of the office whistling.

Cardigan, after a minute, stepped out into the corridor, strolled to the elevator and rang for it. It came up and he rode it down to the basement and walked out into the street. He strode along Twelfth, turned into Olive. His face was dark with anger.

WHEN he entered the Edge Building and banged into the Cosmos office Miss Elfoot said: "Did you meet Pat?"

"No."

"Well, she went out to that Washington Boulevard address after you."

He stopped on his way into the inner office and frowned at Miss Elfoot. "Huhn?"

"Yes. She came back here from headquarters, where she found the slugs were from the same gun. I told her where you'd gone and off she went after you."

"When'd she leave?"

"About twenty minutes after you left. Later, she phoned back and said that the place was empty but that she was going to hang around and watch it."

Cardigan's lips tightened. "Listen. If Shadd shows up, tell him you haven't seen me. I'm going out to the Bundy Real Estate Agency, on Locust. If you hear from Pat, phone me there. If I'm not there, I'll phone you later."

Miss Elfoot said: "You sound as if you're going to town."

"I'm going around in circles," he muttered, "and I got to pull out of them."

He slammed out and went down to the street and climbed into a taxicab. It headed out Lindell while Cardigan sat with his elbows on his knees, his big hands dangling loosely. There was a dark, lowering look on his face, and menace in his eyes. He did not once look out the cab windows but sat staring straight before him. When the cab drew up in front of the office building on Locust he remained seated for a moment, deep in thought. Then he pushed open the door, shoved his leg out and swung to the pavement. He paid the driver and entered the building, climbed upstairs and strode darkly toward the real-estate agency's door. The door was locked.

He opened it with a master key, stepped in and let the snap-lock bolt itself shut. Crossing to the desk, he sat down and pulled out all the drawers, rifled them. He found nothing interesting, so he rose and moved to the filing-cabinets, skimmed through correspondence, cards, real-estate listings. Nothing he found roused his curiosity. He sat down again at the desk, leaned back, pulled out a cigar and nipped off the tip. A match flamed off his thumbnail and he puffed the cigar to a nice red end. Then he drew out his gun and laid it on the desk and swiveled a bit in the chair, to face the door.

It took half an hour to smoke the cigar down. Rising, he tossed the butt out the window, emptied the ashes after it. The phone rang and he looked at it for a few seconds, then picked it up. Miss Elfoot was on the wire. As she spoke, he took out a pencil, scribbled on a piece of paper.

"Sit tight!" he said, and hung up, pocketed his gun.

He strode long-legged to the door, let himself out and heard the lock snap shut. His big feet made a lot of noise on the way down the stairs and he ran out in the middle of the street in order to stop a taxi; gave the address and jumped in, adding: "I don't mind speeding a bit."

THERE was a cluttered cigar store on the corner where Cardigan got out of the cab. He stood for a minute with his hands sunk in his ulster pockets, his old hat crushed down to his eyebrows, a keen windy look in his eyes. Brick and frame buildings jostled one another in the narrow street; there were a few garages, an empty lot, a bottling-plant. The smell of the river came up the street.

Cardigan turned into the cigar store, peered around; went outside again and craned his head, scowling. He returned to the store and asked the sleepy, fuzzy-haired man behind the counter: "Was there a girl here recently—one that made a phone call?"

"*H'm*—yeah, I guess so. You mean about half an hour ago?"

"About that, yes. She was supposed to wait here."

"Well," yawned the man, "she did— for a little while. Then another gal fell over the doorstep coming in and I guess turned her ankle. She could hardly walk. This other gal, the one you asked about, helped her—I guess helped her walk home, I dunno."

"What'd she look like, the one that fell?"

"I dunno. Young—that's all. I can't find my eyeglasses and I can't see good without eyeglasses."

"How long ago did they leave?"

"Oh, maybe ten minutes."

Cardigan pivoted and strode out. Pat had phoned the office and said that she had tailed a man from the Washington Boulevard address to a house in this street. She had given the address of the cigar store from which she had phoned and had told Miss Elfoot to have Cardigan join her there. She had said that the house to which she had followed the man was in the same block but had no number.

• The Cosmos op walked along on a

broken sidewalk. No one seemed to live in the street. There were no dogs, no cats; no sound of any kind. Some of the old buildings were boarded up. Cardigan felt a prickling sensation on the back of his neck. It was in this neighborhood, not far from this very street, that Talbott had been found dead.

He went up one side of the street, listening at doors, at windows; he came back on the other side of the street, crossed and stood in front of the cigar store. He had a feeling that he was being watched, that from an upper window somewhere in this block eyes followed his movements. He walked again over the broken sidewalk, more slowly this time, his hand on the gun in his overcoat pocket.

And then he stopped and looked at something that he had noticed with only idle interest on his first tour: a red smear along the wall of a yellow frame house—a red streak about a foot long. He moved on, saw another similar streak across a door; and two houses farther on, another streak. This time he rubbed with his finger, found his finger smeared with the red stuff. He sniffed it. He figured that it was lip-rouge. Going on, slow step by slow step, he found another streak of red. He began to move faster and then stopped suddenly when he saw a red circle scrawled on a gray wooden door. The house was frame, boxlike, and three-storied. Shades were drawn. Bending, he picked up Pat's lipstick.

Cardigan did not knock. He walked on faster now; reached the empty lot and entered it. At the back of the corner building was a fire-escape and he climbed it, his coat-tails swinging on the way up. He came to the roof and crossed it; dropped to the roof of the next house and went over a ledge to the roof of the third. The fourth was the one he wanted and he walked on his toes when he had reached it. He crossed to a chimney and held his

hand over it and felt warm air rising. He knew the house was not vacant now. There was a fire-escape down the back of it. There was a trap-door in the roof but it was bolted from the inside. He went over the side, took six steps down the fire-ladder to a metal landing outside a window. The window was locked. He could see a small bare room with a closed door at the other end of it.

TAKING out his jack-knife, he went to work on the top center pane of the old-fashioned, six-paned window. He clipped away the old putty, pried out the small metal triangles; then got his knife blade in under the edge of the pane and pried it free of its frame without so much as chipping it. He laid the pane down on the landing, reached in and unbolted the window. Raising the window slowly, he climbed in, left it raised.

He drew his gun and moved across the room, opened the door and looked out into a hallway. There was a room off the left and though it was innocent of a stick of furniture, there were two trunks and three handbags. There were four other rooms on the top floor, all of them empty. He heard a low murmur of voices and turning his head, saw a hot-air radiator in the wall. He put his ear to it but could hear no more than a voice's low murmur.

Going back into the hallway, he made his way down the staircase to the second floor. He paused, heard the sound of voices again; how many voices, he did not know but he figured there were three or four, all downstairs. He went to the front of the hall, pulled up the shade and carefully raised the window, wanting to be sure of a quick way out in the event of an emergency. He stuck his head out and saw that the street was deserted. A gust of wind uprooted his hat and though he tried to recover it, it spun downward and landed in front of the street door. He cursed under his breath, pulled his head in and went down to the lower hall.

The voices were in the rear but he tried a nearer door and it opened at his touch and he found himself entering a gloomy front room containing overstuffed furniture. An open doorway led him into a large bedroom and, though it was daylight outside, this room was bathed in gloom. A door was beyond and beneath it he could see a thread of light. He crossed silently to that door, laid his hand on the knob, turned it, felt the door give.

He yanked it in and said "Don't move!" into the next room.

Four men sitting around a kitchen table moved as though an electric shock had touched them—but they did not move far. Ansel Bundy, looking fat and perturbed and with his hair disheveled, dropped a glass of whisky. A big blond man in a black pull-over sweater shot his mouth tightly over to one side and held it there, rigid. A stumpy, ape-like man with a broken nose choked and spat out a cigarette. John Strawn, who had shot Buddy Miller to death under Cardigan's eyes, wore a cold, gray look. All the shades, of a dark green color, were drawn, and a large electric light glowed against the ceiling.

Ansel Bundy made a sound something like *"Ahnk!"* and swallowed hard. His eyes seemed to bulge from their sockets; fear glazed them and ripped its way down his fat, quaking face.

"I suppose," Cardigan said dully to him, "I'm in the wrong house again."

CHAPTER FIVE

The Real McCoy

ANSEL BUNDY shook all over. The broken-nosed man began to stare hard at the floor, as though he were not concerned with what was taking place.

The big blond man began to scratch his chest. Strawn seemed to be listening for something. There was in the room an atmosphere of a balloon swelling and threatening to burst.

Cardigan's voice chopped into it harshly. "Where's the girl that was brought here?"

Strawn lifted his eyes slowly and said: "What girl?"

"The girl that found this address!" Cardigan snapped. "Pat Seaward!"

"Do you see her?" Strawn inquired.

Cardigan's eyes drilled him. "Never mind trying to uncork an act, brother." His eyes shifted to Bundy. "All right—then you tell me, little fat man—or you're going to have a busy day."

Bundy's fat chin jigged. "I—I don't know a thing. That is a fact, sir. I—"

"Shut up!" Cardigan shouted. "I've got it all figured out. Talbott went to that Washington Boulevard address. Nobody was there. He saw your sign in the window. He went to your office and was killed! You're the mastermind behind all this!"

Bundy waved his fat hands in horror. "No, sir! I assure you, sir!" The sweat began to make his fat face very shiny and his hands pawed the air. Terror had riddled his eyes. "I—I was forced into countenancing certain acts—" He stopped, his voice wheezing, despair hanging at his mouth.

Strawn's lips were taut and his cold eyes were fastened on the fat man. Bundy forced himself to meet that stare—and then shrank away, his mouth contorted with fear. He cried out: "I know nothing, sir! Not a thing!"

Cardigan nodded to a door at the side of the kitchen, said: "What's in there?"

"A servant's room—now unoccupied," Strawn said.

"There's somebody in there," Cardigan growled. "At the door. I hear—"

The knob of the door rattled. The broken-nosed man moved on his chair, making it creak. Strawn seemed to sit straighter in his chair. His face was pale, deathly gray, but not a muscle twitched. Bundy squirmed on his chair and seemed on the point of tears and the blond man pursed his lips and began to whistle.

Suddenly the door swung open and revealed the blonde, Agnes Mahoney, on hands and knees. Her hair was rumpled and there was a handkerchief tied around her mouth and she appeared to be on the point of collapse. Cardigan, saying, "One move out of any of you palookas, and it's root-a-toot-toot," began moving across the floor to where Agnes Mahoney was now crawling slowly into the room. He reached down with his left hand, grabbed hold of her arm and said: "Try to get up, kid, so I can—"

She shot to her feet like a wildcat and her hands clawed down across Cardigan's face. Pain seared his face and a violent kick in the shins sent him staggering. Agnes jumped back and the man with the broken nose jumped in. Cardigan caught a hard fist on the jaw and slammed back against the wall. The blond man came into him headfirst and almost knocked the wind out of him.

Bundy jumped up and ran for the door, terrified.

"Hey, you!" Agnes Mahoney screamed.

Strawn snapped: "Bundy—get back here!"

Cardigan hit the squat man and drove him across the room into a pile of dishes that crashed. But the big blond man had his other hand, his gun-hand, warped high and backward.

BUNDY was trying to get the door open, heedless of the threats of Strawn, the yells of the woman. Bundy got the door open but the woman hit him with a heavy glass pitcher and floored him.

Strawn snapped to the blond man, "Break away, Dutch. I'll cover him. Cardigan, drop that gun!"

"Drop hell!"

"Drop it! Dutch, break, I tell you!"

Cardigan put his heel against the wall, shoved and went banging across the room carrying Dutch with him. Strawn jumped out of the way, hit a chair and fell down. The squat man came up out of the broken dishes pulling a gun. Cardigan tossed Dutch off, shifted, snapped his gun around and cut loose at the squat man. The squat man looked surprised, then stricken, and fell back into the broken dishes.

The woman leaped on Cardigan's back, got her fingers in his eyes. He yelled, heaved and threw her over his shoulders; and as she cleared, her legs flying, Strawn

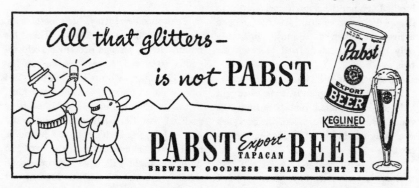

All that glitters — is not PABST

Pabst EXPORT BEER KEGLINED

PABST *Export* TAPACAN BEER

BREWERY GOODNESS SEALED RIGHT IN

stepped in and banged Cardigan across the face with the barrel of his gun. Blood spouted and Cardigan turned around and fell to his knees. He was getting up again when Dutch kicked him and flattened him. But he rolled over and, half blinded, fired upward. Dutch's feet clubbed the floor as he staggered backward and crashed into Strawn. Cardigan shoved himself up to his feet, reeled and went staggering into the side room. He didn't stop until a wall stopped him and then he fell, bounced off a bed. But he felt an arm— soft, small—and then, in the dim light, he saw a form on the bed.

"Pat!" he muttered.

She was bound and gagged and could neither move nor say anything. But he knew she would be in line of fire. Grunting, he grabbed hold of her—but she was lashed to the cot. He had no time to cut away the lashings, so he gripped the cot and tried to slide it out of the way of the door. It swung heavily. He threw his weight against it hard and it rumbled across the floor, stopped against the other wall.

He turned and bounded to the doorway. He saw Bundy again on his feet, clawing toward the hall doorway, trying to get out. He saw Strawn, thin-lipped, aiming his gun at Bundy.

"Strawn!" Cardigan ripped out.

Strawn's gun went off and Bundy lurched against the door frame. Cardigan dropped Strawn with a low shot, hopped across the room as Bundy, apparently only lightly wounded, tried to reach the hall.

"Stop it, Bundy!" Cardigan yelled.

Bundy didn't stop and Cardigan caught hold of him, pulled him back into the room. Bundy sat down on the floor, his eyes bulging, his breath pounding up his throat.

"Listen—listen, I tell you, sir, I had nothing— Look, sir. She—Agnes—I fell for her. Hard, you understand. She wrapped me around her finger. I tell you, sir, I thought it was legitimate at first. Strawn's auto-tourist society. He got me to handle accident insurance for clients. He sent out many letters—had a large mailing list—small country towns. Five-dollar fee, for which members were supposed to get cut-rate gas, lodging, on tourist trips. List of fake lodging-houses, camps, gas-stations. Talbott showed up. Shrewd country editor. First I knew about them using Washington Boulevard address as blind. Agnes did that—gave Strawn the key. Strawn collected mail there every day. Talbott saw my sign in that window, came to my office. Demanded to know my hook-up with the society. Sir, I was in a spot. While we talked, Agnes went out, phoned Strawn. He came and took Talbott away, burnt his baggage, hid his car. I had to play along. Strawn threatened. Canny country editor—"

"You took those letters in the hallway that time?"

"No, sir. Strawn collected the letters. Your Miss Seaward happened to be watching across the street—saw him enter, come out with letters. She followed him. But he happened to notice her there, saw her again in this street. Saw her go in that cigar store—and sent Agnes after her—"

He stopped suddenly, his mouth open, his eyes wide with horror. Then his mouth closed, his lips pressed fiercely together. He saw Agnes creeping up behind Cardigan with a carving knife. But Bundy did not shout, did not warn him; in this terrible minute Bundy must have realized that Cardigan would not, could not let him go. In his fear and terror he must have figured that with Cardigan dead, he might still have a chance—one small, craven snatch at life. He reached up and with both hands gripped Cardigan by the neck.

AGNES lunged. Cardigan lunged right across Bundy's body—so fast, so hard, that his head banged against the wall and stunned him. The knife missed him. It sank in the floor. Agnes went head over heels. There was a crash somewhere else in the house. The sound of it spurred Bundy to a final, miserable grasp at life. He wrenched the knife from the floor, struggled to his feet, swayed a minute and then, with the knife upraised, headed for Cardigan, who was on his knees, shaking his head.

Miss Elfoot came through the door holding a large revolver. Her hat was knocked over one eye. A sucked-in breath hissed through her teeth and she held the revolver out awkwardly, with both hands, and her knees shook, a grimace warped

across her mouth. The gun boomed in her hands and with a little startled cry she let it drop and clapped her hands to her cheeks. Bundy went down on one knee, then toppled over on his back.

Miss Elfoot said "Oh, oh, oh," in a scratchy little voice.

Cardigan looked up at her foggily. "Miss Elfoot," he said.

"Y-yes, sir?"

"Take that knife, go in that room and untie Pat."

He reached over and caught hold of Agnes with one hand. She was a little dazed but she turned on him, tried to bite him. With his other hand he knocked her cold. He rose slowly to his feet, his face bloody, his hair matted.

Pat came out into the room and cried: "Oh . . . chief, you're hurt!"

"Patsy, think nothing of it. That was

WHEN THE REGIMENT'S MOVING FORWARD—

When bullets are waiting under a desert sun, can you expect an old Legionnaire to obey— when you tell him to die in bed?

THE WAY OF THE LEGION

A novelette by Georges Surdez and other outstanding fiction is in the June ADVENTURE.

15c   *Out May 8*

Send a dollar bill to ADVENTURE, 205 E. 42nd St., N.Y.C., for a special eight-months subscription.

a swell idea, the rouge marks on the walls."

"It was a long chance. The minute she got me out of the store, she held a gun on me."

Miss Elfoot came into the room saying: "I know I should have stayed in social service. I—"

"And how did you get in?" Cardigan asked.

She gasped: "Oh, goodness. I wonder—" and ran out into the hall.

Pat said: "Well, what—"

They heard a scraping, rubbing sound, and in a minute saw Miss Elfoot hauling Boze Shadd into the room. Shadd was not on his feet and he looked a bit cracked up. His head was rolling and he was muttering vaguely under his breath.

Miss Elfoot said: "He showed up at the office and when I wouldn't tell him anything, he dragged me over to headquarters. But I figured you might phone, and I wouldn't be in the office—so I had to tell the—well—cluck. I had a hunch you might get tied up in things. We came down to the cigar store, didn't find out anything, and then we walked down the street and I saw your hat on the sidewalk. 'This is it,' I said. We tried the door but it was locked and I said to

Shadd, 'You're tough. Go ahead and bust it down.' Well, he took a running broad-jump and busted it down—and knocked himself out doing it. I—well—grabbed his gun."

Shadd, coming to, began to yell: "It's a lie! I was knocked out and—" He sat up and glared at Miss Elfoot. "You knocked me out! You hit an officer! I'll—"

Miss Elfoot blushed a little. "Well, all right, then I did." She turned to Cardigan. "He broke the door down but when he heard the racket back here he wouldn't go in. He said, 'I'll go get a squad of cops.' I told him there wasn't time. He said there was. So I hooked one on his jaw and knocked him out and took his gun."

Shadd blared: "She hit me with a hammer!"

"I did not," said Miss Elfoot, taking a set of brass knuckles out of her pocket. "I hit you with these. I got them as a present from Honey Boy Potofski, when I was in social-service work."

Cardigan turned and said, "I could go a drink," and headed toward a bottle standing on a shelf.

"Try this," said Miss Elfoot, hauling a half-pint flask out of her pocket. "It's the real McCoy."

The Cards are stacked against you

WHEN YOU BUY THE *unknown*

● You gamble when you buy unknown razor blades! Probak Jr. —priced at 4 for only 10c is produced by the world's largest maker of razor blades. It glides gently over tender faces, shaves tough whiskers without pull or irritation. Buy a package and see!

4 BLADES FOR 10¢

PROBAK JUNIOR

THE DOMINO LADY

In the crime-infested cities and countryside—as portrayed in the pulp magazines—the police were either too weak or too corrupt to contain misdeeds. Powerful and sometimes bizarre evildoers thrived. A handful of athletic, super-intelligent civilians took the law into their own hands. They worked undercover, wearing distinctive dress, aided by faithful agents.

These costumed crime fighters are best exemplified by The Shadow, who battled crooks in 325 issues of the Street & Smith magazine of the same name from 1931 to '49. The Spider fought thugs and super criminals in 118 issues of his own Popular Publications magazine from 1933 to '43. Other super-heroes included The Black Bat (in sixty-two novels published between 1939 and '53), The Crimson Mask (fifteen adventures, 1940–44), The Green Lama (fourteen stories, 1940–43), and The Whisperer (thirty-three tales, 1936–42).

A rare female in this category is Ellen Patrick, alias The Domino Lady. Her handful of exploits, written by Lars Anderson, appeared in *Saucy Romantic Adventures* and *Mystery Adventures Magazine.* These magazines were from a publishing family that emphasized sexiness (though stopped short of outright sex).

"The Domino Lady Doubles Back" is from the June 1936 issue of *Saucy Romantic Adventures.*

The Domino Lady Doubles Back

A modern "Mrs. Robin Hood" rights a great wrong, and wins a detective's approbation

By LARS ANDERSON

CHAPTER I

"**E**LLEN PATRICK, as I live! What are you doing in San Francisco?"

Roge McKane, young private investigator, dropped into a chair opposite Ellen in the Cocktail Room of Frisco's exclusive Hotel Catalan.

"Hello, Roge," she smiled, brown eyes narrowing languorously as she flicked the ashes from her cigarette. "I'm just week-ending, and taking in the Kettrick Ball Masque. How's the sleuthing business since we last met?"

"Fair," drawled McKane, his dark eyes searching Ellen's lovely face and sensuous figure with frankly admiring candor. "But did I hear you mention the Kettrick Ball?"

"Why, yes," she murmured, casually, a tight little smile playing about the corners of her disturbing crimson lips as her great brown eyes swept over the handsome features of the young detective. "I hear it is to be quite an event. Why, Roge?"

"Oh, it should be quite an event," he assured her, "if present indications are to be accepted as a crite-rion. I'll be there myself, in my professional capacity, of course."

She was instantly alert, cautious. "Professional capacity?" she questioned, quickly. "Why, what do you mean? I didn't think. . . . "

He glanced about the rather crowded room, leaned closer to her before replying. "Kettrick's showing his collection tonight!" he confided in a half-whisper. "Them and that ex-movie star wife he brought back from Los Angeles! But wait," he continued, as she started to interrupt, "You haven't heard the half of it, Ellen! He's had a threatening note from that nervy little dame who calls herself The Domino Lady! And . . ."

Ellen broke in with a short laugh. "But the police will protect a big shot like Kettrick." Contemptuously. "And I wouldn't envy anyone who tried to crash the Kettrick mansion tonight! . . . "

McKane laughed, mirthlessly. "Yeah, Ellen, that sounds logical, I know, but Old Boy Kettrick is a slick customer. Rumors are that at least part of his collection is fenced rocks! At any rate, he's not calling in his friends, the police, for protection! And that's where Mrs. Mc-Kane's little boy, Roger, comes in! Some of the boys and me are to be johnnies on the spot tonight, and grab The Domino Lady if she has the nerve to show up, and try anything!".

Ellen smiled, enigmatically.

"It all sounds absurd to me," she exclaimed, "I'd think he'd call the ball off until a more favorable time, if danger threatens. Why, with celebrities from all parts of the state attending, and . . ."

"That's just the point!" he grinned, beckoning to a hovering waiter. "Have another drink, Ellen?"

She shook her golden head, decisively. "Thanks, no, Roge. If I'm attending that masque tonight, and all the intriguing things you say are true, I'll want a clear head so's not to miss a thing!"

McKANE ordered a drink for himself, then leaned across the table again. He grinned. "As I was saying, Ellen. Old Kettrick is a stubborn ass. And he's mighty proud of those diamonds and of that new wife he imported from Hollywood. Hell and high water couldn't stop the festivities tonight, not even if he knew there might be shooting! The lives of his celebrated guests are secondary to him! So it's up to the boys and me to see that nothing happens, no matter where our personal sympathies lie. . . ."

"With you there, Roge," she smiled, seductively, crossing one silken-clad leg over the other in a careless gesture which immediately drew McKane's admiring gaze. "Everyone will be perfectly safe! And here's luck to you, Big Boy!" Ellen raised her half-emptied glass

to her lips, smiled at him over the edge of it as she sipped the amber liquid, slowly.

Roge McKane grinned his appreciation as he raised his own glass.

"And here's to the loveliest girl to grace the Kettrick mansion tonight!" he toasted, boldly, his dark gaze sweeping her seductive figure and piquant face, and centering on her moist, crimson lips.

"But this Domino Lady," she quickly changed the subject "Is she just a money-mad little thief, or . . ."

"I really don't think so, Ellen," he interrupted, quickly. "Perhaps you won't be able to understand, but it's rumored about that she never steals for personal gain. It is said that she is the anonymous donor of much of the money which has been given to worthy charity in this state recently. Why, in this instance, her threat is aimed at the crooked politicians. Ames Kettrick, who owns half the tenements in town. And, not satisfied with penny-grabbing and the ejecting of widows and orphans from his shacks, he flatly refused aid to the Community Orphanage where hundreds of poor kiddies, some of them being victims of Kettrick's greed, are badly in need of help. So he's right in line for a visit from The Domino Lady who intends, according to her letter of warning, to take the Old Boy for his collection of diamonds for the benefit of the charities he persistently ignores. . . ."

Ellen had listened, intently. Now, she interrupted: "You're to guard the place," she murmured, softly, "yet you sound as though you were in sympathy with the lady, Roge!"

He grinned: "Did I say I wasn't? But, although I admire her nerve

With gum, she stuck to the window frame a small, black card.

and principles, personal sympathies don't mean a thing in this game. I'm drawing my salary for guarding something, and that protection holds good, no matter who my employer happens to be, or what I'm retained to guard. You see that, don't you?"

As she began to word a pert reply

there came an interruption. A bellhop entered the Cocktail Room, paging Roge McKane. He frowned. It was an important telephone call, but it was easy to see that the young investigator disliked leaving his charming companion!

"Don't mind me, Roge," Ellen

laughed, tinklingly, "I really must be going. I must look my best to night, and I need the beauty nap, you know. See you at the masque, I suppose?"

"You bet!" McKane told her, enthusiastically. "And if I can manage a dance or two, will you save 'em for me, Ellen?"

With her consenting laugh echoing in his ears, the frowning detective went to answer the telephone summons, and Ellen stood up and walked toward the elevators.

CHAPTER II

PETITE Ellen Patrick had earned her title of "The Domino Lady" through some considerable degree of personal daring, an inherent love of adventure, a willingness to risk life and liberty, and a desire to wreak vengeance upon the crooked political machine which ruled the state.

Her father, Owen Patrick, had been one of the most feared politicians in California at one time. He had been honest. An assassin's bullet had cut him down in his prime, three years before, and it had been whispered about that the killer was a gunman in the employ of the state machine! Ellen had inherited the big Irishman's keen wit and fearless spirit.

The little adventuress had always lived a life of comparative ease as befitted the only child of Owen Patrick. A Berkeley graduate, she was thrilling to a Far Eastern trip when news came that a cowardly slug had robbed her of the one who meant more than life itself to her. From that dark day forward, her life had been devoted to a fearless campaign of vengeance!

At times, Ellen unhesitatingly accepted nigh impossible undertakings simply for the sake of friendship and the love of adventure. At other times she was coldly involved in dangerous schemes merely to embarrass the authorities whom she blamed for her father's death. But, always, her anonymous donations to worthy charity covered the biggest portion of any recompense obtained through her forays against the wealthy. Of late, Ellen had become increasingly well-known and feared as The Domino Lady!

Dealing only with the higher-ups, the social elect, Ellen had no retained corps of informers, nor did she need them. Rumors, whispered gossip, news reports. These were her sources of information, and, moving in the upper strata upon which she preyed, they fell into her dainty hands with regularity and dispatch!

For instance, Ellen Patrick had learned much about Ames Kettrick, big political figure of Frisco. And he was just as crooked as he was big! Kettrick had always added to his wealth in dubious ways. Yet his fortune was immense. His recipe was unfailing. With the political machine behind him, he "got away with" anything crooked from fencing stolen jewels in his two elaborate jewelry establishments to defrauding widows and orphans in shady tenement deals.

Kettrick believed, and there was evidence to sustain his belief, that very few of those in on the "easy money" were saps enough to part with any portion of it under any circumstances. There was, he claimed, no reason why he should bestow part of his takings from the orphans and widows upon a needy orphans' asylum! It was strange!

Innately vain, the politician had recently married a woman thirty years his junior; one Jane Forbes, a dazzling movie queen of pre-talkie days. Jane was still a beauty in spite of her fall from movie grace and she, along with the Kettrick Collection, were the apples of the old crook's eye; he seldom if ever neglected an opportunity of displaying both to advantage. Thus, the much-heralded Ball Masque to be given at the Kettrick Mansion and to which celebrities from all parts of the state were to attend and pay homage to an elderly crook, his youngish wife, and a rather dubious collection of p r i c e l e s s stones!

It had not been easy for Ellen to secure an invitation to the affair, but the Hollywood beauty kept after what she wanted until she got it!

Arriving at the smart Catalan in Frisco two days before, she had at once set about making preparations for another daring coup; one which she fondly hoped would not only put a crimp in Ames Kettrick's vulpine nature, but would enable the hard-pressed orphanage authorities to adequately rebuild their home and finance the proper upbringing of their little charges.

H e r customary white-on-black message of warning had been brief and to the point. Ames Kettrick was to contribute worthwhile funds to worthy charities before Friday afternoon, or take the consequences! And the consequences in this instance, as the missive broadly hinted was to embrace a call from the mysterious Domino Lady, and the loss of his muchly-prized diamond collection which he was determined to display at the Ball Masque!

Of course, Kettrick had scoffed at the message. Who was this Domino Lady? He'd never heard of her! Some Hollywood upstart, trying a new publicity gag? Probably. Yet, in his heart, the crooked politician was sorely troubled and frankly afraid. And even the retaining of competent guards could not dispel that fear, for Kettrick *had* heard of The Domino Lady! H a d heard much, and none of it productive of peace of mind on his part!

WHEN Ellen entered her hotel suite after her enlightening encounter with Roge McKane, she immediately discarded her clothing, and donned *chic* black and white pajamas. Relaxing on the bed in her boudoir, she stretched h e r cramped pink toes, one by one, in luxurious serenity. Slowly, her keen mind clicked over every detail of her daring venture of the night almost at hand. Her plans were perfect. Of course, there was a certain amount of chance, but she was ever ready for that possibility, as she wanted no endeavor where there were no chances to be taken!

Dreamily smiling to herself, her mind turned to Roge McKane. She'd always liked the tall, darkly-handsome ex-collegian. She first remembered him as a backfield ace at Saint Mary's; that had been before his father's death and the subsequent loss of the McKane millions. She'd been a happy-go-lucky Berkeley co-ed in those days. She hadn't seen Roge in ages; of course, she'd enjoy dancing with him, but . she hoped that any possible encounter of the night would not have to be with him. . . . Too bad he had been retained to guard Kettrick's. . . .

So musing, Ellen drifted off into

a peaceful and dreamless sleep!

* * * * *

Later, when it was time to dress, Ellen stripped off the pajamas, drew a tub of warm water which she lavishly scented with an expensive, exotic perfume. Slowly, she immersed her beautifully r o u n d e d body beneath its caressing surface. For long minutes, Ellen luxuriated in the soothing influence of the scented waters before leaping up to massage herself dry with a huge, fluffy towel.

Her butter-hued hair was a crown of enchanting, silken curls when she had finished with it. Crimson for her lips, eye-shadow for allure, perfume, powder. With a feeling of naughtiness, she slipped into a pair of black lace panties. Then, sheerest hose for her shapely legs, black velvet slippers for her dainty feet.

Next, Ellen sheathed her lithe, youthful body in a close-fitting, shining-black evening gown which lent lure and mystery to her every curve and contour. Entirely backless it was, with the front caught about the white column of her neck in a captivating halter-effect. The ensemble, plus a white silken cape and black domino mask, was the identifying costume of the daring Domino Lady!

The costume she had chosen for the masquerade was a voluminous affair of the eighteenth century, and it suited her ravishing Nordic beauty and allure, perfectly. It accentuated the fullness of her shapely bosom, and the boyish slimness of her waist. It also gave her svelte hips a wide sweep which was at the same time beautiful and seductive. And it went on perfectly over the tight-fitting black crepe gown beneath!

A moment later, throwing the white silken cape about her kissable, bare shoulders, Ellen took a final glance into the tall mirror. She felt perfectly satisfied. All plans were perfected; her appearance was almost too perfect to be real; the success of her perilous venture rested squarely upon her own fearlessness and daring, and the element of chance!

With a little smile of confidence curving her cupid's bow crimson lips, she went out and locked the door of her suite behind her.

CHAPTER III

AMES KETTRICK'S mansion, one of the show places of smart San Francisco, was aglow with lights and noisy with music and merriment when Ellen Patrick entered the huge ballroom. Numbered among the masked and costumed guests were leaders in almost every line of human endeavor; politicians, actors, artists, business and social demigods, and the elderly politician was in his element, reveling in the choice opportunity of displaying his great wealth and his pretty, young wife.

Ellen found that the Ball Masque revelers were to unmask at midnight when a showing of the fabulous Kettrick d i a m o n d collection would be accorded them.

In the ballroom proper, the lights were so dim one could hardly see anything. The air was heavy with the scent of a thousand perfumes. Servants glided here and there with loaded trays, and underneath the sensuous strains of the Spanish orchestra, she could hear the swish of feet on the polished floor.

The little adventuress stood in a

shadowed corner and took in the entire layout. Her heart was thumping with the acceleration of the chase, the knowledge that here was new, exciting adventure in the making! It was her life, her greatest thrill of living! Visible through the holes in the orchid mask which concealed the upper half of her lovely face, great brown eyes glowed and smouldered with growing excitement!

Abruptly, she turned at a touch on her arm. She was startled for a brief moment. A tall, wide-shouldered man, dressed as an English knight—helmet, visor and everything, was leaning over her.

"Ellen, herself!" came in the deep tones of Roge McKane. "Couldn't fool me, although you *are* looking extra swellegant tonight! May I have this dance?"

She smiled. "But can you dance in that outfit, Galahad?" she asked, pertly.

"Oh, this isn't real, you know," he returned, quickly. "It's merely a bunch of tinsel hung together. Old Kettrick's idea. Said he thought I'd best mask like the guests so as to be able to mingle freely about and watch for the blonde in the black gown and domino, if she dares attempt anything! How do I look, Ellen?"

"Just lovely!" she smiled, her soft voice throbbing melodiously with a peculiarly emotional quiver, a little trick of hers. "I'd say you'd just left the Round Table, or something of the sort!"

He laughed: "Shall we dance?"

She stepped into his glittering arms, and they glided out into the stream of dancers. For some little time they did not speak, but Ellen thrilled to the feel of his possessive arm about her slender waist. McKane was so tall she couldn't see over his shoulder, and, big as he was, not once did his boots touch her dainty slippers.

Ellen laughed tinklingly as they glided about the ballroom in time with a dreamy waltz. The young investigator's arms clasped her momentarily closer, while her rounded arms were about him. At the moment, she forgot where she was and why she was here. All she realized was that, under the spell of his magnetism and the influence of the sensuous music, she was having the time of her life, and her affectionate little being quivered with suppressed emotion.

However, her fertile brain could not long remain dormant when there was adventure in the offing. It swung back abruptly to the ways and means of accomplishing her set purpose of the evening. Where were the diamonds she sought, and 'ow were they guarded? How was she to get possession of them? It was almost eleven; the unmasking and the display of the stones was scheduled for twelve! She must work fast if she were to succeed before that time!

AS SOON as the dance was ended, Roge McKane entreated her to walk in the garden with him while opportunity presented itself. She yielded, seeing in the invitation a chance of securing needed information. She disliked taking advantage of the young detective's friendship in that manner, but it seemed justified under the circumstances. She would not allow anything to stand between her and ultimate victory!

There was an argent California moon overhead and the air was warm enough to make her cape unnecessary. Laughing and chatting, she allowed the tall investigator to lead her to a marble bench, half concealed from view by shrubbery. When he had lighted her cigarette, Ellen leaned back and gazed absently across the moonlit garden.

"Won't you be missed?" she asked, softly.

"I hardly think so," McKane's thoughts were on other things and he scarcely realized what he said as he answered, "and I can't help it if I am. As long as I'm with you, here in the moonlight, it doesn't matter, Ellen . . . !"

"But the stones?" she interpolated, "will they be safe with you away?"

"The boys are guarding them in a little room off the main corridor," he replied, quickly, "where they are placed for the showing at midnight. The men are not costumed or masked as I am, and they'll keep their eyes peeled every moment. Nothing can happen. "But," he went on, sinking down beside Ellen, "why waste our moment here together with talk of things like that, Honey? I want to talk about you! After all, the stones are adequately protected. . . . "

A FAINT pulse was throbbing visibly at the base of her throat. Roge McKane's dark eyes were on it; he missed the gleam which crept into her brown orbs through the slits in the mask as he gave her the wanted information!

"Well, I hope you're right," she whispered, musically, "because I wouldn't want to be the one to keep you from your duty . . . Roge!"

The slight hesitation before she said the last word made the detective lean forward. Suddenly, he caught her lithe body in his arms

and drew her toward him. His hard lips were pressed to the cerise contours of her dewy mouth!

"You're sweet, Ellen, Honey!" he panted, emotionally. "You're maddening . . . !"

For the moment, Ellen clung to him as he kissed the warm softness of her crimson mouth. It was as though the lonely little adventuress, devoting her life to a campaign of vengeance, had been starved for his affection and could no longer restrain herself. Her seductive figure trembled expectantly in his arms.

Suddenly, she pushed him away, rose to her feet. "Please, Roge!" she breathed, softly. "Not now! You should be thinking of your duty, you know! We'd better be going inside before you're missed . . . !"

Roge McKane grinned like the good fellow he was, and escorted her back into the ballroom. They danced again. Laughing and talking mechanically with the young detective, Ellen's mind switched from the rather thrilling episode in the garden to the grim business directly at hand. Her alert mind toyed with the information obtained from the unsuspecting McKane. She knew that the moment was ripe for her endeavor, and no time must be lost!

It required fifteen minutes of precious time to get rid of McKane. Finally, he left with a word about seeing her later. In a few moments, she had slipped away from the crowded ballroom and was traversing the spacious main corridor. It was deserted and her slippers made no sound on the thick *Roneau*. She moved cautiously forward, keen ears tuned to catch any slight sound in the rooms on either side of the hallway.

Midway of the long corridor, she

heard a faint sound. A droning. She hesitated, listened intently. The sound came from the room at her right. It resolved itself into the subdued buzzing of voices, without audible words. But it was significant that the room was occupied as McKane had intimated it would be!

With racing heart, Ellen crouched with her ear to the door. She strove to catch a word which might tell her that this was indeed the room of the guarded treasure. Finally, a few words came, louder than the rest, and in a heavy masculine voice.

". . . gettin' sleepy, Tom. The rocks look swell, but I don't believe there's any danger at all."

"Almost midnight, Ben," another voice replied, "and I'm thinkin' that Domino Dame is scared out! That is, if there's really such a dame! I'll be glad when this night watch stuff's finished. It's no job for a man with brains. . . ."

Came the sound of raucous laughter, and then the words again became inaudible. Soon, the talking ceased altogether. Ellen stooped, looked through the keyhole. Across the room from the door, two men were lounging in upholstered chairs, smoking cigars. On a heavy teakwood table between them were a pair of capable-looking revolvers, and a large jewel case; a thing of leather and plush and velvet. Inside, no doubt, glittered the wonder collection of flawless diamonds so prized by Ames Kettrick, but Ellen had no sure way of knowing. From the angle of the keyhole, she couldn't see inside the jewel box! But she'd gamble it held the two hundred thousand dollar treasure just the same. . . .

". . . guess the old boy'll be bringing in the guests right soon,

now, Ben," one of the guards was saying. "So I suppose we'd better be gettin' into our coats again. . . ."

Ellen had heard and seen enough. Boldly, she turned and glided to another door directly across the corridor. She opened it softly, an inch at a time, stepped inside into Stygian darkness. No one stirred. She closed the portal in her wake after experiencing the feeling that she was alone. She breathed a deep sigh of relief as she took out her pencil flash and played its tiny beam about. A moment later she had located a switch and the tiny room was flooded with light. She was in a washroom of some sort, although she could tell from its size that it was not the one in general use.

The little adventuress was as cool as the proverbial cucumber as she usually was when under the stress of peril. Her movements were deliberate, but carried off with a speed and precision truly remarkable. First, she bent and grasped the fluffy hem of the eighteenth century gown. Hurriedly, she drew it upward over her youthful body. A moment later the costume was hidden from view behind a large hamper against the wall. This, of course, left her shapely figure sheathed in the form fitting evening gown of black crepe which she had worn under the other one!

THIS black, daringly-cut creation, backless and with halter-neck, was the identifying costume of the mysterious Domino Lady!

Replacing the orchid mask with a domino of shining black silk, and with a tiny black, snub-nosed automatic in her right fist, Ellen switched off the light, and stepped out into the still deserted corridor.

Once more the intrepid Domino Lady was on the prowl, keeping a midnight engagement of vengeance!

FACING the door of the treasure room, Ellen reached into the low-cut decolletage of her evening frock, drew forth a shining metal ball which has rested snugly in the warm valley of her shapely bosom! Small, compact, it was a powerful weapon when properly used. Although harmless, it contained a volatile gas which temporarily rendered powerless those persons unfortunate enough to inhale its sickening and paralyzing vapors!

A wicked little smile lighted her piquant face as she softly tried the knob of the door. It surprised her by giving noiselessly before her even pressure, and she slowly shoved it open. Across the room, the two guards, half dozing and unconscious of her presence, awaited the midnight hour with illy-concealed signs of disgust with their lot. They missed seeing the lovely figure as it crept silently inside!

With a skill born of much practice, Ellen tossed the bomb! The detectives' first intimation of an intrusion was when the gas container shattered into a million tiny fragments on the table between them, and their lungs began to smart from the fumes of the quick-acting agent! They lunged upward, going for their guns.

"What the——" burst from the lips of the taller of the two as he glimpsed the black-clad figure of the Domino Lady for the first time.

"Hold it!"

The command, softly spoken, cut

The Domino Lady tossed the gas bomb to the table

through the stillness of the room, as the tiny automatic was trained upon the reeling detectives. "One move or one cry, and you get it where it'll do you the most good! I mean business, men . . . !"

But the words or the gun were almost superfluous in the face of the volatile gas. It had gotten in its deadly work, and the two detectives slumped groaning to the floor!

The Domino Lady was all speed and precision now. Her left hand whipped a handkerchief from inside her frock—one that had been loaded with a powerful neutralizing powder. Holding it to her nose and mouth, she darted forward toward the glittering baubles on the table!

Slipping her automatic inside her dress, and working with her right hand, she quickly snapped shut the jewel case, locked it. She didn't stop to examine the precious loot, but slipped its container beneath her left arm. A swift glance at the unconscious men convinced her that they would slumber peacefully for some minutes to come. If only someone didn't come in to disturb them before that time was up!

Stooping, she tossed a small black card beside the senseless men. On it, in white ink, was inscribed the legend: *The Domino Lady's Compliments!*

A second later, she had spun around and was making for the

door. It was a supreme test of nerve to step into the hallway in her disguise, and with Kettrick's fortune in stones in plain view beneath her arm. But Ellen was made of stern stuff; she faced the ordeal with a calm fortitude which would have done credit to the fearless Owen Patrick, himself!

She glided into the big corridor, looked swiftly about. It was deserted! The haunting strains of *Beautiful Lady in Blue* came faintly to her ears from the direction of the ballroom. Was Roge McKane there, perhaps looking for her? The thought gave speed to her movements as she closed the door, darted forward and entered the washroom again.

Ellen swiftly manipulated a small metal lever on the wall of the washroom after switching on the lights. With steady hands, she pulled her costume from behind its concealing hamper. The tight-fitting creation came off over her shining head, leaving her shapely body clad only in the lacy black scanties! Stooping, she wadded the black dresses and the domino into a small roll. This she placed on the tile floor near the wall. From her wrist-bag she produced a tiny vial of colorless liquid. The domino and dress, of special construction and previously treated so as to take the acid, were doused with the consuming liquid! A tiny wisp of nauseating smoke eddied upward for a moment, then the gown and domino were nothing but a small pile of dark ashes!

Before dressing, Ellen scooped these ashes up, sifted them into the washbowl. A dash of water from the tap, and they had disappeared from view. Next, she reached for the costume gown, prepared to pull it on

over her shining head. Just as she raised it high, she startled. *Someone was trying the door of the washroom!*

Ellen stood stockstill, the dress suspended in midair while her heart beat like a sledge hammer against her ribs. Was she about to be discovered? *Was this to be the end of the Domino Lady?*

CHAPTER IV

ELLEN listened, intently. Nothing happened. Whoever had tried the door, if indeed someone had actually tried it, had retreated after finding it locked. Or perhaps they awaited her appearance, seeing the light and knowing the single door to be the only means of exit from the washroom! Well, she mused grimly, if that was the way it was, she couldn't help it; she'd have to take that chance.

Quickly she slipped the voluminous costume gown down over her beautiful body, securing it tightly about the waist. Picking up her orchid mask, she fastened it in place, looked about. Everything was in order. No one could ever tell that she had been there. With her wrist-bag in hand, she unlocked the door, stepped out into the large corridor!

It was entirely deserted! With a tight little smile on her face and a prayer of thanks in her heart, Ellen made for the further end of the hallway and the ballroom.

The alarm was sounded shortly after. Ellen had again met Roge McKane and they were waltzing when, suddenly, all the lights in the huge ballroom were snapped into coruscating brilliance. There was tense silence for a moment after the orchestra broke off in the middle of a beat. Then, a very red-faced Ames Kettrick broke into excited speech from the big doorway.

The scowling, heavy-set politician was having difficulty in suppressing his anger. His beautiful wife stood beside him, a bit embarrassed if indications were to be taken at face value. Her dazzling beauty shone through the troubled look on her lovely face. Despite her fall from grace in fickle picturedom, Jane Kettrick was still the possessor of a breath-taking beauty. It requires more than mere symmetry of feature and figure to crash one's personality across to the public through the medium of photographic flashes; and this still-young woman had been a headliner short months before! She squinted her expressive eyes about composedly, in direct contrast with her fiery sixty-year-old husband.

"The Kettrick diamonds have been stolen!" raged Ames Kettrick. "And the thief is still on the premises! Every outlet to the house and grounds have been under the watch of an armed detective! No one was admitted without invitation, and no one has left! Still, two armed men were overcome and the diamonds stolen from under their nose by a person dressed in black and wearing a black domino! The guards seemed to disagree on just what the robber actually looked like, so everyone must be searched! All will immediately unmask, and searching will start at once . . . !"

A little murmur ran about the room. At the first intimation of trouble, Roge McKane excused himself to Ellen and hurried to the side of Kettrick and his wife. The politician swung on the young detective.

"A fine detective you are, McKane!" he cried, hotly. "Letting the thief walk off with my property while you dance about with one of the guests! Get busy! You'll search every single one of the guests! Not a soul leaves this house until the diamonds are found, do you hear? I'm not going to allow a fortune in diamonds to walk off in somebody's pocket!"

"But some had already left, Mr. Kettrick!" stated Roge McKane, coldly eyeing the frantic millionaire. "And besides, many of the guests are prominent people, and old friends of yours! You wouldn't . . ."

"Yes, dear," soothed Jane Kettrick, trying to pacify her infuriated husband. "You wouldn't want to offend . . ."

"You keep out of this, Jane!" he shrilled at her, rudely. "I don't intend to be robbed like this, and let the crook get away with it! If it was man or woman, I'll get my property back, and see to it that the person who calls themself the Domino Lady is put away where they belong . . . !"

JANE KETTRICK stepped back a pace. "Yes, Ames," she placated, "but really . . ."

"Shut up!" he snapped, roughly. "Didn't I tell you to keep out of this?" He swung on McKane. "Search 'em!" he ordered. "Search everyone in the house! You search every single one of them, or I'll search 'em myself. . . . !"

Ellen felt sorry for the ex-actress; it was plain to see, as she retired, that she was badly hurt by her elderly husband's uncouth actions and rough speech. But Ellen had to laugh at the tableau as Roge McKane started his distasteful task as directed by the irate millionaire.

Before giving up, Jane Kettrick

tried to lift her soft voice in protest again, but her husband squelched her with a glare and a curt command. The state beauty turned, then, and left the scene. Kettrick looked after her, running his stubby fingers through his thick, black hair, and cursing beneath his breath.

There ensued a slight delay while McKane summoned a woman operative, and then the searching began. The guests, some of them nationally known figures, submitted without a murmur; but if looks meant anything, the social and political career of the lordly Kettrick died a sudden death right there! While the searching was going on, Ames Kettrick paced up and down like an enraged lion, glaring about as though he were in a den of thieves. His evident suffering brought a tight-lipped smile to Ellen's face as she watched him while awaiting her turn to be searched. It made up to her for all her risks to see the crooked politician writhing under the loss of his beloved diamond collection, and to see him putting himself in bad favor with the most influential people in the entire state!

While the guests were submitting to the searchers, a squad of men, summoned by McKane, went over the premises with a fine tooth comb, but to no avail. After being searched, Ellen walked over to the entrance and talked with Roge McKane who was opening the portal to let out little groups of guests who had undergone Ames Kettrick's idea of hospitality and entertainment by being searched. The young detective grinned somewhat foolishly, though grimly. The women held their wraps closely about their shoulders and departed with their noses in the air.

"A silly business," growled Mc-Kane to Ellen. He squinted at Kettrick who was standing nearby, frowning at the departing guests. "But what can you do with an old fool like that? I can't feel sorry for his loss or for what this insult to his guests will mean to him in lost friendship and prestige, Ellen! He deserves it. . . ."

She smiled, prettily. "Yes, I suppose he does," she murmured, softly, "if all the stories I've heard about him are true. . . ."

"Oh, they're true, right enough!" gritted the disgusted detective. "And I'll be glad when this mess is over with! Hope I never draw an assignment like this again! I'm sorry for your sake, too, Ellen. . . ."

"Why, that's not your fault, Roge!" she told him, evenly.

"Will you let me show you how sorry I am," he asked, softly, "by escorting you to your hotel after this mess is over, Ellen?" His deep voice was softly pleading. "And after I take off this monkey-suit," he added as a grinning afterthought, indicating his costume.

"If you wish," laughed Ellen, softly, "and if it won't be too long until it's over. . . ."

"Oh, it won't take long now," he grinned. "I'll speed things along for the sake of seeing you away from this place, Honey!"

THE last guest left without the diamonds being found. McKane turned with a shrug to his scowling employer.

"Bear in mind," he told Kettrick, precisely, "that this outrage was committed at your express orders. Have you anything further to offer as a suggestion?" There was no mistaking the sneer in his voice.

"I want you to recover my diamonds!" commanded Kettrick, angrily. He thrust out a pugnacious jaw. "They're not on the premises, and the guests who were here did not have them. I'm going to give you a list of the ones who had left before the robbery was discovered. I'll expect you to put a man on each of them, McKane, and have them shadowed night and day until my prop-

McKane drew to the curb near the Catalan, and Ellen allowed him to kiss her. She laughed at his hungry zeal.

"Will I see you again before we leave, Honey?" he pleaded as he stood on the sidewalk beside the car after they had alighted. His boyish eyes burned with a fierce fire.

"If you wish," she told him, softly.

Do you prefer Ellen Patrick, "The Domino Lady"; or would you choose Barbara Ravenal, Southern beauty and Confederate spy, as your type of heroine? In any case, you'll find either one, or both, of the glamorous pair in every issue of "Saucy Romantic Adventures" magazine.

erty is recovered. Do you hear that?"

The young detective grunted, and went to call off his men.

Later, after removing his costume and securing the list of names from Kettrick, McKane rejoined Ellen. He looked very handsome in gray tweeds. Ellen laughed softly as he handed her into his coupe.

"Do you think the Domino Lady was present tonight?" she asked, innocently, "and if so, do you think you'll catch her and recover the diamonds, Roge?"

He was silent as he got the car underway, then he nodded. "Yes, I'm sure she must have been there, Ellen," he said, grimly, "because no one else would have had the nerve to pull a thing like that under our noses! As far as catching her is concerned, I'm not so sure about that. Still, I'd rather someone else had that privilege, anyway. Darned if I can work up any zeal after Kettrick's actions tonight! And I'm rather admiring the little lady's nerve, too!" He chuckled.

"I haven't seen half enough of you, Roge! Shall we make it tomorrow evening at nine o'clock promptly?"

"You bet!" He was enthusiastic. "If we can't make it any sooner!"

He made as if to embrace her right there on the sidewalk, but Ellen eluded him and ran into the hotel. McKane stood for a moment, staring at the doorway through which she had vanished, then turned on his heel and entered the car.

CHAPTER V

DAWN wasn't far off when Ellen Patrick approached the Kettrick mansion for the second time that night. She dismissed the owl cabbie three blocks from the politician's home, and continued on foot. In rubber-heeled and soled evening slippers, she moved along like some silent shadow of the night.

Crossing the spacious lawn to one side of the palatial house, and keeping in the shadows of some overhanging trees, Ellen circled the structure, found a window which was conveniently located, took from her bag a glass cutter and a small roll of chewing gun from her mouth.

Working with silent speed, she circled the glass of the window with the cutter, then, when she had almost completed the circle, placed the gum against the pane. She completed the circle, and the segment of glass from the window, being stuck to the gum, made no noise as she lifted it out.

SHE knew that the burglar alarm would be set. She was prepared for that emergency. She inserted a cautious arm through the opening in the window, felt with trained fingers until she had found and disconnected the alarm. Then, she raised the window, slid her lithe body into the blackness of the interior.

All was still. She drew the tiny automatic from her wrist-bag, moved forward on the balls of her feet, guided by the rays from her pencil flash. Her great brown eyes snapped ominously as she crept along, and it is doubtful if young McKane, had he seen her at that moment, could have readily recognized in her the limpideyed girl he had left at the Catalan several hours earlier that night! Presently, she stood at the head of a narrow stairway, leading downward into a dark basement.

She hesitated a moment. Was there someone lying in wait for her in the silent confines before her? Some detective, perhaps, who would shoot on sight without asking questions? The answer lay fairly in the laps of the gods!

Ellen Patrick slipped slowly down the stairs in the murk. Cautiously, she moved across the concrete floor of the basement. In one corner,

brought into sharp relief by the pencil of light from her flash, stood a huge clothes hamper. Leading into it from above were several chutes by which soiled linen was transported from the rooms of the house to the basement laundry. The hamper was half full of linen.

With pink-tipped hands that trembled slightly, the little intruder began sorting through the linen. Piece after piece was examined as the moments flew rapidly by. In a little while, a little cry of triumph seeped from between her tautened lips. Excitedly, she pulled a jewel case from between the folds of a soiled bath towel where she had placed it several hours before! She had utilized the linen chute and a soiled towel in disposing of her precious loot in the washroom above, after overcoming the detectives and making away with the diamonds! Thus, they had not been found on her person when she was searched! And her plan had worked to perfection, the searchers evidently scorning the basement, and particularly a basket of soiled linen in their search for the missing gems!

The Kettrick diamonds! Ellen turned them over in the case in the glow from her flash, and blinked. Exquisite gems, flawless, ice-blue, perfectly matched, pear-shaped. No mistaking them for what they were! Reluctantly, she locked them in their case, slid the receptacle into a large envelope, stamped and addressed to herself at her apartment on Wiltshire Boulevard, in Hollywood!

"I suppose that puts a crimp in Mr. Ames Kettrick!" she murmured, with innate satisfaction, "and I'm not taking a chance on keeping them at the hotel until I leave, either! Fenced properly, these stones will bring a fortune in New York. After that, I suppose the kiddies at the orphanage will be brought up properly at Kettrick's expense, whether he likes it or not! And that is just as it should be, considering that the diamonds were bought with dishonest money, stolen from the needy!"

Ellen slipped back across the basement, up the stairs, and to the window. She slipped out the way she had come, through the window. She closed the window; and left, also, stuck to the window frame with gum, a small, black card. On it in white ink, was inscribed the words: *The Domino Lady's Compliments!*

At the corner, she dropped the bulky envelope into the postal box. And as she walked hotel-ward, there was a grim little smile playing about her mouth as she thought of her father, and of how he must be enjoying her successful campaign of vengeance, wherever he was!

In her room, Ellen undressed slowly, and got into bed. Her thoughts reverted to Roge McKane, and the night that was to come. For a long time she lay, smiling up at the ceiling in the early morning light. But at last, she drifted off to sleep, another daring exploit triumphantly concluded!

Romance in Eastern Canada

CANADA'S maritime provinces beckon to the motor tourist this year. Hitlerized Germany, militarized Italy and communistic Russia no longer lure the American traveler to Europe. Romance, peace, joy and happiness lie in your vacation right at home—in eastern Canada.

Splendid hotels and wonderful opportunities for fishing, rest and relaxation exist in New Brunswick at McAdam or St. Andrews-by-the-Sea. In Nova Scotia you'll find Digby and "The Pines," Kentville and Grand Pré; Yarmouth and the inn fronting Milo Lake, and Halifax and "The Lord Nelson" offering wondrous opportunities for happy

week ends or months of pleasant stay. The Hon. D. Leo Dolan, of the Canadian Travel Bureau, R. U. Parker, of the Eastern Steamship Lines, and O. C. Jones, of the Canadian Pacific Hotels, have done everything they could to promote travel to the Dominion's Maritime Provinces—a land so pregnant with the background and tie-ups in our own American history. According to Col. Walter W. Hubbard, well known travel authority and radio lecturer, both Nova Scotia and New Brunswick are due for splendid vacation seasons and a record-breaking influx of pleasure-seeking and appreciative tourists.

SUE McEWEN

The magazine *10 Detective Aces* was published from 1933 to
'49 by Ace Periodicals. It offered several series characters,
among them Emile G. Teppermann's Marty McQuade, Richard B. Sale's Cobra, and Norman A. Daniel's Russian detective, Renouf.

Another in its stable was Frederick C. Davis (1902–
1977), one of the more prolific pulp writers, who turned in
work for *Black Mask, Detective Fiction Weekly, Dime Detective Magazine,* and *Secret Agent X.* He was "Curtis
Steele" when writing Operator 5's adventures for the magazine of the same title. And he created the team of Schuyler
Cole and Luke Speare for a mystery novel series.

Davis explained his work methods in an article in the
March 1942 *Writer's Digest:* "Good craftsmanship demands,
almost categorically, that the mystery story writer start off
the plotting process by deciding upon the reasons for the
culprit's homicidal deeds. By logically developing the story
action *resulting* from this single *cause* he is assured of producing a more clear-cut, more convincing, and more closely
knit plot."

Davis wrote thirty-eight Moon Man stories for *10 Detective Aces.* In the series, a major secondary character is Sue
McEwen, daughter of ace cop Gilbert McEwen. Being the
daughter of a policeman was common, in the vigilante
pulps: Carol Baldwin was the offspring of a police sergeant

in the Black Bat series in *Black Book Detective,* and Tiny Traeger was the daughter of Richard "Quick Trigger" Traeger in The Whisperer stories, from the publication of that title.

"Fingers of Fear" is from the September 1934 issue of *10 Detective Aces.*

Steve Thatcher Feels the Clutch of

Fingers of Fear

"Moon Man" Novel

By
FREDERICK C. DAVIS
Author of
"Calling Car 13!" "Moon Doom," etc.

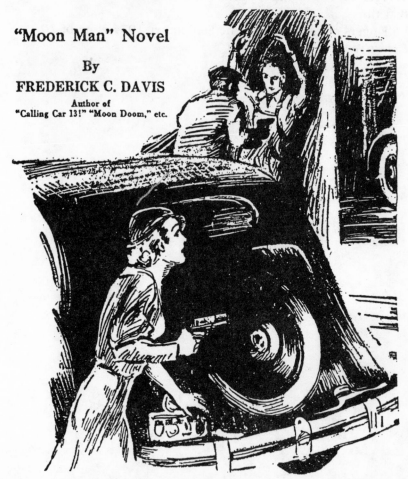

CHAPTER I

BEHIND SECRET DOORS

BLAZING bulbs on the marquee of the Masque Theatre had brought moths and people swarming into the glare.

Newest Musical Hit! HOT STUFF! *Girls—Stars—Girls!*

Chauffeured limousines had whirled bejeweled women and silk-hatted men to the doors. The orchestra had trumpeted a throbbing overture. Bare-legged choruses, torch singers, putty-nosed comics had paraded in the foot-light shine. Late-comers filing to the box office saw a sign announcing: *Standing Room Only.*

Dicks die hard! Gil McEwen, ace sleuth of Great City, gets kicked off the force for failing to bring in the Moon Man. Gil McEwen, whose very life's breath is the police department, is forced to turn in his shield . . . . And Detective Sergeant Steve Thatcher—the notorious Moon Man—has to get Gil McEwen back on the cops—without exposing himself.

The Moon Man captured the police commissioner.

Curious "standees" in the foyer noted that many chairs in the orchestra section were, none the less, empty. Richly dressed women and men holding ticket stubs occasionally sauntered to an exit at the side of the theatre and did not return. The show was a stand-out, yet more and more seats were left unoccupied and the dark side door mysteriously opened and closed.

The orchestra was screeching the climax of the first act finale, a fashion-parade number that suffused the stage with bird-of-paradise color, when a young man—clean-cut, brisk-mannered, sharp-eyed—rose quietly from his chair at the extreme end of the first row. He was the son of the chief of police of Great City—Detective Sergeant Stephen Thatcher.

Unobserved in the blue light, he moved into the dark space behind the lower boxes. He pressed through a fireproof door into the gloom behind the stage scenery. Unseen, he rapidly climbed an iron ladder that lifted him to a narrow runway. Unnoticed by the electricians who were shooting baby spots downward, he climbed still higher into the flies.

Far up in a maze of ropes and drops and counterweights he saw the curtain lower, the chorus herd off, overalled men crowd to unbrace the jig-saw sections of scenery. At a corner of a black platform he pushed up an overhead door, lifted himself through, and stood in cool night air on the roof of the theatre.

From a shadowed corner of the cornice he lifted a black case, and out of it he took a coil of rope. He looped one end of the strand around a pipe and the other to the handle of the case; he lowered it, legged over, and went after it hand under hand.

On the adjoining roof he untied the case and walked quickly to the housing of a skylight. While the glow shone in his face, he opened the case again and brought from it a pair of black gloves, a long black robe and an automatic.

He pulled on the gloves. He shook the robe over his shoulders. Lastly he lifted from the case a spherical, silvered glass shell, its halves hinged, and carefully fitted it over his head. He became a grotesque, shadow-figure whose head was a gleaming ball.

Steve Thatcher, detective sergeant, had in one moment transformed himself into the most notorious criminal Great City had ever known—the Moon Man.

THE shining head of the Moon Man lowered as he opened a leaf of the skylight. His mask was mirror-bright; but through the Argus glass he could see as clearly as though it were crystal. He looked down into a hallway. It was empty.

He lowered himself through the skylight and dropped. He stood in the silent corridor, peering at closed doors, at a stairway. Automatic leveled, he strode silently and quickly toward the stairs. His globular head glittered, turning from side to side, as he listened.

He drifted down into another hallway, also empty, though it bustled with busy noises penetrating the doors which lined it.

He moved to the first, moved a flap aside, and brought his silver sphere of a head close to a peep-hole.

The man who had no eyes looked through upon a roulette table, surrounded by women in costly evening gowns and men in full dress, their faces flushed with gambling fever. The wheel whirred and the ball clicked. The croupier droned the winning number and his rake swept chips. The Moon Man drew away.

He moved silently to another door, then to a third. He observed other members of the élite of Great City playing b a c c a r a t, *chemin-de-fer*, "bird-cage"; he saw eminent men intent upon a glorified crap game in which the stakes were thousands. He strode on.

The last door in the hallway had no peep-hole. Behind it lay silence. The Moon Man very slowly twisted the knob. A lock barred the way. Through a slit in his cape he brought out a packet of master keys. The bolt drew back. Through a crack he peered into the glow of a shaded light turned upon an ornate desk in a corner. He stepped in quickly, and closed the door.

The Moon Man was probing into the drawers of the desk when footfalls sounded near. He whirled; his black robe flapped as long strides took him to another door; he snapped it open to reveal a deep closet. He closed himself in thick blackness and tensely listened.

Quiet steps came into the room. The desk-chair moved; there was silence again. The Moon Man heard a voice speak quietly, as if into a telephone. A single word:

"Report." Again: "Report." And again: "Report."

The response came almost immediately: footfalls in the corridor. The hallway entrance opened and closed four times. The Moon Man, easing to the closet door, twisted the knob very carefully, and opened it a crack. He saw on the desk four trays heaped with high-denomination currency.

Four men had brought the loaded trays; the shaded light of the desk had been turned to shine full into their faces, faces which the Moon Man recognized: Dino Gardini, Lanny Hegg, Pete Wycoff, Angy Oliver. Ex-racketeers all. Together they formed a criminal quartette that might justifiably worry any police force.

The glare of light hid the man who sat behind the desk. Only his hands, gloved in gray mocha, were visible. They took check slips from the piles of currency and drew them into the darkness behind the shaded light; they returned to gesture the four crooks away. The four men stepped out the door, and closed it.

The gray-gloved hands reached again from the dark corner and dug avariciously into the money. The Moon Man saw them tremble. One of the fingers, he noticed, bent back as if double-jointed when it pressed the desk top. They wadded handfuls of banknotes into a briefcase that fattened with thousand upon thousand.

The Moon Man straightened. His hand gripped the knob of the door to thrust it wide. He was about to step out when—

A buzzer sounded in the room, rasping a signal swiftly repeated. One of the gray-gloved hands shot to a cam of the dictograph on the desk. A whisper rushed from the blackness behind the light.

"What is it?"

Through the instrument another voice sang.

"A raid! A raid!"

TO the front of the theatre where *Hot Stuff*, the newest musical hit, was playing to S.R.O., four police cars had come skirting. Out of them uniformed men crowded, led by another in plainclothes who was hard-faced, stony-eyed, grim.

He was Detective Lieutenant Gilbert McEwen, relentless crook-hunter, ace man of action of the Great City detective division, the sworn nemesis of the notorious criminal known as the Moon Man.

McEwen snapped: "Right in! Don't give 'em a chance!"

He strode, flanked by his men, into the lobby of the Masque. They brushed aside the ticket taker. They ignored the startled standees who stared. They marched toward the door at the side of the theatre, where a hard-faced man in evening clothes stood warily.

McEwen grabbed him aside. "Hold him!"

He pushed through the mysterious door. His men crowded after him into the narrow space of a stairway which had been walled in at the rail. The flight descended to a door in a partition. As McEwen tramped in, a greasy-faced man sidled through from beyond.

McEwen commanded, before that man could utter a word, "Pipe down!"

He looked out the door. The stairway had been walled off from a small restaurant. The large room was crowded with tables at which men and women were eating *hors d'ouvres*, nibbling crusty bread, drinking red wine. McEwen shut the door.

The unceremonious entrance of the headquarters men had attracted attention in the theatre. The audience twisted in its seats, curiously staring back. The leg-swinging chorus peered worriedly across the footlights. On the far side of a foyer an usher touched the base of a bowl of plaster flowers, leaned close and spoke into a microphone hidden in the dusty artificial blooms:

"McEwen coming up."

McEwen was already up. He hammered at a door. When a latch clicked he pushed into a room which was divided into large booths. Men and women seated in the booths were talking, laughing, drinking. Another waiter flustered toward McEwen.

"What's matter? What's matter?"

"Saw us coming, did you?" McEwen snapped coldly, and spun to his men. "Tear into this place! They've ditched the tables! Find 'em!"

The uniformed men spread down the hallway. McEwen tramped after them, looking into other rooms. Each was the same as the first, filled with booths where couples were apparently dining with the utmost innocence. McEwen's eyes grew harder and colder.

The headwaiter trotted after McEwen, hands fluttering. "Nice people come here to eat! They like our place. They come to enjoy—"

"Shut up!" McEwen snapped.

He trod toward the rear. Through a forward door another waiter observed the move, raised a hand to a coat hook and tugged at it. He whispered to an oil-painted nude on the wall.

In the rear room, where the light glared over the desk, a voice rasped out of the dictograph:

"McEwen going back!"

THE Moon Man, peering through the crack of the door, had seen the gray-gloved hands vanish out of the light, one of them gripping the handle of the brief-case. He had stepped into the room, automatic leveled. He had swung to face the darkness in the corner behind the desk.

"McEwen going back!" the dictograph warned.

The Moon Man's muffled voice rang behind his leveled gun.

"Put the case on the desk!"

No answer came from through the curtain of darkness. The Moon Man's arm shot out, struck the shade of the lamp and shifted its glare to illuminate the corner. The Moon Man's gun jerked with surprise.

The chair behind the desk was empty. The entire space behind the desk was empty. Gray-gloved man, brief-case and all, had vanished.

In the corridor heavy, tramping, footfalls were sounding. The dogged strides meant McEwen. The Moon Man's hand touched the catch of the spring lock and the bolt clicked into its socket.

The knob rattled. Knuckles rapped. "Open that door!" boomed in McEwen's voice.

The Moon Man tugged at the desk and swung it outward, opening the corner. He stepped into the triangular space and ran his fingers quickly, searchingly, over the walls. He was stooping, his globular head glittering, to examine the floor, when a hard shock jarred the door and a panel splintered.

"Break it open!" McEwen's voice roared.

The Moon Man's long robe flapped as he crossed the room. He peered out the windows and saw a sheer drop through darkness to a brick-paved alleyway. Below, squad-car cops were on watch. The panel of the hallway door cracked again as he spun back.

"Smash it!"

The black-robed man stepped into the darkness of the closet, and closed the door. Wood splintered again as he crowded back into a far corner. He crouched, raising a full-sleeved arm to cover his silver head. Within the glass shell his breath whistled as he steadied his gun toward the door.

A shattering crash sounded in the room. Heavy heels beat inward. Just outside the Moon Man's hiding-place McEwen's voice boomed again:

"Search this room!"

The knob of the closet rattled. The door swung wide. Light shafted in as McEwen stepped through.

THE Moon Man ceased breathing. Shrouded by darkness, the one crouched, the other erect and alert,

FINGERS OF FEAR

the notorious criminal and the relentless detective came within a few feet of each other.

For months the Moon Man's amazing crimes had blackened the front pages of the newspapers with sensational headlines. He had robbed again and again. He had twice committed the capital crime of abduction. He was wanted for murder. The fact that he had not committed the murder meant nothing: completely unable to prove his innocence, his capture by McEwen would mean his certain conviction. The fact that every dollar stolen by the Moon Man had been contributed to the care of the sick and to the help of the needy was also meaningless in the eyes of the law: the criminal must pay for his crimes.

Again and again Gil McEwen had brought the Moon Man to the point of capture. Each time the notorious criminal had managed to escape.

Now in the darkness of the closet, he crouched within a few feet of the detective who had sworn to destroy him.

The man who wore the silver mask knew full well that no power on earth could swerve McEwen from the full performance of his duty. The consequences of the Moon Man's crimes would be meted out to him regardless of his identity. McEwen had promised him "the works," and McEwen would keep that promise, even if he learned that the Moon Man was his friend, Steve Thatcher . . . . Steve Thatcher, detective sergeant. Steve Thatcher, son of the kindly old chief of police. Steve Thatcher, fiancé of Sue McEwen, the grizzled detective's only daughter.

No one realized better than the Moon Man the inevitable, tragic results of the exposure that was so imminent now. The revelation would break the old chief's heart—almost certainly it would kill him. It would crush even as hard a man as Gil McEwen. It would bring keenest grief to Sue. It would irretrievably wreck the life of Steve Thatcher.

The motive behind the Moon Man's crimes was unselfish generosity, obedience to the higher law of human mercy, and an unquenchable desire to help unfortunates who must have help or perish. The result of his exposure would be disgrace, dishonor and the electric chair.

HUDDLED in the corner of the closet, gun gripped, silver head shielded against the glow of light that shafted through the door, the Moon Man dared not breathe. He heard McEwen step closer. He heard McEwen's voice rasp:

"Looks empty, but—bring a light!"

Footfalls told that a squad cop was moving to obey the order.

Another man spoke quickly: "Gil! Look at this! A trap in the floor!"

McEwen snapped: "By damn!"

The Moon Man ventured a long, silent sigh as the detective stepped out the door. The men in the room crowded toward the desk in the corner. In the triangular space a rug had been pulled aside. Cracks in the woodwork had disclosed the outline of a secret exit. It yawned open now, disclosing a dark well into which a flight of narrow stairs descended.

"By damn!" McEwen exploded. "I knew there was somebody in this room! He got out that way!"

The Moon Man listened. He heard men climbing down the hidden steps. Hollow footfalls rang from a passage below. McEwen's voice grew muffled as he descended into the opening.

"Beat it outside! Watch the theatre next door. This thing leads back of the stage."

The Moon Man remained unmoving as men crowded out the door, as silence came. At last he rose slowly, and looked into the empty room. He stepped to the outer door and listened. A glance outward showed him that there were no headquarters men in the hallway.

Quickly he lifted off the precious, fragile mask of Argus glass. He whipped out of his robe, tugged off his gloves. He rolled the sphere in the black garment, and tucked the bundle under his arm. He stepped into the hallway, and darted to the stairs.

In the upper hall he paused beneath the open skylight. With the utmost care he tucked the black bundle under his left arm. Steve Thatcher reached high and jumped. He gripped, pulled, swung himself up with his right arm. He gingerly lifted the black bundle through the skylight, then wriggled onto the roof . . . .

A long time later the stage door of the Masque Theatre opened. The performance was ended. The auditorium was empty. The stage was bare, flatly lighted by a pilot. It was a place of gloomy desertion. Steve Thatcher left it unseen.

He walked a block quickly, carrying the black case, and climbed into his roadster. He swung from the curb with a sigh, his face anxious, his heart still pounding with dread.

"You almost got me that time, Gil!" he said as the motor sang. "Almost!"

CHAPTER II
BROKEN DICK

STEVE THATCHER entered the office of the chief of police next morning to find Gil McEwen slumped in a chair, gnawing angrily on an unlighted cigar. McEwen's greeting was a sour glance.

The white-haired man seated behind the old roll-top desk smiled and said, "Morning, son."

A girl rose quickly from a chair, and came into Steve Thatcher's arms.

Sue McEwen was in her early twenties, strikingly pretty, with a shrewd mind inherited from her father. She kissed Steve Thatcher lingeringly. She said:

"Look out for dad, Steve. He's been eating raw meat."

"By damn!" McEwen exploded. "Savage, am I? All right! By damn!"

Thatcher asked: "What's up, Gil?"

"Plenty! The biggest damn gambling ring that ever operated in this town is going full blast! There's a whole chain of places. They're crowded every night. The best people are crazy enough to play a lot of crooked games they've got running! Merchants in this town are going broke because of poor business, and this gang of crooks is raking in big coin night after night!"

"You mean the raid on *Le Petit Paris?*" Thatcher asked. "Sorry I wasn't in on it, Gil."

"By damn!" McEwen stormed. "Petty Paree my hat! Monte Carlo would be a more appropriate name for it. People going there to eat—hell! Before I got through with that place I found the tables. I made enough pinches to fill every cell in the cooler. What galls me is that the Big Shot slipped out before I could grab him!"

"Got any idea who he is, Gil?" Thatcher asked.

"No. But if you ask me, he's no stranger in this town. He knows his way around, all right! By damn! As if I didn't have my hands full enough trying to grab the Moon Man, now this gambling ring starts operating!"

A knock sounded at the door, and it opened immediately. A man strode in briskly, rod-backed, stern, nodding curt greetings. McEwen straightened from his chair and said, "Morning, Mr. Mead."

Chief Thatcher rose and extended a blue-veined hand: "How are you, commissioner?"

Curtis Mead, attorney-at-law, president of the Police Board, cleared his throat with threatening brusqueness.

"I've come here this morning, gentlemen," he declared, "for a very important reason. I regret the necessity. Perhaps it will be a shock to you, but we, the police commissioners, have been forced to drastic measures."

McEwen blinked. Chief Thatcher asked slowly: "What do you mean, commissioner?"

"I mean that this department has shown an appalling inability to get results in the most important case facing it. I mean failure to bring to justice the crook who has defied you again and again—the Moon Man."

STEVE THATCHER searched Curtis Mead's stern face. He felt Sue's hand steal into his. Intently he listened.

"First of all, Chief Thatcher," Mead continued, "let me say that this is no reflection upon you personally. You have ably headed this department a good many years. You've stayed in office because you choose, though you might have retired long ago. We're proud to continue you in office. The fact is that your position is almost an honorary one. The active head of the police department in this city is Lieutenant McEwen."

"Yes," the chief agreed. "Gil is far more able than I to handle—"

"McEwen's ability," Mead broke in brusquely, "is precisely the point at issue."

McEwen glared and demanded: "Well?"

"You know the facts as well as we do, McEwen," the commissioner continued bluntly. "The Moon Man began operating in this city well over a year ago. He has brazenly defied the law and this department. He has gone so far on several occasions as to enter this headquarters and escape uncaught. At one time he achieved the incredible mockery of kidnaping your own daughter. He has, to put it flatly, laughed in your face and gotten away with it!"

McEwen scowled. "I've sworn I'm going to get the Moon Man," he declared, "and I'm going to do it!"

"But," Mead retorted, "you haven't done it. He has demonstrated that he is cleverer than you are. He has made you a laughingstock. At this very moment he is in this city, uncaught, doubtless planning new crimes, confident that when he wishes he can defy the law again and escape untouched. That, McEwen, is a sad comment upon your detective ability."

McEwen grated: "It is, is it?

Perhaps, Mr. Mead, you'd like the job of catching the Moon Man yourself!"

"It's not my office to capture him, McEwen, and it is yours!" Mead snapped. "On two previous occasions the Police Board has issued ultimatums to you to get the Moon Man. In both cases you failed, and we chose to give you another chance. This time we are at the end of our patience. You have had every possible chance to make good your promise to apprehend the Moon Man—and you have failed."

Mead's glance from face to face was defiant.

"The Police Board is taking this action," he declared, "at the urgent demand of the Governors of the Chamber of Commerce. Our leading business men have revolted against police inefficiency. They have petitioned a drastic clean-up. Gentlemen, they are getting it!"

McEwen began: "What the hell does the Chamber of Commerce know about grabbing—"

"They are entitled to police protection which they have scarcely received from you, McEwen!" Mead said bitingly.

"By damn!" McEwen snapped. "My record speaks for itself. The Moon Man is the only crook who ever—"

"The Moon Man has defeated you decisively, again and again. The Police Board can no longer condone your ineffectual handling of the case!"

Color drained from Steve Thatcher's face. The old chief gazed appalled at the grim face of Curtis Mead. The commissioner returned McEwen's glare stonily.

" 'Can no longer'—what?" McEwen blurted.

"This," Mead declared, "will speak for itself." He thrust a letter at McEwen. "The man who takes your place, as active head of this police department, is going to produce results!"

McEwen's cigar dangled. "Who—who takes my place?" he asked blankly.

Curtis Mead turned. He strode to the door. He said, "Good morning, gentlemen!" and slammed out.

GIL McEWEN stared down at the folded letter which Mead had put into his hands. He looked at the chief. He looked at Steve Thatcher.

Sue said in anguish, "Oh, Dad!" as his glittering gaze turned to her.

He snapped the letter open, said dazedly: "By damn!"

"Gil—good Lord!" Steve Thatcher blurted. "Mead can't do a think like that to you!"

"No?" McEwen asked slowly. "He can't, can't he? Let me tell you something. He's done it."

Sue reached for the letter. "Dad, please—"

"By damn! The Commerce Club is howling, is it? A lawyer's telling us how I should go about grabbing a crook, is he?" McEwen laughed bitterly. "He wants the Moon Man got, does he?"

Steve Thatcher took the letter from McEwen's wrath-tightened fingers. He uncrumpled it as Sue came quickly to his shoulder. They read a terse, ironic sentence.

The Board of Police Commissioners herewith accepts the resignation of Detective Lieutenant Gilbert McEwen, effective at once.
    CURTIS MEAD, President.
    MOFFETT MERRITT,
    JOHN SUTTON.

Sue's trembling hand closed tightly about Steve Thatcher's. His throat burned tightly. He raised haggard eyes to the hardened face of McEwen.

The grizzled detective slowly drew his wallet from his pocket and opened it. He gazed at the gold badge pinned to a flap inside. His lips curved in a sour smile.

"Chief—" his voice was husky—"I guess I'm off the force."

He unpinned the badge; he placed it on the chief's desk while those around him stared incredulously. He dropped beside it his folded, dog-

eared credentials. He moved toward the door with lagging steps and paused to say:

"I guess I'd better clean out my desk."

Sue McEwen watched her father's grayed face. She sensed, as no one else could, the devouring agony that filled him. She felt the stunned groping of his mind as it endeavored to grasp the fact that he was no longer Detective Lieutenant McEwen. That suddenly, in a moment, after years of unremitting devotion to the force—he was broken.

Broken because he had failed to capture the Moon Man—the Moon Man who was Steve Thatcher, her fiancé!

McEwen opened the door. He paused and turned back, glaring.

"By damn!" he exploded. "They've broken me, have they? They've kicked me out! They've fired me off the force! By damn, let 'em! Let 'em do anything they damn' please! Writing me a letter can't make me stop being a copper!"

He swallowed; his fists clenched unconsciously.

"Copper or not, I've sworn to get the Moon Man, and I'm going to do it! No matter if I don't wear a gold badge any more! No matter if I've got no business any longer in this headquarters. I'm going to get the Moon Man! *I'm going to grab that crook!*"

The door slammed hard. McEwen's heels pounded away. Steve Thatcher stood gazing in agony at the panels, and Sue's cold hand trembled in his.

CHAPTER III

DICKS DIE HARD

STEVE THATCHER left his roadster at a downtown corner, entered a cigar store and sidled into a telephone booth. The number he called was that of Dr. Tryce's Sanitarium, which was located outside the city.

"How is our patient, doctor?" he asked the directing physician.

"Excellent!" Dr. Tryce answered. "His scalp is almost completely healed.

He can leave any time he likes. Want to talk to him? He's right here."

An eager voice sang over the wire: "Boss!"

"Angel! Okay, Angel?"

"I'm swell again, Boss!"

"Steady," Thatcher warned. "Remember you're there as a detective."

A chuckle sounded. "I haven't forgotten, Boss!"

Ned Dargan, ex-pug, secret emissary of the Moon Man, was not likely to forget, ever, his unbounded admiration and complete loyalty to the man who had once saved him from poverty and starvation. He could not forget that scarcely a month ago the notorious crook had rescued him from capture by McEwen—had, amazingly, spirited him out of headquarters.

At the beginning not even Dargan had known that the Moon Man was Steve Thatcher. He had acted as the Moon Man's ambassador, distributing to the needy the money which the Moon Man stole. When circumstances had revealed the Moon Man's identity to him, he had continued to stand at the side of "the Boss" loyally. He, as the Moon Man's partner in crime, was being even at that moment hunted by the police.

Ned Dargan was one of the only two persons in the world who shared Steve Thatcher's secret; the other was Sue McEwen.

"Angel, I need your help. Will you take a chance and come back to town?"

"Sure, Boss! Anything you say!"

"I'll send Sue in a car for you, Angel. Get yourself a room somewhere, and let me know where you are. Stay handy. We've got a big job ahead of us, Angel—a big job!"

"Sure, Boss!"

"Can't explain now. See you later. Watch sharp, Angel!"

"Depend on me, Boss!"

Thatcher hung the receiver. Thoughtfully he called another number, that of Gil McEwen's home. The voice that answered was Sue's.

"Steve!" the girl exclaimed anxiously. "Have you seen dad?"

"Not a glimpse, dear, since he—"

"He's not here. He went off somewhere without telling me. I'm worried about him, Steve. He's not his old self at all. It's been a terrific blow to him. It's hurt him so deeply—"

"I know, Sue," Thatcher said gravely. "According to Mead, Gil's in this jam because of me. It's up to me to help him out of it."

"But, Steve, he's already broken. And anything you try to do to help him will be a dreadful risk. Darling, please—"

"I'm damned if I'll let them do a thing like that to Gil!" Thatcher said. "He doesn't deserve it. It'll kill him. Sue, will you help me?"

"Of course, Steve!"

"Angel's at Tryce's Sanitarium. I want you to drive out and get him. Be sure nobody sees you bringing him back. Start right away, but watch yourself, Sue! It's a chance!"

"Steve, I want to help dad, too. But if your helping him should mean that the chief learned, and dad too, that you're—"

"We can't think of that, Sue! On your way! Good-bye, dear. Watch sharp!"

STEVE THATCHER strode out to his car, reached for the door handle, and paused. He had left it empty, but now a man sat slumped in the front seat. Thatcher said quietly:

"Hello, Gil."

McEwen forced a wry smile. "Hello, Steve. I was just wandering by and saw your car and got in. Sort of lost, I guess. Mind if I ride along?"

"Im mighty glad you're here, Gil."

Thatcher turned the roadster into the evening traffic. From the radio under the dash, which was tuned to the police wave-length, twanged the voice of the headquarters announcer droning a signal about a routine disturbance. McEwen made a growling noise.

"Habit, I guess. I keep listening. No

use for it at all, now, but—I can't help watching for some new lead to the Moon Man."

Thatcher was grimly silent. The car stopped at a red-lighted corner where newsboys were howling. Their shrieks made McEwen wince.

"Detective McEwen discharged by Police Board!"

"McEwen kicked out following successful gambling raid!"

"McEwen broken by commissioners!"

Thatcher said bitterly: "It was a damned dirty thing to do, Gil."

"I've got a queer feeling, Steve," McEwen answered quietly, "that my not grabbing the Moon Man isn't the real reason at all."

Thatcher tightened. "Then what is, Gil?"

"I broke up one of the gambling ring's houses last night. This morning I got kicked off the force. Maybe there's a connection."

"Good Lord, Gil!" Thatcher blurted. "You're not suggesting that Mead, the president of the Board of Police Commissioners, is in with the ring!"

"Not directly, that couldn't be. But even a man like Mead can get the thumbscrews clamped on him. Those crooks know how to put 'em on. And Mead's human."

The car turned a corner. Thatcher said: "Mead wouldn't knowingly yield to pressure of that kind."

"Not knowingly, of course," McEwen said grimly. "But it could be done, to him and the Governors of the Chamber of Commerce, too." McEwen eyed the lighted entrance of the Continental Hotel as they began to pass it. "That damned bunch of bluebloods who run the Chamber of Commerce—"

"Don't let it get you, Gill," Thatcher cautioned. "Don't let it—"

"'Get me'!" McEwen snapped. "By damn, I've been a cop all my life! I started as a third-class patrolman pounding the gas-house beat! I've fought for every inch of the way up.

It's in my blood. It's *me*—being a cop. 'Don't let it get me' when—Stop this car!"

HE thrust open the door and edged out while the roadster was still moving. Jaw clamped, eyes blazing, he strode through the entrance of the hotel. Thatcher parked quickly and followed to see him glaring at a bulletin board in the lobby.

Chamber of Commerce Dinner
8 p. m., Florentine Room

McEwen marched to a broad, swinging door and pushed through it. He paused, Thatcher coming anxiously to his side, peering into the huge dining hall. At a great U-shaped table impressive-looking men, leaders in business in Great City, were ashing cigars into empty coffee cups while, at the head of a table, a man spoke.

The speaker was Barron Thayer, broker, chairman of the Board of Governors of the Chamber of Commerce.

"Gentlemen, we are no longer the victims of police inefficiency!" he was declaring, gesturing with a closed fist. "We have demanded adequate police protection, and we are going to get it. Ineffectuals on the force are being eliminated and the men who take their place will be capable of coping with our crime problem. Our first step has been decisively taken. I promise you we will not stop until—"

McEwen had strode close to the head of the table, gray eyes glittering, jaw clamped hard. Steve Thatcher's hand taking his arm protestingly, had been shrugged off. McEwen's ringing voice broke into the oratory of Barron Thayer with:

"Until—what?"

Thayer's fist raised in gesture, remained poised. He looked dismayed and indignant.

"So," McEwen shot out, his edged voice reaching the far end of the hall, "I'm an example of police inefficiency, am I? I haven't given you adequate police protection, have I? I'm an ineffectual, am I? That sounds very pretty, Mr. Thayer, but you know it's a damned lie!"

Barron Thayer protested: "You can't come in here and—"

"Easy, Gil!" Steve Thatcher cautioned.

"I can't, can't I?" McEwen raged. "I'm telling you! You think you've kicked me off the force. You think you've broken me. By damn, you can't do it! You've taken my badge from me but you can't make me quit being a copper!"

"McEwen, you're off the force and you might as well accept it!" Thayer asserted. "Now, leave us—"

"I don't accept it!" McEwen snapped. "By damn, I don't! I may be off the force but I'm not off my cases. I promised myself that I'm going to grab the Moon Man and I'm still going to do it!"

"See here, McEwen!"

"Remember that!" McEwen roared. "I find it a rare pleasure to invite all you gentlemen, and you in particular, Mr. Thayer, chairman of the Board of Governors, to go to hell! Good night!"

McEwen stamped out of the hushed hall.

Steve Thatcher, hurrying after him, did not find him in the lobby, nor on the street, nor in the roadster. Steve Thatcher, his ears still ringing with that violent denunciation, could not find McEwen at all.

E X-DETECTIVE McEwen h a d pushed angrily out a side entrance of the hotel. He tramped along the street with fists clenched and heels hammering. At each corner the shouts of newsboys mocked him. Red-faced with wrath he got a paper, snapped it under his arm, and then strode on. Blocks away he paused in the light of a show window to read headlines that stung his eyes.

The body of the item announcing the discharge of McEwen from the force dealt with his record and his most recent raid.

McEwen's invasion of *Le Petit Paris* last night followed close upon the heels of confidential information he received from James Kelton, well known in society circles, who attempted suicide yesterday.

Kelton, McEwen learned, attempted to kill himself in despair over having lost a large sum of money at gambling. From Kelton, McEwen obtained information which disclosed that a huge gambling ring is operating in the city and catering to the wealthiest classes who are continually seeking new thrills. The raid followed. Two known criminals, Lanny Hegg and Angy Oliver, were arrested.

McEwen discovered that *Le Petit Paris* was a blind, that the chief entrance to the gambling hall was through the foyer of the Masque Theatre. It was the first of a series of raids planned by McEwen. His dismissal leaves the next move up in the air.

McEwen probed grimly into his pocket for a slip of paper. It was a small sheet he had found in the desk of the office hidden above the restaurant. He had characteristically kept it to himself; following events had crowded it from his mind. Now he studied it intently.

It bore three words, *Paris, Slipper, Nu-Way*, each followed by figures denoting tens of thousands of dollars.

McEwen thrust the slip into his pocket and tramped on. He turned corners until he came to a canopied doorway framed with photographs of nude show girls. He pushed past a doorman, left his hat at a check stand, and climbed a thickly carpeted flight.

A square-faced man eyed him frostily as he reached the upper landing, where tom-toming music reverberated and girls' voices shrilled in chorus through swinging doors.

"What's up, McEwen?"

"A guy has to get his mind off things, hasn't he?" McEwen grated, and strode past.

He entered a huge ornate room where tables were crowded and spotlights were playing over short-skirted girls prancing across a narrow stage. He demanded a rear table and got it. Through a fog of smoke he glanced about curiously, and ordered a drink, as a slick-haired master of ceremonies on the stage announced through a loud speaker:

"The Golden Slipper Girls in the daring Babylonian dance that has the town talking!"

Indigo light stained the haze as the orchestra pounded a sensuous melody. McEwen ignored the unclothed Babylonians. He noticed deserted tables, drinks left scarcely touched. He watched couples wind their way toward a shadowed corner and disappear. Presently he rose and sidled in the same direction. He found a door unattended. He sidled through into a dark corridor.

Two hard-eyed men stepped to bar his way.

"You can't go back there," one of them warned. "Dressing rooms."

McEwen asked: "Meaning the dressing-down rooms for the suckers."

"You can't go back!"

McEwen commanded: "One side!"

He started on. Huge hands gripped his arms. He wrenched away wrathfully. A fist hissed toward his face. He side-stepped as knuckles clicked to his jaw. Fury burst out of McEwen. He straight-armed, and grabbed for his armpit holster.

"I'll see those games!"

Four hundred pounds of fighting muscle drove at him. He was slammed hard against a wall. Fists rammed into his face like kicking mule hoofs. Desperately he tried to tear away as two more men came running along the corridor. He went down, gripped by gorilla arms. Something hard and sharp clicked to his head.

Blinded, stunned, overwhelmed, he felt himself dragged. He was jerked down flights of stairs. Fists hit him again as cold air gushed around him. He was flung. He whirled and stumbled across a sidewalk, slipped off the curb, sprawled in the street. Headlights glared and brakes shrieked.

A voice gasped: "It's McEwen—getting bounced!"

McEwen staggered up, pushing aside arms that groped for him. He tottered into a blear of light he knew was a drug store. Feminine shrieks sounded as he fumbled into a telephone booth, scalp bloody, cheek cut, mouth trickling red.

He called headquarters and looked out to see a face he recognized—that of Tom Barrett, reporter. He groaned. When a voice answered he gasped:

"Garrity! McEwen talking! Signal a dozen squad cars to the Golden Slipper! They've got gambling rooms hidden behind it. They're running full blast now. Get going!"

He dropped the receiver and sagged, mopping dizzily at his bleeding head.

CHAPTER IV

THE ANGEL TRAILS

GIL McEWEN leaned grimly over the desk of Chief of Police Peter Thatcher. A bandage encircled his head. His face bore patches of plaster. A split in his lip was still seeping red. He demanded gratingly:

"What do you mean, chief—you didn't find anything?"

Chief Thatcher's head wagged. "Just that, Gil. There was not a game in the place. Private dining rooms, that's all."

"Sure!" McEwen blurted. "Because they had plenty of time to ditch everything before the squad cars got there. Chief, I tell you I know. The Golden Slipper is only a blind for another of the layouts that the gambling ring is running in this town!"

Again the chief's head wagged. "We didn't get a thing, Gil, but maybe you're right. Maybe another time will—"

"Another time, hell!" McEwen snapped. "The Big Shot of this gambling ring is slick as the very devil. He'll never use that place again. He'll have another some place else tomorrow night, working like a clock. Now, by damn, you'll have to begin all over again!"

Steve Thatcher was watching Gil

anxiously. At his side Sue stood. They had come together from McEwen's home when a radioed news-dispatch had told them of the episode. They had found McEwen receiving first aid at headquarters. Unmindful of his injuries, the grim ex-detective had insisted upon hearing the report of the raid.

"I'm convinced of it!" McEwen raged. "I wasn't kicked off this force because I haven't grabbed the Moon Man. I was broken because I staged that first raid. Somebody in this town is clamping down. Some big guy behind this ring clamping down so hard that—"

McEwen broke off as the door opened, and moaned when he saw the furious-eyed Curtis Mead striding into the room. Mead was garbed in evening dress. He was gripping a rolled newspaper in his hand. He glared at McEwen.

McEwen asked disgustedly: "Well?"

"What," Mead demanded harshly, "is the meaning of this?"

He unfolded the newspaper on which a red-printed "EXTRA!" blazed. Huge headlines screamed across the front page:

EX-DETECTIVE BOUNCED FROM NIGHT CLUB FOLLOWING FIGHT!

—

Gil McEwen Creates Disturbance At
Golden Slipper, And is
Thrown Out!

—

ONE-MAN RAID SHOWS NO RESULTS

—

Had Astounded Commerce Club
by Denouncing Them
at Banquet

—

"Well?" McEwen growled again defiantly.

"You've made an inspiring spectacle of yourself, McEwen!" Mead denounced. "You've acted in a most disgraceful manner. What is worse, your high-handed tactics are in violation of the law which you once swore to uphold!"

McEwen bade grimly: "Go ahead!" His eyes narrowed suspiciously.

"You had no right to try to search that night club," Mead asserted. "You're not a police officer any longer. You're a civilian. You are expected to conduct yourself accordingly. You attempted an act which would have been unlawful even if you were still a member of this force—search without warrant."

"What the hell? You think carrying out the letter of police procedure is more important than getting the goods on a gang of crooks?" McEwen challenged.

"You had no authority to attempt to find evidence!" Mead countered. "You assumed official powers which you no longer possess. You've disgraced yourself and this department!"

McEwen sighed: "I have, have I?"

"I'm here to warn you, McEwen. Listen to me carefully. I mean every word I say. On this occasion the Police Board can overlook your offense, but not a second time. If you overstep the mark again—mind you—I shall order your arrest!"

McEwen gulped: "You'll—*what?*"

"We'll handle you in exactly the same manner as any other citizen guilty of breaking the law. Understand that!"

Curtis Mead turned indignantly to the door. Gil McEwen took quick steps after him. His grip on Mead's arm brought the commissioner to a stop.

"One moment," McEwen said very quietly. "One moment."

Curtis Mead glared.

"Suppose," McEwen said, "that within one hour I capture the Moon Man and lock him in a cell in this headquarters. Will that be sufficient to reinstate me?"

Steve Thatcher's breath stopped. Sue glanced at him anxiously. The same burning question sprang into both their minds. Had Gil McEwen come upon a new clue to the Moon Man's identity? Had he found a fresh trail that would lead to the apprehension and unmasking of the notorious criminal? And if he had—

Steve Thatcher waited tautly for the answer.

"Considering the circumstances, McEwen," Mead declared, "there is no need for my answering that question."

"No?" McEwen drawled. "Then I'll ask you another. If I hadn't begun these raids on the gambling rooms, would I still be a member of this police force?"

Mead flushed. "That question is an insult! You infer that the Police Board removed you from the force because they wish to stop the raids, because they desire the gambling ring to continue to operate. Insulting, sir—and absurd!"

McEwen's eyes blazed. "All right. Now listen to me a minute. All the righteous indignation you can muster, Mr. Mead, is not going to stop me. All the threats you can make are not going to hold me back. Nothing you can say is going to keep me from following these cases through to the end. My answer to you, Mr. Mead, is exactly the same as my answer to the Governors of the Chamber of Commerce . . . . You can go to hell!"

McEwen brushed Mead aside. He tramped into the hall and down the stairs. The commissioner stood pale and trembling with anger until the heavy heel-beats died away. He turned cold eyes toward the appalled Chief Thatcher.

"Chief, if McEwen persists in his actions, I will order his arrest. If I order his arrest, I expect you to carry out those orders to the letter, instantly. If you refuse to carry out my orders, I'll replace you, and every man under you, with others who will!"

Chief Thatcher sank slowly into his chair and rubbed blue-veined hands at his wrinkled face. He said nothing because words were beyond him.

Curtis Mead strode out. Steve Thatcher glanced wretchedly at Sue,

and quietly left the room. They opened McEwen's office and found it empty. The desk, once littered with reports, once the working-place of a dynamically driven man, was now cleared and empty. McEwen was not seated in the worn chair, was not in the room at all.

Sue's eyes pleaded with Steve Thatcher's. "Oh, Steve! Gil will do it. He'll go right ahead! He'll wreck himself so that there'll never be a chance of his getting reinstated. Steve dear, what can we do?"

Thatcher's hand took Sue's shoulders firmly. "Darling, he's got to be kept from it. *We've* got to keep him from it. You and I and Dargan. It's the most important thing in the world. You know that!"

"Yes, Steve!"

Thatcher turned away anxiously, opened the door and paused.

"Stick with him, Sue. Don't let him out of your sight if you can help it. If he starts going wild again, for God's sake let me know!"

He stepped out. "Most of all," he said very quietly, "it's up to me—saving Gil," and he strode away.

IT was mid-evening when Steve Thatcher brought his roadster to a stop in front of a row of gloomy tenement houses in an unsavory district of the city. He pushed through a paint-peeled entrance and climbed two flights of bare steps. He knocked at a door and called softly:

"Angel!"

The door opened into a dark room. When it closed behind Thatcher a switch clicked. White glare fell into the face of the neckless, cauliflower-eared ex-pug who gripped Thatcher's hand warmly.

"Boss!" Dargan exclaimed. "Gee, Boss! I've been walking the floor, waiting for you!"

Thatcher smiled. "All safe, Angel? Sue got you here without anyone's spotting you?"

"All safe, Boss!"

"Angel," Thatcher said breathily, "we're facing a ticklish job. Since he was broken, McEwen's more determined than ever to grab us. He means to do it, Angel. He'll let nothing stop him."

"Gosh, Boss! We can't ever let him find out about you! What happens to me don't matter. But you—"

"Good guy, Angel. But right now," Thatcher interrupted, "neither of us matters as much as McEwen. Getting kicked off the force has hit him hard. It's driving him crazy. He's apt to do things that will wreck him completely, wipe out his last chance of ever getting back into the department. McEwen's swore to get us, Angel, but we've got to forget it."

"*He* won't, Boss!"

"He never will, Angel. But listen. It's going to be your job to keep an eye on McEwen. Sue's watching him, but we've got to make double sure. I want you to plant yourself near McEwen's home. You're to shadow him. Wherever he goes, you're to keep him in sight. It'll be a chance, Angel, with every cop and dick in town watching for you."

"Never mind that, Boss! I'll do it, sure!"

"Report to me if anything goes wrong. I'll be at headquarters, handling another tough job. One of the toughest I've ever faced—taking over McEwen's duties. I'd quit the force myself rather than do it, but I've got to stick for dad's sake. You can reach me there, Angel. On your toes!"

Dargan pulled on a cap. "Sure, Boss! Trust me, Boss!"

They went down the stairs and warily into the street.

"Here's money, Angel. Rent a car. Live in it. Watch McEwen's every move!"

"He won't slip me, Boss. I promise you that. I'm on my way. So long." Dargan hurried a few steps, paused, and looked back. His fist-marked lips, scarred during his days in the ring, widened in a grin. "Gee, Boss," he said warmly. "I think you're one hell of a swell guy!"

Thatcher's q u i c k smile came. "Bless you, Angel!" He slipped into his car, glanced back, and saw Dargan hurrying along the gloomy street, daring to move into the open while hundreds of headquarters men were alert to sight him and capture him and fry him for the Moon Man's crimes.

CHAPTER V

WALLS KEEP SECRETS

GIL McEWEN strode back and forth, back and forth across the living room of his home. Fists thrust into his pockets, teeth clenched into an unlighted cigar, gray eyes shining like metal, he tramped across and back.

Sue McEwen watched him anxiously. "Take it easy, Dad," she pleaded. "Please! You need rest."

McEwen said "Huh!" and kept striding.

"You're driving yourself crazy, thinking about it so much, Dad!" the girl protested. "Listen. It's terribly unfair. But does it really mean so much? It doesn't to me, Dad. No matter what they've done to you, I think you're the best detective that ever lived."

McEwen smiled and said "Good girl!" and sat stiffly. He brought from his pocket a slip of paper and studied it. His lips formed the coined word "Nu-Way." He picked up the telephone directory, thumbed to the classified section, and eyed the columns.

"It's getting late, Dad," Sue pleaded.

McEwen kept searching, under one heading after another. Suddenly he sat straight. He peered into the air thoughtfully, rose abruptly, grabbed his hat, and started for the door. Instantly Sue came after him.

Hand on the knob he paused and asked: "Where're *you* going?"

"With you, Dad."

"No, you're not!"

Sue's chin raised. "I certainly am.

Just try getting out of here without me. Just try it!"

McEwen saw unquenchable determination in her eyes. He frowned as he turned back. "Aw, well," he said. "Nothing important. I guess you're right. We'd better go to bed."

He trod up the stairs and Sue followed to see him stride into his room. She entered hers and sank wearily to the edge of the bed. The day had torn at her nerves. She kicked off pumps, peeled off stockings, began slipping her dress over her head.

A sound froze her. It was the grating of a car starter, snarling in the garage behind the house.

She whirled to the window, pulled her dress down, slipped into her shoes, and ran. She flung out the door, whirled to the driveway and sprang upon the running-board of a car that was sliding toward the street.

From the darkness inside it came a discouraged grunt: "Huh!"

Sue opened the door and settled to the seat as though determined that no power could move her.

"Where," she asked, "are we going, Dad?"

Again: "Huh!" McEwen switched on the lights. In the glow the ex-detective looked grimly into his daughter's shining eyes.

"Will you go back to bed, Sue, please?"

"No," Sue said. "You thought you'd slip out on me, didn't you? Unfortunately for you, my father is a detective. I'm not so easy to fool. And I'm just as stubborn as he is."

"Go back, Sue!" McEwen asked again.

"No!"

The car backed out the driveway. McEwen sent it rolling quickly along the street. He felt Sue's eyes studying his face, but he did not glance at her.

"Dad, what's up? No answer? All right, I'll tell you something. If you start doing anything that's apt to get you into more trouble I'll scratch and

kick and scream to keep you from it."

"I believe it!" McEwen said, and nothing more.

Staring straight ahead, he did not notice that a car was following him. He had not seen it spurt from the curb half a block from his house a moment after he had started, did not realize that it was cautiously duplicating each turn he made. He did not dream that the man at the wheel was one upon whom he would delight to get his hands—Ned Dargan.

Dargan, driving warily, followed the red beacon of McEwen's tail-light into a district neighboring "automobile row."

McEwen turned at an intersection, spurted, then swung sharply into an alleyway. By the time Dargan reached the corner, the ex-detective's car was out of sight. Puzzled, Dargan eased to the curb. He knew that McEwen had had no time to reach the next corner. He was sure McEwen had ducked for cover somewhere. He cut the motor and alertly waited.

McEwen, at that moment, was easing from his car. He stepped into the shadow behind a telephone pole near the alleyway entrance. He looked across the street at a squat, square brick building with a broad door over which a sign swung:

NU-WAY GARAGE

He turned back, and through the window of the car said quietly to Sue:

"I'm going to keep an eye on a place across the street. You stick here. I won't be long."

Sue saw him melt again into the blackness behind the telephone pole. She adjusted the rear-view mirror to watch him. Minute after minute ticked by. She grew puzzled, then anxious, then alarmed. She slipped out of the seat and walked toward the telephone pole.

Stopping short, she peered into emptiness.

"Dad!" broke from the girl's lips unconsciously. She looked up and down the street. She retreated into the gloom, hand raising unconsciously to her parted lips, eyes widened apprehensively.

Gil McEwen had slipped away unseen. Not anywhere was there a sign of him.

NED DARGAN, hunched on the seat of the rented car parked near the corner, had seen McEwen slip quickly from the alleyway. He had watched the ex-detective ease into the dark entrance of a store. McEwen had dissolved from sight, but Dargan's eyes stayed on that black rectangle.

From his position McEwen could see part of the interior of the Nu-Way Garage. Against the whitewashed walls expensive cars sat in glistening rows. Farther back stood a huge curtain-sided van. The place was quiet.

Presently headlamps gleamed down the street, a heavy limousine turned into the garage. Two women and two men, modishly dressed, alighted from it as an attendant approached. They moved out of view. McEwen waited alertly; they did not reappear.

Soon an imported coupé swung from the street into the garage. A couple whom McEwen recognized as fast-living socialites climbed from it. They too stepped out of sight. They too failed to emerge. McEwen's eyebrows slid suspiciously low.

Ned Dargan saw him ease cautiously from the shadows, dart across the street, and vanish into the alleyway opposite.

Dargan emerged from his rented car, hurried through the shadows, and took the position McEwen had deserted. In the alleyway opposite he could see nothing of the ex-detective.

McEwen had stepped into an open space behind the building where several dismantled cars lay rusting. He eased to a window in the rear wall of the garage. The panes were painted over, but a triangular splinter had been broken out and through it McEwen could see a section of the interior. The six stylishly dressed persons who had entered were not inside now.

McEwen noticed a second truck behind the first, in the corner, and a man in overalls perched on a step-ladder, painting it yellow.

Headlights gleamed again through the street-entrance of the garage. A costly roadster stopped inside: two men and a woman, dressed for evening, alighted from it, and walked into the space between the two trucks. The painter stopped wielding his brush and scrutinized them.

He drew his step-ladder to the side of the curtained truck. The woman ascended, drew the rubber curtain aside, and stepped through into dark space. The two men followed her. The painter replaced his ladder and resumed slapping his brush.

McEwen breathed "By damn!"

The overalled attendant sauntered close, and McEwen heard the painter say:

"I sure as hell get tired of painting this damn truck over and over again every night. Bet there's fifty coats on it now."

McEwen drew back thoughtfully. He searched about and found several bricks lying near one dismantled car. With one in his hand he moved back to the alleyway. He scanned the street, slid to the entrance of the garage, and peered in.

The attendant was now inside a partitioned office at the front, reading a tabloid newspaper. McEwen ducked beneath the panes, and slipped in between two cars. Alertly listening, he eased to the side of the curtained truck farther from the painter and silently drew the tarpaulin back.

The slats were set too close together; on this side there was no way in.

McEWEN stole to a position near the hood of the truck, peered at a rear window and gauged its distance carefully. He heaved the brick. It twirled through the panes with a splintering crash that sounded like a thunder-clap in the garage.

The painter ejaculated "Geez!" The overalled attendant came from the partitioned office on a trot. The two men advanced toward the shattered window and one of them exclaimed: "Somebody out there. Maybe kids playin'!"

Their backs were turned a moment, and the moment was long enough for McEwen. He darted to the other side of the covered truck. He jerked aside the curtain and heaved h i m s e l f through an opening cut in the slats. He got to his feet in thick darkness, gun in hand, listening.

The truck was backed within an inch or two of the brick side wall. A square of the wall had been ripped out. Darkness lay beyond.

McEwen eased to the hidden aperture, heard nothing, and went down steps. He found himself in what was evidently the rear room of an adjoining, empty store building.

The hum of a motor in the garage whirled him into a dark corner. He waited tensely, and saw dark figures appear inside the covered truck. They came through the opening in the wall, and moved to a door on the opposite side. They knocked; a slit of light appeared and a shadowed head looked out at them.

"Friday," came a quiet password.

The door opened; the newcomers passed through it; the door closed.

McEwen, blood running hot, stole from the corner to the inner door. He knocked. Again the slit appeared, again the eye looked out.

"Friday," McEwen said.

The door swung, and he stepped into a dimly lighted cubicle. A man with steely eyes examined McEwen's face intently as he swung open another door. McEwen walked through, and it closed behind him.

He could not see the finger of the man at the door press a button in the wall three times, then once.

He walked along thick carpet in a narrow corridor recently built of com-position board and gilded. From somewhere came the rattling of chips, the whirring of a roulette wheel. McEwen realized that he had entered a hidden space cleverly shielded from the street by a row of apparently innocent store fronts.

He strode alertly toward the far end of the corridor. His muscles jerked tight when a door opened suddenly a few feet ahead of him. He stopped short as two bull-necked men, heads lowered, eyes gleaming, stepped to bar his way.

One of them said: "Wait a minute, friend."

The other swung a blackjack.

McEwen's arm angled upward swiftly—an instant too late. Terrific power exploded on his skull. He thumped to his knees, head lolling, his other hand dropping from his armpit holster. He was spilling forward when the two men gripped him.

They whisked him through the door from which they had come, closed it, bolted it. Again the corridor was empty and quiet.

WORKING at his desk in police headquarters, Detective Sergeant Steve Thatcher took up the jangling telephone, and heard a voice exclaim:

"Boss!"

Thatcher tightened and said warily: "Hell, Joe. Anything wrong?"

"Plenty!" Dargan whispered. "McEwen—"

"Too bad, Joe. Wait." Thatcher flattened a vest-pocket notebook and read a number aloud. "Ring it in exactly five minutes, Joe."

"Okay, Boss!"

He pronged the receiver, then gave the sergeant at the headquarters switchboard a call to put through for him. The line fluttered as the telephone bell rang in Gil McEwen's home. No answer. Anxiously Thatcher left the office.

He hurried into a booth in a cigar store on the opposite corner. Minutes passed before he touched the telephone. When its bell shrilled he quickly unforked the receiver.

"Angel!"

"Boss! Something's happened to McEwen! God knows what, but you'd better come!"

"Coming, Angel! Where are you?" As he heard the address he added anxiously: "Where's Sue?"

"I don't know, Boss!"

Thatcher strode quickly to his roadster, unlocked the rumble compartment, made sure the black case was inside, and slipped behind the wheel.

Singing tires carried him across town. He swerved past a corner and drew to the curb behind a light car. Dargan strode toward him as he slipped out.

"I don't know what the hell's up, Boss!" Dargan said. "I saw McEwen duck into that garage, but he hasn't come out. And he's not in there now!"

Steve Thatcher listened anxiously to the details as he strode to the alleyway opposite. They became silent when they entered the space behind the garage. Inside the shattered window, an overalled man was tacking a piece of canvas to the sash to blanket the hole.

It was still uncovered when headlights shafted from the street beyond into the garage. Hastily the attendant drove another tack, shutting off Thatcher's view. Thatcher eased closer, listening, carefully reaching for the greasy flap.

Dargan was at his shoulder when he peeled it back and saw two men, who had alighted from the sedan that had just come in, climb a ladder and duck into the interior of the covered truck through its side. When the attendant approached the window again he was forced to retreat.

Quickly he strode with Dargan into the alley, into the street. He was passing the open door of the garage when a startled, whispering cry came from somewhere in the gloom. Thatcher heard it, jerked, and strode on as it came again:

"Steve!"

HE stopped in front of one of a row of empty stores beyond the garage. He saw a dark figure hurrying across the street. He stepped into the blackness of a doorway with Dargan as the figure hastened close.

"Steve!"

"Sue! In here!"

The girl came breathlessly to Steve Thatcher's side. His hand closed snugly around her arm as she talked. He cupped hands and peered through a grimy pane into the store interior.

"Something's happened to dad. I know it!"

Steve Thatcher urged: "Steady, Sue! Watch, Angel!"

He slipped from his pocket his leather case of master keys. When the bolt drew back, he guided Sue in and gestured Dargan to follow. They stood in musty gloom, listening.

"Stay here!"

Thatcher groped to the back of the store. In a rear partition in a wall which seemed new, he found a locked door. Again his master keys came into play. He was about to step through when a sound from beyond froze him.

He peered into a crack to see a man and a woman appear in a square opening in the wall of the rear room. He saw them cross to another door opposite. He heard a whispered word, "Friday," and saw them disappear into a corridor beyond.

Steve Thatcher backed, peered about, strode quickly to the entrance, and eased out, signaling Sue and Dargan with him. He stepped to the second in the row of empty stores and again used his keys.

The three entered a cold, dark space. A hacked counter, glass display cases, and a huge three-legged block disclosed that this had been a butcher shop. At the rear Thatcher again found a wall apparently new, which flanked a huge ceiling-high refrigerator.

Ear pressed to the composition wall he heard, very faintly, a hum of voices. He searched for a door but found none. He was feeling his way along when

Dargan's voice called huskily from the front.

"Boss! Somebody coming!"

Dargan and Sue hurried back. A vague shadow was moving against the show-window panes. It glided to the door, and an echoing click told that a key had slid into the entrance lock.

Steve Thatcher exclaimed: "Down! Behind the counter!"

They ducked out of sight as the store entrance swung open. Footfalls came closer quickly, as though the man who had entered knew his way perfectly in the dark. They saw his legs swing into the open space behind the counter.

He tugged open the heavy door of the refrigerator; he stepped inside; he thumped the door shut behind him.

Thatcher waited tensely, a long time. He slid close to the refrigerator door, and listened. He ventured to open it, very slowly. He brought a vest pocket light into his hand and touched the button.

The gleam showed him hooked meat racks, a chopping block, cleavers and knives hanging on the walls, but otherwise—emptiness.

DARGAN and Sue eased near Steve Thatcher. He whispered: "Wait here." He stepped into the uniced refrigerator, and ran his hands along the walls. He felt a crack and the shine showed him the rectangular outline of a recently cut door, without keyhole and without handle.

Thatcher pulled on the meat-hooks bolted through the wood. The concealed door did not yield. He pushed. The door swung back three inches and stopped. Thatcher shoved it toward one side, then the other. It slid noiselessly into a recess, opening a dark space beyond.

Thatcher's automatic nestled in his hand as he stepped into a small space walled by composition board. At the far end there was a reinforced section, a door. Gliding to it, he listened.

There was no sound. He took a handle and drew back cautiously.

A slit of light appeared, shining from a bulb goosenecked above a desk in the room beyond; its shade was turned to illuminate all the space except a section behind it. From the dark corner movements sounded. Into the glare came—a pair of hands.

The hands were gloved in gray. One of them picked a pencil from the desk. As the fingertips touched the blotter, Thatcher saw one of them bend backward as if double-jointed. The pencil-point scratched on a pad of paper as Thatcher watched.

He closed the crack and stepped into the refrigerator. He slid the connecting door shut, and pushed out into the store. His hand clasped Sue's.

"Game to help me?"

"Anything, Steve!"

"Angel, got your gun?"

"Sure, Boss!"

Thatcher's fingers took the automatic and eased it into Sue's hand.

"Stay here, Sue. Watch that door. If anybody goes in through it, keep out of sight and let them. But if anybody comes out, stop them. Particularly a man wearing gray gloves, Sue —you've got to keep him in here."

Sue asked, "You—you're going, Steve?"

"Going," Thatcher echoed. "Angel with me. We'll be back soon. Angel, come on!"

They strode to the entrance, looked back and saw Sue stationed beside the huge black box, gun steadied. Leaving the girl alone, because the quick desperate plan that had formed in Steve Thatcher's mind demanded it, they swung away.

CHAPTER VI

VOICE OF THE MOON

IT was a gala night at the home of Mr. Curtis Mead. Many cars were parked along the street on which the imposing residence stood. The tinkle of a dance orchestra filled the huge conservatory where crowding couples swayed. Fragrant blooms were everywhere. Champagne flowed. Laughter filled the house.

On her eighteenth birthday Miss Martha Mead, only daughter of the eminent attorney, was "coming out."

It was an exclusive affair to which engraved invitations had summoned hundreds; but lack of an invitation did not deter a "guest" who, when the festivities were at their height, made his entrance through an upstairs bedroom window.

Steve Thatcher had left his roadster near the house. With Dargan he had stolen to the rear of the grounds, carrying his black case. He had whipped on the black robe, pulled on the gloves, fitted the precious shell of Argus glass over his head. He had climbed a trellis. Now, cautiously, he slipped across a windowsill and stood with glittering head bowed, gun waving—the Moon Man.

The master bedroom was empty. The Moon Man circled it quickly, swinging hanging pictures on their nails. Behind one he found the circular front of a wall safe. His black-gloved hand twirled the combination while his silver head bent low to listen.

The man who had no ears heard tumblers click. He opened the safe. Removing a jewel case, he inspected a delicate filigree necklace with an emerald pendant. He replaced it in the case, the case in the safe, and spun the combination.

He moved to a telephone standing on the table. It must be, he knew, one of a number of extension instruments scattered about the big house. He lifted the receiver and, when the operator's voice answered, his muffled voice directed:

"When I hang up please ring this number."

He broke the connection. Almost immediately the bell in the room, and all others in the house, rang. Again the Moon Man lifted the receiver. A coolish voice come over the line:

"Mr. Mead's residence. Betlow speaking."

The butler had answered the call in one of the lower rooms.

"Police headquarters calling," the Moon Man said in his muffled tones. "Mr. Mead, please—it's highly important."

In a moment another voice said: "Curtis Mead speaking."

"Headquarters, Mr. Mead," said the Moon Man. "We have just arrested a crook, and we've found a jewel case on him. There's an emerald pendant necklace in it which seems to tally with a description we have on file of one of Mrs. Mead's pieces of jewelry. Will you check up, please, to see whether or not it belongs to her?"

Mead exclaimed: "Certainly! Hold the line."

The Moon Man did not hold the line. He pronged the receiver; his robe flapped as he strode to the door connecting with the hallway beyond. His glittering head lowered when he heard quick footfalls approach. He stepped forward alertly as the door was flung open.

"Mr. Mead," he commanded, thrusting his automatic hard against the police commissioner's back, "oblige me by raising your hands!"

CURTIS MEAD made a choking noise. He twisted and saw the moon-like head of the cloaked figure behind him, as the prodding gun forced his hands up.

"This—this is an outrage!" he blurted.

"No doubt," the muffled voice answered. "Don't worry about your wife's necklace, Mr. Mead. It has not been stolen. And have no concern about yourself. I do not intend to harm you. You are, however, coming with me."

Mead blurted: "Are you attempting to kidnap me? You don't dare—"

"At the moment," the Moon Man interrupted firmly, "I am daring a great deal. I won't tolerate any resistance from you, Mr. Mead. I should regret having to knock you unconscious. You will regret trying to raise an alarm. Come with me quietly, and I will release you very soon."

Mead sputtered wordlessly.

"Climb out that window," the Moon Man directed. "Go down the trellis. I warn you again—don't raise an alarm. The window—do you hear? Obey me!"

The ringing command brought paleness to Mead's face. The glittering gun waved its silent warning. The police commissioner, red-faced, trembling with rage, faced no choice. He went to the window.

While the Moon Man's head shone above him, while the Moon Man's gun watched his every move, he climbed down the trellis. When he reached the ground he whirled, as if to dart away, but instantly he became enclosed in a crushing embrace. He squirmed toward the man who had grabbed him and saw eyes shining brightly above a tightly drawn handkerchief mask.

"Steady!" warned Ned Dargan.

The Moon Man dropped to the ground beside Mead. The commissioner responded to the prodding automatic. Striding between the white-masked man and the moon-headed criminal, he was guided across the grounds and through a hedge.

Quickly the Moon Man and Dargan hustled Mead into the seat of the roadster. The gun, now in Dargan's hand, pushed hard against the commissioner's ribs as the Moon Man took the wheel.

The roadster spurted. Each time Mead began to speak his indignant wrath, Dargan's gun poked him into silence. Dark streets blurred past. The Moon Man kept away from lights and busy sections. He circled swiftly into a gloomy thoroughfare removed from the center of the city. He shot past the lighted entrance of the Nu-Way Garage and braked to the curb just beyond.

Cautiously he ducked out. Dargan

thrust Mead close behind him at the door of the deserted butcher-shop. The Moon Man's master keys opened the way, and they stepped into the musty quiet of the store.

THE Moon Man took the gun and grasped Dargan's arm. His voice was a muffled breath.

"Get her out of sight, Angel. We're going in."

Dargan darted rearward. Whispers sounded. Dargan called: "All clear!" The Moon Man marched behind Mead and brought him to a stop inside the huge refrigerator.

Dargan now had the gun he had left with Sue. He held Mead at a standstill with it as the Moon Man whirled from the heavy door. The girl was huddling in a dark corner.

"Did anybody come out?"

"No!"

"Good! Listen! I'm taking Mead in there. I intend to bring him out again —but something may go wrong. If we don't come back within a few minutes, go to the nearest telephone and call headquarters. Order every squad car in the district to surround this place and crash it."

"If—if you don't come back?" Sue faltered. "But if I do that, they'll find you in there! They'll—"

"You've got to do it! There's no other way. Promise me! Promise!"

"I—I promise."

The Moon Man whipped away. He found Dargan flattening Mead against the refrigerator wall. His black hands pressed the secret door, and slid it aside. He warned Mead "Keep quiet!" and stepped in. Dargan eased Mead along as the Moon Man stole to the hidden door beyond.

No sound came through. He eased the door back a crack and the slit of light sparkled on his mask. He saw again the shaded bulb, the black corner, the gray hands. Now the hands were pawing heaps of currency out of trays into a briefcase. Except for the man blanketed by the glare, the room was empty.

Suddenly the Moon Man stepped into the light, gun pointed. His muffled voice rang!

"Keep your hands in the light! Move them and I'll shoot!"

The gray gloves closed quickly, tensing into fists. The Moon Man's robe flapped as he strode to a door beside the desk and sank a bolt into its socket. Over his shoulder he ordered: "Bring Mead in."

The gray-gloved hands flattened on the desk top; a gasp sounded in the shrouding darkness of the corner.

Through the door Curtis Mead appeared, prodded by Dargan's gun. The three faced the corner.

The Moon Man's voice came muffled while the police commissioner stared.

"You are standing, Mr. Mead, in the office of a suite of secret gambling rooms. The man behind that desk is the organizer and master mind of the ring. Into his pockets goes the greatest share of the winnings. He, Mr. Mead, is the biggest crook operating in this city today—possibly excepting, depending on your personal viewpoint, myself."

Mead stood speechless.

"I believe, Mr. Mead," the Moon Man continued quietly, "you will find that man to be one who has, by day, played the respectable citizen. By night he has operated his series of gambling dens and taken with his crooked games thousands that should be going to legitimate business. Perhaps you will recognize him."

Still Mead stared.

The gray hands were curling, the fingertips clawing at the desk.

"Observe, Mr. Mead, that finger of our crook's right hand. See it bend. The glove finger bends because the first joint is missing. Do you know, Mr. Mead, a man who has the tip of that finger missing?"

Mead exclaimed: "Good God!"

"I think," the Moon Man's muffled voice came, "you do. Suddenly it is all clear to you. Very well. We have

seen enough. We will go." The Moon Man took slow steps backward. "To you, sir," he addressed the man hidden by the glare, "good night."

Dargan pulled Mead quickly through the secret door. The Moon Man's gun waved a threat as he followed. Swiftly he swung the door shut. He dropped into place a stout bolt to bar it. He whirled Mead into the black refrigerator.

Dargan held the commissioner motionless as the Moon Man stepped out. He strode to the girl huddling in the corner. His muffled voice commanded: "Find a telephone! Put that squad call through now—now!"

HE hurried the startled girl to the door. She hesitated, tortured eyes turning to the shining spherical head; then she ran. The Moon Man left the street door open and called: "Angel! This way out!"

Dargan came trotting. Together they swiftly crossed the sidewalk. The Moon Man slipped to the wheel of the roadster as Dargan clambered in. The motor sang as the car spurted away. The Moon Man shot it swiftly into the opposite alleyway, sped into a shadow at the far end, and sharply stopped.

"Boss!" Dargan gasped. "You've got me guessing!"

Slipping out, the Moon Man shrugged off his black robe. He jerked out of his black gloves. Carefully he removed the fragile mask. In the gloom the Moon Man vanished and Steve Thatcher, detective sergeant, reappeared.

He stowed the regalia in the case and locked the case in the rumble compartment as he urged Dargan:

"Back to your car, Angel! Head for your room! Stay out of sight! The rest is up to me alone!"

Dargan gasped. "Gosh, Boss! Gosh, you're taking an awful chance!"

"Back, Angel! Hurry!"

Dargan's hot hand sought Steve Thatcher's and clamped it before he sprinted out of the alley. Thatcher swung his roadster into the street and saw Dargan hurrying along, circling to the rented car. He swung in the opposite direction, then near the corner which opened toward the Nu-Way Garage he stopped.

As he waited he clicked the switch of the car radio. The tubes warmed on the police announcer's strident voice.

"Calling all cars in District B! All cars, District B! Code 4. Place, Code T-8. Emergency! Look for Miss Sue McEwen, follow her orders!"

Steve Thatcher saw a hatless, breathless man hurry to the intersection—Curtis Mead. He saw Mead signal a cruising taxi and duck in.

Steve Thatcher followed.

He trailed the cab out of the automobile district, into the business center, into a residential section. He parked quickly when he saw Mead's taxi stop in front of an imposing, castlelike house. He slipped from the car as Mead hurried in. He went up the street carrying his precious black case.

When he reached the corner of the grounds of the house which Mead had entered, he slipped through a hedge. A shine of window light drew him. He glided across a garden, and paused, looking through filmy curtains into a paneled library. Within the room Curtis Mead, pale and agitated, was striding back and forth.

Minutes passed.

Mead turned quickly as another man entered the room. That man's back was turned to the window. Voices came through the panes to Steve Thatcher.

"By God, sir!" Mead declared gratingly. "You've used me as a dupe! You lied to me and tricked me! By God, you'll pay for that!"

The other man asked tonelessly: "What're you going to do, Curtis?"

"I have no choice in the matter!" Mead's voice rang. "I'll expose you. Regardless of consequences, I'll see that you are properly punished! I promise you that!"

Steve Thatcher drew back. He clicked his black case open. He tugged on the black gloves, the black robe; he fitted the precious mask to his head. Again the detective sergeant vanished; again the Moon Man appeared.

He slipped along the garden to a rear door. He tried it and found it locked. He unsheathed his master keys and opened it.

The crash of a shot rang through the house.

The Moon Man pushed through the door of the library with gun leveled. Curtis Mead was retreating from a desk that sat near the shelved wall, face deathly white, jaw dropped. He gave one swift, dazed glance at the black-robed figure, then peered again at the man lying slumped on the floor.

The Moon Man looked down at the lax face of Mr. Barron Thayer, at Thayer's right hand, at the smoking gun which lay beside it. That hand had swung the gun to Thayer's temple. A finger from which the first joint was missing had pulled the trigger.

THE Moon Man faced Curtis Mead. "It will not make a pretty story," he declared, "when the newspapers publish the facts."

Mead blurted: "Good God, I didn't suspect him! I didn't know!"

"But he influenced you to discharge McEwen," the Moon Man insisted. "He forced you to do that because McEwen was raiding his gambling rooms and wrecking his ring. That was the real reason behind McEwen's discharge—not the fact that he hadn't yet captured me."

"I realize that now!" Mead exclaimed. "I didn't know it at the time. By God, sir, I would not knowingly be a party to such a thing! Thayer seemed to be acting in good faith. I didn't dare ignore his demand for McEwen's removal."

"Why not?" the Moon Man demanded. "Why didn't you dare?"

Mead sank exhaustedly into a chair. "Thayer was my richest client. He paid me a large yearly retainer. Lately his retainer was all that kept me going. If I lost it, I'd go bankrupt—be penniless. I couldn't risk his disfavor. When he told me the Governors of the Commerce Club were demanding McEwen's removal—I had to go through with it."

"A mistake, Mr. Mead," the Moon Man declared. "You admit that now."

Mead exclaimed: "Now I know! I was tricked! You—you've revealed it to me. For God's sake, why have you done it?"

"Perhaps," the Moon Man's muffled tones came, "because I wish to convince you that I am not as reprehensible as you think me. Perhaps because I could not endure to see McEwen broken unjustly. That does not matter now. There, on that desk, Mr. Mead, is a typewriter. Use it!"

Mead stared at it. In the silence the Moon Man's silver head glittered, his automatic gleamed. The commissioner drew the typewriter toward him. He fumbled a sheet of paper into the roller. His trembling fingers tapped the keys. He snatched the letter out and scrawled his name under it.

The Moon Man said: "I'll take that!"

Again Curtis Mead stared at the still form on the floor. He heard a rustling movement, looked up and found the black-robed figure gone.

Half a block from the home of Barron Thayer a roadster started up. Steve Thatcher, again unrobed, again unmasked, sent it whirring toward the center of the city. He parked outside the postoffice building, and in the gleam of the dash-light he read the letter that Curtis Mead had typed.

Lips twirked tightly, Thatcher crudely printed *Chief of Police, City,* on an envelope and pressed a stamp on it.

His wry smile growing, he moistened the ball of his right thumb with the inky point of his fountain-pen. He pressed the thumb to the paper and left a clear-cut print.

It was an impression that McEwen would recognize instantly—the mark of the Moon Man.

Again he read the letter:

Gilbert McEwen is herewith reinstated to his former rank in the Police Department, effective at once.   CURTIS MEAD.

Steve Thatcher dropped the letter into the mail-slot and sighed "Thank God!"

THE morning newspapers howled. "Thayer revealed as head of gambling ring!"

"Hidden rooms raided!"

"McEwen found prisoner in secret den!"

"Ace detective reinstated!"

"Curtis Mead reveals full facts, resigns from Police Board!"

In the chief's office at headquarters, Gil McEwen sat grinning. Behind his roll-top desk Chief Thatcher smiled. Sue McEwen echoed the triumphant gleam in her father's eyes.

"By damn, I'm a different man!" McEwen chuckled. "By damn, I feel good!"

Steve Thatcher was standing with his right hand thrust into his pocket, concealing the inky smudge on the ball of the thumb.

"I think," he said fervently, "we all do, Gil."

Sue's warm hand stole into his; she raised happy, proud eyes.

Her father read again the amazing letter that had come through the morning mail.

"This guy, now—the Moon Man!" McEwen said. "I'm going to get him! By damn, I'm a cop, and he's a crook, and there's only one possible end to that. When I get my hands on him I'm going to give him the chair!"

Steve Thatcher's smile faded: but it came again in a moment.

"If I knew where that crook is hiding right now," McEwen declared tersely, "if I knew where I could reach him—" the detective's smile showed like the sun through storm-clouds— "I'd send him a letter of thanks, by damn!"

KATIE BLAYNE

A market note in *Writer's Digest* for January 1937 describes the pulp *Detective Fiction Weekly* as follows: "The magazine runs a variety of crime fiction. It uses humor and an occasional—very occasional—semi-tragic story; it uses crook pattern stories and stories told from the viewpoint of the hero. It uses stories of a hero against the villain who is a respected member of society who has committed his first crime. . . ."

In other words, the magazine was open to many styles of crime and detective stories. It certainly never shied from trying out women as leading characters.

Whitman Chambers (b. 1896) wrote about Katie Blayne for the magazine. Nicknamed "The Duchess," she is a competitive reporter for *The Sun,* working the police beat. She often follows her intuition to solve the crime.

"The Duchess Pulls a Fast One" originally appeared in *DFW*'s September 19, 1936, issue.

Katie Blayne's Bluff Forces a Mysterious Insurance Murderer into the Open

Bergstrom directed them toward the closet

The
Duchess Pulls a Fast One

By Whitman Chambers

THE three of us, Spike and Katie Blayne and I, were alone in the City Hall press room. It was six thirty of a dark and rainy evening. I'd just taken over the beat from Spike, for the *Telegram*, and Katie was waiting for the *Sun's* night police reporter to come on the job.

"Duchess," Spike Kaylor beefed, "why don't you scram out of here and go home?"

"Spike, why don't you give yourself

up?" the Duchess retorted, smiling.

"Pinky, doesn't she get in your hair the way she hangs around and hangs around, all the time?" Spike persisted.

I didn't say anything. I didn't want to be drawn into their quarrel which, for seven months, had kept the press room on pins and needles. In the first place, Spike Kaylor is my best friend. And in the second place, Katie Blayne—well, never mind about Katie Blayne.

THE DUCHESS PULLS A FAST ONE

The fire alarm gong tapped out 236. Spike strode over to the card tacked on the bulletin board. "Fifth and Chestnut." He looked more cheerful. "Our City Hall apparatus will roll on the deuce."

"And you, dear little boys, I suppose, will take a ride on the big old fire engine," Katie jeered. "Won't that be just ducky!"

"Well," I said, "it's some consolation to be able to do something that you can't do."

Katie's blue eyes twinkled. "Maybe you think I can't."

"Skip it," I said. "You're not going kiting around on any fire truck. Not the way these lunatics drive."

At that instant the second alarm clanged in. "There's the deuce!" Spike shouted, and leaped toward the door.

I was on his heels and I realized, unhappily, that Katie was on mine. We tore down the corridor and into the fire house. The big pumper was just starting to roll. The three of us caught the hand rail and swung onto the running board. Two firemen up beside the driver looked back and yelled at Katie. The roar of the powerful engines drowned their words and the Duchess looked the other way.

As the pumper turned into the street with a breath-taking skid and roared away with bell clanging and siren wailing, Katie swayed toward me and shouted happily: "I've always wanted to do this."

"It's just the little girl in you," I growled.

We saw the red glow in the sky while we were still blocks away from the fire. Huge clouds of yellow smoke were rolling upward.

"Kurt Bergstrom's chemical plant is at Fourth and Chesnut," I yelled.

"Fine!" Spike shouted. "And if Bergstrom is going up in smoke with his chemicals, I'll buy the drinks."

Which is the way most newspaper men feel about Kurt Bergstrom. The head of the Bergstrom Chemical Company is an inventor, a nationally known chemist, a man of wealth and substance. But! He'll stoop to any gag, short of murder, to get his name in the papers. And reporters do not like publicity hounds.

The pumper pulled up a block from the fire. Katie and Spike and I piled off and started down the street as one of the firemen yelled: "Hey, Duchess! Next time you want to go to a fire, hire a cab!"

"Thanks for the buggy ride," Katie called sweetly, and blew him a kiss.

THE fire, we discovered with some disappointment, was confined to the north wing of the two-story brick building. It was evidently already under control, despite the billowing clouds of acrid smoke which rolled out of the shattered windows.

"Not much to this," I remarked.

Then we saw an elderly man talking excitedly to Battalion Chief Murphy. We pegged him for the night watchman and ran over.

"He was in the chem lab in the north wing when I come on at six," the old man was saying. "He was alone, workin' on some experiment. I goes over the plant and I'm down in my room makin' some coffee, when I smell smoke. That's about a half hour later. I runs upstairs and the whole chem lab is in flames. I never seen him go out. His car's right there in front of the office where he parked it, but he ain't nowheres around."

"Who?" Spike bellowed. "Who?"

The watchman blinked at us. "Mr.

Hamlin. Mr. John Hamlin. He's Mr. Bergstrom's assistant in the lab."

Chief Murphy grunted. "Well, we'll find out if he's in there in a few minutes. I'll send in a couple of men with gas masks."

A little later they found the body, or what was left of it. They didn't even try to carry it out. They left that grisly job to the coroner. In the confined space of the laboratory the heat had been intense.

We cleaned up as many angles of the story as we could and then Spike called a cab. The Duchess, as usual, was right on our heels. She climbed into the taxi with us and sat down calmly between Spike and me.

Spike stared straight ahead as the cab pulled away from the curb. "My nose tells me it's still with us," he commented acidly.

"My Christmas Night perfume," Katie said blandly. "Don't you adore it?"

"I'd adore to drop you down a manhole," Spike groused.

She let that pass. "Are you by any chance going to the Hotel Drake?" she asked. "Because if you are, I'll go with you and we'll interview Kurt Bergstrom together."

Spike groaned, but didn't argue.

The clerk at the Drake directed us to the dining room and the head waiter told us Bergstrom was eating alone in the south alcove. Spike started off, then checked himself. A cagey look came into his eyes as he asked casually: "How long has Mr. Bergstrom been in the dining room?"

"Since a little after six, sir."

As we paraded through the room, a bit damp and sooty and bedraggled, Katie asked:

"Now what was the occasion for that question?"

"Did you ever hear, my little cabbage, of the crime called arson?"

"Yes," Katie said promptly, "and I've also heard of the crime called murder. But if you're thinking of them in connection with Kurt Bergstrom, you'd best forget them. Mr. Bergstrom is a wealthy man. He had no reason to stoop to arson, much less to murder."

"That mugg would stoop to anything to get his name in the papers."

BERGSTROM rose when he saw us coming. He's a heavy-set chap of fifty, with very pink cheeks, keen blue eyes and close-clipped blond hair.

"Goot evening, gentlemen. Goot evening, Miss Blayne." He knew every reporter in the city. "There is something I can do for you?"

"There sure is," Spike said. "Who is John Hamlin?"

"Hamlin is my assistant in the laboratory."

"Not any more he isn't your assistant." Spike never beat around the bush. "The north wing of your plant was just gutted by fire. Hamlin was burned to death, or so the watchman believes. Anyway, the firemen found a body in the lab. Hamlin's car is out in front but Hamlin is missing."

Bergstrom took it calmly but that didn't prove anything. He's the type who never shows emotion.

"Now about this man Hamlin," Spike hurried on. "Was he married?"

"Yes. He lived with his wife at 17 Bay Terrace."

"Why was he down there after hours?"

"An experimental chemist," Bergstrom proclaimed, "has no hours. He was working nights on an experiment of his own. Only during the day did he help me with one of my inventions."

"Which is?"

Bergstrom brightened. "An inexpensive device for recording sound on motion picture film. An attachment for the home movie camera, selling for only a few dollars, which—"

"Give the details to the advertising department," Spike broke in. "We're not handing out any free publicity for your invention." He paused, looked the big German straight in the eye. "Do you believe, Mr. Bergstrom, that the body found was John Hamlin's?"

Bergstrom shrugged, said cautiously: "You say Hamlin iss missing und a body was found in the laboratory. Surely you, as a brilliant young newspaper man, should be able to draw the obvious conclusion."

"But perhaps," Spike said slowly, "the conclusion is too *damned* obvious!" He glared at the bristling Bergstrom. "Have you stopped to think of that?"

"I haff hardly had time," Bergstrom retorted stiffly, "to think of anything. Und now if you excuse me please, I run oud to the plant."

We followed him out of the dining room. In the lobby Katie asked: "Are you going out to see Mrs. Hamlin?"

"Yes, *darling!*" Spike shot back. "And I suppose you'd like to tag along."

"Yes, *dear!* I'd love it. You know how I enjoy your company."

WE found Mrs. Hamlin dry-eyed and calm, though we knew immediately we saw her that she had been informed of her husband's death. She was a tall, big-boned woman with black hair that looked dyed and dark, close-set eyes.

She invited us into the living room and asked us to sit down. "I knew that those experiments would end in tragedy," she told us calmly. "You

see, my husband was developing a high explosive."

"So far as anyone knows," Spike pointed out, "there was no explosion."

"The chemicals he used were highly inflammable."

"I see." Spike didn't look as though he saw at all. "Did your husband come home for dinner tonight, Mrs Hamlin?"

"He came home, yes. He ate an early dinner, as always, and rushed back to the laboratory. He must have got there a little before six. I did my dishes and sat down and tried to read. I had planned to go to a movie. But, somehow, I didn't dare leave the house. I was sitting here on the Chesterfield when the coroner phoned. I was neither surprised nor shocked. You see, I have been expecting this." She wiped her dry eyes with a folded handkerchief. "I suppose you will want pictures?"

She turned to a table, picked up three large snapshots and handed them to me. "They were taken a year ago today. Our wedding day."

Well, it should have been pretty pathetic, but somehow it wasn't. I looked at the pictures. Mr. and Mrs. John Hamlin on somebody's lawn. A little guy with a head too big for his stooped shoulders, his thin arm held in the possessive grip of a smirking, overdressed Amazon.

Spike asked quietly: "Did Mr. Hamlin carry any insurance?"

"Yes. He took it out before we were married."

"A large amount?"

"Eighty thousand dollars."

Spike peered around the room. "Quite a sizable policy for a man in his circumstances, wouldn't you say?"

I could see her stiffen as she glared at Spike. "Considering the dangers of his work, no. He wished me to be provided for if anything happened."

"Well, we'll hope his wish is granted," Spike said, rubbing a smile off his lips. "Although insurance companies sometimes get tough about things like this. Any further questions, —children? If not, that will be all, Mrs. Hamlin. Sorry to trouble you, and thanks for the pictures."

We filed out, climbed into our cab and started back to the Hall.

"What a story, what a story!" Spike chortled. "If we can only crack it!"

"You mean this poor woman's losing her husband on their wedding anniversary?" Katie asked.

Spike moaned. "Brilliance. That's it. Positive brilliance. Duchess, don't you know a Schwartz when one jumps up and spits in your face?"

"A Schwartz?"

"Tell her, Pinky. She was still in kindergarden when the Schwartz case broke."

"This Schwartz was a chemist and inventor too," I said. "He had a laboratory out in Walnut Creek where he was working on a process for manufacturing artificial silk. One night there was an explosion and the joint burned down. They found a man's body in the ashes. Everybody thought, of course, that Schwartz had cashed his checks. His wife put in for the hundred grand insurance he carried.

"Then it developed that the body wasn't Schwartz's at all. The dead guy was an itinerant preacher whom the chemist had lured into the laboratory and knocked over the head. Schwartz, in the meantime, had holed up in an apartment he'd rented weeks before he pulled the hoax. The dicks got on his trail and were closing in on him when Schwartz put a .45 slug between his eyes. Since then, Katie, an insurance

hoax of that type has been known as a Schwartz."

The Duchess took one of my cigarettes and lit it with hands that weren't very steady. "And you think this is an insurance hoax?"

"Cinch," Spike declared flatly.

"Why?"

"Because it's too damned pat and because that guy Hamlin carried too much insurance."

"And who was the man they found in the laboratory?"

"Some hobo who'll never be missed. Hamlin got him in there on the pretext of giving him a job, slapped him over the conk and fired the joint. Simple, Duchess."

"And you think Kurt Bergstrom was in on the hoax?" Katie pursued.

"Cinch." Spike nodded gleefully. "The way I dope it, the time of the fire was prearranged to put Bergstrom in the clear. John Hamlin is a weak sister and the whole plot was cooked up by Bergstrom and Mrs. Hamlin. Hamlin is safely holed up somewhere, and when the heat is off he and the dame'll scram to South America with forty grand."

"And the other forty grand?"

"Into Kurt Bergstrom's sock. Well, what do you think of it, Duchess?"

"I think the whole thing," Katie promptly retorted, "is a silly machination of a disordered brain."

WHEN we got back to the press room I called the beat while Spike and the Duchess phoned their offices. Then, on a hunch, I rang the morgue and by sheer good luck got hold of the coroner himself.

"Pinky Kane," I said. "Look, coroner. About that man who was burned to death in the Bergstrom fire. Have you got around to a p.m. yet?"

" We've made a cursory examination at the request of Captain Wallis."

" What'd you find?"

" Perhaps you'd better ask Wallis. He ordered me not to give out any details."

Katie and Spike were still in the phone booths as I impatiently jiggled the hook, got the operator and asked for the Captain of Detectives. Wallis came on almost immediately.

" This is Kane, skipper. Understand you ordered a post mortem on Hamlin's body."

" That's right, Pinky."

" What'd you find out?"

" Well, his height and build approximate that of John Hamlin. He carried a gold watch on which Hamlin's initials are still discernible. He wore a full denture—not a tooth in his head. Same as Hamlin. And that, Kane, is about the works."

" Come on, skipper. Kick in."

" I said that was the works."

" Now look here. You were on that Schwartz case and so was I. And I haven't forgotten it. Now what else did your medical examiner discover when he went over that body? Tell me everything."

" Well," Captain Wallis sighed, " you'll get it sooner or later, so I might as well give it to you now. The man's skull had been fractured."

" Uh-huh, I thought you were holding out something like that. Hamlin's skull couldn't have been cracked in the fire, could it?"

" Chief Murphy said nothing fell on him and if he had a fractured skull he must have got it before the fire broke out."

" Well, what do you think?" I asked.

" I don't know how you spotted it, Pinky, but I think you're on the right track. Another Schwartz."

" How about Bergstrom? Do you think he's in on it?"

" If I answered that question I'd be guessing. So let's pass it."

"And Mrs. Hamlin?"

" I've only talked to her on the phone. She may be a party to the hoax and she may not. Probably not. Schwartz's wife wasn't, you know. He planned to contact her after the pay-off and, as the saying goes, tell all. Anyway, I've just sent out an all-state teletype with Hamlin's description. I've ordered him held."

" On what charge, skipper?"

" Murder, my boy. Murder," Captain Wallis said cheerfully.

I hung up, a bit breathless all of a sudden.

The Captain certainly had been working fast.

Katie came out of the *Sun* booth. " You've been talking to Bodie Wallis, haven't you?" she said, smiling.

" Bodie did most of the talking. I listened. He's sent out an all-state teletype to pick up John Hamlin."

Katie's laugh told me what she thought of Bodie Wallis. "John Hamlin has already been picked up. In a basket, by a couple of coroner's deputies."

" Captain Wallis doesn't think so."

" String with Captain Wallis, Pinky, and you'll sleep in the street," she said airily.

Spike tumbled out of the telephone booth bellowing:

" Hey, Pink! The office just got a flash from Duke Wayland on the lower beat. Captain Wallis—"

" I know. I was just talking to him."

" That guy had a fractured skull!" Spike exclaimed excitedly.

" Yeah," I said.

Katie's jaw dropped as she looked from Spike to me. " What guy had a fractured skull?" she asked in a small voice.

"The guy they picked up in a basket. The guy you were dumb enough to think was John Hamlin."

KATIE sat down abruptly. Spike and I stood looking at her, gloating a little. It wasn't often that the Duchess put her money on the wrong number.

"Well, muh frand?" Spike grinned at last.

She shrugged. "It looks bad but it isn't hopeless. I'm banking on one thing: the integrity of Kurt Bergstrom. I've known him for several years and I can't see him getting mixed up in an insurance hoax involving murder. And I can't see that meek and mild person, John Hamlin, hitting a man over the head and burning his body."

"That's logic for you," Spike jeered. "Kurt Bergstrom looks too honest to go in for murder. And John Hamlin looks too meek to kill anybody. Forget, for a minute, the looks of those two guys and where are you? Well, I'll tell you. You're stringing along with Pinky and me and Captain Wallis."

"Three," Katie said sarcastically, "of the most brilliant minds in the city. Well, if you three are brilliant, I'm a low moron. Good night."

Katie breezed, slamming the door.

Spike chuckled. "Did we get the little lady's goat, all right. But I'd much rather get John Hamlin."

"And maybe you think we won't. Now look. It's a ten to one shot the guy never left the city. His best bet was to establish a residence in some quiet apartment house. He's probably had the apartment for weeks, just like Schwartz did. All right. So what?"

"I'll bite."

"We smoke him out."

"You and me?"

"Don't be a sap. We got a staff, haven't we. We got three or four cubs sitting over there in the office wearing out the seats of their pants, haven't we? Oke! Tomorrow morning early we turn 'em loose, along with anybody else Andy can spare. We contact every hotel and apartment and rooming house in the city."

"The dicks will be doing just that," I pointed out.

"What of it? We can put as many men on the job as Bodie Wallis. We got just as good a chance as he has of turning up Hamlin. And if we get a break—well, will Katie's face be red? Dunt esk!"

WE went to work the next morning. It was house-to-house stuff and it was tiring. But we didn't care. Spike and I felt, the whole *Telegram* staff felt, that we were on the right track.

As we read John Hamlin's mind, he never expected any hue and cry. He thought the corpse would be accepted as his, and the pay-off would be a pushover. He'd made only one mistake. He'd hit the poor devil he'd hired to double for him too hard a blow. The body wasn't wholly consumed, as he'd expected it to be, and the skull fracture showed up in the post mortem. John Hamlin, we reasoned, must have got quite a shock when he read the papers in the morning and learned that every law enforcement officer in the state was looking for him.

It was a long hard day and we found no trace of John Hamlin. Something, however, was in our blood. The thrill of the chase. We felt, Spike and I and the cubs, as though surely we'd locate him in the next apartment house, the next hotel. We kept doggedly at it all day, all the day following, all the day after that.

At five in the afternoon of the third day, dead on my feet, I strolled into the City Hall press room. The reporters on the afternoon papers had gone home and Katie, looking fresh and spruce and more than a little like a million dollars, was all alone.

"You looked dragged out, Pinky," she smiled. "Where have you been all day?"

"Hunting John Hamlin," I said, slumping into a chair.

"Why, don't you read the papers? Hamlin was buried today. I covered the funeral."

I sighed. "You don't really think that was Hamlin, do you? I know you're silly, Duchess, and I know your judgment isn't very good. But you're not that silly, are you?"

She looked at me hard for a long minute. Then:

"See here, Pinky Kane. I don't like that. I don't like it even a little bit. You can call me almost anything else, but I draw the line at being called silly. I was going to spare you this, but on second thought I won't. I'll go out of my way, for once, just to show you how silly *you* are. Will you meet me at the Drake Hotel at eight tonight?"

"What for?"

"For the pay-off," Katie said.

The door had opened and Spike Kaylor stood on the threshold. "Where's the pay-off?" he demanded.

"At the Drake, tonight," the Duchess told him. "You're invited."

"Thanks," Spike grinned. "Will this affair be formal, or shall I—"

"Wear tails, by all means," Katie shot back, and left the room.

"What's the kid got on her mind?" Spike asked.

"You can't prove anything by me."

"Do you really think she has a hot lead?"

"I wouldn't put it beyond her."

"But what is it? She hasn't found John Hamlin, has she?"

"No. She insists Hamlin is dead and buried."

"But maybe that's just to throw us off the track." Spike eased into a chair. "Pay-off, huh? Pay-off," he mused. "Pink, there's something screwy about this picture. If she was ready to crack this story, would she invite us to the party? Not any! She'd tell us something was due to pop and let us stew in our own juices until two o'clock tomorrow morning when the final edition of the *Sun* comes out."

"That's what you'd think, all right. So what?"

"So we take her up. What the hell else can we do?"

We found the Duchess, sitting off by herself, in the lobby of the Drake at eight o'clock.

"Well, keed, when does the curtain go up?" Spike asked.

"Almost any minute," Katie returned shortly. "Just keep your shirts on and your mouths shut."

She lit a fresh cigarette off a glowing butt.

Her hands were shaking and I saw that the palms were moist. Her eyes were bright, feverish, as she kept watching the door.

"Our little pal seems a bit nervous," Spike grinned.

"We can do without your puerile mouthings for a while, Mr. Kaylor," the Duchess told him.

THEN Kurt Bergstrom strode into the lobby and Katie rose. The chemist spotted her and came over. He looked keyed up and he didn't smile as he bowed perfunctorily over her hand.

"These are your friends?" he asked, looking at Spike and me with cold and fishy eyes.

"Not my friends, but they'll do as witnesses."

"Goot! Bring them up in ten minutes."

Bergstrom turned and walked briskly toward the elevators. Katie sat down and lit another cigarette. She was plenty nervous.

I began to feel restive myself. Even Spike, who is almost irrepressible, didn't have anything to say. We watched ten slow minutes tick off on the clock over the desk. Then Katie stood up.

"When we go up to Bergstrom's room," she said, "you two will do as you're told and ask no questions. Have you got that straight?"

"Oke, kid," Spike nodded. "Lead the way."

Bergstrom received us in the living room of his suite. He waved Katie to a chair and then stood for a minute eying Spike and me. You could see he didn't like us. You could see he wished we were a long way from there. Finally he said:

"I hope we can trust them, Miss Blayne."

"They'll do as they're told and like it," the Duchess said.

"That all depends," Spike said, "on what you tell us to do."

Bergstrom threw open a door to a clothes closet. "You will go in there und stay there und keep quiet," he said crisply. "You will leaf the door oben two or three inches, joost enough so you can see und hear what goes on. You will nod come oudt until you are told to come oudt. All right?"

"All right," Spike agreed.

"I will tell you when to go in. In the meantime, please to sit down und be comfortable."

We sat down diffidently. So help me, I couldn't get the angle. I couldn't make head or tail of the layout. Spike caught my eye, while Bergstrom paced briskly up and down the room, and signalled: "Watch yourself. I don't trust this guy." I didn't trust him either.

After a time the telephone rang. Bergstrom took it up, listened a moment, ordered: "Show him up at once."

Spike started to rise.

"No, no. Nod yet," Bergstrom said irritably. "It iss only Captain Wallis."

Spike sat down again, looking a bit deflated. Bodie Wallis came in after a few minutes. In his quiet blue serge business suit, he didn't look much like a detective.

He nodded to Katie and Bergstrom, grinned at Spike and me.

"You two boys don't miss anything, do you?" he chuckled.

"Not if we can help it," Spike admitted, a bit boastfully.

"I might point out," Katie remarked, "that they are here at my invitation. And anything they see or hear won't be reported in the *Telegram* until it has appeared exclusively in the *Sun*. Right, Mr. Kaylor?"

"Wrong, Miss Blayne!" Spike bristled. "That wasn't part of the bargain."

"It's part of the bargain now."

"Sister, it takes two to make a bargain. And as long as I have two legs and can run to the nearest telephone—"

THE phone buzzed at that instant and Bergstrom raised his hand authoritatively. "Silence, if you please!" He picked up the instrument, said after a moment: "Show her up at once."

He turned and waved us toward the closet. We got up and went in and closed the door to a two-inch crack. Spike jammed his foot against the door and I pulled on the knob, to hold it steady open. Spike, kneeling at the crack, whispered:

"It's a funny one, Pink. You got any ideas?"

"No ideas, but I got a good hunch," I whispered. "Bergstrom is on the spot. With Katie's unwitting help, he's trying to slide out from under."

"Yeah. That's the way I dope it. He's about to pull a fast one. And when it comes down the groove, we'll pole it over the right-field fence for a home run. How's about it?"

"That's oke by me."

We didn't say any more, because Bergstrom had stepped to the hall door and was admitting—Mrs. John Hamlin! She wore black and she looked tense and watchful and cool. Bergstrom was saying:

"Miss Blayne you haff met, I believe. Und this, Mrs. Hamlin iss Mr. Wallis."

Mister Wallis! Well, why not? The whole situation was cockeyed anyway.

"Please to sit down, Mrs. Hamlin," Bergstrom said, helping her to a chair with great solicitude. "We haff wonderful news for you. Your husband, my dear, iss *alive*!"

Mrs. Hamlin sat on the edge of her chair, stiffly, blinking up at him. She said carefully: "I buried my husband this afternoon."

Bergstrom smiled down at her gently, shook his head. "The man you buried vas nod your husband. John iss alive. He vas badly burned in the fire und he sustained a severe injury to the head. He hass been suffering from amnesia ever since. In fact, even now he iss delirious. But the doctor assures me that his chances for pulling through are excellent."

The woman never moved but I could see the last of the color in her cheeks fade out.

Spike whispered: "Amnesia! Did I tell you a fast one was coming down the groove? Amnesia!"

Well, it was easy enough for a couple of smart reporters to dope the play. I saw it this way: When Bergstrom and Hamlin realized their hoax wasn't going over, they got together and devised this amnesia gag. Burned Hamlin with a little acid, probably. Cooked up a good story. "I don't remember anything that happened till I woke up in the hospital." That sort of thing—it's pulled every day.

YES, it was all pretty smart. Just about the type of stuff you'd expect a bright lad like Herr Bergstrom to pull. Having Captain Wallis there on the job was just the right touch. It showed the supreme confidence and egoism of the chemist.

"I feel certain there has been some mistake," Mrs. Hamlin said slowly, gripping the arms of her chair. "I did not see John's body. I did not want to look at it. But I knew, as I sat there staring at the coffin this afternoon, that my husband was in it."

"But," Bergstrom pointed out calmly, "there iss no way you *could* know, Mrs. Hamlin. No way in the world, because—John iss in bed in the next room. Alive. Delirious, seriously burned, very ill—but *alive*!"

He shouted that last word in a way that sent a chill down my spine—even though I'd suspected all along that Hamlin wasn't dead.

And then all at once I was conscious

of a voice from the room on the far side. Someone in there had been talking for quite a while, talking very softly. And now, as Spike and I and the people in the living room listened, the voice grew louder. We could catch a word or two: " Valence of three. . . . calcium chloride . . . neutralized . . ."

What a shock to that woman who was sitting there so white and rigid. A voice, literally, from the dead!

I felt my hair standing on end. I heard Spike's fast and unsteady breathing. I could feel his body shaking with the tension of nerves about to snap. Let me tell you, it was electric!

Bergstrom stepped to the other door. He threw it open. The room was dark but we heard that rasping voice going on monotonously: " . . . carbon union in the aliphatic hydrocarbons has apparently the same effect on the boiling point as two hydrogen atoms. But as I was telling you, Kurt, an acetylenic or triple linkage is associated with a rise in the boiling point. However . . ."

Mrs. Hamlin was on her feet, staring into the darkened room. She screamed: " No! No!"

Bergstrom said patiently, gently: " But yes, Mrs. Hamlin. Surely you recognize John's voice."

The woman caught the arm of a chair, steadied herself. " I tell you," she cried hysterically, " John is *dead!*"

" No. John iss very much alive."

Bergstrom reached inside the door, flipped the switch. The bedroom was bright with light. Looking straight across the living room, I could see a figure in the bed. I caught a glimpse of a head swathed in bandages. I saw lips moving. I heard the deadly monotonous voice going on and on.

" . . . true of the fatty acid series, Kurt, and the corresponding ketones and . . . "

THEN the bedroom door was blocked by the angular figure of Mrs. Hamlin. She swayed against the frame, caught herself, screamed: " No, no, I tell you! It can't be true! He can't be alive! I killed him myself with a hammer. I got into the plant with a key to the back door. I've had it for months. I crept up behind him. I knocked him down. I poured gasoline over him and struck a match. I saw him burn. *I saw him burn!*"

All this in a wild screech that sent icy chills up and down my spine. John Hamlin's voice went on:

" . . . although, Kurt, the correlation of melting point with constitution has not . . ."

The tall woman covered her face with her angular hands She screamed through her bony fingers: " *I tell you I killed him!*"

Then she dropped in a dead faint.

" . . . symmetry of the resulting molecule may exert such a lowering effect that the final result . . ."

" Westoby!" Bergstrom yelled. " Ged oud uf bed und turn that damn' thing off. If I haff to listen to John Hamlin's voice one minute longer I shall haff hysterics!"

Well, after Mrs. Hamlin had snapped out of her faint and Captain Wallis had taken her away, we were all pretty limp. Bergstrom brought out a bottle and some ice, and we all sat down and tried to come back to earth. The chemist remarked finally:

" Fortunately, Hamlin had been helping me with my sount devize. I suppose I haff a mile or two uf film on which his voice iss recorded."

Westoby, who is one of the chemist's lab men, added: " Lucky, too, the film was stored in the physical laboratory in the south wing, which the fire didn't touch."

The Duchess was smiling. "And speaking of luck, wasn't it a break that I brushed against Mrs. Hamlin's coat in her hallway the other night?"

"Huh?" Spike grunted. "What's Mrs. Hamlin's coat got to do with it?"

"It was wet, darling," Katie said pleasantly. "There were beads of rain on the fur collar. And Mrs. Hamlin had told us she hadn't left the house that evening."

"Look here!" Spike snorted. "Do you mean to tell me you had the play doped from the beginning?"

"I had it doped, as you put it, within an hour or two after I brushed against that wet coat."

"Well, Duchess, I got to hand it to you. You're the top." He drained his glass and stood up. "Bergstrom, you've put on a grand show and we'll give your sound recorder a million dollars' worth of publicity. Now I've got to hit a phone with the story. Okay to use yours?"

"No," Bergstrom said steadily. "It iss most decidedly nod okay to use mine."

"Huh?" Spike gasped. "Wha-zat?"

Bergstrom, still smiling, bowed to Katie. And the Duchess rose.

"Mr. Bergstrom has ordered the operator to accept no out-going calls," she informed us. "So if you want to give your office the story, Spike, you'll have to find another telephone."

She moved toward the door, adding over her shoulder: "If you can, and that will be quite a job!"

"If I can!" Spike bellowed, and started after her. "While I've got the use of my legs, I guess—"

Katie threw open the door. Lounging in the hall outside I caught a glimpse of half a dozen of the toughest looking punks I ever saw outside of a penitentiary—or a morning paper's circulation department. Spike stopped in his tracks.

"Keep them here, boys, until midnight," the Duchess ordered cheerfully. "And try not to hurt them too badly if they make a break."

"We won't hurt 'em, Miss Katie," a big bruiser grinned. "Not *much*!"

Well, they didn't hurt us—because we didn't make a break. We stayed there till midnight, drinking very good whisky with Kurt Bergstrom and wondering where we ever got the idea that the Duchess was silly, and dumb, and slow on the pick-up.

Steals Five Truck Loads in Four Years

KLEPTOMANIACS are persons who cannot resist the impulse to steal. Many shoplifters properly belong in this class and, although money may mean nothing to them, they continue to lift things from the stores and homes which they visit. One psychological treatment which has been found to be effective is to get the kleptomaniac interested in collecting as a hobby which enables theft to be avoided.

Some kleptomaniacs are able to steal over a period of years and escape detection. As an example, a kleptomaniac of Woodburn, Oregon, lifted things for four years and the quantity of the stolen merchandise was so great that five truck loads were carried from his home when he was finally caught.

—*John Berry.*

DINAH MASON

Journalism was a popular vocation for female secondary characters in pulp series. Christine Stuart was a reporter in the Candid Camera Kid tales in *Detective Novels*. Diane Elliot was a newshound in *Operator 5*. Betty Dale worked a beat in *Secret Agent X,* as did Doro Kelly in *Captain Zero* and Winnie Bligh in *The Masked Detective*.

And Dinah Mason pounded the typewriter in the Daffy Dill series in *Detective Fiction Weekly*. Dinah is described as "something out of a Petty cartoon only mildly better, and I could go on about her in an unbecoming manner for a long time. In other words, she is in the groove, and her heart belongs to Daffy, although she has persisted in her procrastination of the legal act of holy wedlock. We have been engaged for some time now, and she is weakening daily."

Author Richard Sale, born in 1911, is a former newspaperman. He began writing for *Black Mask, Argosy, Adventure, Blue Book, Dime Mystery Magazine,* and other pulps in the early 1930s. He wrote more than 350 short stories. He went on to script Hollywood movies (*The Oscar* is his work) and eventually switched to directing movies and television programs.

His story "Double Trouble" is reprinted from *DFW*'s October 31, 1936, issue.

Double Trouble

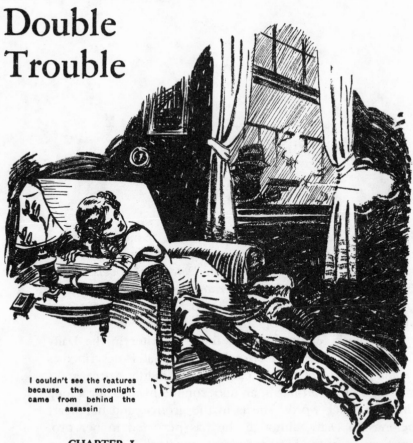

I couldn't see the features because the moonlight came from behind the assassin

CHAPTER I

When an Undertaker Dies—

I WAS sitting at my desk in the darkest corner of the New York *Chronicle* city room and I was taking it easy and trying to appear as inconspicuous as possible, when the telephone jingled a couple of times. I picked it up and said hello and it was the Old Man.

For those who came in late, the Old Man is an anonymous goblin who edits the *Chronicle* which is published by Vincent Kendril, a wealthy and courageous little guy who is too fat in front of himself. As for the Old Man —when I said goblin I meant goblin. He's bald. He hasn't a hair on his head. He always wears a green eyeshade far down over his eyes so that

---

Daffy Dill, Whirlwind Reporter for the New York Chronicle, Risks His Precious Neck in Order to Follow Dinah's Brainstorm Hunch!

I pulled up my revolver, took a
quick bead and fired

DFW
COMPLETE
NOVELETTE

By Richard Sale

you sometimes wonder what he looks
like. He's only about five feet tall and
thin as a Roosevelt dollar and when he
squats behind his big desk under a
green-coned light, he looks like a
gnome. But he hasn't got a gnome's
voice.

"Good morning, Daffy," he said
with heavy sarcasm. "I see by the
clock that you have arrived only two
hours late for work."

I said: "Chief, I'm a hard sleeper.
I sleep so hard my housekeeper thought
I was dead when she found me this

morning. She even called a doctor for the resurrection."

"It worked, apparently," he said drily. "Too bad. . . . Well, since this newspaper pays you the sum of fifty-five dollars a week to garner news for its colyums, would you mind stepping into my office and receiving an assignment."

"Not only a pleasure," I said, "but a duty!"

I hung up and got my hat because the tone of his voice told me I was going sightseeing, and then I went into his private doghouse at the end of the city room and eased myself into a chair.

"Daffy," the Old Man said without looking at me, "did you ever hear of Gregory Cain?"

I sighed. "Did I ever hear of Gertrude Stein? Did I ever hear of George Washington? What a memory you must have! Sure I remember Gregory Cain. When Luke Terk and his boys tried to snatch the brain of Fern Woodruf after Woodruf had died and was being embalmed at the Wagnall Funeral Parlors, I met Cain. He was one of the men who worked on the embalming of Woodruf."

I TOLD you about that case in the Fifty Grand Brain story. Woodruf's brain had been insured for fifty grand because he was such a brilliant scientist. Luke Terk tried to hold the brain for ransom after Woodruf's death.

"Excellent!" said the Old Man. "*My* memory was perfect. I was merely testing yours. What else do you know about Cain?"

"Well," I said, "I learned several things about him later on. I used to go with a girl named Belle Randall before Dinah Mason appeared in the

picture. Belle was a sweet, sensitive kid. She danced at the Tip Top Club before repeal. She married Cain two years ago."

"And?"

"And she began to find out what a guy he was. He beat her. He was a tinhorn gambler who welched every chance he could get. He'd been in the con racket. He should have made blackmail a life's work. Years ago he used to work in a clip joint—a small-time museum on Fourteenth Street. Belle used to tell me all this stuff to get it off her chest. She was afraid of him; that's why she wouldn't leave him."

"Not a very good citizen," the Old Man smiled. "Maybe it's all for the best."

"Maybe what's all for the best?"

"That's he's dead."

I stared. "Dead? You don't say! Happy days are here again. I hope the driver who hit him got away clean."

The Old Man grunted, "Nix, clown. Shot and killed."

"Murder?"

"All the way. . . . Bill Hanley gave you a buzz here around nine o'clock this morning. You weren't in, but I expected you right away so he gave me the tip. Cain was bumped off sometime last night in the Lab of the Wagnall Funeral Parlors on Sixty-sixth and Broadway. He was working on a stiff, doing an embalming job when he caught the slug."

"Verily, verily," I said, "this is a surprise!"

"How about it?" the Old Man asked. "Got any ideas?"

"Oh, scads," I said. "But I wouldn't print one. Whoever killed that rat should get the Congressional Medal. If you expect me to get on the scent you're pixalated. Not Daffy, Chief. That's one killer can go skip rope for all I care. I wouldn't touch him with a ten-foot pole."

"A hell of a citizen you turn out to be," the Old Man snapped. "First story in two weeks with any novelty and you get cold. Don't you see the set-up? It's man bites dog. When an undertaker dies—that's news!"

"How you do go on. . . ." I murmured. "Fact is: I'm adamant. No killer-chasing on this one. If you want me to cover for the sheet, I'll cover. But that's all."

"Well, aren't you hell?" he growled, looking disgusted with me. "Go on. Get out of here. If you're a newspaperman, then I'm Rasputin. Scram!"

"So long, Rasputin," I said. "Catch on?"

He tossed a book at me and I departed.

But that was on the level. I didn't care who had killed Gregory Cain. If you've known a nice girl and you've seen her go all to pieces with a guy you know is an overgrown rodent, you wouldn't care either. As a matter of fact, I was seriously considering the fact that Belle herself might have done the job, and I wasn't going to get her in any jams. . . .

Dinah Mason was outside in the city room. Lest you forget, Dinah is the light of my life, the reason why I pay a medico regularly to stethoscope my heart. She'd turned down two hundred and thirty-one proposals of marriage from me. You remember, she went to Alabam U. and got a burning ambition to do a George Jean Nathan. The Old Man put her on the switchboard as an apprenticeship, and she'd just been promoted to the rank of sob-sister, covering the human side of the news.

She looked a knockout there, dressed in a smart purple suit with her blond hair glistening under her hat. "Hi," she said laconically. "If it isn't Custer's last stand!"

"Out of my way, Garbo," I said. "I'm on my way to look at a corpse."

"Who died?" Dinah said, tugging on my tie.

"Gregory Cain. You know. Belle Randall's ball and chain. Shot last night."

Dinah knew Belle pretty well. The news made her gasp. She whispered. "You don't think Belle—"

"I don't know a thing," I said. "Come on along and I'll take you to lunch afterwards."

"You couldn't pry me loose," she said.

We went downstairs and we caught a cab on West Street and in a few minutes we were heading uptown.

CHAPTER II

The Dead Man

THE Wagnall Funeral Parlors were the best in the city. At least they always seemed to bury the most exclusive corpses. They even said so in their ads. And over the door of their building on Sixty-sixth and Broadway, they had a big neon sign that read: WE BURY THE BEST PEOPLE. MAY WE COUNT ON YOU? You don't mind interment by an undertaker with a sense of humor.

It was quarter of twelve when we reached the spot and got out. I paid off the driver and made a mental note of the sum for the dear old swindle sheet. Then I took Dinah's arm and we went in.

There was a flatfoot inside who immediately collared us. Strange to say, he stood aside and honored our press passes—a minor miracle in itself.

"Where's the *situs criminis?*" I asked.

"The what?" he queried dully.

"Where," Dinah interpreted, "did the holocaust transpire?"

"Oh," he said. "The Lab. Straight back and then down the stairs."

"That's right," I remarked. "The Old Man told me. I should have remembered."

We walked through the resplendent hall of the place which was lined with doors where the dead could lie in state before burial. When we reached the stairs we went on down until we came to a door twice as wide as an ordinary door with LABORATORY printed nicely on it.

We went in without knocking.

I'd been in this Lab before—as I told you—and it hadn't changed much in two years. It was a large room with white enameled tables all around it and plenty of instruments and medications on the tables. In the center of the room, there were mobile operating tables—four of them. Three were empty. One held a body covered with a sheet.

This was the stiff that Cain had been working on when he died.

I saw Lieutenant Bill Hanley first. He was close to the door, talking with two of his scentless bloodhounds, Detectives Babcock and Claghorn. Hanley and I had been together on more criminal cases than we could remember. He gave me a *carte-blanche* in an investigation and sometimes let me in on stuff his bureau didn't know about.

There was an unlighted cigar in the left corner of his mouth and he chewed on it thoughtfully while he talked with his men. His homely red face was lined from eyes to mouth and he looked worried.

"Hello, Poppa!" I called. "How goes it?"

"Hello, Daffy," Hanley replied with a brief flip of his hand. "Hiyah, Dinah. Better come in and shut the door."

Dinah stared at the cigar, fascinated. "Don't you ever light that thing, Poppa?"

Hanley looked at me and grinned. "Why, Daffy," he said, "I thought you once told her that I never smoked a cigar in my life."

Over on the other side of the Lab, there was a closet door. I saw several men moving around in front of this door and I recognized the Buzzard—Dr. Kerr Kyne, chief medical examiner of New York County—and Louis Scanzone who is the official police photographer and can put any picture snatcher on the *Chronicle* to shame.

I collared Poppa Hanley and we went over. "Any leads?" I asked. "The Old Man wants news."

Hanley shook his head. "We got clues," he said. "I figured at first that maybe his wife—Belle Randall—had knocked him off, but she has an alibi and it looks honest. I don't think a woman would have used a forty-five anyhow. Takes pretty good shooting to put one between the eyes with a heavy pistol. Have a look at the stiff and see what you think, Daffy."

"Thankee, my fran." I went over and had a look.

Gregory Cain had been a good-looking devil. Dark and sleek and smooth with oily black hair that was never out of place and a tricky waxed mustachio. He still held his good looks despite the fact that his skin had that yellowish waxiness that only death can paint.

His features seemed much sharper, too, his cheeks having fallen in and his mouth hanging open.

JUST over the eyes and exactly between them, I saw the raised blue welt of the bullet-hole with tiny red flecks of blood all around the rim. The center of the hole was black. There were no powder burns. The pale blue eyes were open and the horror in them was quite plain. His fists were clenched tightly and his upper teeth were bared.

"You ought to see the back of his head," Poppa Hanley grunted. "It just *ain't*. I tell you, Daffy, a .45 can take away a lot of skull on the way out."

I asked: "Find him like this?"

"Naw. He was in the closet. One of Wagnall's other assistants opened the closet this morning and out popped Cain. He fell on his face. We did the turning to get a look. We got the slug, too. Ain't it pretty?"

He handed it to me. It was a steel-jacketed .45 caliber bullet. The nose was slightly turned. "Where'd you find it?"

"Dug it out of the wall opposite the closet. Now if I know anything about ballistics, Cain was standing over there facing the closet. He must have been close to the wall. The killer came in this back door which opens between that wall there and the closet here. The killer fired. Cain fell. Then the killer propped Cain in the closet and beat it out the back door again. . . . What've you found, doc?"

Dr. Kerr Kyne sniffed and looked annoyed. "I," he replied acidly, "have found nothing. I leave the solution of such cases to the doubtful ability of the homicide squad. I can set the time. It's twelve now. I'll put time of death at one o'clock A.M."

Hanley nodded. "I guessed that."

"Anyone hear a shot?" I said.

"No."

"Well, look," I said, "here's monkey business. No powder burns on Cain's forehead. The distance between the closet and the wall is about eight feet. If the killer came in this door, he was only six feet away when he fired. By holding out his arm to aim—it was no hip shot certainly—he cut the distance down to five feet. Why no powder burns?"

"You mean — maybe it had a silencer?"

"Sure."

"Then that would make it an automatic for sure," Hanley replied. "And from the look of that slug, I'd hazard maybe it was an Army Colt. Eh?"

"Very good for you," I said. "You've been eating your spinach, I see. . . . Well, Poppa, it's your headache. I'll be phoning the yarn in."

"Hey," Hanley exclaimed, "I figured maybe you'd have some ideas on this one, Daffy!"

"Not me," I said. "If I knew the killer's name and address, I'd still play dumb. Why, Poppa, don't you realize it yet? This fair city has been done a good turn and now they're employing you to be vindictive about it. I'm surprised!"

I went back and I got Dinah who had avoided the body like she avoids Pasquale, my pet mouse who lives under the left hind leg of my desk, and then we both waved to Hanley and went out.

"A fine guy you are," Hanley growled.

Dinah and I went upstairs.

"Listen, Maestro Dill," Dinah said presently, "I was just thinking."

"Ha-ha," I said sadly.

"Isn't this the place where Have-

lock Pendleton laid in state two weeks
ago? You know who I mean—Pendleton the coal baron who died of infantile."

"That's right," I said. "What
of it?"

"Nothing," Dinah sighed. "Only,
wouldn't it have been a swell story if
Cain had been killed trying to stop a
pair of body-snatchers from hoisting
Pendleton's body and holding it for a
piece of the coal baron's estate?"

I shook my head. "What are you
asking for?"

"Double trouble," Dinah said. "I
get good ideas."

"You get pipe dreams," I said. "I
don't know what brand of opium
you've been inhaling, but I do know
that it's a shame 'n' pity the way crime
has ruined a perfectly good college
education. You ought to hear yourself. Such language, Garbo, such
language!"

Dinah threw up her hands. "You
can't win. So let's eat."

CHAPTER III

Sybl Pendleton's Offer

IT was after midnight that same
night when the pulchritudinous
Dinah and I trekked into the resplendent reaches of the famed Hideaway Club on Broadway in the heart
of the Roaring Forties, all set for a
go at old-fashions and lilting fan-
dangos.

Since neither of us had been to the
Hideaway for a month or so, it was
like old home week. The place was
owned and operated by Bill Latham—
as nice a guy as ever donated free
drinks on the house. Since I'd practically lived in the Hideaway once upon
a time, Latham and I were like that.
As for the old-fashions I just

mentioned, they were thrown together
by a barkeep named Shorty McInnis
who was an Irish ex-boxer with a grin
that cut his red face in half. When it
came to highballs and cocktails, the
Rialto had to admit that McInnis's
hand had never lost its touch. He was
a miracle-maker.

This night, after the theater crowds
had all piled into the club, it was alive
with voices and music and clinking
glasses. Dinah and I had telephoned
for reservations and when we got
there, who should do the greeting at
the door but Latham himself.

"Daffy Dill?" Latham exclaimed.
"It does this old heart good to see you
again!"

"Stop grinning," I said. "You look
like a Siamese cat. I know the coins
are clinking in the cash register but
can't you be more subtle about it?"

"He sure is hopped up," said Dinah.

"I'm just glad to see you," Latham
replied, hitting my back. "And to
show you how much I've missed you,
anything you have tonight is on the
house!"

"On the house, you said. Not on
the cuff?"

"That's it!"

"Good. Send over a case of champagne," I said. "I always did like some
one else to pay for my delicious de-
bauchery."

"With pretzels," said Dinah.

We muscled our way across the
dance floor and we went up through
the rising tiers around it to the booth
which we had reserved. We waved to
Shorty McInnis on the way. He looked
like he was being worked to death but
he waved in reply and called that he
wanted to see me later.

We sat down and lighted cigarettes
and pretty soon Latham arrives followed by a waiter who had champagne.

Latham sat down with us and had a drink. He said, " I see by the *Chronicle* this afternoon that you covered the Cain killing."

I told him I had.

" I *know* you did," Latham said. "They're still giving you by-lines. Why I don't know. My gosh, Daffy, where are the days when we used to have a little excitement around this good old street?"

" I'm getting older and seriouser," I grinned.

" The hell you are. You're getting to be a sissy. Is there anything new on the Cain thing?"

" I wouldn't know."

LATHAM leaned over close to me. " Well I would. I could name you four guys who might have done that job. Four guys that Cain welched on. He owed twenty-two grand. Did you know that?"

I shrugged. " Makes no dif. Not interested."

" Oh." Latham regarded me owlishly. " You've got your reasons, I suppose. By the way—a dame was asking for you. I didn't know you were getting up into the four hundred."

" Meaning what?" Dinah asked. " Who is the dame and what's her business with Daffy?"

" Why, look at the green in her eye!" I exclaimed. " Garbo, can it be that you care?"

" What about it, Bill?" Dinah persisted, ignoring me completely.

" It's Sybl Pendleton," Latham said, frowning at Dinah. " She's the daughter of the coal baron they buried last week."

" Two weeks ago," Dinah said.

" If you say so. Anyway, she's worth about five million bucks roughly. You see, when old man Pendleton cashed in,

he split the family fortune four ways. Sybl got five; her brother Val got five; her uncle Stephen got five; and Stephen's daughter, Rita, got five. That makes twenty million. Nice mazuma, huh?"

I asked: " Where'd you get all this stuff?"

" In the paper, dope. The will's been probated. If you read your own rag once in awhile, you'd know."

Dinah squinted. " Is this Sybl goodlooking?"

Latham snapped his fingers. " Knockout!"

" What'd she want with Daffy?"

" I don't know. She's around somewhere. I told her I'd let her know— wait a second! Here she comes now! The tall dark dame with the ivory satin gown!"

I saw her. She *was* a knockout. She was tall and willowy with a thin, fine face, and she had dark hair that looked better than the five million fish she now owned. There was a man with her, a big broad blond guy who looked like a football player and had a pleasant grin on his face. His eyes sat too close together and he didn't have much of a brow, but he looked hot in tails.

I nudged Latham. " Who's the man?"

" I dunno," Latham answered, peering. " Oh, yeah—the same one. She's been hitting the Hideaway regularly with him. Before her old man died. This is the first time they've been out since the funeral."

" Who is he?"

" Harry McFee," said Latham. " Used to be a stunt man in Hollywood but he got banged up in an airplane accident and quit the racket. Here they are."

They reached us and Sybl immediately said, " Hello again, Mr. Latham.

I wondered if Daffy Dill had arrived yet?"

I got up and said: "That's my name."

"The *Chronicle's* claim to fame," Dinah cracked.

"How do you do?" Sybl said nicely. "I'm Sybl Pendleton. I've been wanting to talk with you. This is Mr. Mc-Fee."

"And this is Miss Mason," I said. "Have a seat, Miss Pendleton. What can I do for you?"

Sybl sat down. "It's rather private. Run along, Harry, like a good boy. You know the story anyhow."

"I'll hit out too," Latham said and he left.

I whispered to Dinah, "Scram, Evangeline."

"She sees you alone over my lifeless form," Dinah said. "I stay or else. Besides, I'm curious."

SYBL was eyeing Dinah warily, so I explained: "You can say anything you want in front of Miss Mason. She and I are practically married and she'd only wheedle it out of me later on. Go ahead."

"Well . . ."

Dinah smiled at her disarmingly. "Go ahead, Miss Pendleton. I'm as safe and sane as the Fourth of July. And I work on the same paper as Daffy anyhow."

"Oh, please!" Sybl cried suddenly. "this is not for publication! In fact my whole purpose in contacting you is to avert very unpleasant notoriety."

"Off the record it is then," I said, nudging Dinah to be still. "Let's hear the dilemma."

"My father is—" she paused, "was, I mean, Havelock Pendleton, as you may know. He passed away only recently. He'd been quite ill from in-

fantile paralysis for the past year and we had expected his death. He was buried from the Wagnall Parlors two weeks ago in Woodlawn Cemetery."

Dinah looked at me and frowned.

"Now," Sybl continued, "my uncle, Stephen Pendleton—who was very close to my father—is very suspicious concerning my father's death."

I asked: "How do you mean?"

Sybl replied: "Uncle Stephen believes that father did not die naturally." Her voice was very low and husky.

"You mean your uncle believes that your father was murdered."

"Yes, to put it bluntly."

Dinah nervously lighted a cigarette and leaned forward tensely, puffing on it. I said to Sybl: "Keep talking."

"Uncle Steve is quite set upon an exhumation of father's body," Sybl explained quietly. "He wants a thorough autopsy. I wonder if you can appreciate the publicity that will cause when he sees the District Attorney. . . . Well, I don't want such publicity. At least—not without some facts."

"So?"

"That's why I wanted to see you. I'll pay you a thousand dollars if you'll look into my father's death and find out what happened to him one way or the other. If you think there was foul play, then we'll exhume. If not, we'll drop the whole business. Uncle Steve is quite agreed that if you think things are all right, he'll be satisfied."

I took a deep breath. "What makes your uncle think something isn't kosher?"

Sybl shrugged. "Motives, I expect. I can't see them myself, but he seems to think that Val—my brother—wanted his inheritance very badly. Val gambles some. Then, too, he knows very well that my father was not at all in accord with Rita—Steve's own daughter. Rita wanted to marry a boy named Frank Fisher. Father said he would cut her off if she did. He didn't like Frank Fisher. The boy was too independent. Perhaps Uncle Steve has a motive for me, too. I don't know—"

"All right," I said suddenly. "I'll cover for a thousand dollars payable when I come to you and say it's one thing or another. Check?"

Sybl smiled. "Double-check," she said. She rose and extended her hand. "And thanks very much for being a good sport. . . ." Turning, she called, "Harry! Oh, Harry . . ." and she went off to rejoin her escort.

Dinah stared after her morosely. "If her father was bumped," she said, "that dame did it herself. She's too beautiful."

"Cut it out," I said. "That's no motive."

"I know it," Dinah said. "But with those looks and five million besides, even a cluck like you isn't safe." She stared at me. "Remember what I said about double trouble? I've got a hunch I wasn't wrong. It wouldn't make me flick an eyelash if you found out that Gregory Cain's murder had plenty to do with this Pendleton fracas."

"All right," I said, imitating Major Bowes. "Let's dance. . . ."

CHAPTER IV

The Shadow in the Window

I TOOK Dinah home around two-thirty A.M. and Bill Latham was glad to see us go since we'd nearly eaten him out of house and home.

Then I took a cab back to West Forty-fifth Street where I dwell in the Castle which is a three-room apartment on the fourth and top floor of an old brownstone house. It isn't much but I call it home.

When I unlocked the door and stepped into my place the telephone was ringing madly.

I ran over to it and picked up and said: "Hello?"

"Daffy?"

It was Dinah. She sounded terrified. I never heard her voice so hoarse and taut with fright.

"What's the matter, Angel-Eyes?"

"For gosh' sake, darling—"

"Talk, damn it!"

"Belle Randall is here—she just came—she's got a load on her mind that she wants to— Daffy, listen—"

"For Pete's sake, Dinah," I snapped, "skip the hysterics and get to the point! What's wrong?"

"Somebody followed her," Dinah said hollowly. "Somebody followed her and fired at her! She's got a crease on her left arm that's bleeding! Somebody thinks she knows too much about Greg Cain's killing and now—hurry up, Daffy, because—"

"Dinah," I said evenly when she stopped talking. "Dinah—listen."

"Can't talk," she whispered. "Someone is on the roof. Heard 'em walking across it. *I'm scared!*"

"Get this. Lock doors and windows and get under cover. Lights out. I'm on the way."

"Hurry, hurry . . . !"

I hung up.

I went to my desk and unlocked it and I took out the Smith and Wesson .32 caliber revolver which I had there and I made sure that each chamber was primed to blow. Then I slipped it into my jeans and went downstairs like a bat out of hell.

I couldn't find a cab anywhere on Forty-Fifth Street and I was frantic. I ran down to Broadway and I grabbed a hack there. Shouting Dinah's address —which is Central Park West—I sat back, studded with cold sweat, while the driver gave his can the gun.

It was pretty late and there was no traffic at all. At first I thought I'd have trouble with the driver but I waved a fin under his nose and he jumped at the chance to earn it.

It was two-forty A.M. when he squealed to a stop in front of Dinah's apartment.

I threw the five spot at him and I leaped out of the car. In the vestibule I buzzed Dinah's bell one long, two short, our own signal, and she promptly let me in downstairs. She must have been sitting by the clicker.

The automatic self-operating elevator was waiting conveniently on the main floor. I pressed the button for the sixth—and top—floor and went up.

When I got out upstairs, the hall looked gloomy. There was only one forty-watt light glowing and it cast dark shadows across the silence.

When I got to Dinah's door, it was open a crack and her right eye peered out at me.

" Garbo?"

" Shh!" she said in a raucous whisper. " Ease in and keep quiet. Things are happening. Darling, I'm certainly glad to see you for once in my life!"

I eased in. Dinah closed the door behind me and locked it. Her apartment was dark. Moonlight cast a square patch on the rug to the left side of the window in her living room.

I asked: " Is Belle Randall okay?"

Belle answered for herself. She was across the room, sitting in a chair in pitch blackness. I recognized her tight contralto at once. " I'm all right, Daffy. I'm here."

" Good. What's new?"

" Shh!" Dinah said again. " Watch the window. Some one came down the ladder from the roof. Out on the fire-

escape now. Been peering around the left side, waiting. I've died from a bullet in the heart ten times in the last fifteen minutes. Ah me, I'll never be my old self again... Watch...."

I DIDN'T see anything. I stared at the moonlight patch instead. The slightest movement outside would make a spot in the patch. I said, " All right, keep talking. What happened to Belle?"

" I'll tell you," Belle replied softly from the other side of the room. " It must have been near two o'clock and I'd been sitting around in the apartment. I had a bad case of jitters, Daffy, because I knew why Greg had been murdered. I got to thinking about it until finally I said to myself I had to tell some one. . . . So I called Dinah and I asked her if I could come over and she said yes."

" Go on."

" No sooner had I put down the phone than I heard the sound of a window opening in my bedroom. I went in to see what it was. A man stepped across the sill and fired a pistol at me. Just one shot. He nicked my arm. I screamed and ran—"

" Wait a minute!" Dinah gasped. " There it is—the shadow at the—"

I had seen it too. A round pock crept into the moonlight patch upon the floor, black and grotesque as it increased in size.

I snapped up my eyes at the window. Half a man's face was there. I couldn't see the features because the moonlight came from behind it, silhouetting it against the glass pane.

In another instant a big pistol was also there with a stubby cylinder perched on the end of the barrel.

I shoved Dinah. " Hit the floor!"

She dove, calling to Belle to lay low

at the same time. I pulled up my revolver and took a quick bead on the side of the pistol's gleaming barrel and I fired.

The gun made an awful racket and for a second there was too much smoke to see what had happened and I swore to myself I'd get smokeless powder slugs for that gun next time. But to make sure I snapped: " Stand still, sport, the gun's on your skull!"

I'd missed his pistol. I knew that the next second when I saw the stab of orange flame in the darkness, and heard a hot bullet slap the wall at the left of me.

I'd forgotten one thing. He couldn't hear me through the locked window. He'd thought it was gunfight.

Next thing I knew, he was gone. No more shadow in the window nor on the floor.

I sprang to the window and unlocked and climbed out on the fire-escape.

Two more shots. The steel-latticed floor of the fire-escape seemed to jerk under the impact of those bullets and after that, the slugs went off in a loud whining richochet and I got an idea that they were steel-jacketed. He'd fired straight down at me from the roof.

I didn't even see him then. I stuck my rod over my head and pulled the trigger four times. It made a lot of noise and sent up a couple of sky-rocket bullets which probably fell in the Hudson River, but it did the trick.

He lammed. He wasn't taking any chances on being hit by anything.

When I got to the roof he had disappeared entirely. I gave the roof the once-over lightly and cautiously but it was easy to see he'd probably hit out across the roof of the house next door and maybe the one after that. They were all on the same level.

I climbed down the ladder and went back into the apartment.

" Daffy," Dinah called, " are you hurt?"

" I'm okay," I said, frowning. " He took a powder. Good one too. He's gone...." I turned around and snapped on the lights. Belle had returned to her chair. I could see her arm was bandaged from the wound which she'd gotten earlier. She looked pretty changed. Her youth seemed to have ebbed out of her and while she still had her looks, her blond hair was wispy and her face looked haggard. Greg Cain had taken it out of her and no error.

" Hello, Daffy," she said tiredly. " Thanks for everything."

"H ELLO, Belle," I said. " Sorry there's no time for sweet amenities, but get this. Somebody probably heard those shots and telephoned the police. They'll be here quicker than an income tax collector. I'm going to turn you over to them—"

" Listen, you dope," Dinah said, " you can't do that to—"

" Cut it out," I snapped. " Emote in pictures. I know what I'm doing. Jail's the only place where Belle'll be safe. Some one's trying to plug her. Why not stick her in a calaboose?" I wheeled around. " But before you go, Belle, give."

Belle scowled. " Give?"

" That guy tried to knock you off. Why? Because he killed Greg Cain. And you know why he killed Greg Cain. And because you know _who_ he is! Come across."

" Daffy, please," Belle said quickly. " You're right and you're wrong. I know why Greg was killed. But I don't know who killed him even if the killer thinks I do."

"No riddles, Belle. You sound like an enigma. Why was Greg murdered?"

"Because he was blackmailing some one," she said.

"Who?"

"I don't know, I don't know," she cried. "Don't you see? If I knew I could tell who killed him—who tried to kill me—but Greg never told me."

"What did he tell you?" I asked.

"He came home a little over two weeks ago," Belle replied, "and he was a little drunk. He kissed me and then he slapped me and he said that we were in the money. 'Belle,' he said, 'what do you think the cops would say if they knew that Havelock Pendleton had been murdered?' I asked him what he meant. He told me that he had embalmed Pendleton's body and that he had discovered that Pendleton had been poisoned. Then he said he knew who had done it and that he was going to get plenty for his silence and that if I breathed a word, he'd kill me. . . . That's all, Daffy, and that's the truth."

"It's enough," I said.

Dinah's eyes were shining. "Golly, Adonis," she breathed. "How about changing your mind? You weren't interested in who killed Greg Cain, but now—"

"I've changed my mind," I said thoughtfully. I put my gun away. "It's a matter of self-defense now. That guy—whoever he is—will figure we three all know him now. That calls for action. . . . Did you say double trouble, Dinah?"

"I said double trouble," Dinah said. "I didn't mean to be taken up on it so doggoned quick."

Down in the street, a siren was howling.

I sighed.

"Here comes your homicide squad," Dinah said.

"Let me do the chatting," I said.

I spent the rest of the night explaining what had happened to Poppa Hanley. I didn't get home until quarter of five and even then I didn't sleep.

CHAPTER V

The Missing Pistol

THE *Chronicle* is an afternoon paper. It hits the newsstands at 12:30 P.M. That left me plenty of time to catch up on sleep and still get to the office to write the inside story of Gregory Cain's death. I didn't spare anything because if worst came to worst, I wanted Cain's killer after me and not after Belle or Dinah.

I wrote a pretty good yarn. I told about the A.M. attack, about the fact that Cain had been blackmailing an unknown, and I hit a climax when I wrote that Havelock Pendleton had been murdered.

The Old Man whistled when he read it. "Jeepers creepers, Daffy," he said, startled out of his usual diffidence, "I hope you know whereof you write."

"Scared?" I said

"Not me," he said. "It's good stuff—the best you've done in many a blue moon. But there's criminal libel in it and I haven't any particular desire to spend some time in the local jug."

"Listen, boss," I said, "there won't be any criminal libel suit in this job. At least not one that can't be beaten. Gregory Cain was blackmailing the murderer of Havelock Pendleton. That—in short and long—is the fact. And if I don't have an exhumation of Pendleton's body by tonight, you can watch me eat my hat."

"I'd love to," grinned the Old Man. "What's on your mind now?"

"I want to see Poppa Hanley," I said, "and find out if there's anything new. And then I'm going to run up to the Pendleton place and have a long talk with Stephen Pendleton. He suspected that something was out of focus."

"I'll know where to reach you," the Old Man said. "Keep going the way you are and I'll begin to think you have the makings once more."

"Phooey to you from me," and I went out.

Dinah was at her desk typing an eye-witness story of the same attack when I came up and booed at her behind her back. She nearly left her clothes. "Goshamighty!" she breathed, casting venomous looks down my throat. "A nice way to say good morning. Daffy, I was so scared after you left last night. What am I going to do tonight? Suppose Killer Joe comes back for *my* scalp? I know Belle is safe. She's in jail. But how about me?"

"You might marry me this afternoon," I said. "Then you could stay at my house tonight."

"What a price to pay!" Dinah said, shaking her head and tsk-tsking. "If you don't mind I'll risk my life. Where bound, lunatic?"

"Homicide bureau," I said, "to see what I can see."

I walked over to Centre Street and since it was only a couple of blocks from the *Chronicle* building, I reached it in nothing flat. I went upstairs to the offices of the homicide bureau and found Poppa Hanley there, chewing on his cigar—it might have been the same one—and looking very chipper and cheerful.

"Hi-ho, Poppa," I said. "What's new?"

"I was just thinking of you," Hanley replied gruffly. "I wondered when you'd blow in. . . . Well, we matched those slugs we got outa Dinah's wall with the slug we got outa Gregory Cain."

"And—?"

"Same rod. You knew that. Why ask?" Hanley grunted and stared at his desk. "You see the set-up, don't you? The killer thinks Belle knows who he is. If we could only keep him coming. I found out something else. Gregory Cain used to work in a clip museum joint on Fourteenth Street. Eight years ago."

I said, "I knew that."

"Sure, sure, but you didn't know this. Another guy worked with him. They roomed together. This other guy's name was Harry McFee. And he's *in* town!"

"Harry McFee?" I said thoughtfully. "Hell, Poppa, I met that man last night!"

"You did?" Hanley said. "Where?"

"At the Hideaway Club. He was with Sybl Pendleton."

"With Sybl Pendleton!" Hanley snapped. "What is this? . . . Lemme think, lemme think. You figure we could locate him?"

"Easily."

"Good. All I want from him is one answer. When I ask him if he knew Gregory Cain and he says he never heard of him, by God, we'll have nabbed the right guy!"

"You sound like a cop," I said. "All right, let's go and see."

JUST then the telephone rang and Poppa answered it and looked at me. "It's for you," he said. "The Old Man."

I took the handset and said hello.

"Get back here," the Old Man said.

" Hell and thunder's broken loose. Val Pendleton just got a load of your story on the streets and he's out for your neck."

" I'll be right over."

Poppa Hanley went with me. We found Valentine Pendleton in the Old Man's doghouse. He didn't shake hands with us. He looked mad. Tall and wiry, slicked blond hair, a receding chin, prominent buck teeth. " I want to see you alone," he said to me. " You're the chap who wrote that story?"

" I am."

" I want to talk with you alone."

The Old Man got up without a word and took Hanley by the arm and the two of them walked out.

Val Pendleton sat down and stared at me coldly, his lip curling into a faint leer. " I suppose you know I could have you jailed for criminal libel on my father's name," he said. " A nice stretch too. You sensationalists deserve such treatment."

" Oh, I dunno," I said casually, watching him.

" However," he went on, " I don't want the publicity. I want a retraction from you."

" You won't get it," I said.

" I want a prominent retraction in cold print," he said. " A full retraction."

" Veddy sorry," I said. " No can do."

He leaned forward and looked at me pleadingly. " Now listen, Dill, you've got brains, you're clever, and you know a good thing when you see one. I'll pay you two grand to print a retraction and drop that angle overboard."

I smiled. " Know what I think, sport? I think you're a phony. In the first place, you know that I know that

your father *was* murdered. Why would you be willing to pay me two thousand smackers when you could do it legally for nothing? You see? Publicity, hell! You know that if you brought suit and had me jugged, it would be the best publicity in the world. It would prove that your father died naturally. . . . But you won't bring suit. You're like the others in your family—your uncle excepted. Everybody trying to hush it up. Why?"

He stared at me but didn't say anything.

" Maybe because you bumped off your father yourself," I said. " You know how it is—you gamble—you go in the hole—you need mazuma—maybe the old man's cut you down to a mere pittance—you're desperate—"

" Cut that!" Val Pendleton snapped. " Cut that!"

" Sure," I said. " Jimmy LaVerne —for instance—he owns the Three Penny Club which is the smartest gambling house in town and while Jimmy LaVerne is a white guy and a square gambler, he doesn't like welchers, and if you happened to welch on him—"

Val Pendleton was white. My crack about Jimmy LaVerne had been in the dark but I saw the guess was red hot. Suddenly, Pendleton came out of his chair and at me with his arms swinging. He was wide open and he didn't have enough *umph* to crack a peanut with his fists. It was a shame to do it but I didn't like him at all.

I jabbed him gently behind the ear and rocked him onto the floor.

Then I went out to where the Old Man and Poppa Hanley were waiting. I said: " Now I've committed assault and battery and mayhem and what not. He swung on me and missed. I swung back."

"You didn't miss," Hanley grinned. "Good."

"I didn't like him either," said the Old Man. "You go along with Hanley, Daffy. There'll be no retractions on that story. I think you've got ze goods."

So Poppa Hanley and I went downstairs and got into his prowl car and headed uptown.

The Pendleton home was located on Riverside Drive near Seventh-ninth Street. It was a granite three-story house of the old régime, wedged tightly in between two gigantic new apartment houses.

WE'D no sooner gotten out of the prowl car when a red and black roadster pulled up behind us and Sybl Pendleton and Harry McFee got out of it and approached us.

"Hello!" Sybl called. "This is a surprise! Harry and I were downtown for lunch and we just returned. When I saw you—have you any news?"

"Hello," McFee said, with a flip of his hand. He grinned at us cockily.

"Wait a minute," Poppa Hanley said to me in a low voice. "This Harry ginzo—is he McFee?"

"He is," I said. "But steer clear until after we see Stephen Pendleton...." To Sybl, I said, "Your offer is null and void, Miss Pendleton."

"Oh?"

"I didn't have to do any sleuthing at all to find out that your father had been murdered. I don't want the money."

Sybl looked at me strangely, her tongue playing across her mouth, while McFee said, "Say, are you serious? Did you really find—?"

"Yeah," Poppa Hanley said.

"Who is this?" McFee asked, putting his arm around the girl.

"My name's Hanley," Poppa replied evenly. "I'm head of the homicide squad of this city."

There was a short silence. Then I spoke up. "I want to see your uncle, Miss Pendleton. We want an exhumation. If he doesn't consent, then the D. A.'s office will have to do it on their own. Right, Poppa?"

"Right, Daffy."

"C-come in," Sybl faltered. "I'll see—if he's home."

We went in. The house, richly furnished, looked desolate somehow. There wasn't a soul around. Sybl called and when there was no reply, she said to McFee, "Run up and see if Uncle Steve's in his room, Harry."

"Which is his room?" McFee asked, frowning.

"Third from the top of the stair," she said. "Hurry and tell him these gentlemen wish to speak with him."

McFee nodded, vaguely disturbed by her pallor. He left the room and we could hear his footsteps creaking up the staircase in the hall.

As soon as McFee was out of sight, Poppa Hanley wheeled on Sybl Pendleton and asked brusquely, "Did your old—did your father have a gun?"

"Yes," Sybl replied. "He kept one in his desk drawer upstairs. I've seen it many times. After he died, we put it in the desk here." She pointed to a tall mahogany desk which sat in a corner of the living-room.

"Let's see it."

Sybl rose and went to the desk and opened the first drawer. From it she extracted a .25 caliber pearl-handled revolver which she handed to Hanley. Poppa was disappointed of course. He didn't care a lick about this gun. He weighed it in his hand and asked: "Was your father ever in the Army?"

"No," said Sybl. "But Uncle Steve

was. He saw service in France. He was a captain."

" Did he have a gun?"

" Yes—a big pistol—a forty-five he used to tell us. But it isn't around. It's been missing for over two weeks."

" Eureka!" Hanley roared. " I knew it!"

Simultaneously, Harry McFee came tearing down the stairs and burst into the room. His face was scarlet with excitement and exertion and he was panting like a dog.

" Hey!" he gasped, grabbing at the doorway to steady himself. " Steve Pendleton's dead!"

Hanley reached out, grabbed McFee, jerked the man toward him. " Dead? Dead, you say?"

"*Murdered!*" McFee breathed, terrified. " His head—shot—"

Poppa Hanley and I were upstairs in zero flat.

CHAPTER VI

Questions and Answers

STEPHEN PENDLETON would never be deader. He was lying on the floor of his room, face down. It looked as though he had just leaped up from his chair when the bullet caught him. The body was still warm, the blood still fresh. The back of his head had been torn out and the sight wasn't pretty. Poppa closed the door and locked it so that Sybl couldn't get in to see.

We followed the line of the bullet, estimating by Pendleton's height, and we finally found the hole in the wall behind the chair where the bullet had hit after passing through the dead man's head.

Poppa Hanley found a paper knife and he used it to excavate that wall. It took a long time but he finally caught the bullet in his hand. It had been banged up badly, but there it was. A .45 slug, steel-jacketed.

We locked the room and went downstairs and after Poppa phoned for the M.E., I called the *Chronicle* and spilled the story to the Old Man who squeaked like a ghoul at the news beat and promptly made generous offers—which he later took back or forgot about—about the raising of my salary.

Then Hanley got the telephone again. He called the District Attorney's office and when he got the D. A. — who was Fighting Tom O'Brien, Fusion-elect—he talked. " I want an exhumation order for Havelock Pendleton," he roared. " I know what I'm doing, Tom, and I've got the dope. A guy was just kicked in here because he wanted an exhumation too. Get the papers over to my office and I'll detail Claghorn and Babcock to handle the job. I want that body in the morgue by nightfall. How about it?"

Tom O'Brien knew Poppa Hanley who *never* went off half-cocked. He okayed the exhumation order.

Then we went into the living room. Hanley started right in. " All right, you two, where have you been in the last two hours?"

They'd been down to Schrafft's for luncheon. They had left the house at twelve. It was now two. It was a straight alibi. No phony. We could tell.

" Haven't you got servants here?" Hanley asked.

" Yes," Sybl said. " There's Walter, the butler. I'll call him."

She brought the butler from his room and Hanley went to work on the poor guy.

" Where's everybody in this crazy house?" He looked like a lion and

Walter—who was a diminutive guy—trembled in his boots. " Was anyone besides yourself here from twelve to two?"

" Y-yes, s-s-sir," Walter faltered. " That is, Mr. Stephen was here and should still be here. Miss Rita—his daughter you understand—was here until about twelve-thirty. Then Mr. Frank Fisher arrived and they went upstairs together.

" About ten minutes later, I saw them go out the back door. They seemed very excited. They had valises and they went to the garages in the back and took the yellow Daimler roadster and drove out. They were in a great hurry. . . ."

Hanley snapped his fingers. He grabbed Sybl and pulled her into the hall where the telephone was located. Then he called the Telegraph Bureau and said, " Hello, Mac? I want this on the air and over the teletype. Hear me? . . . Get it right. It's murder. Want these two people held. May be dangerous. Don't know. Approach with caution. First, Rita Pendleton—" and then with Sybl's aid, he gave a tight description of the girl and followed it with, " Frank Fisher, age thirty, hair brown, eyes blue, height six feet, small circular scar under left eye . . ." and so forth, Sybl still supplying the details. He wound up with a description of the car.

They came back into the living room. Hanley stared at McFee and then asked, " I've been meaning to slip you a question or two, mister."

McFee wiped his face with a handkerchief. " Gladly, officer. If you'll—"

" Ever hear of a guy named Gregory Cain?"

" Ever hear of him?" McFee cried. " I roomed with him for a year and a half! We used to work together in a little museum down on Fourteenth Street. Greg had a bunch of trained snakes in a pit and he'd tease them and show them off for the customers. I helped him. Sometimes he'd put a rat in with a rattler and—"

" That's enough," Hanley said, his face falling. " You know he's dead?"

" I read about it in the papers," McFee replied.

Hanley turned to Sybl. " Where did you first meet Mr. McFee?"

" In Hollywood," she said. " I spent four months out in Brentwood this spring and I met Harry at Epic Studios one afternoon."

McFEE was trembling. " Why—why these questions, officer? You act as though you thought I might have—"

" Sure. I was thinking that."

" I didn't do anything," McFee gasped. " Gee—" He looked funny, such a big guy with such a bad case of jitters. Poppa Hanley had to smile. He turned to me. " Daffy, I figure it's over. Looks pretty plain to me. Havelock Pendleton said he'd disinherit Rita Pendleton if she married Frank Fisher. When he said that, Rita was probably already married to Fisher. So Fisher—who was coming into five million through his wife—bumped off the old man. Then Greg Cain, who embalmed the old man, learned of the murder by examining Pendleton's body, and he got an idea that Fisher had done it. He blackmailed Fisher and Fisher murdered him. Then Steve Pendleton was pushing for an exhumation. So Fisher bumped him, too, got his wife, Rita, and they both took it on the lam."

" It sounds good," I said. " But how did Fisher kill Havelock Pendleton without the family medico getting wise.... Who *is* the family medico, Miss Pendleton?"

"Dr. Karl Riker," she said.

I asked for Riker's telephone number and when she gave it to me, Hanley and I went out into the hall and I called the doctor. Hanley winked at me, so I knew I had a free rein. When Dr. Riker answered, I said, "Hello? My name is Holmes — homicide bureau."

"Yes?" Dr. Riker said precisely and warily.

"I'm investigating the Pendleton case."

"I didn't know there *was* a Pendleton case," Dr. Riker said stiffly, "except for some hair-brained news story I just read, which is insipid."

"Then it may interest you to know," I said, "that Stephen Pendleton was shot and killed this afternoon because he thought that his brother had been murdered and wanted an investigation. How do you like them berries?"

Dr. Riker didn't say anything.

I asked, "Now what was your diagnosis of the cause of death?"

"Havelock had been suffering from progressive infantile paralysis for two years," Dr. Riker replied. "He'd been bed-ridden the entire time. When I found him that morning recently, he had strangled from paralysis of the respiratory centers. He couldn't breathe. It was the same paralysis, no doubt. Reached his lungs and heart and finished him."

"No post-mortem?"

"No. . . . I'm very sorry about Stephen."

"Okay, doc. I hope you're telling the truth. We're exhuming Havelock Pendleton. If it turns out—well you know. Goodby practice for you." I hung up.

"Kind of a queer bird," I said when we returned to the living-room. "Sounds screwy."

"I've always thought so," McFee said. "He's got a regular Loki den over at his place. Experiments with a lot of snake poisons, trying to make a serum or something for cancer and tuberculosis from them."

"That is very interesting," I said, staring hard. "Yes, indeed."

Outside, a siren filled the street, and I gathered that Poppa Hanley's faithful minions of the law had arrived on the scene at last. I told Poppa, "I got things to do," and with a brief wave of the fist, I left and took a cab downtown to the *Chronicle* building.

CHAPTER VII

A Body, a Verdict, a Confession

"VAL PENDLETON," the Old Man said to me, "did not like that jab in the jaw which you kindly donated to his cause."

"It wasn't exactly a jab," I said modestly. "It was kind of a Facisti salute with a fist on the end of it. Besides, he was a babe in the wood."

"Hmm!" The Old Man studied me. "And just suppose Val Pendleton is the nassy man who's been killing people? Suppose he's the nassy man with the big gun? How do you feel now?"

"If Val is Killer Joe," I said, "and tried or did shoot me because I had a better right hand than he did, why he'd give himself away, don't you see?"

The Old Man sighed. "You mean, if we find your lifeless young body perched on some stray ashcan, then we have sure proof that Val did the job? If you find any consolation in that, it's all right with me.... What's new?"

"The D. A.'s exhuming," I said. "Rita Pendleton— dead man's daughter—has flown the roost with friend F. Fisher. Hanley thinks they did the whole job—at least Fisher did. Secret marriage and all that. It's hot. I think he can give Fisher the works on it."

" What do you think?"

" About Rita and Fisher? Phooey. I can't see a thing that ties them up except theory. No one knows whether they're married or not and so forth. As a matter of fact, if they *are* married, they were probably married after Havelock's death."

" Yeah," said the Old Man, " but suppose Fisher knocked off Havelock so that he could marry Rita—as an heiress."

" Well," I said, " I'll tell you. Right now I have no facts to show that Gregory Cain ever heard of or knew Frank Fisher. But get this : Cain knew Harry McFee very well. Roomed and worked with him years ago."

" Ah !"

" And Cain had trucking with Val Pendleton. Val owed Cain money at the time of Havelock's death."

The Old Man gasped. " That's *news.* Where did you find that out?"

" I stopped in at Jimmy LaVerne's Three Penny Club and had a talk with Jimmy on the way down here. Before Havelock Pendleton died, Cain came to Jimmy and gave Jimmy an I.O.U. for five grand. It was Val's I.O.U. Cain needed money and sold the I.O.U. to LaVerne for half price. Then LaVerne collected the full five grand from Val after he got his inheritance. Furthermore, Val owed LaVerne—for money lost on LaVerne's wheels—a measly thirty thousand dollars."

" There's your man," the Old Man snapped.

" Uh-uh," I said. " Not unless he's a trickster. The night Cain was killed, Val Pendleton was at the Three Penny

Club. The alibi isn't airtight but it's pretty good stuff.

" What *the* hell. This is a mess."

" You've called it. Now, listen, Chief, I have a great big hunch of my own. You said you knew a guy on the Los Angeles *Times,* didn't you?"

" Sure. Ray Gilly. Used to work for me here."

" Would he do a bit of investigating for you?"

" The shirt off his back."

" Then send him this wire and let me know what you get back in reply to it." I handed him a message I had scribbled out on some copy paper while talking to him.

The Old Man picked it up and read it and then looked at me and wiped his chin. " Sybl, uh? Now that's smart. Nobody's figured her in this at all."

" Just send that wire," I said, " and we shall see what we shall see."

About four-thirty P.M., while I was sitting at my desk working up a new lead, my telephone rang and when I answered it, it was Poppa Hanley. " I'm at h.q., Daffy," he said. " Come on over."

" What is it, Poppa?"

" Havelock's body is here in the morgue," Poppa answered. " Doc Kyne is giving it the once-over right now. He ought to be through by the time you come over."

" Be right over," I said.

" With me," Dinah said, handing me my hat. " I don't know where you're going, but my daily stint is done and my time's my own. Let's go."

" Where did you come from, Garbo?" I asked, surprised.

" Oh, I had to review a movie for our erstwhile cinema reviewer this afternoon. A little gem called Dry

Gulch Days. I've recovered. Where away?"

I patted her cheek. "To the Morgue, little girl. Still want to play dolls there?"

Dinah swallowed. "If you can stand it, I can."

WE went out and walked over to Centre Street and we found Poppa Hanley waiting for us. Then the three of us skedaddled for the Morgue and when we got there, Dr. Kerr Kyne was just washing up after having finished his dirty job.

"Well, Doc?" Hanley grunted.

"Corpse in remarkably good shape," Dr. Kyne sniffed loudly. "Very good shape."

"I don't give a hoot if the corpse was resurrected!" Hanley said. "Was it natural or was it murder?"

"It was murder," Dr. Kyne replied. "Pendleton received an injection in the small of the back, some sort of poison. Just broke his respiratory system to pieces. Paralyzed the vasomotor mechanism, made him strangle, then suffocate.

"What kind of poison?"

Dr. Kyne shrugged. "Don't know. Can't tell. What more do you want?"

"Say!" Dinah cried excitedly. "I once read in a scientific book about some one in South America being bitten by a rattlesnake and the venom made it look as though the neck had been broken and the victim had strangled. Maybe it's the same—"

"No," I said. "I know that case. That was—wait a minute! You've given me an idea. Where's a phone; where's a phone?"

We finally found a telephone and I called Dr. Lewis Coxe, curator of the Zoological Park for the last twelve years. You may remember him. He figured in that case of the strangler without hands—the time a man named Laney attempted some wholesale and ghostly slaughter with the use of venoms.

"Doc," I said, "this is your old pal, Daffy Dill. I'm on a murder case and we need a snake expert. I'm at the morgue. Could you come down? It's very important."

"Hello, Daffy," Dr. Coxe said. "It's good to hear you again. Of course, I'll come right down."

He made it in half an hour. We took him in and gave him all the facts and then we let him see the body. After this he had a consultation with Dr. Kyne and finally he shot the works.

"Your murderer is very clever," Dr. Coxe said slowly. "To have used this respective venom in connection with an infantile case, I mean. Really now, only a rigorous examination would have told that anything was amiss. And I'm quite sure that this particular venom was the one which did the work."

I asked, "Which one, doc?"

"The venom of *Dendrascips augustinceps*—the black mamba, Atilla of all snakes, the deadliest, fiercest reptile of them all."

"It wasn't snake-bite?"

"Oh, no. Hypodermic injection. . . . What puzzles me is how anyone could find black mamba venom in New York, unless they were herpetologists—"

Hunches wet me down. I grabbed Dinah and made very hasty farewells and then I found a telephone book, got an address and we took a cab uptown.

Dr. Riker was in when we got there. He was very short and had a gray Van Dyke beard and his eyes were gray and very quiet. "Ah!" he murmured when I told him who I was. "Then it is all over. There is no use in my pretending any further. Will you kindly step in? I will give you a statement."

Which was what I wanted terrifically.

We sat down in his study and he held his head in his hands and studied the floor. He explained in a low voice, "I did not know that Havelock had been murdered until several days after he had been buried. You see, I have been conducting several experiments in my laboratory here which necessitated the use of venoms. I had centrifuge tubes of cobra, rattlesnake and mamba venoms for such use. When I found that a tube of my mamba venom was missing, I realized why Havelock Pendleton's vasomotor system failed.

"I have been a friend of the Pendleton family for twenty years. I instantly suspected that Valentine Pendleton had killed his father. But the thought of the ensuing shame and disgrace should he be found out distressed me. I decided to forget the whole thing."

"Did you tell him that you knew?" I asked.

"Yes. I thought it best we had an understanding. He denied it, of course, but I also pointed out that he had incurred numerous gambling debts and was the only one in the family who had any motive. Furthermore—I regret to say—his character was not of the best. I knew that Rita and Sybl and Stephen could never have done such a thing."

"I see," I said. "But could the others have taken the venom?"

Dr. Riker shrugged. "As for that —anyone could have sneaked into my laboratory and stolen the venom. My consulting room is divided from my lab by a waiting-room for patients. Any patient could have entered the lab

while I was with another patient in the consulting room. . . . Are there any other questions, young man?"

"No," I said. "That ties it."

He smiled faintly. "Then we will consider this confession at an end. Good day. . . ."

CHAPTER VIII

Dinah Gets Her Man

THINGS slowed down then. I telephoned Poppa Hanley to see what was new and he told me that Rita Pendleton and Frank Fisher had been apprehended in Weehawken, New Jersey, heading north in the Daimler for parts unknown.

"I'm holding them incommunicado for forty-eight hours," Hanley said. "I don't know what to do now. Their story sounds honest. They say they were eloping. Maybe they were. How the hell am I supposed to know?"

I said, "Sit tight, Poppa. There'll be a break in the case tomorrow. I've traced the mamba venom."

"You have? Who had it?"

"Riker. The Pendleton medico. It was stolen from him. He thought Valentine Pendleton had done the job."

"Swell!" Hanley said acidly. "And how did he bump Steve Pendleton when he was at the *Chronicle* unconscious from your jab?"

"I'm just telling you."

"Well, look at it, Daffy. Rita and Fisher say they were eloping. They were in the house from twelve to twelve-thirty. They say Stephen was alive then because they told him they were eloping and he waved them on. I think—between us—the yarn is on the level. This kid, Rita, is throwing genuine hysterics. We've got a doctor working on her now. She nearly died when we told her. So much for that.

Sybl and Harry McFee were out riding. The butler saw them go and saw them return. Sure, they might have come back and sneaked in. But here's something *you* didn't know. That butler—Walter—says he was talking with Stephen Pendleton fifteen minutes before we got there! How do you like them berries?"

I didn't say anything.

"Now will you kindly tell me who bumped Steve?" Hanley asked.

"Maybe Steve did the whole works and then committed suicide," I kidded. Hanley really sounded like he was perturbed.

"Yeah, and then hid the gun after he was dead. . . . It leaves one man, Daffy. That's Dr. Riker."

"Look into it," I said. "I'm awaiting a message." And I hung up.

I called the *Chronicle* but the Old Man said that nothing had come in yet, so I took Dinah out to dinner.

About nine thirty P.M., we wound up at my apartment where I planned to call the Old Man again. We'd picked up some cold cuts and potato salad for a snack and we'd been having a pretty good time, forgetting the whole case.

When I unlocked the door and went in, I gave the food to Dinah and told her to fix it. She went into my kitchen and I picked up Alexander Bell's folly on my desk and gave the Old Man another ring.

"Ray Gilly just wired me," he said abruptly. "Your hunch was right. Sybl pulled the stunt all right."

"When and where?" I asked.

"Altadena, California on May 14 last spring. I guess that is that. Looks like we've beaten the field again. I'll hang onto this wire and guard it with my life. What are you going to do?"

"Let it hatch," I said. "I'll break the case tomorrow. I'll see Hanley in the morning or maybe tonight. I want things to be set when we let go with the story."

"Double-check," said the Old Man. "I hate to say it, Daffy, but I'm afraid you're a good newspaperman."

"So sweet of you, Rasputin," I said. "*Bon soir.*"

"*Bon soir,*" he said, and he hung up the receiver.

Dinah came in from the kitchen. "The podado salad is ready, sire," she said, salaaming. Then she frowned at me. "You look awfully pleased with yourself, lunatic. Tell a girl who died?"

"Garbo," I smiled, "here's something for you to sleep on. I know who killed Havelock Pendleton, Gregory Cain and Stephen Pendleton."

"The deuce you say!"

"It's a fact. And I think I can prove it. Stand by." I got the handset again and I called the Pendleton house. Walter, the butler, answered. I said, "May I speak with Sybl Pendleton, please?"

"Jeepers!" Dinah exclaimed. "I always said that dame did it! Too beautiful and too much gelt!"

"Miss Pendleton is not at home," Walter told me. I hung up. I said, "She isn't home."

"No," a voice said from the doorway. "She's here, Mr. Dill."

DINAH and I wheeled around like a shot. Sybl Pendleton was standing in the doorway with her hand still on the knob. "I didn't bother to knock," she said. "The door was open a crack. I couldn't help hearing what you were saying."

Dinah ran to my desk and opened the top drawer and jerked out my Smith and Wesson revolver. She turned around and held it close to her on a line with Sybl's stomach.

I said, amazed, "For Pete's sake, Garbo, what's the matter with you?"

"You dope!" Dinah cried. "Don't you see? She's come to knock you off because you know too much!"

I shook my head sadly. "Cut it out, cut it out. Sybl didn't do these killings. What's the matter with you?"

"But you said—"

"I didn't say anything. I just telephoned her at her house and you immediately jumped to a conclusion."

Sybl Pendleton smiled wearily and closed the door. "I can't blame her," she said, her eyes drooping. "All our nerves have been jumpy with this ghastly business." She was very pale and so nervous that her full mouth twitched to the left side and she couldn't keep her hands still.

"Have a seat," I said. "Dinah—put that rod away."

"Not me," Dinah said acidly. "It's put away over my prostrate figure."

"All right, then keep it and shoot yourself by accident," I said, annoyed. "Well, Miss Pendleton?"

"I—I heard you say that you know who killed my father," Sybl faltered.

"You can't hush this up with money, lady."

"Hush it up?" she murmured. "I don't want it hushed up any more. None of us are safe now. I—I want to help. You see—I know, too!"

"Oh," I said. "What makes you think so?"

"I found the gun. Stephen's pistol. It had a silencer on it."

"Where did you find it?"

"Where—" her voice broke and her hands plucked at her face, "—where—Val hid it—in the top of his closet—"

I didn't blink an eye. "So Val, your brother, hid the pistol in the top

of his closet, eh? Did you bring it with you?"

Sybl shook her head. "N-no. I didn't think I'd better touch it. I came straight to you. I thought—"

"Skip it!" I said harshly and abruptly. "All I can say is: you're a damned bigger fool than I gave you credit for, Miss Pendleton!"

She sprang to her feet. "What do you—how dare—?"

"Never mind that," I went on quickly. "You're flirting with death and you don't know it! How long are you going to play along like this? Don't you realize that you're next on his little list? Don't you realize that your dad was . . . and that you were intended to be second all along? And just the same you go merrily on your way, making alibis and protecting a guy who'll kill you as soon as—"

Then, like a lightning bolt, Dinah shrieked.

"Daffy! Look out—"

There was no sound of a shot, but the window in my living room tinkled as the glass broke, a dull plop seemed to echo across toward me, and like a panther, Sybl Pendleton sprang to my left, rigid with shock and collapsed on the floor clawing at her shoulder.

Simultaneously there was another shot. This one wasn't silenced. It cracked sharply in the confines of the room and there was a short jagged stick of orange flame and a lot of billowing smoke and the window tinkled again as a slug went out of the room, fired from the gun in Dinah's hand.

Out on the fire-escape went up the most gruesome scream of pain and surprise I've ever heard and then it seemed to fade away very slowly until it died.

I saw what had happened. I sprang to the window and looked out. The fire-escape was absolutely empty.

I RAN to the door. Dinah was standing there, looking stupidly at me, my gun still in her hand, while Sybl, who was still conscious, began to groan on the floor.

"Garbo," I snapped, "get a grip on yourself. This is the finish. Call an ambulance and get that kid to a hospital. Call Poppa Hanley at h.q. and tell him to come running. We've got the Pendleton killer. Then call the Old Man and break the yarn. I'll be back. . . ." And I tore out and down the stairs.

I found the body in the street. It was lying on the sidewalk, its hand still clenching Stephen Pendleton's .45 pistol. It was all bashed up from the four-story fall but one look at the bullet hole over the heart told me that Harry McFee had been dead long before he ever hit the cement.

I was still standing there when Poppa Hanley flew up in his prowl car, along with Detectives Babcock and Claghorn. Poppa immediately put the two dicks to keeping the body clear of morbidly curious pedestrians who gathered round. Then he said, "Murder?"

"Murderer," I said.

"What?" Hanley roared. "Impossible! He couldn't have killed Stephen Pendleton. According to Walter's testimony, Stephen was alive when we arrived at the house. McFee arrived with us. So how—"

"Sometimes," I murmured, "you disappoint me, Poppa. How indeed? Didn't Sybl ask him to go up and tell her uncle we wanted to see him? Sure. So McFee went up and he plugged Stephen while we were downstairs!"

"There wasn't any shot!"

"Of course not! The rod's silenced!"

We went upstairs. Dinah had put Sybl Pendleton in my bed and was washing her wound. Sybl was conscious. Dinah said, "I don't think it is bad. It's in the shoulder. She says she feels all right."

Hanley had a look. "Just a flesh wound. Too close for comfort though."

"Who—who was he?" Dinah asked.

"I didn't see the face. I saw the hand and gun."

"Harry McFee," I said.

"You get him, Daffy?" Poppa Hanley asked.

"Dinah did. I was talking to Sybl when he tried to pump one into Sybl. Listen, Miss Pendleton, you were lying when you said McFee was out with you the night Cain died, weren't you?"

"Yes," Sybl whispered. "He asked me to say that. Said he was innocent but might get in trouble. I believed him. But tonight I found the gun in his coat pocket—he threatened to kill me unless I did as he said—he made me come to you and blame Val—"

"I don't get this at all," Hanley said. "Explain it to me, Daffy."

"Look. On May 14th in Altadena, California, McFee married Sybl here. He was a fortune hunter and she was good pickings, on account of her father was sick and due to pass out of the picture leaving her five million. But Havelock Pendleton hung onto life. So McFee helped him along with a shot of mamba venom which he had heard Dr. Riker had and which he stole from Riker. Remember he said that Riker's lab looked like a Loki den? How else would he have known unless he'd seen it?"

"Go on."

"Gregory Cain embalmed Pendleton's body, saw that snake venom had been used. Investigation proved that McFee was chummy with Sybl. Cain jumped at the conclusion and blackmailed McFee, knowing McFee had

had experience with snakes in that 14th Street museum years ago when they were together."

"So McFee bumped Cain."

"Sure. And then Stephen Pendleton, either because Steve wanted the exhumation or because Steve suspected him. All the time he tried to throw the shadow on Val Pendleton—the old black sheep of the family.

"Then Sybl here learned that Harry McFee had the gun. He made her come to me and say she found the gun in Val's closet. He meant to finish her here, leaving her naming Val as her killer. Who could contradict a dead woman? That had been the original plan all along. To kill Havelock Pendleton. And then Sybl. Cain and Steve just got in the way."

"Because," Hanley said slowly, "with Sybl dead, McFee was suddenly worth five million dollars. . . . How did you find out they were married, Daffy?"

"They were too used to each other. I got suspicious. Figured the knot had been hitched on the West Coast. So I had the Old Man wire a friend out there to do a little investigaitng. He found it out and wired back. And there's your case on a silver platter."

"Sure, sure," Hanley nodded. "It's okay. . . . But if Val was innocent, why

in hell did he try to pay you to stop the story?"

"Because Riker had told him that his father had been murdered. And Riker openly suspected Val of having done it. And after the Cain killing—with the IOU tying Val to Cain, Val was petrified that he'd be framed for the murder—which McFee actually was trying to do. . . . Go on home, will you? I've got a dish of potato salad waiting for me in the kitchen."

"For you maybe," Dinah said, heaving a mournful sigh. "But not for me. I couldn't eat a thing."

"What's the matter?"

"I was thinking—about killing that man tonight—I never killed anyone before in my life—but—" she broke down and started to cry real tears.

"TAKE it easy, Garbo," I said. "It couldn't have been different. Think of it this way. You saved Sybl's life. You saved my life. You saved your own life. And, say, you saved the State $230. It would've taken that to execute him. That's nothing to cry about."

"I'm not crying about that," she said tearfully. "I was just thinking what that awful man might have done to you if I'd missed him."

So there's a woman for you.

I WONDER WHY I FEEL SO LOW, I DIDN'T OVER-DO IT.

JUST TAKE AN ALKA-SELTZER, JOE,-- AND THERE'LL BE NOTHING TO IT.

IF I COULD ONLY EAT THE THINGS I LIKE, AND HAVE NO FEAR.

THAT'S JUST WHAT YOU ARE GOING TO DO, AND ALKALIZE, MY DEAR.

Be Wise— Alkalize

MORNING MISERY

SOUR STOMACH

Alka-Seltzer Makes a sparkling alkalizing solution containing an analgesic (acetyl salicylate). You drink it and it gives prompt, pleasant relief for Headaches, Sour Stomach, Distress after Meals, Colds and other minor Aches and Pains

Alkalize with Alka-Seltzer   AT ALL DRUGGISTS   30¢ 60¢   SLIGHTLY MORE IN CANADA

IVY TRASK

"The earliest book of short stories relating the criminal deeds of a woman is probably Mrs. L. T. Meade's and Robert Eustace's *The Sorceress of the Strand* (1903), about the infamous Madame Sara," says Ellery Queen in the introduction to *The Females of the Species: The Great Women Detectives and Criminals.*

The pulps nurtured a number of series women characters with dark reputations. Judson P. Philips's criminal woman, Ivy Trask, for instance, was featured in a short series for *Detective Fiction Weekly* in the early 1930s. "The readers couldn't seem to accept women as action figures," says the writer. So he went on to create the Park Avenue Hunt Club—which was composed of four male members.

Philips, born in 1903 in Massachusetts, was educated in England. He wrote for radio, for Street & Smith, Munsey, and other pulp publishers, for television and for the stage, and for hardcover book publishers. He was early on known for his "vocational" stories, tales that revolved around specific professions or settings. The author of more than eighty mystery books, many published as by "Hugh Pentecost," he was awarded the Mystery Writers of America Grand Master Award in 1973.

"Death to the Hunter" is from the February 18, 1933, issue of *Detective Fiction Weekly.*

DETECTIVE
FICTION WEEKLY

"The Magazine With the Detective Shield On the Cover"

| VOLUME LXXIV | SATURDAY, FEBRUARY 18, 1933 | NUMBER 2 |

Death to the Hunter

A Novelette

By Judson P. Philips

*She Tracked Them Both, the Hunted and
the Hunter—Ivy Trask, Whose Beauty
Hid a Cruel and Dangerous Soul*

CHAPTER I

The Man from the West

DANIEL LEVERING thought, a trifle ironically, that the city officials were making a little too much of a hippodrome out of his so-called "crusade." Of course it was all a necessary part of politics, he supposed. Everything that could possibly reflect credit on the administration must be ballyhooed, especially with another election coming on in the near future. But to Daniel Levering, grim-lipped and with steady, unwavering blue eyes, what he was going to attempt was simply his duty as an American. It was high time that drastic steps were taken to rid the city of its domination by the g a n g s t e r s and racketeers that had turned law and order into a mockery, and made

person in the city was behind him . . . that he was to have his efforts given full coöperation by all officials. He wished eagerly for the next day to

"Force that door, and for God's sake hurry!"

come and for the beginning of his crusade.

a travesty of justice. Daniel Levering, a Westerner, had dealt in a summary fashion with a similar situation in a small Western city, he had been imported by the city administration, made a special deputy police commissioner, and told to go ahead in any way he saw fit.

Levering was a man of firm convictions, high ideals, and a great deal of confidence in his own ability to meet this situation and deal with it. After listening to the resounding speeches of the city officials that had been made at a dinner for him, he found himself enjoying a feeling that every respectable

But first, of course, this evening a celebration must be gone through. Levering would have preferred to have spent it with his wife and his small son, who was the apple of his eye. He would have liked to skip away after the dinner instead of going on the theatre party which had been planned for him. But he couldn't do that . . . not on this first night. After tonight, however, he would wash his slate clean of all social obligations until such time as his job had been successfully completed.

Levering didn't drink, and he found himself much less gay than the rest of the party that was driven from the banquet hall to the theatre. Bolton, the police commissioner, who rode next to Levering in his car, was in a particularly mellow mood. Secretly Bolton thought that Levering was a great fool. Bolton knew what this crusader from the West was up against; knew how almost impossible it was to deal with a situation so honeycombed by corruption and dishonesty. But it suited Bolton, for he would now get a little respite from the continued attacks levelled at him by high-minded civic organizations.

Oh, Bolton felt a great feeling of friendliness for Daniel Levering on this particular evening! Levering, with his square jaw, his fearless eyes, and his broad-brimmed black felt hat that made him resemble one of the pioneer politicians of old, could bear the criticism on his broad shoulders for a while and give Bolton a chance to have a little fun. Perhaps when he too failed to put a stop to wholesale crime in the city, the people would realize that Bolton wasn't such a bad commissioner after all . . . even if he did share rather handsomely in certain slices of the graft "melon."

DANIEL LEVERING imagined that these gay politicians would take him to some musical comedy, loaded with pretty girls and amusing comedians, and the prospect bored him. He was much fonder of the drama, though he knew almost nothing about the theatre and had very little occasion in his busy life to see much of it. When their car arrived at the theatre and he saw that they were to attend " Woman Courageous," starring Ivy Trask, it meant nothing to him. He had not heard of the play, and, moreover, he had not heard of Ivy Trask.

Levering was restless as they waited for the play to begin. He wanted to smoke, but he felt it was silly to light a cigar for the few minutes that re-

mained, and he simply couldn't smoke cigarettes. He wished he could call up his wife and tell her what a dull time he was having. He wished he could be at home, reading aloud to his kid. A great boy! He wished he didn't have to listen to the coarse jokes of the men he was with, and that he didn't have to force a rather frosty smile of appreciation for this type of wit.

Then the house lights darkened and they sought their seats. Levering sat, with his head sunk forward on his chest, steeling himself against what he felt would be a boring ordeal. Thank the Lord this was apparently a straight play and not a musical comedy. He listened only vaguely to the prattle of a butler and a maid about something or other. Then came a moment that Daniel Levering never forgot as long as he lived. Ivy Trask made her entrance. The house applauded. Bolton, sitting next to Levering, gave the Westerner a poke in the ribs.

" Not bad, eh?" he chuckled.

Daniel Levering was an idealist. Not only that, he belonged to the old school of chivalrous gentlemen who looked upon women as goddesses to be worshiped and revered. And here was a goddess . . . a pale, golden goddess, with a low, soft voice that struck a strangely exciting chord in Daniel Levering's emotional fibre. He sat listening, scarcely following the thread of the play, watching Ivy Trask as she moved quietly, gracefully, about the stage. There was strength of character behind those eyes, strength and sympathy. Hers was the beauty of a madonna! And yet there was enough of worldliness to make one feel unconsciously that she was not altogether unattainable if one had the strength of character sufficient to match hers.

The lights went down on what

seemed to Levering an all too short first act. He sat without applauding, too deeply impressed by this woman to show outwardly what he felt.

"Not bad, eh?" Bolton repeated. It seemed to Levering that the commissioner's smile was rather unpleasantly like a leer.

"She seems to typify everything fine in womanhood," said the Westerner, ponderously.

"She's the nuts," agreed Bolton.

Daniel Levering would have liked to protest at the use of such a vulgarism in describing Ivy Trask. Like many others before him, this man had failed to pierce the outer surface of that pale, golden loveliness. He knew nothing of the trail of tragedy stretched out behind her; tragedy caused by a sinister and evil quality which Ivy Trask possessed to a highly developed degree, but of which almost no one but her victims had ever learned.

CHAPTER II

Behind the Mask of Beauty

"WOMAN Courageous" was a play which dealt with the struggle of a fine woman to save her husband from his own weakness. So great was Ivy's skill as an actress, that somehow one could not help but feel that here was something real! That this woman was really pitting her courage and faith against the forces of evil. Daniel Levering found himself completely under the spell of this illusion; he watched the play fascinated. Here was the sort of woman one dreamed of . . . a woman who combined all the fine qualities one could wish for in a wife, along with a breathless beauty. When the curtain went down on the last act, he felt a sense of personal loss, as though a

precious friend had suddenly gone out of his life forever.

"How would you like to go back stage and meet the lady?" Bolton asked.

Levering stared at him, almost unbelieving. "You mean . . ."

"I've met her several times. Strange thing . . . we're hunting for a crook who is apparently her double. I've had several laughs with her about it. She might even go to Ross' with us."

"Ross?"

Bolton chuckled. "Sure. We're giving you a real send-off, Levering. Clark Ross runs a gambling house. He's probably the most dangerous man in New York. Thought you might like to have a glimpse of him socially before you begin to run up against him in an official capacity."

"You mean he'd let us into his place?" asked Levering.

"Why not? If you went over it with a fine comb you could not find anything the matter with it. Oh, of course there is gambling . . . and they sell liquor. But nothing crooked, I mean." Bolton laughed at his own wit.

Levering's lips tightened. "I shall enjoy meeting Mr. Ross," he said.

"And the lady?" asked Bolton slyly.

"I should consider it an honor," said Levering gravely.

Bolton smiled to himself. What a stuffed shirt this Levering was! He would have liked to give him a good riding, but it wouldn't do. He was Levering's official host. He led the way up the little alley to the stage door and sent in his card to Ivy Trask. Levering, standing first on one foot and then on the other, was a little fearful of this meeting. Perhaps this woman in real life would be different from the woman he had seen on the stage. He dreaded a disillusionment. But there could be no turning back now for the doorman had returned with the information that Miss Trask would be happy to see them.

They walked across the stage to the door of her dressing room and she called out pleasantly to them to come in. Levering felt his heart beating a little more rapidly. Then he came face to face with her. He heard vaguely Bolton's introduction.

"Mr. Daniel Levering . . . who's going to clean up our fair city . . ."

THERE had been mockery in Bolton's tone, but Ivy Trask's lovely blue eyes met Levering's gravely.

"You have a big job on your hands, Mr. Levering. One that calls for courage and perseverance. You look like the sort of man who might accomplish it." It was the same low, soft voice he had heard on the stage. The same graciousness of manner, the same pale, golden loveliness.

Levering moistened his lips. "I— I'd like to pay you a—a sort of backhanded compliment, Miss Trask," he said.

"Compliments of any sort are always charming," she said.

Levering was twisting his black hat round and round in his big hands. Daniel Levering could face gun-fire without turning a hair, but somehow in the presence of this woman he had lost his poise. "I thought the woman you portrayed in the play was a pretty wonderful woman," he said, "and I thought you were a great actress to make her so real. But now I see that it really wasn't such great acting. You are that woman yourself."

It takes a person of really great poise to accept compliments gracefully, and Ivy Trask had that poise. "That is one of the nicest things anyone has ever said to me," she said quietly.

"I meant it in all sincerity," said Levering.

"I felt that you did," she said. "No one could doubt your sincerity."

"And now," said Bolton, rather loudly, "that you two have crowned each other with laurel wreaths, let's get down to business. We're taking Mr. Levering to Clark Ross' place, Miss Trask. Want him to meet the big shot socially before they cross swords. Would you like to come?"

Ivy hesitated. It was just the proper amount of hesitation.

"It would be a great pleasure to have you," said Levering. He had suddenly forgotten his desire to go home. He felt that he must talk to this woman . . . that she would understand the problem he was undertaking. He couldn't know that already he had opened himself to a mortal attack, for the golden-haired woman who looked at him so steadily was in reality his enemy . . . the enemy of any man who fell under her spell.

"How can I refuse two such charming people?" she said. "If you'll excuse me for a moment . . . wait for me on the stage . . . I'll join you."

The two men left her and she turned to her dressing table. If Daniel Levering could have looked over her shoulder at the reflection in the mirror, he would have been startled. Her face was suddenly hard and cold. The softness in her eyes had been replaced by a strange, rather frightening glitter.

When she had added the final touches to her make-up, she took a small beaded bag from the drawer of her dressing table and opened it. For just a second her hand closed over the butt of a small, pearl-handled revolver. Her lips twisted into a hard, satisfied smile. Then she turned off the lights and went out onto the stage to join her two escorts. When she reached them she was once more soft, lovely, pale gold.

CHAPTER III

Two Cups of Coffee

CLARK ROSS sat behind the big flat desk in the private office of the gambling house he ran on the smart side of town. Ross had a face which is typical of comedians or killers; it was expressionless except for the deep-set dark eyes. When he spoke it seemed as though only his lips and eyes moved, the rest of the muscles of his face appearing to be utterly immobile. He was tall, with a good figure, and rather finely chiselled features, for all the fact that his lips were a trifle too thinly drawn and his eyes just a bit too closely placed. He was immaculately dressed in a smartly tailored dinner coat which gave him at least the outward veneer of a gentleman of position in the world.

After all, Clark Ross *was* a man of position. Those wiry fingers of his pulled the strings that made a good portion of the underworld dance at his will. His was not the domination of showy violence, but of cool, unrelenting scheming. When he moved against an opponent he was like a chess player calmly making the vital play which checkmates the enemy king. No fireworks, no theatre; but devastatingly certain.

At this moment he leaned back in his chair, smoking a cigarette with an appearance of intense enjoyment. Each time he drew the smoke down deeply into his lungs he exhaled it in a little column that drifted ceilingward in a spiral cone. On the desk was a bottle of Scotch and beside it stood a small whiskey glass; however it was not Ross who drank. It was the thick-set blond youth who paced nervously back and forth in front of the desk, puffing at his cigarette like a racing steam engine. About every half dozen turns across the room he paused to pour himself a short drink and down it.

"I tell you, Clark," he blurted out, "you're a fool to let that man in your place. He isn't like the others. He can't be bought . . . and he won't play ball. He'd just as soon give us the works tonight as any other time."

Clark Ross flicked the ash from his cigarette into a tray on his desk with meticulous care. "Your education in tactics has been sadly neglected, Dutch," he said. His voice was monotonously level, as unemotional as the expression of his face. "Always give your opponent a slight opening early in the battle and you'll learn a good deal about his methods. Levering can't do us any harm by coming here tonight. I want to see him, gauge his capabilities. Then perhaps *we* can move first. The best defense in the world is a sharp and sudden attack."

Dutch Slade shook his head and tossed off another shot of whiskey. "This guy ain't like the rest of the crooks in the political racket. He won't play ball, I tell you."

Clark Ross' face was completely expressionless. "You are hired, Dutch, to protect me from gunmen . . . to take care of any fireworks that may take place. When it comes to handling Daniel Levering you leave the worry and the planning to me. And you'd better lay off the booze from now on. They'll be coming in a few moments." His eyes narrowed for a moment. "It's just possible that I will decide to stop Levering before he ever gets started. It would be just too bad if the papers carried headlines tomorrow describing the sudden and unexpected death of Daniel Levering from heart failure."

Slade's face twitched as he looked into the keen eyes of his employer. "You mean . . ."

"Send McCarthy in here," rapped Ross. He seemed suddenly engrossed with an idea. He sat motionless as Slade left the room until the ash from his cigarette dropped onto the lapel of his dinner coat. He leaned forward and crushed out the stub of that cigarette and lit a fresh one.

SLADE came back into the room with a man in waiter's garb.

Ross stared at him moodily for a minute, and then nodded toward the bottle. "Have a drink, McCarthy?"

"Thanks, Mr. Ross."

Ross leaned back, the tips of his thin, wiry fingers together. "There's a man coming here with a party tonight that may need taking care of, Mac," he said quietly. "You may have heard of him, Daniel Levering."

"Sure, Mr. Ross. The big clean-up man from Oshkosh or somewhere."

"That's the general idea, Mac. He's paying us a visit tonight . . . a purely social visit. But it may be that we'll determine not to monkey with him at all if he looks as though he'd make trouble. That's where you come in."

"Yes, Mr. Ross."

Ross opened his desk drawer, and then, with a small key on his watch chain, unlocked an inner drawer and pulled it forward. From it he took a small box, and from the box, a thin, folded slip of paper, sufficiently transparent to show that it contained a small quantity of a white, powdery substance.

"In his drink?" asked McCarthy, matter of factly.

Ross shook his head. "He's a tee-totaler, I believe. We'll have a bit of

supper in here perhaps. You'll do the serving. And you'll not use this stuff unless you get the word from me. If I give you the high sign slip it into his coffee."

"Yes, Mr. Ross."

"You understand? Nothing doing unless I give you the high sign."

"Yes, Mr. Ross."

"Good. Now slip this in your vest pocket, and don't give it to anyone you like. Scram."

"Yes, Mr. Ross."

Dutch Slade waited until the waiter left the room and then he turned almost fiercely to his employer. "You can't give a guy as big as Levering the business! They'll run you down sure as hell."

Ross gave the gunman a straight look. "What do you think I paid out so much dough to that German chemist for, Dutch? To get hold of something that is easy to trace? If we give Daniel Levering the business he will simply pass quietly away in his sleep from heart failure. And no doctor or medical examiner in the world can trace poison in his system."

"What is the stuff?" asked Slade doubtfully.

"You wouldn't know if I told you."

"Well, it's your funeral, not mine," said Slade.

"If there's any funeral, Dutch, it will be Levering's," said Ross.

The door to the office opened and a man stuck his head in. "The police commissioner and his party are here, Mr. Ross. Bolton's asking for you."

"How many in the party?"

"Well, there's Bolton, and Daniel Levering, and Grover, that assistant D. A., and a woman. A swell looker."

"Probably Levering's wife," said Ross, rising. He turned to Slade. "Have McCarthy set a table for five in one of the private dining rooms, and let us know when the supper is ready. Better serve champagne . . . and coffee. Plenty of black coffee for Mr. Daniel Levering."

Ross walked out along the corridor from his office to the main reception room, and there he saw Bolton and Levering and Grover. The police commissioner's face was flushed, and it was apparent that both he and Grover had been drinking. Levering seemed to tower above them, grim as a block of gray rock, scowling at what he saw about him. Ross' eyes narrowed as he studied the man for a moment, for he recognized that in Daniel Levering he had an opponent who would not fail for lack of courage or steadfastness of purpose. Then he saw the woman, and for just a moment his hands clenched tightly. Ivy Trask . . . the ten most beautiful women in the world rolled into one! He had always wanted to meet her. Levering wasn't doing so badly for a stranger in town.

Ross crossed to meet his guests and Bolton shook hands with him warmly. " Hello, Clark! Still working at the same old stand, eh? Thought we'd drop in for a chat and a little iced tea!" He winked, and then laughed heartily at what he considered was a sly joke. Not a muscle of Ross' face moved. " Want to present you to Miss Ivy Trask," Bolton continued. " And this is Mr. Daniel Levering . . . you'll hear a lot about him, Clark. A hell of a lot!"

Ross nodded perfunctorily to Levering and then his eyes, close-set and steely, met Ivy's pale blue ones. Ivy Trask had wanted to meet Clark Ross almost as badly a he wanted to meet her . . . but of course he couldn't know that. He couldn't know that Ivy's activities outside the world of the the-

atre had reached a point where it was absolutely necessary for her to have someone to turn to for help in moments of danger, and that she had made up her mind that Clark Ross was the man who could do most for her. It was a moment of importance to both of them, but only Ivy realized it at the time.

Yet Ivy found her attention distracted, for across the room she caught a glimpse of the man who had made it necessary to seek out Clark Ross' help. The one man who knew the truth about her, but who had failed so far to get sufficient concrete evidence to make things dangerous for her. Geoffrey Malvern, the dramatic critic, was sitting in an arm chair in the corner of the room, idly smoking a cigarette, and watching the people at the gambling tables.

Geoffrey Malvern had sworn to get Ivy because she had been the cause of his brother's suicide. She knew he was the one great menace to her safety and happiness, yet somehow the sight of him roused in her the spirit of combat. It was the thrill of danger which made life worth living to Ivy.

Malvern saw her and nodded coldly. The lines about the corners of his mouth hardened, for the sight of Ivy always brought back to him the picture of his brother—the one person he had adored—lying cold and dead with a round black bullet hole in his pale forehead. Some day he would square accounts with this woman. Some day he would get the evidence that would make her pay in full for what she had done to him and a score of others. Ivy saw the look of hatred in his eyes, and for a second her hands closed tightly. Then with an effort she turned back to Clark Ross.

"One hears of you often, Mr. Ross," she said.

"I'm afraid there's a great deal of unpleasant gossip," he said. "It's the penalty one pays for running a place of this sort."

"I was thinking less about what one hears of your business than what one hears about you as a man, Mr. Ross." Her wide eyes met his coolly. One thing that everyone said about Clark Ross was that he was not susceptible to feminine charms, and as she looked at his almost mask-like face, she knew that she would never be able to read anything there. She knew that the way to make the grade with Clark Ross was not to attempt the simple tricks of flirtation.

"I can only hope that your presence here indicates that those things were not too bad," said Ross. He turned to the others. "I have arranged to have a little supper served in a private dining room. I hope you will all be my guests."

DANIEL LEVERING'S jaw was set grimly. He had come here only because he had been swept off his feet by the charm of Ivy Trask, but he recognized that Clark Ross was his sworn enemy, and he had old-fashioned ideas about that sort of thing.

"It would hardly do for me to break bread with you, Ross," he said, a little pompously. "I am out to get you, and you know it."

Ivy, watching Ross' expressionless face, felt admiration for him. There was not a quiver of an eyelash as Levering made his pronouncement. "I understood you were not taking up your duties until tomorrow, Mr. Levering," Ross remarked quietly. "Certainly there is no reason why tonight we should refuse to have supper together."

"I can only tell you," said Levering grimly, "that though I don't take on my job until tomorrow, I should feel thoroughly justified in using anything I might see here tonight against you."

"My dear sir," said Ross suavely, "you are at perfect liberty to use anything you can find against me here tonight or any other time. And now shall we go into the dining room? I see that the waiter is signalling me that supper is ready."

It was Ivy who turned the tide. "I am simply famished," she said. "I don't eat anything before the theatre and after a performance I am usually starved. I for one accept your invitation gladly, Mr. Ross."

Ross offered her his arm, and as Ivy slipped her hand through it she felt the ripple of hard muscles under his coat sleeve. She felt, somehow, that for all Daniel Levering's square-jawed tenacity of purpose, that he was up against an opponent in Clark Ross who would give him cards and spades and still win.

The table was tastefully set for them in a small dining room. There were little copper chafing dishes before each place, and a large silver ice bucket containing several quarts of champagne. Ross seated his guests at the oblong table so that Ivy was on his right with Levering next to her; Bolton and Grover faced them, and the sideboard from which McCarthy served was behind Levering's back. For Ross had made up his mind. For all his blundering pomposity Daniel Levering was going to be decidedly dangerous, and at the moment Ross was not interested in trying to cope with him. Better to have him out of the way without any further delay.

The chafing dishes contained a delicious chicken à la king, cooked in real sherry, and even Levering seemed grudgingly to enjoy it, although he refused the excellent champagne which the others drank. He believed that if there was a prohibition law that each citizen should observe it by not drinking. Ross was watching him with unfathomable eyes. He leaned forward slightly.

" Would you like your coffee now, Mr. Levering?"

" Thanks," said Levering shortly.

Ross turned to McCarthy at the sideboard. He answered the questioning look on the Irishman's face with a slight nod of his head. Then he leaned back in his chair and very carefully lit a cigarette. Suddenly Ivy spoke up.

" I think I'd like my coffee too," she said. Her eyes were strangely bright, but Clark Ross was too much absorbed in what was about to take place to notice it. He was too absorbed to realize that he had made a fatal mistake and that this woman had found him out.

McCarthy came to the table and placed a cup of coffee at Ivy's place. Then he went back to the sideboard and returned with a cup of coffee for Levering. Bolton and Grover were laughing a little boisterously over some joke. Ross sat like an image in his chair, watching, fascinated, as Daniel Levering reached for the small silver coffee spoon by his cup.

Ivy, her eyes very bright, turned suddenly to Levering. " Do you ever have peculiar and very foolish desires, Mr. Levering? Things like wanting one piece of toast rather than another at the breakfast table. Or to want to change something you have for something else that is exactly like it?"

" Why—why, I don't know."

" Well, I have a perfectly ridiculous desire to trade cups of coffee with you, Mr. Levering. Will you do it?"

He laughed. " Of course," he said.

A strange, choking noise came from McCarthy at the sideboard. Not a muscle moved on Clark Ross' face, but every bit of color had drained from it. His hands closed very tightly over the arms of his chair, but he remained perfectly motionless. To make any move to repair this horrible mistake might expose his whole hand, and that was a risk he dared not run, even to save a beautiful woman. Then he saw that her eyes were meeting his, and that there was a faint twinkle of amusement in them.

" And now, being a woman," she said lightly, " I shall prove that we are all quite insane. I don't think I want any coffee at all."

With almost indecent haste McCarthy removed the cup, and Clark Ross took a handkerchief very slowly from his pocket and wiped away the little beads of perspiration on his white forehead.

CHAPTER IV

A Proposition

SUPPER was finally over . . . a supper over which the shadow of death had hovered without the intended victim or the police commissioner or the District Attorney knowing that anything had happened. Ivy knew that she had won the victory she had hoped for, and as she watched Ross, sitting quietly at the head of the table, she knew that from now on this man would have to be on her side. She turned to him when Bolton and Levering started an argument about some sort of police procedure.

" I'd like to see the sights," she told him.

" For example?" he asked coolly.

" Haven't you a private office? I've always heard that the proprietors of gambling houses had private offices with sliding panels, and mysterious hiding places."

He stood up with alacrity. "I should be delighted to show you my office," he said. "Come along."

He took her down the corridor to his office, ushered her in and then very carefully locked the door. His eyes were grim, intense, watchful. She perched herself on the edge of his desk, and despite the fact that Ross knew that this woman had caught him in an attempted murder, he could not for the moment help but admire her. Yet there was something about her at the moment that he couldn't understand. She seemed changed; certain hard little lines about the corners of her eyes; a tightening of her lovely lips that gave them a cruel contour.

"I am very interested to know," he said steadily, "just how you knew there was something wrong with that cup of coffee, Miss Trask. Don't tell me it was feminine intuition, because I don't believe in it."

"I should like to give you a much cleverer explanation than I can, Mr. Clark Ross," Ivy said, "but it's really quite simple. You put me with my back to the sideboard but you neglected to remove the mirror from the opposite wall which gave a very clear picture of what was going on."

"And just by chance you saw Mc-Carthy doctor that cup?"

"Not entirely by chance. I saw you give him a sort of signal and I was interested to know what it meant, so I watched him." She gave her shoulders, pale white shoulders, a charming little shrug. "The rest was simple."

Ross lit a cigarette with a hand that was quite steady. "You had with you the police commissioner, a s p e c i a l deputy commissioner, and a district attorney and you see a murder about to be committed, yet you go to great pains to prevent it without letting them know about it. Why didn't you turn me over to the police? What is your game? What is it you want of me?"

"I want to be counted in," Ivy said quickly.

"Counted in?"

"There are moments when I can be of help to you and you can be of help to me," she said.

"Just how can you help me?" he asked.

"I can help you get rid of that fool Levering," she said promptly.

"But you just prevented my getting rid of him," he said, puzzled.

"I had to make you see that I wasn't just a stupid woman . . . that I had a talent which would be useful to you. In return for it you can help me."

"What is it you want?" he said impatiently. "Money to back a play? What is it?"

Ivy laughed, a hard, metallic laugh. This man was being more stupid than she had anticipated. "Don't be a fool. You've heard of the robbery and murder that took place at Angus McPherson's place on Long Island? You've heard that the woman accomplice escaped and that she is supposed to look like me? Well, she does . . . because I was that woman! Of course no one believes that it could have been the famous Ivy Trask. But it was!"

Her voice had risen a little with excitement and her eyes were very bright. Ross listened, nothing in his face betraying surprise. "You remember when Cyrus Mortimer's son was killed in an automobile accident? It was because I had just separated his father from a hundred thousand dollars by making him believe that his son was a thief. Do you remember the suicide of Geoffrey Malvern's brother? I was behind that. Do you see now, Mr. Clark Ross, why I want to join forces with you? Because we can use each other. Because the theatre is just a blind for the kind of life that means everything to me!"

SHE paused. Her eyes were very bright, almost glittering, and her hands were clenched so tightly together that the sharp-pointed nails bit into the palms.

Clark Ross' close-set eyes met hers searchingly. "You're an actress, Miss Trask," he said. "Is this a performance for my benefit, or are you by any chance trying to work some racket for Levering?"

"If I were working for Levering," she said, "why didn't I turn you in the minute I saw your man poisoning that cup of coffee? I'm telling you the truth, and unless you're more stupid than I think, you'll believe me. You can't have reached the position of power you hold here in the city without being a good judge of character."

He blew a thin cloud of blue smoke through his tightly compressed lips, and took a step or two across the room. It was the first sign Ivy had seen in him that indicated the slightest break in his poise.

"You're like a chameleon," he said almost irritably. "At one moment you look like an angel . . . like the finest ideal that one has of woman. Then at the next moment you look like what the Devil would look like if he was a woman. Which is acting? God knows I can't tell!"

Ivy leaned forward eagerly. "If I were working for Levering you'll at least admit we couldn't have foreseen that you would try to poison him tonight. Why, there was enough to hang

you if I'd cared to expose you . . . Levering wouldn't have needed any more."

Ross smiled crookedly. "You would still have to get out of here, Miss Trask." He smoked for a moment thoughtfully. "I've got to nail Levering, and nail him quickly," he said, thinking aloud. "Perhaps you could help . . . and if you did I would pay you handsomely for it. I don't believe there is anything that produces loyalty so readily as money. We can't shoot Levering down in the street. We don't want to make a public martyr of him. It's got to be a great deal more subtle than that, and perhaps your woman's brain can help devise the proper method." He flicked away his cigarette. "I'm damned if I don't think you might do something."

She gave him an arch smile. "You mentioned money, Mr. Ross."

He leaned forward. "If you can devise the method by which I can safely rid myself of the menace of Levering it will be worth just fifty thousand dollars to you." His eyes glittered. "If you could find out from him what his plans are . . . get him to talk . . . we may be able to crucify his campaign before it gets started."

CHAPTER V
The Black Room

GET Levering to talk! Ivy, sitting in the corner of a taxicab with the big Westerner, smiled to herself. Why, this man was ready to pour out the most intimate secrets of his life after only a few hours' acquaintance. He had begged for permission to take her home . . . "act as your escort," he had said in his pompous fashion. Already she felt that she held him very tightly in the palm of her hand . . .

And it was that sense of power, the feeling that she had it within her to grind this man's hopes and plans under her heel that brought Ivy the only joy she had in life. She had a strange urge, an urge that she could never entirely satisfy, to twist the rack beyond the point of endurance; to turn the screw tighter and tighter until it could no longer be borne.

She watched his face as he talked. It was an open, guileless face . . . the face of a man who believes sublimely in the power of right. He was perfectly sure that because of the justice of the crusade he was about to undertake, that he could not fail. He didn't know that but for a woman's whim he might at this very minute have been at the gates of death. He didn't know that he had been spared simply because of this woman's lust for cruelty. He didn't know that he was now in a trap far more difficult to free himself from than any Clark Ross could have set for him.

"I suppose it's presumptuous of me," he was saying, in deep, rather ecclesiastical tones, "to talk to you about my work . . . my plans, but somehow I feel that you are a person who will sympathize . . . understand and help. I felt it the first time I saw you walk out on the stage tonight. You have a sort of magic, Miss Trask . . . a sort of magic that makes one feel at peace."

Black magic, if he could have known it. Black magic that would presently turn everything to pain. There were others who would have warned him—young Malvern, Barry Fielding, Guy Mortimer—that he was on the brink of hell at the very moment that he imagined his eyes to be upon the stars.

"I was worried tonight," he said. "I can see how a man of sinister qualities like Ross would interest you. But I was afraid you wouldn't realize the danger of going off with him alone. I confess I was almost tempted to interfere."

"Is Ross really as bad as he's painted?" she asked innocently.

"He's the most dangerous man in the city," said Levering, "and I'll tell you why. He's not one of these gunmen who goes around murdering people with a machine gun. Did you notice that he just barely sipped his champagne tonight? I understand he doesn't drink at all. He's always cool, collected, playing his hand with the utmost skill. No one has ever pinned anything on him because he never lets down the bars for a minute. He's always on his guard . . . always covering up. If we could rid the city of that one man we would break the back of gangster domination."

"But what are his crimes?" she asked.

"Murder, blackmail, bootlegging, dope peddling . . . every vile practice on the calendar."

"And yet you have no definite evidence against him?"

"Not a shred," said Levering. He smiled a grim smile. "But at this time tomorrow the menace of Clark Ross will have been removed forever from this city."

Ivy was above everything an actress. There was not a trace of the eagerness she felt in her voice as she asked the next question. "How on earth are you going to do that, Mr. Levering?"

Levering laughed softly. "I was brought up in a country that is famous for establishing law and order, Miss Trask. Out West, when the law failed, the citizens got together and made it work by force. Well, gangsters are running this city by force and the only way to fight them is with their own methods. Fight murder with murder! Do you get the idea?"

"BUT how can you do that, Mr. Levering, without laying yourself open to the penalties of the law?" Her tone was still casual, but her eyes were bright steel points in the darkness.

"It's a pretty grim business," he said. "Perhaps I'd better not tell you . . . It's a man's job. Not the sort of thing you should trouble your lovely head with."

Ivy laughed, a light, gay little laugh. "There is one crime worse than murder or dope peddling, Mr. Levering," she said. "That is arousing a woman's curiosity and then failing to satisfy it. You've simply got to tell me how you are going to handle Ross so quickly when no one else has ever been able to touch him."

"You mustn't tell anyone," he said. "A person could sell this information to Ross for a fortune."

"I won't breathe a word of it," Ivy said.

A hard note crept into his voice. "It's quite simple," he said. "Tomorrow night we raid Ross' gambling house . . . ostensibly to prove liquor violation. Actually we are going there to finish Mr. Clark Ross. Someone starts trouble and in the excitement Mr. Clark Ross will find a bullet lodged very neatly between his eyes."

"But . . . but that's murder!" Ivy drew in her breath sharply.

"Is it murder to kill a man who is responsible for hundreds of deaths? Is it murder to kill a man who has made a travesty of the law? Is it murder to kill a man who is aiding and abetting in the corruption of the youth of our country? No, by God, Miss Trask, it isn't murder! It is a public benefac-

tion!" There was a fine conviction in his manner.

"And . . . and you will do the killing?" she asked, in a small voice.

"I know that shocks you," he said. "Let me tell you why I can do it without one qualm of conscience. I have a boy, Miss Trask . . . a little son four years old." He was tender now. The hard lines about his mouth were suddenly gentle, and his eyes which had flashed a moment before in righteous anger, were just a little misty. "That boy has the greatest heritage in the world, Miss Trask. He is an American—an American of the old pioneer stock.

"He has a right to be proud of his country. It has always stood for liberty, for fine, clean ideals. I want him to be proud of it when he grows old enough to realize and understand. I want him to have the same thrill that I have when he realizes that he is an American! Can he feel that thrill if men like Clark Ross have injected the poison of treachery and evil into the very fibre of our country? No! And I owe it to that boy of mine to stamp out this rottenness . . . to give him back the thing that every boy deserves; the right to be proud of his country!"

"But the danger to you?" she suggested.

Levering laughed softly. "Next to his country I want my boy to be proud of his dad," he said. "Would he be proud of me if I shirked this great opportunity to break the back of corruption and vice just because it involved a little personal hazard?"

They rode on for a minute or two in silence. Ivy was thinking fast; thinking of a way that would rid Clark Ross of this menace . . . a menace that was great because of the tremendous conviction behind it.

"You love your boy, don't you, Mr. Levering?" she said quietly.

"Love him?" Levering's voice shook just a trifle. "I'd give my right arm, my heart's blood for him, Miss Trask." He looked at her with shining eyes. "Some day you'll have children of your own . . . A woman of your type should have children. When you do, you'll understand why I want to make this world a place my boy will be glad to live in. The least we can do for our kids is fight for them."

The taxi was drawing up in front of Ivy's apartment. "I'd like to see your son," she said. "I should like to call on your wife. One of the things that my career has cost me is a home." She said it very convincingly, so convincingly that Levering could not guess that there was sardonic laughter behind what she was saying. "May I call some time?"

"Any time! Mrs. Levering and I would be delighted." He stood on the sidewalk, holding open the door of the cab for her. "I want to say," he added haltingly, "that meeting you has made it seem even more important to me to go on with my plan. Good night . . . and thank you."

She held out her hand to him. In the soft light from the hall of the apartment building she was especially lovely. "Take care of yourself," she said. "Faith is sometimes very costly. I hope your faith will not be too costly to you."

IVY hurried into the building, leaving Levering on the pavement, looking after her. Marcelle, her maid, opened the door for her and she went quickly into the entrance hall. Downstairs of Ivy Trask's duplex apartment, rich colors exhibited a fine, feminine taste. Soft, creamy woodwork served to show off her lovely, golden beauty. Flowers tastefully arranged . . . everything in place, and yet everything that suggested comfort.

But this was not the room that Ivy lived in. It was just a setting, a setting for Ivy Trask the actress, the woman of fine, noble character. The woman that in reality didn't exist. There was another room that was a setting for the real Ivy, and it was to this room that Ivy hurried now, for it was in this room that she found her whole attitude adjusted and attuned in a fashion that pleased her. Up a winding stairway to a door . . . a door that promised little as she opened it and stepped in.

Behind that door was the strangest room a woman ever called her own. It was a room of black and gold . . . a room of black and gold, pervaded by a strange, elusive perfume that somehow suggested the sinister Ivy Trask. It was a room of straight, hard black lines . . . a room with uncomfortable, hard black chairs. A room decorated with strange figures . . . figures in black marble . . . cruel figures. The central decoration in the room was a black marble statuette standing on a small black table. It was the familiar trilogy of "The Laocoön" . . . a father and two sons caught in the murderous embrace of a twisting serpent, their faces mirroring the terrible agony that was theirs as they were slowly crushed to death.

Not what one would expect in a lady's boudoir. And yet it seemed to fit in with the scheme of things, for this woman had apparently made a hobby of collecting statuettes which depicted physical suffering in some form or other. And there were strange objects; a whip hung over her dressing table . . . a black leather whip with three leather thongs, cruelly knotted. It was a whip that had been used, for the handle was well worn, and it was the first thing that Ivy glanced at as she came into the room. Hatred, intense, vicious fury clouded her eyes for a moment. The lovely, pale gold Ivy Trask was transformed into something unbelievably sinister.

She crossed the room and sat before the dressing table . . . a black table facing a gold mirror. She sat in silence for a minute or two, her narrowed eyes fixed on a small object on the table. It was a replica of a crouching black panther who clutched a small child in steely paws. One white hand reached out and seemed to caress this symbol of ruthlessness. Then she reached for the telephone, and in an almost harsh voice, called a number.

" I want to speak to Mr. Clark Ross." A pause, and then his voice came over the wire. " Listen," she continued coolly. " I've found out all you need to know. Levering will raid your place tomorrow night, and in the scuffle you are to be shot down in cold blood. They're not going to bother to get anything on you."

" Thanks," came the laconic reply across the wire.

" What are you going to do?"

" It seems that Mr. Daniel Levering will have to be shot down in cold blood first," said Clark Ross.

Ivy put her lips so close to the black mouthpiece of the telephone they almost touched it. " There is a better way," she said, in a low, purring voice. " A much better way. A way that will silence Mr. Daniel Levering forever, without running the risk of having a murder traced to you."

" Well?"

" Levering has a son . . . a small boy of four . . ."

As she talked, her hand gently caressed the figure of the crouching black panther.

CHAPTER VI

While Ivy Plans

IVY TRASK sat in the corner of her big limousine, driving up town to Clark Ross' office. She had not had much sleep. Most of that night she had walked the floor of that strange room of black and gold thinking . . . thinking. In those early morning hours she had evolved a scheme, a scheme that outranked anything she had done in her career. Clark Ross and Daniel Levering . . . king of the underworld and head of the forces of the law respectively. She suddenly realized that Fate had delivered both these men into her hands, and she meant to take advantage of it. This morning she would collect fifty thousand dollars from Ross, and before twenty-four hours had passed she fully expected to get twice that amount from Daniel Levering. She smiled faintly to herself . . . a hard, cruel smile.

When her car reached the gambling club she ordered Fanshawe, her chauffeur, to wait, and hurried upstairs. The main rooms of the club were in the hands of the charwomen, preparing it for the night's play. Ivy went back along the corridor to Clark Ross' office and rapped sharply on the door.

" Come in !"

Ross was seated at his desk. He rose as she entered and came forward eagerly to meet her. His face was expressionless as ever, but there was an excited gleam in his eyes.

" So you got Levering to spill the beans !" He pulled a comfortable chair close to his desk and passed her cigarettes. When she had lit one she leaned back and smiled at him.

"Have I earned my fifty thousand, Mr. Ross?"

"You can have it now—in cash—if you want it," he said. He opened the desk drawer and tossed her a bundle of bills which had been prepared for her. "I pay my debts promptly, Miss Trask."

"Well, I think we know enough to checkmate Levering permanently," she said. She paused for just a second, moistening her lips. "Do you want me to outline my idea to you?"

He inhaled deeply on his cigarette. "Shoot," he said.

"Levering plans to raid your place at midnight," she said coolly. "In the course of the raid you are to be shot down. If we could stop that raid . . ."

"You're sure," he cut in, sharply, "that it is scheduled for exactly midnight?"

"Positive," Ivy said, steadily. As she said it she could see Levering sitting in the back of the car the night before. Eleven sharp, he had said. "I asked him very definitely and he told me. Now here is my idea. Levering's one vulnerable spot is that kid of his. If the boy was to be kidnapped just a short time before the raid is scheduled, with a threat that if the raid is carried out it will finish him, Levering will back down in a second. You see the point? You can force him to resign from the force, save the raid on this club, and be clear of him for good."

"Why do you make a point of the kidnapping taking place a short time before the raid is scheduled? Wouldn't it be better to go to work on it now?"

"No," said Ivy, decisively, "for two reasons. First, if Levering has several hours to hunt for the boy something might go wrong . . . He might find him and then your goose would be cooked to a turn. Secondly, if you put off

stealing the boy till, let us say, eleven o'clock, Levering will be out of the house getting ready to make the raid. Probably only Mrs. Levering and the maids will be on hand, and you can take care of them easily enough. Levering won't have time to make any counter move and he'll have to call off the raid. Then you can refuse to return the boy until he has given up this vice crusade. Also you can probably make him pay that fifty thousand dollars you have just given me."

Ross studied the end of his cigarette thoughtfully. He could see the value in drawing the time element fine, but there was a definite risk involved. It meant that four of his best men would have to be out of the club until just before the scheduled time of the raid. If anything went wrong . . .

"It doesn't give us the slightest leeway for a slip-up of any sort," he said doubtfully.

"There simply must not be any slip-up," she said. "Surely you have three or four men that are clever enough to manage the kidnapping of that boy successfully? With only a couple of women in the house to deal with it should be simple."

"It's not that," he said. "But if the raid should, by any chance, come off ahead of schedule, I'd be in a tough spot with those four men missing. Because," he added grimly, "if there's to be any shooting we're not going to let it be one-sided."

"There won't be any raid . . . You can bank on that," said Ivy. "When Levering hears that his boy is missing he will agree to any terms."

CLARK ROSS was a man who made decisions quickly. His snap judgment on matters of importance had always been good . . . always until the night before when he had allowed himself to take on Ivy Trask as an ally. For shrewd as he was Clark Ross could not see the trap into which he was walking. He rang the buzzer on the desk.

"I'll send for the boys and tell them just exactly what they are to do. The kid is to be stolen at eleven sharp, and Levering is to be notified at once that unless he calls off the raid and resigns his position that it will be just too bad."

"You'd better leave a note in the house . . . something for Mrs. Levering to find. She'll have a tremendous influence on him," said Ivy, shrewdly. "Shall I write it for you?"

"Go ahead, while I talk to the boys," said Ross.

She moved around to his chair behind the desk, her eyes narrowed. So far things were going exactly as she had planned them.

Meanwhile, other plans were being made. Daniel Levering was at police headquarters in conference with Captain Danning, the head of the flying squadron that had been put at the Westerner's disposal. Danning was a shrewd policeman, who knew his underworld inside out and had a certain amount of scepticism when it came to Levering's schemes. But he was prepared to obey orders to the letter.

"We must be sure that the time element is properly synchronized," said Levering, puffing on a cigar. "We will have men ready at all the entrances to the club and they must be ready to go in at exactly the same instant."

"There'll be no trouble about that, Mr. Levering."

"I'll get down here to the station at ten and we'll get under way shortly after that. At precisely eleven o'clock we enter the club. I am counting very definitely on the element of surprise. I don't think Ross has the slightest idea that we'll act against him so soon. He knows we have nothing against him and he thinks he's safe."

Danning chewed on the stem of his pipe. "I hope you haven't mentioned this affair to anyone, Mr. Levering. Ross is a powerful man . . . He has ways of getting information that would surprise you. If he knows you're planning a raid, and knows that you plan in the course of that raid to finish him . . . Well, we're apt to be met with a machine gun barrage instead of surprise."

"I haven't talked to a soul," said Levering. Already he had forgotten that he had let slip the salient details of his plan to Ivy Trask, and if he had remembered he would have felt perfectly safe, for she was the type of woman a man could trust. She had sympathized and understood his passionate desire to make the city a place worth living in.

"I'm relieved to hear it, sir," said Danning.

Levering was thinking ahead. "There won't be many patrons at the club as early as eleven," he said. "The crowd doesn't begin to arrive until after the theatre . . . but there will be some. I want them got out of the place as quickly as possible. When the showdown comes I want no one there but our men."

"Yes, sir."

"And one more thing, Danning. If I can come face to face with Ross alone, so much the better. The fewer people who are in on the know, the better. I suppose most of your men are trustworthy, but what they don't know won't hurt them."

Danning shook his head. "I'm afraid of what will happen to you afterwards. Ross' mob will put you on the spot, sure as hell!"

Levering laughed. "They're all yellow rats, Danning, and once they haven't Ross to guide them they'll all fade away out of sight. I'm not alarmed about any aftermath."

Danning shrugged. "Of course, that's your concern, sir."

"Of course it is, Danning. Now have we got all the details straight? You are to allot the men to their various stations and at precisely eleven we all enter. Whatever patrons there are will be hustled out and then we have our little showdown with Ross. Your men are to watch his men, but I will personally attend to Mr. Clark Ross. And I expect to eat my usual dish of ham and eggs tomorrow morning, Danning."

"There won't be any slip-up as far as the men are concerned," said Danning.

CHAPTER VII

The Raid

A QUARTER to eleven. Clark Ross, usually in complete control of his nerves, paced restlessly up and down the floor of his office. In fifteen minutes Dutch Slade and three other of his men would enter the Levering house and take the Westerner's small son. They planned to leave the child at a hideaway in town, one that they could reach within ten minutes of the time they got him. Another ten minutes would see them back here at the club— roughly eleven twenty-five. That gave them thirty-five minutes in which to get word to Daniel Levering that he must call off the raid or forfeit his son's life. It was drawing things pretty fine . . . Almost too fine for comfort now that the time had arrived. Perhaps he had trusted too much to Ivy Trask's judgment in this affair, yet there had been

a cool-headedness and a directness about her planning that had convinced him of its soundness. Well, it was too late to make any changes now. Ivy had promised to come direct from her performance at the theatre to the club so that they could celebrate their victory over the crusader together, and wait for him to kick in with his resignation and his ransom for the child.

Ten minutes to eleven. Ross lit a cigarette and blew the acrid gray smoke toward the ceiling. He hated inaction. He hated to sit back and entrust such an important job to his men, but it had seemed unwise for him to leave the club. Levering might be having it watched, and if Ross acted in any suspicious fashion it might serve to precipitate the raid, and everything depended on the raid being pulled off on scheduled time . . . midnight.

He wished that he might talk to someone about it, but only Ivy Trask and the four men who had been commissioned to the kidnaping job were in the know. It was best not to take any unnecessary people into their confidence on this thing. He walked down the corridor to the main gambling room and saw that already a handful of customers had arrived and were playing at the roulette wheels and the table for chemin-de-fer. Then back to his office.

Five minutes to eleven . . . Slade and the boys would be almost ready now. In five minutes they would be in the house and off with Bobby Levering, and in fifteen minutes he would get the tip-off on it over the phone. Then he would feel a little easier. Not that he wouldn't be ready for Levering when he arrived at midnight if things *did* go wrong. No mug from the Middle West was going to put anything over on him; but it would mean ducking out into hiding and inactivity for an indefinite period of time.

Well, there was no reason why Slade and the boys should fail. It had all been carefully worked out in detail. It was going to be just too bad for Mr. Daniel Levering, with all his high sounding talk about driving crime out of the city. There was a lucrative graft here that Ross expected to avail himself of for a good many years to come.

Across the street, in the shadow of a protecting doorway, Daniel Levering stood with his eyes glued on the phosphorescent dial of his wrist watch. One minute to go. He felt a strange exhilaration about the adventure that lay ahead of him. A rat like Clark Ross should be exterminated like all other rats. Thirty seconds to go . . .

Out of the darkness men appeared and started across the street. The uniformed doorman who stood outside the club saw them coming and turned apprehensively toward the entrance, but if he intended to warn his employers all idea of loyalty ended when he felt the steel barrel of a pistol stuck into the small of his back. Levering nodded to the men who were grouped about the front door, and, pulling the brim of his black felt hat down over his eyes, he led the way into the club and up the stairway to the main floor.

The men who had come in the back way had already reached this floor, and the guests playing at the tables saw at once that something was up. There was no sign of resistance from the croupiers or other employees of the club, and Levering noticed that none of Ross' hangers-on seemed to be in evidence. For just a moment he had a sinking sensation. Had Ross got wind of this thing somehow and skipped?

"We have no intention of causing any of the patrons any trouble," he said briefly. "Get your coats and hats and leave quietly. Our business is with the management." Then he spied Mc-Carthy, the waiter who had served him the night before. "Is Ross in?" he asked.

McCarthy gave him a vapid, unintelligent look. He shrugged his shoulders. "I don't keep tabs on the boss," he said.

Levering smiled grimly. "We'll soon find out," he said. "You take charge here, Danning. I'm going back to Ross' office."

He dropped his hand into the pocket of his coat and strode off down the corridor. Unceremoniously he flung open the office door and stepped in.

The entrance of the police had been so quiet that until he swung around to see who had entered his office, Clark Ross was unaware of what had happened. At the sight of Levering his eyes narrowed, but he stood quite still, his masklike face betraying nothing of what he felt. Something had gone wrong . . . desperately wrong.

"Hello, Levering," he said softly.

"You're being raided, Ross," said Levering harshly. "My men are all over the club. There's no use trying any rough stuff."

"WHO is trying any?" asked Ross, coolly. He moved slowly toward his desk, took a cigarette from the box and lit it. He was thinking fast. If Ivy Trask had been right about what Levering intended to do he was in a tight spot. His gun was in the top drawer of his desk, and if he made a move for it Levering would probably plug him. He could see the bulge of the gun in Levering's coat pocket, and saw that it was already trained on him. "I told you last night, Levering, that I was willing to have you raid the club any time you cared to. You'll find nothing incriminating here."

He shifted his position so that he was standing directly in front of the desk drawer. Levering hadn't asked him to raise his hands. Apparently he was waiting, as Ivy had said, for the slightest provocation to pull his trigger.

"There isn't much need for incriminating evidence, Ross," said Levering, sternly. "I know what you are and what you are doing. Liquor, dope—everything vile. You've gotten away with it long enough, Ross. You're through—washed up."

"Interesting if true," said Ross casually. His long, slender fingers were resting on the edge of the desk now, not six inches from his gun. Could he wrench open that drawer and get it before Levering would fire? Ross was at his best in a situation of this sort. His brain working coolly, quickly.

"It is true, and you might as well know that the game's up," rapped Levering.

Ross looked straight into Levering's burning eyes. "Just what do you propose to do?" he asked calmly. "You have no legal charge that you can bring against me. Do you propose to shoot me down in cold blood, Mr. Levering?" One hand dropped slowly down over the edge of the desk toward the handle of the drawer. He would have to act in a split second if he was going to save himself. There was a look of almost fanatical righteousness on Levering's face, and it was obvious to Ross that the man in front of him had quite definitely justified the course he was going to pursue. He must either act quickly or stall for time. In a few minutes Slade and the others would be back . . . he might trade his life for the boy's.

Then the door to the study opened once more . . . a rustle of silk, a faint exotic perfume, and Ivy Trask stood there. Levering saw her out of the corner of his eye, and his lips parted in a grim smile.

"Well, Miss Trask, I told you I'd be here at eleven o'clock, and here I am."

Clark Ross stiffened, and his keen eyes shifted to the woman's face. It was pale, lovely, wide-eyed with horror. For just a second Ross was uncertain.

"You say you told Miss Trask you would be here at eleven?" he repeated slowly.

"Yes," said Levering. "I told her last night I was coming. If I were you, Miss Trask, I'd leave. I have a little score to settle here that might prove unpleasant for you to witness."

Clark Ross' lips had narrowed into a thin slit, and his eyes glittered like splintered ice. In a clear flash he saw the whole thing, saw that he had been played for a fool. With him out of the way she would be able to take the big share of the kidnap ransom; she had already hooked him for fifty thousand dollars and then betrayed him into the hands of his enemy. For the first time in his life, Clark Ross lost all control of his emotions. His face was chalk white as he stared at Ivy. Then suddenly his rage knew no bounds.

He sprang around the corner of the desk, a mad desire to sink his fingers into that lovely white throat.

Levering's gun roared in the close confines of the room. Halfway between the desk and Ivy, Ross stopped abruptly, strangely rigid, surprise and dismay on his face. Then with a grotesque spin he fell in a heap on the floor, a little trickle of crimson running from his temple.

Captain Danning came running into the room and took in the picture with a quick, comprehensive glance.

"He tried to attack Miss Trask," said Levering quietly. "I had to shoot him."

"I was on my way back here to get you when I heard the shot," said Danning. "Your wife wants to speak to you on the phone."

"My wife!" Levering was incredulous. "Why should she call me at a time like this?"

"She said it was vitally important—a matter of life and death," said Danning. "Perhaps you can get her on that extension phone there."

Levering went to the telephone and lifted the receiver to his ear. "Hello!" He listened, and Ivy, watching him intently, saw his great body sag and every vestige of color leave his face. His voice was thick, choking when he spoke.

"I'll come at once," he said.

He put down the phone and looked dully from Ivy to Danning. It was as though he couldn't take in what he had heard . . . as though he was numb, unable to move. Then suddenly the words broke from him in something that was very like a sob.

"The devils! The devils! They've taken my boy . . . my Bobby. Take charge here, Danning. I've got to go . . . I've got to go." He staggered blindly out of the room.

CHAPTER VIII

Before Police Guns

AT eleven sharp a tragedy took place at the Levering house in the east eighties. Mrs. Levering had long since steeled herself to the fact that her husband was constantly running risks, but somehow it had never occurred to her that she, or the rest of her household, was in any danger. She knew that her husband was staging a raid this evening, but raids were not particularly dangerous as a general thing, and she had taught herself to control her nerves at such a time.

Thus, when, at eleven o'clock, the front door bell rang, Mrs. Levering was not disturbed. She had told the servants that they might go to bed so that the opening of the door had devolved upon her. With no thought that danger was at hand she went to the door and opened it. At once three men crowded into the entryway . . . three men flourishing pistols, their faces covered with black masks. Even then Mrs. Levering kept her nerve. She had heard of hold-up men, and she assumed that these masked bandits were here to steal her silver or jewelry.

"You take Mrs. Levering back in the living room, Benny," said the leader. "You, Rossi, keep your eyes peeled for the servants. I'll get the kid."

It was all so fast, so ruthlessly quick, that Mrs. Levering was scarcely able to undertand what was going on. It couldn't be that they were taking her Bobby. The leader reappeared.

"We are kidnaping your baby, Mrs. Levering," he said quietly. "There is no use your attempting to phone the police, because your telephone wires have been cut." He handed her a thin white envelope. "You will discover in this note the terms upon which you can get your son back. I advise you to get in immediate touch with your husband, for it depends almost entirely upon him whether you ever see the boy alive again. Good night."

The leader hurried out, and the man called Rossi, keeping her covered with the gun, backed out after him. Mrs.

Levering ripped open the note. It was addressed to her husband.

You will not communicate with police. At twelve-thirty tonight you will stand at the corner of Fiftieth Street and Lexington Avenue. A driver will approach you in a taxi and speak to you by name. You will hand him fifty thousand dollars in unmarked bills. If you have the police with you, or have this taxi followed you will never see your son alive again.

An attempt to use the telephone proved that the kidnapers had spoken the truth, for she was unable to raise the operator. After rousing the maids, she hurried out to the corner and called Police Headquarters. From there she learned where her husband was and managed to get Clark Ross' club on the wire. Breathless, choked with grief and horror, she told him what had happened.

There was nothing to do now but wait . . . wait and torture herself with imaginary pictures of what was happening to Bobby. It seemed hours to her before her white-faced husband arrived. He read the note, his face grim.

"There's nothing to do but follow instructions," he said.

"But can you raise that much cash at this time of night?"

"Certainly; if I have to get a bank president out of bed! You sit tight, mother, and keep your courage."

Meanwhile, two blocks away from the appointed place for the pay-off, a taxi was parked at the curb. The driver, lolling behind the wheel, glanced from time to time at his watch. It was a dark spot in the middle of a block where this taxi was parked, for the driver had no intention of taking a fare. He paid little or no attention to passing traffic, and so it was that he failed to notice that a big, handsomely equipped limousine had drawn up about twenty yards behind him. He failed to notice that the chauffeur had slipped out from behind the wheel and was coming slowly, but quite nonchalantly, along the sidewalk toward him. And even if he had seen the chauffeur he would probably not have guessed that the man had a short piece of iron pipe concealed up the sleeve of his coat.

The chauffeur was Fanshawe, Ivy Trask's man. His movements were casual, yet alert, as he approached the taxi. The last few feet he traversed boldly and openly.

" Got a match, buddy?"

" Sure." The man in the taxi reached leisurely into his pocket.

Down came the piece of pipe over the back of his head in a sharp, vicious blow that left him crumpled, unconscious. Fanshawe worked quickly. The block was deserted for the moment and he dragged the unconscious form of the driver out of the front of the taxi and bundled it into the back. Hands and feet were securely bound and the man was gagged. Then, with another look to be sure he had been unobserved, Fanshawe got in behind the wheel of the taxi. A glance at his wrist watch told him that it was just about time to start.

Meanwhile Daniel Levering had worked fast, and at exactly twelve thirty he stood at the appointed corner waiting to do business with the kidnapers. He hadn't long to wait, for presently Fanshawe, driving the taxi, drew up alongside.

" Mr. Levering?" he said, in a disguised voice. A pair of huge dark glasses pretty well eliminated the chance that Levering would recognize him if he ever saw him again.

Silently Levering held out the package containing the money. His lips were tightly compressed, and he was struggling against an overwhelming desire to take this man by the throat and tear from him the information as to where Bobby was hidden and who was back of this outrage.

Fanshawe took the package. " Go back to your house and wait for instructions. If everything is in order you will be given information as to how to reach your son." Without anything further he drove off.

LEVERING went back to his house and to his anxious wife. Nothing to do but wait . . . wait, and agonize over the possibilities. Levering paced the floor of his living room, his teeth clamped tightly over the butt of a dead cigar. Mrs. Levering sat quietly in a chair, her red-rimmed eyes looking into space, in the grip of that deadly sort of calm that is almost worse than hysterics. At last, after nearly three-quarters of an hour, there came a ring at the front door bell. Levering literally ran to open it, not knowing what to expect. He was confronted by a Western Union messenger.

" Telegram for Mr. Levering."

" Right. Wait . . . there may be an answer." Levering ripped open the yellow envelope. *Boy held by Ross men at 162 E. 48.* Advise immediate action. Levering saw there was no signature. " No answer," he said. He went back into the house and showed the wire to his wife.

" This sounds as though it might come from someone else beside the kitnapers to me," he said. " If Bobby was taken by Ross' mob I'm afraid they'll double-cross us when they learn that Ross is dead. I'm going to follow the advice in this wire and act."

Twenty minutes later Levering had rejoined Danning and the flying squad and they were heading toward the ad-

dress on East Forty-eighth. Danning was inclined to agree that the fact that the ransom money had been paid would not cut much ice with Ross' men when they learned that their leader had been killed. The best chance there was for Bobby was to trade his life for the lives of the men in the house.

A block away from the hideout the policemen got out of their cars. They were all heavily armed and two of them carried sub-machine guns with them. Danning issued crisp, concise orders for surrounding the house, an old brownstone structure with heavily boarded windows which kept out all light. From the sidewalk it was impossible to tell whether or not there was anybody inside or not. When part of the squad had had time enough to surround the house, Levering, Danning, and half a dozen other men hurried up the steps to the front door. Sharp knocking brought no response. Levering spoke up, loudly.

" You fellows inside! The house is surrounded. You haven't a chance to get away. If you turn over my boy to me safe and sound you'll all be given a chance to get away. If you don't not one of you will get out alive. Will you open up?"

No answer.

" If you don't open up in fifteen seconds," said Levering, grimly, " we force our way in. And if you've harmed the boy, God help you." He turned to one of the men. " Stand by with that machine gun," he said loudly. " You with the axes, get ready to force the door." He glanced at his watch. " Five seconds left . . ."

From the back of the house came the sharp reports of half a dozen pistol shots. Levering motioned to his men. " Force that door, and for God's sake hurry !"

A dozen lusty blows with an axe, and then the broad shoulders of Levering and Danning smashed the door open and they rushed into the hall with drawn guns. The house was lighted, and just as they entered three men came running down the stairs.

"Quick! Stick 'em up!" rapped Levering.

Dutch Slade and his two men hesitated only a second. The sight of the attacking force with pistols and machine guns settled the issue. Their hands went up to the ceiling.

"Come down here. Now get this straight," said Levering. "I want my boy, and I want him quick. If you haven't harmed him I'll promise you all twenty-four unmolested hours in which to get out of town. If you have harmed him . . . well, no power on earth can save you."

Slade and his men exchanged glances.

"You've got to think for yourselves, boys," growled Danning. "Clark Ross is dead."

The color faded slowly from Slade's face. He made a quick gesture with his upraised hand. "The kid's in the room at the head of the stairs," he said hoarsely.

Levering bounded past him and up the stairs. He pushed open the door of the room, and there, lying on the bed was Bobby. Levering caught the faint odor of chloroform. He knelt beside the boy, his heart pounding. He examined the unconscious lad quickly and was relieved to discover that he was breathing regularly and without difficulty. Gently he picked him up in his arms and went out and down the stairs. At the bottom of the stairs he turned to Slade and his men who had been disarmed by Danning.

"I always keep my word," he said, sternly. "You birds have just twenty-four hours in which to get out of town. After that this town is going to turn into a hell for you and your kind."

He turned and hurried out of the house, young Bobby held tightly in his arms.

Captain Danning jerked his thumb toward the door. "Scram!" he said, dryly.

GEOFFREY MALVERN stood on the threshold of that room of black and gold. His keen eye took in the picture of Ivy Trask, lying gracefully on the chaise longue, her pale gold head against a black pillow. She was smiling at him mockingly.

"Why this early morning call, my dear Geoffrey? Can it be that you were concerned about my health?"

"Not in the slightest," he said.

"My habits, then? I saw you looking disapprovingly at me the other night at Ross' gambling house. Still, you were there yourself so I guess you don't mind gambling. I am consumed with curiosity, my dear Geoffrey."

Malvern took from his pocket a folded copy of the morning paper. He opened it and very slowly read the headlines to her. "*Underworld King Killed in Vice Raid. Daniel Levering Strikes First Blow in Crusade Against Crime. Later Rescues Small Son Kidnaped by Mobsters After Paying Fifty Thousand Dollar Ransom. Gangsters' Hideout Revealed in Anonymous Telegram.*" Malvern paused to look at her quizzically. "I talked to McCarthy, a waiter at Ross' place. He said that Ross was ready for the raid . . . someone had told him exactly what to expect. But somehow there was a mistake about the time of the raid."

Ivy's eyes were very bright. "Surely you haven't called at this hour of the morning to read out loud to me, Geoffrey. I have seen all that in my own paper."

"How much did Ross pay you for the information you got from Levering . . . and on which you double-crossed him?" asked Malvern.

"Rather warm for this time of year, don't you think, Geoffrey?"

"Did you collect the ransom money, too?" Malvern persisted, grimly.

Ivy got up from the chaise longue and crossed the room to the telephone on her dressing table. With her eyes still on Malvern she called a number. "I'd like to speak to Mr. Daniel Levering," she said. Then presently, in a voice that was rich with sympathy and understanding, "This is Ivy Trask, Mr. Levering. I wanted to tell you how glad I am to know your boy is all right . . . And he's suffered no ill effects? . . . Splendid! . . . Why, yes. When you and Mrs. Levering have recovered from the shock I should be glad to come to tea . . . Good-by."

She put down the phone and reached for a cigarette. Malvern's eyes were hard and cold.

"You are a great actress, Ivy . . . and the evilest woman I have ever known. Somehow I'm always just a step behind you. I know . . . but I can't prove. But the day is coming . . ."

"Oh, please, Geoffrey. I get enough of the theatre at night. You're so dreadfully melodramatic. Do come back when you're feeling better."

"I'll come back, Ivy," he said, slowly. "Some day I'll come back with the evidence that will put a rope around that lovely white throat of yours. Good morning."

DIZZY MALONE

Pulp magazines took advantage of the big crime era, issuing titles such as *The Underworld, Gangland Stories, Racketeer Stories, Gang World, Speakeasy Stories, Mobsters, Underworld Romances, Prison Stories, Underworld Love,* and *Mobs.*

Of course, on the other side, there were *G-Men Detective, Feds, Ace G-Man Stories, Federal Agent,* and other titles favoring the law-and-order view.

Perry Paul created two women series for *Gun Molls Magazine,* a publication that began in 1930. One offered Dizzy Malone; "The Jane from Hell's Kitchen" from the October 1930 issue is reprinted here. The other featured Madame, a "mystery moll of the underworld."

"These stories aren't long on literary quality," says pulp historian Bill Blackbeard, "but they are marvelous period pieces."

In a letter appearing in the same issue as "The Jane from Hell's Kitchen," author Paul, a former crime reporter, expressed his enthusiasm for the magazine "because the moll is the real thing around which underworld's life revolves. . . ."

"Somebody'll get it in the neck," said Dizzy, "and don't

The Jane from Hell's Kitchen

By PERRY PAUL

CHAPTER I

DIZZY MALONE

THE grizzled district attorney stood over a newspaper spread out on his desk, scare heads staring up at him in crude challenge.

*CHICAGO PROSECUTOR
VANISHES IN NEW YORK*

**Mysterious Kidnaper Demands
Huge Ransom**

*Local District Attorney Scouts
Gangster Vengeance Motive*

The district attorney, scourge of

forget I told you to keep your eyes off the ground!"

Things happened quickly to Dizzy Malone—because Dizzy was a real gun moll—a jane with a purple paradise and a red past—but a sport.

New York's underworld, glanced nervously from the headlines to the watch on his wrist and showed his teeth in a smile of cynical satisfaction.

Behind him the door opened noiselessly—a flash of chiffon and silk—the door closed and a girl backed her quivering body against it, her mouth open, panting.

Her high, pointed heels ground into the heavy rug as she struggled for self-control. Her lithe, supple body tautened. Her lips hardened into a thin scarlet line. The grey eyes, shadowed by a tight-fitting crimson bit of a hat, tempered to the glitter of new steel.

Sensing an alien presence, the district attorney's head came up sharply.

" 'Local D. A. scouts gangster

vengeance motive!'" the scarlet lips jeered.

The man sprang round to face the door with the agility of a jungle beast of prey.

"Dizzy Malone," he gasped, "the same, gorgeous body and all!"

The girl swung her slender hips across the room until she faced the man.

James Mitchell, veteran district attorney of New York, looked down at her lovely blonde bravado with the expression of a man charmed against his will by some exotic yet poisonous serpent.

Dizzy Malone was like that. She went to men's heads. Her moniker was a stall. They called her Dizzy because she most decidedly wasn't any way you looked at it.

"Well, when did you get back to your purple paradise in Hell's Kitchen?" the district attorney demanded. He was a tough baby. He knew all the dodges. He talked gangster talk and every crook in New York feared him. "I thought you lammed it to Europe with the Ghost when he finished his rap up the river."

The girl's sensitive nostrils quivered.

"Yeah? You *thought* so!" she sneered. "Well, I didn't. The Ghost saw to it that I missed the boat. He'd decided to change his luck, I guess. Anyway Spanish Lil went with him. Her hair is black, mine's blonde. And that's why——"

"Say, wait a minute!" Mitchell interrupted. "I'm not running any lovelorn bureau. What's the idea? How did you get in here, anyway?"

"That's my business!" she flared. "Now collapse, stuffed-shirt, while I put on the loud speaker!"

The D. A. opened his mouth—and closed it again. When Dizzy made up her mind to talk, she talked, and everyone else listened.

"Now, get a load of this," Dizzy snapped. "It's about that guy Burke, the D. A. from Chicago, that's disappeared. I gotta hunch who lifted him."

It was Mitchell's turn to sneer.

"So you want to squeal, huh, Dizzy?"

"Squeal?" Dizzy panted. "You— you——!"

She crouched like a feline killer ready to spring. Coral-tipped fingers that could tear a man's face to ribbons, tensed. Her lips curled back from her teeth in a fighting snarl of defiance.

"Now calm down, Dizzy. Calm down."

The girl's rage did a quick fadeout, leaving in its place a cold, calculating grimness that was a sure danger signal.

"No more cracks like that then, big boy." Her voice grated slightly on a note of savage restraint. "Get this through your smart legal mind— I came here to make you a proposition, not to turn anyone up. Get that straight!"

"All right, Dizzy," the D. A. growled, glancing hastily at his watch. "Shoot."

"You gotta job to do, Mitchell. I gotta job to do. You help me. I help you. See?"

The district attorney waited.

"Now about this D. A. from Chicago. His disappearing act puts you in a tough spot, doesn't it? Looks like a smart game to me. He gets a phoney wire to come see you. He hops the Century and walks into this office the next morning. You don't know what it's all about. You didn't send any wire. Burke walks outa here and disappears. You get a letter demanding a big ransom for his return. Your job is to get Burke back and turn up the guy that pulled the job. Right?"

"Right, Dizzy."

"My job's a little different. A guy

—yes, it was the Ghost—put the double-x on me. I was his moll. We worked a good racket. We piled up a stake, a big one. We were all set to beat it for the sticks, get married and settle down respectable, and forget about rackets. My man was clever, he never let the coppers get anything on us. Then some fly dick framed a rap on him."

"Oh, yeah?"

"Yeah! I said framed. My man went stir-bugs up there in the Big House, and no wonder. Baldy Ross, his partner, and a straight-shooting guy, gets lit out in Chi with a cokie that's a rat. A copper gets bumped off and the rat turns states evidence to save his stinking hide. Baldy swings because my man's in stir and can't spring him."

Her pink fists clenched.

"The cokie that shot the copper's dead now—they put him on the spot for the rat he was."

The girl's grey eyes narrowed.

"Then what happens? Well, if there's one guy the Ghost's crazy about, it's his kid brother. The Kid's a wild one but my man can hold him. He keeps him outa the racket, sends him to college. While the Ghost's in the "Can" some wise yegg gets the Kid coked up and they pull a job. A watchman gets knocked off. You got nothing on the Kid but circumstantial evidence, but you send him up the river and he fries, across the court from where the Ghost is raving in a strait-jacket.

"The Ghost's already a little nuts from the bullets he gets in his head when that German ace shoots him down in France—but he's a genius just the same. He comes outa the Big House completely bugs. What they did to Baldy and the Kid turns him into a mad killer.

"I been waiting for him, not touching our stake. I figure if I can get him to Europe I can nurse that killer streak outa him.

"Then what happens? That black-haired flossie, Spanish Lil gets her hooks into him and he takes the stake I'd helped him make, and lams it with her. She takes him for the wad and the Ghost is flat, and more bugs than ever."

"Well, what of it, Dizzy?" the D. A. cut in impatiently, shooting a hurried look at his watch.

"Just this, big boy. The Ghost taught me all he knows. He taught me how to fly, among other things, and how to work rackets the flatties never heard of. And I can spot the Ghost's technique through a flock of stone walls. Just about now he's got two things on his mind—dough and revenge.

"Listen! Someone will pay handsome to get this D. A. from Chi back. And don't forget—he prosecuted Baldey Ross—he's the guy that swung Baldy!"

She paused a moment to let her words sink in.

"This is the Ghost's work all right. You'll never find him but I think I can. And I can spring this bozo Burke for you, and get the guy that double-crossed me. But I want to do it legal. All I ask is a plane, a fast one, with a machine-gun on it, and your say so to go ahead."

The district attorney's laugh grated through the silence of the room.

"For once I think you're really dizzy," he said.

His sarcasm cut the girl like the flick of a whip. Her face went white.

"Then you won't——"

"Take it easy for a minute, Dizzy, and let me talk," the big man interrupted not unkindly. The beaten look in the girl's eyes touched him in spite of himself. "In the first place the Ghost is still in Europe. I'd have been tipped-off the moment he stepped off a boat."

"I think you're wrong there, big boy, but—go on."

The man took another surreptitious glance at his watch.

"It won't be long now, Dizzy, so I don't mind telling you a few things," he went on. "We've got this Burke business on ice."

He took an envelope from his pocket and drew out a soiled sheet of paper.

"Here is the ransom letter. For once we outsmarted the newspaper boys. They know it exists but they *don't* know what it says. Listen!"

He read:

" 'UNLESS HALF A MILLION DOLLARS IS FORTHCOMING BURKE WILL NEVER BE SEEN ALIVE AGAIN. FOLLOW THESE DIRECTIONS. THE MONEY, IN GRAND NOTES, IS TO BE TIED SECURELY IN A MARKET BASKET PAINTED WHITE. PLACE MONEY AND BASKET IN THE EXACT CENTER OF VAN CORTLANDT PARK PARADE GROUND AT 7:30 P. M. TODAY AND CLEAR A SPACE FOR A QUARTER OF A MILE AROUND IT. IF THERE IS A PERSON WITHIN THAT AREA BURKE WILL BE PUT ON THE SPOT AT ONCE. THE MONEY WILL BE CALLED FOR AT 7:55 AND BURKE WILL BE DELIVERED AT THE CITY HALL ALIVE AT 8:00 IF DIRECTIONS ARE FOLLOWED IMPLICITLY. ONE FALSE MOVE QUEERS THE GAME.' "

Mitchell looked up and grinned.

"We followed the directions all right, but there's a cordon of police around the park that a midget louse couldn't get through. They wait for a flash from us and make the pinch, exactly at the moment Burke is being returned to City Hall. Furthermore, the money in the basket is phoney and there's a ring of plainclothesmen for five blocks each way around City Hall. Whoever made way with Burke won't stand a show. We'll nab them sure."

"Clever, all right," Dizzy admitted, "but you can't outsmart the Ghost. He's a genius, I tell you, a crazy genius. And there's only one person can put the skids under him, and I'm that baby."

"Okay, okay, Dizzy," the man replied genially, "but whoever pulled this Burke coup is going to get it in the neck in a few minutes."

The girl hunched her shoulders.

"*Somebody'll* get it in the neck, all right," she said cryptically. "And don't forget I told you to keep your eyes off the ground."

Her remark went unheeded, however, for a rap sounded on the door and the next instant it was flung open admitting the slick, dark head of Tom Louden, the D. A.'s shrewd, young assistant.

"Seven forty-five, Chief," he reminded Mitchell. "Most time for the show to start."

"All right, Tom. Is the car ready?"

"Yes, sir."

"Good. Come on, Dizzy. You offered to help us so we'll let you in on the pay-off."

The girl followed them to a low, black police car that waited at the curb in front of the Tombs. She took her place in the back seat between Mitchell and the assistant D. A. without a word.

A sign from the district attorney and the car purred down Centre Street.

Mitchell rubbed his hands with keen anticipation. A suspicion of doubt drew Louden's lips down in a faint frown. Dizzy's face was a blank.

THE car swung into Chambers Street and stopped opposite the rear entrance to City Hall. They were out and hurrying around the grimy, outmoded building.

The plaza in front wore a peculiarly deserted appearance. Walks and benches were empty. The statue of Civic Virtue thrust its marble chest upward, unwatched by newsboy or tattered bench-warmer.

Broadway and Park Row were still literally sprinkled with homeward-bound workers, but they shunned the plaza as though it bore a curse. An atmosphere of tense expectancy hung over it, brooding, sinister, almost palpable in the gathering summer dusk.

Dizzy found herself on the broad steps before City Hall in the midst of a group of grim, tight-lipped men.

The district attorney held his watch in his hand.

"Seven fifty-five," he muttered. "Five minutes to go."

The familiar sounds of traffic came to them in a muted murmur as though muffled by the wall of silence that ringed them in.

"Fifty-seven."

Bodies tautened.

"Fifty-nine."

Keen eyes swept the approaches to the plaza—right hands flicked furtively to bulging pockets.

Dizzy's shoulders slumped forward in a nonchalant slouch, her eyes rose in slow boredom toward the darkening heavens.

A low rumble impinged upon the silence, like the growl of distant thunder. Into it burst the first booming note of the clock in the tower.

The rumble increased to a roar. filled the air with a howl of sound, snuffed out the metallic clang of the clock's second note. The screaming drone of wind through wires.

Eyes snapped upward.

Then it came.

Sweeping in low over the Municipal building hurtled a black shadow —a low wing, streamline racing monoplane. It banked sharply as though to give its pilot a view of the square below him, then disappeared behind the Woolworth building.

The watchers stood petrified.

Once more the black ship swung into their range of vision, lower this time, banked, and circled the cramped area like a hovering eagle.

No one moved.

Suddenly the pilot pulled his somber-hued bus into a steep zoom above the Municipal Building, fluttered up into a graceful reversement and hurled his crate across the plaza again directly at the grey Woolworth tower. Swooping down he pulled the screaming ship up into a sharp inside loop that almost scraped the walls and reached its apex directly above the huddled group on the steps.

As it hung there for an instant, upside down, a black shape dropped like a plummet from the auxiliary cockpit. The pilot brought his plane out of the loop and scudded out of sight toward the south.

THE black object fell writhing. A flutter of black sprang from it, mushroomed out, breaking the swift descent with a jerk.

"A parachute!"

The cry broke like a single word from the lips of the stunned watchers, a moan of mingled surprise and relief.

The thud, thud of running feet as the nucleus of a crowd closed in.

Slowly, silently the 'chute floated down through the windless dusk, the figure suspended beneath it swinging back and forth in an ever-lessening arc.

The group on the steps scattered from beneath it.

A flash of sudden enlightenment burst upon the district attorney. His cry split the silence like the shrill of a siren.

"Burke!"

The kidnaper had kept his word.

A ragged cheer rose. It changed to a gasp of horror, an instant later, as the 'chute deposited its burden with a dull crash on the stone plaza and its black silken folds crumpled slowly over it.

There it lay in a huddled heap, unmoving.

The D. A. sprang toward it, followed closely by his men. Hands tore eagerly at the enveloping silk. A cordon of police appeared as if from nowhere to hold back the milling crowd.

Dizzy Malone stood unnoticed in the excitement, watching slit-eyed.

The black silk came away disclosing the still figure of a man crumpled on the pavement.

It was Burke, district attorney of the city of Chicago.

"He's stunned by the fall!" Louden cried. "Broken bones, maybe! Call an ambulance!"

Mitchell bent over the huddled body, fingers probing deftly.

He straightened up again.

"No need," he said, simply. "Burke is dead—hung."

A spasm of rage swept him. He shook his fists at the sky overhead and cursed the vanishing plane and its pilot with blasting, withering oaths.

"Hung him, the carrion!" he shrilled. "Burke was alive when he dropped. His body's still warm. The parachute was attached to a noose around his neck. When it opened, it hung him—hung him by the neck until he was dead!"

He covered his face with his hands.

AN examniation of the corpse proved that he was right.

It was a clever job and timed to the second.

The shrouds of the 'chute had been fastened to a rope which ended in a noose. The noose circled the dead man's neck, a knot like a hangman's protruding from beneath one ear. His hands were wired together.

When the plane went into a loop and hung there bottom side up, the man had been catapulted downward from his seat. The 'chute opened automatically and snapped his neck with the dispatch of a hangman's sprung trap.

An ambulance jangled up.

From Centre Street came the roar of a motorcycle. A police-runner elbowed his way to the district attorney.

"Flash from Van Cortlandt Park, Chief. At 7:55, a black plane swooped down over the parade ground and scooped up the basket with the ransom. Got into the air again before anyone could get near him."

The D. A.'s big shoulders drooped.

"And then he got wise to how we'd tried to frame him," the big man mumbled. "Poor Burke. My God! Oh, my God!"

His shoulders quivered spasmodically.

In the confusion, Dizzy Malone edged her way in until she stood beside him.

Her words dripped across his numbed mind—measured, stinging, calculated to cut with the bite of a steel-tipped lash.

"Yes, hung by the neck until he was dead—*like he hung Baldy Ross on a frame-up!*" The voice went on, its words searing themselves across the district attorney's soul. "And remember, big boy, *you sealed the death warrant that sent the Kid to the Big House to fry!"*

CHAPTER II

THE MOLL PAYS A VISIT

DIZZY MALONE nodded her way between the huddle of tables that shouldered each other for space around the El Dorado's gleaming dance floor. With a crooked grin and a toss of her smoothly-waved blonde hair she dismissed half a dozen offers of parking space at as many tables.

She wanted to be alone—to think —and it was in the strident, blaring heart of a night club that her mind worked best. About her beat waves of flesh-tingling, erotic sounds—rising and falling rhythmically from brazen throats, from tense, stretched strings, from the quivering bellies of drums—the swirling, clamoring pulse of Broadway's night life.

Dizzy loved it.

She chose a table in the corner and sat down facing the writhing mass of lights and color.

Against its bizarre background the scene in the district attorney's office and the mad happenings in front of the City Hall that afternoon passed rapidly in review.

The job had all the ear-marks of the Ghost. She snarled the name hatefully into the drunken medley of sound. The Ghost must be back then, and broke.

Yes, it all fitted in perfectly. A quick recoup of the stake—part of it hers—that he'd thrown away on that flossie, Spanish Lil—and—revenge. A double-barreled goad that would eat into his twisted mind like acid.

It was like the Ghost to combine business with—revenge.

First this bird Burke who had convicted Baldy, and then——

A waiter with a broken nose and a livid scar that stretched from lip to ear bent over her solicitously, yet with an air of being in the know, of belonging.

"Scotch," Dizzy said, automatically.

The waiter disappeared.

Dizzy's shrewd mind pieced together the scattered bits of the puzzle. With Burke out of the way who would be next? Who, but——

The waiter again.

He placed the drink before her, bent close to her ear as he smoothed the rumpled tablecloth.

"I hear Spanish Lil is back."

Dizzy stiffened.

"Where?"

The words seemed to slip out of the corner of her mouth. Her lips did not move.

"At Sugar Foot's in Harlem, throwin' coin around like a coked-up bootlegger."

"Thanks."

The grapevine! System of underworld news.

The waiter moved away.

Dizzy made a pretense of drinking, smiled woodenly at a shrill-voiced entertainer, and rose.

Where Spanish Lil was, there the Ghost would be.

OUTSIDE the El Dorado, Dizzy climbed into a low, nondescript hulk of a roadster. There was class about the roadster. Its dull, grey finish gleamed in the lamp light. Its nickle fittings were spotless.

When she stepped on the starter, the car's real class became apparent, for under her hand pulsed the steady flow of a V-16 Cadillac. The long, grey hood covered a sixteen cylinder motor mounted on the very latest in chassis.

The gears meshed and the iron brute rolled away with scarcely a sound.

Dizzy swung the wheel and they

turned south into Seventh Avenue, then west to skirt the uppermost extremity of Times Square, south on Ninth, then west again and the grey snout of the roadster buried itself deep into the heart of the sink of gangland—Hell's Kitchen.

Before an inconspicuous brownstone front in the odd Forties the car drew up. The motor hissed into silence.

Dizzy climbed the battered stone steps and let herself into an ill-lit hallway. Two steep flights of stairs —another door. It yielded to her key and she stepped into her purple paradise and snapped on the lights. Behind her the door swung to with the solid clang of steel meeting steel and the snap of a double lock.

The room was a perfect foil for Dizzy Malone's blonde, gaming beauty, and truly a purple paradise. It ran the gamut of shades of that royal color, from the light orchid of the silk-draped walls to the almost-violet of the deep, cushion-drenched divans that lined three walls. Into the fourth was built a miniature bar whose dark, blood-purple mahogany gleamed dully in the subdued light of innumerable silken-covered lamps.

Cigarette tables on tall, slender legs flanked the divans; a massive radio was half-concealed by an exquisite Spanish shawl, worked with intricate mauve embroidery and surmounted by a silver vase holding a gigantic spotted orchid. There was not a book to be seen—not even "Indian Love Lyrics," acme of chorine literary taste and attainment; or Nietzsche's "Thus Spake Zarathustra" which is now considered passé by Broadway beauties; or Durant's "History of Philosophy," displayed, but never read.

Dizzy's purple paradise was, indeed, an institution.

She crossed its thick, soft carpet with a hurried step and entered the bedroom.

It was done entirely in the same color-scheme as the outer room, but, unlike it, was strictly private.

Dizzy tossed her hat on the square, purple bed that stood on a raised dais in the center of the room. From two wardrobes that squatted against the wall she took the flimsy garments she figured to need and spread them in readiness on the chaise-lounge stretching in luxurious abandon beneath the heavily-shaded casement window.

Then the clothes Dizzy had on fell at her feet in a crumpled shower and she stood, stretching her arms above her head, in provocative marble-pink nakedness.

But not for long. There was work to be done.

Throwing a smock about her slender shoulders she sat down before a make-up table that would have done credit to the current reigning dramatic favorite, and switched on the blinding frame of electrics that threw its mirror into a pool of dazzling brilliance.

For several minutes her gaze concentrated on the reflected image of herself, then she rubbed the make-up off with cold cream and set to work.

Dark shadows blended in skillfully around her eyes, made their grey depths even deeper, faint penciled lines gave them a slanting oval appearance. She blocked her eyebrows out with grease paint and drew fine, arching ones over them. Deft dabs of rouge close up under the eyes and flanking her nose aided in completely changing the round, youthful contour of her face. It was the long, smouldering, passionate countenance of the Slav. She clinched the impression by drawing out her lips in two thin crimson lines.

DIZZY gazed at the reflection and grinned. Even she failed to recognize herself. The make-up was perfect.

To complete the illusion, she combed the smooth waves of her blonde bobbed hair flatly down on her little head, then searched through the drawers until she found a flaming red wig.

It was a work of art, that wig, and so expertly made as to defy discovery of its artificiality.

Carefully Dizzy fitted it into place.

An exclamation of delight slipped between her lips.

Perfect, indeed!

Satisfied, Dizzy dressed slowly, choosing a scanty gown that hinted broadly at the palpitating curves beneath. Its vivid, jealous-eyed green threw into hot relief the flaming flower of her hair.

Throwing a light wrap about her, she descended the stairs to her roadster, eased in behind the wheel and gunned the grey hulk toward the river. She swung north on deserted lower West End Avenue, breezing along easily. There was no hurry and she had no desire to run into the drunken crush that marked the three o'clock closing hour of most of Broadway's night clubs.

The blocks slipped past.

At Cathedral Parkway she turned right, passed Morningside Park, and left into Lenox Avenue, the great pulsing artery of Harlem.

Into the maze of side streets the roadster nosed and came to a stop at last before a row of lightless, grimy stone fronts.

Dizzy climbed out and walked around the corner to where an awning stretched across the sidewalk.

In its shadow, towered an ebony doorman.

He scrutinized her closely but at the mention of the name she snarled into his ear, he began to bow and scrape frantically. Flinging the locked doors behind him open, he admitted her to deep-carpeted stairs.

DOWN them she went, and at the bottom there rushed to meet her the hot music, the din, the flashing movement and color that was the underworld's basement-haven—Sugar Foot's.

Her eyes swept the crowded room in the split second before it was plunged into darkness punctured by a spotlight that picked out a brown-skinned girl in the center of the dance floor. The orchestra throbbed into a barbaric African rhythm and the girl flung herself into a writhing, shuddering dance.

Under cover of it, Dizzy threaded her way to an empty corner-table near the door, which she had spotted in that brief instant, before the lights went out.

When the lights flooded on again she was seated behind the table facing the room. She leaned one elbow negligently on its checked calico-top and joined in the applause. To all appearances she had been there for hours.

A boisterous waiter came and hung over her shoulder.

"Scotch!" Dizzy snapped.

There was that in her tone which sent him away on the jump, respectful, in spite of the aura of flaunted lure that clung about her.

In a moment he was on his way back, skipping, sliding, weaving his way across the dance floor in perfect time to the music. He lowered his tray and placed the drink before her, a tall glass, soda, ginger ale, a bowl of cracked ice, and melted away again.

Slowly, lingeringly, Dizzy mixed the drink, sipped it and settled to the business of looking over the crowd that jammed the stifling room to capacity.

Everyone was there — sporting gents flush from the race-track; sinister underworld figures, suave, shifty-eyed; a heavyweight contender with his wizened-faced manager; a florid police sergeant from the tenderloin; the principals of a smash colored review; a sprinkling of tight-lipped gamblers and individuals who fitted into no particular category. All their women—good, bad, and so-so.

But nowhere on the dance floor could Dizzy find the sunken, grey, cadaverous face of the Ghost, or the long, gangling stretch of his emaciated limbs. He would surely be there. He loved to dance, almost as much as Dizzy, herself.

The saxophones sobbed their quivering "That's All!" and the dancers made for their tables.

The lights went out—the spotlight fell upon a black Amazon in a glittering, skin-tight gown. Swaying sensuously to the beat of the music, she broke into a wailing, throbbing blues. Wild applause.

Lights again—the beat of the music quickened—couples left the tables for the dance floor and locked themselves in shuddering embraces to the fervent tempo of the band.

Dizzy's eyes swept the tables.

There—ah! Dizzy's fists clenched. The pink nails went white.

At a ringside table sat Spanish Lil, high-bosomed, languorous, drunk.

The shimmer of new steel gleamed out from the slits that were Dizzy's eyes. They probed at each of the faces that swarmed around Spanish Lil, each one a worthless hanger-on scenting dough. For an instant they paused at a bloated face faintly reminiscent of the Ghost.

Her heart flopped over and beat wildly.

But no! The man's nose was small and straight, nothing like the Ghost's colorless, almost transparent hooked beak. His shoulders were square, not round and sloping; his eyes puffed and bleary.

A keen stab of disappointment tore at her throat.

Her eyes passed on.

Everywhere she met hot stares, pleading, offering, suggesting unmentionable things. Her own swept them coldly.

A PIE-EYED newspaper reporter slouched over her table and began to talk. Dizzy knew him, but to add authenticity to her changed character she sent him away with a stinging rebuff that made even his calloused sensibilities writhe.

Darkness and the spotlight again. A dusky chorus hurled itself into an abysmal jungle dance. A roar of applause.

Lights.

Dizzy rose and made her way toward the ladies' room, taking care to pass close to the table where Spanish Lil and her satelites clustered.

The man with the bloated face looked up and caught her eye for an instant as she went past.

On the way back he was waiting for her. When she came abreast of the table he swayed to his feet.

"Dance, kid?" he mumbled thickly.

Something made Dizzy hesitate instead of brushing quickly by him. Misinterpreting it for assent he insinuated his hand under her elbow.

Spanish Lil leaped to her feet.

"Lay off that, you—you——!" she shrilled.

Her eyes burned with anger and liquor as she seized the man's arm and dragged him away.

"Come on, we're going home."

Dizzy eased out of the jam and returned to her table. She sat down watching every move of Spanish Lil and the man with the bloated face as they stumbled toward the door. Suddenly, with a half-stifled cry, Dizzy sprang upright.

There was no mistaking that shuffling gait, that gangling length of limb. A plastic surgeon could chisel away the hooked beak, booze and coke could bloat the sunken, cadaverous face, a tailor could pad the round sloping shoulders; but nothing could disguise that shuffling, long-legged gait.

It was the Ghost.

DIZZY flung a bill down on the table and plunged after them, fighting her way through the crowd, taking the stairs two at a time.

As she burst through the outer door to the sidewalk faint streaks of dawn were silvering the sky.

Spanish Lil and the Ghost were in the back of a waiting taxi. The driver slammed the door and spurted away.

Dizzy dashed round the corner, wrap trailing—scrambled into the grey roadster without opening the door—clawed the ignition switch—kicked the starter.

The iron brute leaped ahead—swung — backed into the curb — hurtled ahead once more — bumped over the opposite curb — and took the corner into the avenue with a screaming skid.

A red tail-light was just visible in the distance.

Dizzy booted the accelerator to the floor and the sixteen cylinders responded with a lurching burst of speed.

The red light drew rapidly nearer and she eased off the terrific pace.

A slit-lipped grin broke across her face, mirthless, cruel.

She was on the trail of the Ghost at last, the only man who had ever double-crossed her.

"There's only one person that can put the skids under him," she muttered through clenched teeth. _"And I'm that baby!"_

CHAPTER III

IN THE DSTRICT ATTORNEY'S OFFICE

IT WAS well into the afternoon before Dizzy finally slid her roadster to the curb before the brownstone front in the Forties that masked her purple paradise.

A drizzling summer rain fell steadily.

She climbed out and looked the iron-gutted monster over affectionately. It was spattered with mud and one of the rear tires was flat, cut to ribbons. Like its owner it seemed to droop with the fatigue of a sleepless night and almost continuous driving.

As Dizzy turned wearily toward the house a smile of grim satisfaction creased the corners of her mouth

She knew all that she needed to know—now! It _was_ the Ghost!

Stiffly she plodded up the stairs and let herself into the purple salon. Slamming the door behind her, she crossed to the bedroom leaving a trail of sodden garments in her wake. Her white body disappeared into the bathroom to be followed almost instantly by the hiss of a shower.

She came out in a few minutes, fresh, almost radiant, all traces of her character of the night before completely removed.

It was a 100 per cent Dizzy Malone again who chose a quietly expensive street dress from a wardrobe and drew it on over her head.

When she stepped into the purple salon once more she was as modishly dressed, as cool and collected, as any millionaire broker's private secretary. And probably infinitely more beautiful. She looked, indeed, as though she had stepped out of the proverbial bandbox.

But then, Dizzy was Dizzy, and just at the moment she was ravenously hungry.

From the refrigerator behind the bar she salvaged half a grapefruit; set a percolator brewing coffee and made toast in a complicated electrical gadget.

When breakfast was ready she disposed of it with neatness and dispatch. Into the second cup of coffee she poured a generous slug of cognac and sipped it leisurely. Then she lit a cigarette.

AT LAST Dizzy Malone was herself again and ready for whatever the day would bring, which, she figured, would be plenty.

And in that she was right, as she usually was, although things did not begin to happen as soon as she expected.

Calmly, at first, she sat smoking cigarettes and waiting while the rain dripped dolefully outside. Then she got up and began pacing the room, smoking with short nervous puffs.

Finally the break came.

An ominous rapping on the door.

Dizzy started, pulled herself together and ground the cigarette into an over-full ash-tray.

"Who is it?" she called.

"Horowitz and Rourke from Headquarters. The D. A. says you should take a walk to see him."

"Just a second, boys."

The expected had happened.

Dizzy straightened her hat in front of a mirror and opened the door. Outside were two plainclothes men.

"Hello, Dizzy."

Dizzy grinned.

Together they descended the stairs and made a dash through the rain for the black sedan with the P. D. shield on its radiator that was parked behind her roadster.

Instantly the police chauffeur was on his way, siren shrieking.

"What's the big idea of the ride?" the girl asked.

The dicks shrugged.

"We don't know ourselves."

And it was obvious to her that they didn't, although it was evident, too, that they were laboring under an over-dose of suppressed excitement. But they offered nothing and Dizzy asked no questions.

THE remainder of the ride to the grim building on Centre Street was accomplished in silence. Once there she was conducted immediately to the office where she had had the futile conference exactly twenty-four hours before.

The district attorney sat at his desk, Tom Louden beside him.

"Fade!" the D. A. snapped at the plainclothes men and they backed out, closing the door behind them.

Dizzy stood in the middl. of the room waiting, watching.

Mitchell looked up at her out of eyes deep-sunken and blood-shot. His face showed lines of worry and strain. Even his grizzled hair seemed a trifle greyer. It was a cinch that his nerves were keyed close to the breaking point.

What had happened to the big boy, Dizzy wondered. It would surely take more than that business in front of the City Hall to throw a veteran like himself so completely haywire.

His eyes bored into her and a flush slowly rose to his cheekbones.

"You damned little punk!" he roared, suddenly, springing to his feet.

"But, Chief——"

"Shut up!" he snarled at his assistant. "Let me handle this!"

THE JANE FROM HELL'S KITCHEN

Seizing the girl's arm he twisted it savagely.

"Now come clean! What do you know about that Burke job?"

Dizzy looked him in the eye.

"I told you what I knew yesterday," she said coldly. "I made you a proposition purely on a hunch. The offer still holds. Give me a plane, a fast one, with a machine-gun on it, and your say-so to go ahead, and maybe I can get the Ghost for you. And when I say 'get' I mean 'get'! That's all."

"It is, huh?"

The D. A. dragged her roughly to the desk.

"Well, what about *this?*"

He snatched a sheet of paper from its top and thrust it in front of her eyes.

It was in the same handwriting as the Burke ransom letter and on the same type paper.

Dizzy read it hurriedly.

"You see what happens when you try to double-cross us, Mitchell! Don't try to chisel again. Unless you announce through the papers that you will comply with our demand for $500,000 as we shall direct, you will be dead by midnight!"

"Well?"

The district attorney pointed to a newspaper scare head.

DISTRICT ATTORNEY DEFIES BURKE KILLERS

"Now what have you got to say?" he asked fiercely.

"My proposition is still open. And remember, big boy, you prosecuted The Ghost's kid brother. *You sent him up to fry in the chair.*"

"Is that all?"

"Yes."

The D. A. stood over the girl threateningly.

"Listen, baby, you know plenty and you're going to spill it. Now are you ready to talk nice?"

Dizzy shrugged.

"You heard me the first time, big boy."

Mitchell's big hand shot out and clamped over her slim arm.

"You're gonna come clean with what you know, see, baby!" he snarled. "Or else I'll give you the works!"

"I'm no squealer!" Dizzy spit the words in his face.

The D. A. flung her savagely into a chair.

"All right, then, you little punk, *I'll just sweat it out of you!*"

"GOOD Heavens, Chief! Can't you see she's had enough?" Tom Louden's voice quivered. "Lay off her. She won't talk."

The D. A. turned his back on the crumpled heap that lay whimpering piteously in the chair.

"All right, Tom. Jug her then for safe keeping. She's dangerous."

"Oh, go easy, Chief! Don't do that. I'll be personally responsible for her. I don't think she's in the know anyway."

Dizzy looked up gratefully at the young assistant D. A. out of a face that had become pinched and drawn. Racking sobs shook her, but she bit her lips to keep them back.

Mitchell gave tacit consent to his assistant's plea by ignoring it.

"Well, guess I'll call it a day," he said gruffly, pulling out his watch. "Eleven-thirty. The buzzards have got half an hour yet to keep their promise, *but they won't get me!*"

Mitchell turned abruptly on his heel and left the room.

When the door closed Louden crossed to the shuddering heap in the chair.

"I'm sorry, kid," he said with real emotion. "Feeling better?"

Dizzy nodded and tried to smile.

"Good kid. Now promise that you won't take it on the lam and I'll run you home in my car."

"I won't lam it—now!"

"Let's go then, Dizzy," Tom urged as he helped her gently to her feet. "We'll just trail along behind the Chief to see that *he* gets home all right, then I'll chance Hell's Kitchen and drop you at your door."

Dizzy gulped her thanks and clung to his arm for support as they hurried to the street.

WHAT amounted to a riot squad had been called out to escort the D. A. to his home. It roared away from the big grey building while Dizzy and Tom climbed into his modest sedan. An armored motorcycle preceded and followed Mitchell's limousine. On the seat beside him sat a pair of plainclothes men.

Mitchell had boasted that the buzzards who knocked off his colleague from Chicago wouldn't get him, but he was taking no chances.

Tom Louden's sedan stuck its nose into the drizzle of rain and scampered after the cavalcade as it streaked away northward.

Into Fifth Avenue they raced, sirens shrieking; past red lights and green alike, the smooth wet asphalt flowing behind them like a black ribbon.

Forty-second Street slid by and the rain-drenched statue of General Sherman dripping in its tiny park at Fifty-ninth.

A few blocks further on they turned right, bumped across the car tracks at Madison Avenue, past the great church on the corner of Park. It was dark except for the illuminated dial of the clock on its steeple whose hands quivered on the edge of midnight.

Half way up the block the caval-

cade stopped before the private residence of the D. A.

Louden pulled in behind the limousine. The coppers leaped to their stations, guns drawn. The D. A. stepped out, chuckling, and headed for his door, waving aside the proffered umbrella of the plainclothes men who walked beside him.

"The buzzards won't get me," he gloated. "Not tonight they won't."

He reached the door and stood on the mat, regardless of the pelting rain, drawing out his key.

The first stroke of midnight clanged hollowly from the church on the corner.

"I fooled 'em this time," the D. A. laughed.

He thrust the wet key in the lock.

As it touched, a point of blue flame appeared, sputtered into a glow that ran hissing across his hand and up his arm. The D. A.'s body stiffened. Blue sparks cascaded from his feet. His bulky frame writhed in spasmodic jerks, thin spirals of smoke rising from his seared flesh. His features convulsed in agony.

Then, its work done, the burning wave of electricity flung the charred body of New York's district attorney shuddering to the sidewalk.

When his bodyguard bent over him, Mitchell was dead.

In Tom Louden's sedan Dizzy's white lips framed scarcely audible words—"He fried—just like the Ghost's kid brother!"

CHAPTER IV

ANOTHER DEMAND

DIZZY MALONE threw off the purple coverlet of her bed and reached for the morning papers. There was one thing she wanted to find out—how the trick had been turned.

The papers exposed the ingenious device in detail. She lapped them up as she munched rolls and drank coffee prepared by her cleaning woman.

A man had called at the D. A.'s house with the forged identification card of an inspector for the Electric Light Company. He wished to inspect the meter. He was admitted without question by an unsuspecting servant.

The meter was out of order, he said. He would fix it. As well as the servant could remember he had mentioned something about the wiring of the doorbell fouling the house current.

The bogus inspector set to work. What he really did was to install a transformer which stepped-up the house current to a deadly degree. Ingenius wiring of the metal door frame and the steel door mat completed the trap, which was set by simply connecting a wire outside the door. An apparently innocent passerby could stoop over and make the connection. That done the victim stepped on the mat, inserted the key and completed the circuit that electrocuted him. The rain, of course, aided the design materially.

DIZZY shuddered at its utter hellishness.

It smacked lustily of the Ghost, but a Ghost goaded by homicidal mania, a Ghost stooping to the exhibitionism born of illusions of grandeur, a Ghost whose twisted mind was disintegrating in a final burst of fiendish bravado.

If it *was* The Ghost he had gone stark mad. And as such he was doubly dangerous.

But even Dizzy had no real evidence to pin the two killings on her former partner. From long experience with his methods she sensed,

however, that he would have executed them in practically the same manner, as the unknown. And then, too, there was the element of poetic justice in the two slayings that she had hunched in the very beginning.

She was two points up on the police any way you looked at it— she knew the Ghost was in New York and she knew his hideaway. And those two bits of information she intended to keep to herself, to be used to bring to a successful ending her vendetta of hate.

She would put the bee on the Ghost, and she would do it herself —that was her right—but she was smart enough to realize there must be a semblance of legality about it or it would be bars, and possibly the chair, for her.

The next move was up to the Ghost.

It came even as she wondered what it would be.

The faint buzz of the telephone.

Dizzy snatched for the French phone in its recess under the bed.

Tom Louden, acting district attorney for the city of New York, was on the wire. Mr. Louden's compliments and would Miss Malone be so kind as to come to Headquarters immediately?

Miss Malone would.

She held the hook down for a few seconds, then called the garage around the corner for her car. Tumbling out of bed she made a hurried toilette and dashed down the stairs. the grey roadster was waiting at the curb, motor running.

Dizzy craved action and she got plenty of it from the crowds of early bargain-shoppers on the drive to the big grim building on Centre Street.

IT WAS the third time in three days that she had crossed the threshold of the district attorney's office, but this time she entered with a perky smile and a jaunty step, for she realized that she was master of the situation. It was her turn to dictate.

Tom Louden greeted her with a harassed smile.

"There's hell to pay, Dizzy," he said, running his hand wearily through his hair. "Look!"

She took the extended sheet of paper, recognizing with an ominous shiver the soiled foolscap of the two previous ransom letters.

"This just queers everything," Tom Louden groaned. "Read it."

Dizzy's eyes swept back and forth across the paper.

"You see we mean business! The ante is raised to $1,000,000. Follow these directions exactly. Wrap the dough (grand notes only) in a bundle and attach same to an automatically opening parachute. A pilot is to take a single-seater up from Roosevelt Flying Field with the dough and parachute today at 2 P. M. and head due east out over the ocean, flying 100 miles an hour at 5,000 feet. Plane is to be plainly marked with alternating black and white stripes. When pilot sees a yacht whose decks are similarly painted he is to descend, drop the parachute and return. Bets are off if any attempt is made to follow plane or discover yacht. No tricks this time! We see all, know all!

"If these directions are not followed to the letter within twenty-four hours we will bump off Jake Levine!"

A cry of horror burst from Dizzy's lips at sight of the sinister name.

Jake Levine—Boss Fixer of gangland, human octopus in whose tentacles danced dip and judge alike, maker and breaker of politicians, super-fence, master blackmailer, banker for anything from petty larceny to murder if the return was not less than fifty per cent, chiseler and double-crosser feared from the lowest sink in the tenderloin to the highest holder of the public trust.

"You see what I'm up against on my first job, Dizzy," Tom growled hopelessly. "Levine got a duplicate of this letter. He's been down here already—he's here yet. Says he'll blow the lid off, knock the legs out from under the administration—and he will, too—if something isn't done. The party leaders have been on my neck since daylight, and I'm half crazy."

He looked up to the girl appealingly.

"What I heard of that dope of yours about the Ghost sounded pretty sensible and I'd like——"

The door of the office burst open and an undersized, rat-faced man burst into the room.

"What the hell you going to do about this, Louden?" he demanded, his voice high pitched with panic.

He was trembling violently. The sickly sallow pallor of fear showed through his natural swarthiness. His eyes, beady and set close together, jerked furtively about the room. The aggressive loudness of his clothes even had lost their swagger and he stood revealed as the yellow rat he was.

"You've gotta do something, I say!" he almost screamed. "Listen, you heel! When I got that letter I fixed it so there'll be hell to pay for *certain parties"*—he emphasized the words slyly—"if anything happens to me, and they know it. Have they come through with the dough that bum wants?"

"Why—a—not yet, Mr. Levine," Louden stalled. "You see——"

"The hell I see! That guy means business. Look who he's bumped off already. He ain't fooling, and if you don't do something for me damn soon I'll start talking and break every punk in this administration."

His yellow teeth showed in a snarl. "And don't make a false play either, boy. Remember—if I go on the spot, I wreck the grafters just the same. Nobody ever made a heel outa Jake Levine. Now what kinda protection you givin' me?"

"I can lock you up in a cell, Mr. Levine," Louden suggested. "You would be safe there."

"In a cell—a cell!" the man shrieked. "Listen to him! Maybe that bum's got somebody planted to get me there—some lousy screw maybe. I don't trust nobody."

He paused a moment.

"I know where I'll go!" he burst out again. "I'll stick to one of those *certain parties* until he gets me out of this."

Turning abruptly he flung himself through the door.

"Well, it won't be long now before the axe falls," Tom muttered.

"And it won't be long before the time set by that letter is up, too," Dizzy cut in from where she had flattened herself against the wall. "It's almost noon now."

The acting D. A.'s eyes lit up hopefully.

"Oh, yes. That dope of yours about the Ghost—what was it?"

DIZZY gave him the same story she had Mitchell. It was all good hunching, she knew, but not tangible enough evidence on which to make a pinch. She even told Louden that she had positively seen the Ghost the night before, but she carefully refrained from any mention of having trailed him. It was too late to nail him at his hide-away, and even if she *had* been a squealer.

"And my proposition remains practically the same," she finished. "Let me fly that striped ransom plane from Roosevelt's Field at two o'clock this afternoon. Be sure it's a fast one and have a machine-gun mounted on it—and *I'll get the Ghost* for you."

Suspicion flashed squint-eyed across Louden's face.

"Say!" he demanded sharply. "How do I know *you're* not in on this game too? You were his moll."

Hot hate flushed Dizzy's face which changed, gradually, to the amused expression she might have worn when watching the helpless squirming of a newborn puppy.

"Listen, stupid," she laughed. "I don't carry any dough. You weigh the 'chute with a flock of bricks. Everything's like it should be except for that, and the machine-gun, and Dizzy Malone flying the ship."

Louden considered.

"No, no, Dizzy," he burst out petulantly. "It's impossible. I can't take upon myself the responsibility of sending you of all people. It's a job for the police. Your proposition is absurd. I've a Boeing pursuit plane out at the field ready and waiting. It's camouflaged to look like an old crate that's about ready to fall to pieces, and it's striped black and white. The parachute is waiting for its load of a million dollars."

He laughed harshly.

"A million dollars! And I'm sitting here doing nothing. Why, look here! The thing to do is to lay a trap for the boat that's to pick up all that money."

"Don't be dumb!" Dizzy snapped. "I know the way the Ghost's mind works. He's a racketeer and a flier. He don't play with rowboats. I know him like a book and I'm the only one who can get him. Give me a chance!"

The preemptory jangling of the telephone cut in on the voice that had become low and pleading.

Louden picked up the receiver. His face went white as he listened.

"Yes, sir. Yes, sir . . . I'm doing the best I can . . . No, nothing definite yet . . . I'll give you a ring . . . Yes."

His hands trembled violently as he replaced the receiver.

"Come on, Tom." Dizzy was at him again. "Take a chance. Stall those certain parties off. Tell them someone's come through with the dough and you've sent it out. Call the field about the machine-gun. It's the Ghost — I know it's the Ghost and I'll get him so he won't bother anyone again. If I don't get him I won't come back," she finished simply.

Louden's eyes fixed themselves despairingly on hers and slowly a look almost of relief came into them.

He stood up and squared his shoulders with decision.

"I'll do it!"

Dizzy was across the room. Her arms went around his neck and she pressed a red kiss full on his lips. Before he knew what had happened she was half-way through the door. There she turned.

"Plenty gas in the Boeing and two motorcycle cops to shoot me through traffic," she shouted with a wave of the hand.

Then she tore.

Louden stood there, stunned, his mouth open.

"Gas—— cops——" he mumbled, nodding his head dumbly.

But when Dizzy reached her grey roadster, two red motorcycles were coughing impatiently beside it. Their drivers were looking with some disdain at the unpromising hulk, but before they had gone two blocks they **were pleasantly disillusioned.**

THEN, sirens, shrieking, they proceeded to do their stuff and, for the first time in her life, Dizzy looked at a copper with favor. The baby in front of her could ride, and he did so.

Through traffic they wailed their way, screamed across crowded Queensborough Bridge and on to Long Island.

There, Dizzy gunned the V-16, worrying the heels of the man in front. In the mirror she could see the man behind grin as he hung on doggedly.

Then all three went raving speedmad.

It was with fifteen minutes still to spare that they whined through the entrance to Roosevelt Field.

The coppers flung wearily off their busses and kicked them into their rests. But they stood to attention and brought their fingers to their caps with real admiration when Dizzy stepped jauntily to the ground and hurried to where she saw a battered looking crate, striped black and white, being warmed up on the line.

A field official stepped forward.

"The ship is ready," he said, waving his hand.

"Gas?" Dizzy snapped.

"Full tanks."

"Cruising radius?"

"A thousand miles."

"Good!"

Dizzy stepped into the flying suit he held toward her and adjusted helmet and goggles.

She waved aside the parachute straps he started to buckle about her with a grim: "That won't do *me* any good!"

It was to be a battle to the death.

Dizzy climbed aboard and the man explained the manipulation of the machine-gun that had been hastily geared to the motor and camouflaged showed her where the auxiliary belts of ammunition were nested in the cockpit.

"This is a regulation army pursuit ship," he said, "with complete equipment, Very pistol and lights, earth inductor compass——"

"Okay, okay!"

The girl checked the details as he pointed them out and shot a glance at her wrist watch.

Two o'clock!

She revved the motor, thrilling to the smooth precision of its whining roar as the man snapped the buckles of the safety-belt.

"Money 'chute!" she cried.

The man brought it and stowed it away within easy reach.

"Bricks!" he shouted with a grin.

Dizzy nodded.

"Let's go!"

THE chocks were pulled from the wheels. She gave it the gun and the crate rolled into the runway, hurtled forward. A slight pull on the stick and it catapulted into the air.

Climbing in a tight spiral she watched the altimeter—a thousand feet, two, three, four, five. Then she leveled off and threw the ship into a series of intricate maneuvers. She had been taught by a master—the Ghost—and had proved a more than apt pupil. The Boeing responded to the slightest touch on rudder and stick. Never had she flown such a ship.

She leveled off again and, putting the blazing disc of the sun at her back, set her course by the compass dead into the east. Full gun she watched the speed indicator climb to its maximum, then throttled down to an easy hundred miles an hour. No need to figure drift—not a breath of air stirred.

Long Island slid out from under her and the Boeing nosed out over the Atlantic.

Dizzy dipped her left wing and scanned the smooth blue expanse of water. No yacht with striped deck met her eager gaze; in fact, there was no boat of any sort to be seen, no smudge of black smoke, even, on the horizon ahead. She wormed round in the cockpit as far as the safety-straps would permit and scanned the air.

Nothing.

The scorching sun beat blindingly into her eyes.

A sense of utter loneliness settled depressingly about her.

She shot the moon to warm her guns, quivering with a throb of power at their chattering death-talk.

An hour spun round on the dial of her watch.

The sea below her was a round blue waste circled by a shimmering heat haze.

Another hour——

She dispelled a growing uneasiness with a screaming burst of the guns.

The sun settled slowly behind her. The Boeing roared on into the east.

Another hour——

The ship, perceptibly lightened of its load of gas, floated easily in the air. She flew left-wing low, now, searching the water for a striped-deck yacht.

Still nothing. The sea was as barren as a deserted mill-pond. She searched the sky above and behind. Nothing but the red round of the sun, slowly sinking.

The vague restlessness of fear shuddered along her nerves that the staccato of the guns failed to dispel. The gas was almost half gone and still the bare, tenantless reach of water stretched below her.

Where was the yacht?

The suspicion born in the D. A.'s office that it was only a stall grew into a certainty. Real fear gripped her. What was this all about? Should she turn back?

No! She remembered her boast

and screamed it into the surrounding void.

"Damn the Ghost! I'll get him or I won't come back!"

As if in answer to her screamed challenge a black shadow seemed to sweep out of the sun.

Her eyes jerked to the side, her body went rigid.

Beside her floated a low-winged black Lockhead Sirius monoplane.

Her gaze probed through the pilot's goggles, locked with the pale smoldering eyes of—the Ghost!

He waggled his wings and motioned over the side with a long-armed gesture.

Dizzy held up the readied 'chute. The Ghost nodded and she flung it clear.

A cold dash of warning from some seventh sense sent her up in a steep zoom and she fell off on one wing.

And none too soon for a spatter of holes ripped through the doped linen of one wing. The Ghost was heeled too.

She banked to see the man pull his ship out of a zoom that had been intended to rake her bus from prop to tail assembly, and dive for the opened 'chute. He caught it deftly on a hook suspended from the undercarriage and hauled it rapidly aboard.

Dizzy rammed forward on the stick, the wind droned through the wires as she dropped down and threw a burst of steel into the Sirius. It dropped off clumsily on one wing and pulled itself up heavily.

With that maneuver the insane daring of the Ghost's final gesture came clear. The Sirius with its cruising radius of 4,300 miles was fueled to capacity. The Ghost gambled to blast the ransom plane out of the sky with a single burst, pick up the money 'chute and head for Europe.

Dizzy thrilled in spite of herself at the very audacity of the thing, its colossal bluff.

Then the red mantle of hate dropped over her.

She dropped the Boeing down out of the sky and swept alongside the black ship. This would be a fair fight and to the death. She would get him, if she could, and on the level.

Dizzy tore off goggles and helmet, noting with satisfaction the cringe of recognition that swept across the Ghost's face.

She shook her fist at him and motioned him to dump his gas.

He accepted the challenge and a sheet of spray gushed downward. The black ship, lightened of its load, leaped upward.

They were on even terms now.

DIZZY tripped her guns and the man answered the salute—the salute of death, for one of them at least and perhaps both.

They flung their ships at each other, guns flaming.

Steel seared Dizzy's cockpit, rocking the Boeing. She dove, zoomed up in a loop and stood on her head pumping chattering hail into the Sirius.

The Ghost wing-slipped out of the way and they clawed down the sky to get at each other's bellies, then roared upward, guns raving.

Dizzy's instrument-board went to pieces. Stunned, the Boeing slipped into a spin, the Ghost on its heels waiting to rip in the coup de grace.

The girl threw the stick into neutral and when her crate steadied, sat on her tail and clawed for altitude.

Sirius steel tore into the Boeing. Dizzy pulled into a reversement and for an instant the black crate was glued to her ring-sights. She pressed the trips. Steel gutted the black ship.

It wabbled. She was under it, ripping, tearing.

The Sirius nosed over into a spin, flame streaming behind.

The Boeing nosed in for the kill, wires screaming, guns raving.

A black wing collapsed and the Sirius spun faster, down, down.

Dizzy leveled off, banked and leaned over the side.

Below her a flaming ball cometed down through the dusk to be extinguished, suddenly, in a mighty geyser of spray——

Dizzy was limp and trembling when she pulled back on the stick and gunned the Boeing into a staggering climb. The motor missed, caught again and roared on as she leveled off and stuck its nose into the faint afterglow that streaked upward into the gathering darkness.

She rode the air alone, sky-victor in a riddled ship. Ominous metallic growlings broke the smooth beat of the motor from time to time. The instrument-board was shot away, but she realized that her gas must be running low.

The compass needle wabbled perilously on its luminous dial.

She nursed the game crate on—on.

The motor began to miss badly. Her eyes strained into the blackness below, but she remembered the deserted sea and gave up hope of distinguishing a light. A thin, complaining whine from the iron guts of the motor.

Bullet through the oil tanks, she thought. This can't last much longer.

But she kept on, content to take death as it should come, but still fighting. The score was even—victory hers even though she would never enjoy its spoils.

The whine of the motor was rising in a screaming crescendo—she felt the Boeing settle.

Her hands unloosed the buckles of the safety-belt, grazed the butt of a Very pistol. Her fingers closed about it and tore it out of its holster.

Pointing the Very gun over her head a rocket of light shot upward, burst in a shower of colored stars.

With a final shrill of protest the motor clanked into silence.

She nosed the ship down in a long easy glide.

The face of Spanish Lil sneered up out of her mind. Dizzy gritted her teeth. That score would have to go unsettled.

The Very pistol spurted another streamer of light that rocketed into twinkling stars.

The ship nosed down, a darker blackness rising to meet it. Wave crests slapped at the undercarriage, a spurt of spray dashed upward from the dead prop and the Boeing settled gently into the arms of the sea.

UNCOMPREHENDINGLY, at first, Dizzy Malone's eyes took in the little white room, the stiffly-uniformed nurse, the white iron bed; came to rest on the face of the man bending over her—Tom Louden.

Realization filtered gradually into her mind.

Tom grinned.

"Feeling better?"

Dizzy nodded feebly.

"I may get myself into a jam for —ah—commandeering that sea sled but—it was worth the chance. And I was just in time."

"Thanks," she whispered. "You took a chance for me, huh? Well, I'm just dizzy enough to take one myself—now. I'll chance the straight and narrow, if you—think——"

Tom Louden's face bent closer— closer——.

QUEEN SUE CARLTON

Harold Hersey says in his autobiographical *Pulpwood Editor:* "The public fancy was engrossed with the amazing spectacle of racketeers enjoying a fabulous prosperity in the period of the Noble Experiment, when the newspapers made heroes out of the great gangsters. . . ."

Hersey edited magazines for Clayton and later headed his own publishing company, which put out such titles as *Gun Molls Magazine* and *Gangster Stories.* While some expressed dismay at the immoral tone of his titles, Hersey says, "I was careful never to permit an underworldling to triumph over justice. He gets his desserts—and no mistake—in the end. . . ."

C. B. Yorke's Queen Sue Carlton was a series character in *Gangster Stories,* which was published from 1929 to '32. As tough a woman as you'll meet in the pulps, she is seen here in "Snowbound," from the October 1931 issue.

Snowbound

Another Queen Sue Novelette Complete in this Issue

By C. B. YORKE

*Queen Sue was the toughest moll that ever pulled a gat this side of
Hades—she was in the rackets for what she could get out of
'em—But peddlin' snow was entirely out of her line, and
not even Garland's "persuasive" methods could
make this baby change her mind!!*

CHAPTER I

OVER HER HEAD

SHE was nervous from the moment she entered my apartment.
I didn't blame her much. Suds Garland had given her a tough job.

"Here's the money," she said, fumbling in her purse with trembling hands. "Five grand, cash."

I laughed softly. The girl looked up at me with wide eyes. Something in her gaze told me she feared more than what I might do to her.

"Chicken feed," I said, still smiling.

"Seven thousand?" she countered. "That's funny!"

"Ten grand? That's a lot of money."

Perhaps ten thousand was a lot to her. She looked like a kid who wasn't accustomed to dealing in big figures when it came to cold cash. But as for me, ten thousand dollars didn't even get me interested in her proposition, and I told her so.

"Well," she went on, her thin voice shaking slightly from excitement and nervousness, "I'll give you fifteen thousand. Suds will go that high just to get you—"

"Make it fifty grand," I told her sharply.

A little gasp escaped her. I knew she didn't have fifty grand with her, and in all probability Suds wouldn't consider that price. It made no difference to me. So when she got over the shock of the figure I'd named I gave it to her straight.

"Listen, kid," I explained quietly. "I was just kidding about that fifty grand limit. No matter what—"

"Then you'll take fifteen grand?" she interrupted.

"No. Now listen closely. No matter what Suds Garland offers I'm not accepting it. See? Not even fifty grand in cash could tempt me to tie up with him in the dope racket. And that's final. What's your name?"

THE GIRL looked at me with troubled eyes. She had come to my apartment that afternoon to try to get me to change my mind. I'd already told Suds that I wasn't interested in dope, wouldn't be interested, and couldn't be interested. He had sent the girl over to my place to see if money talked louder than words.

That had been a smart move on his part, but not smart enough. Had he known the real Queen Sue he wouldn't have wasted his time. Sure, I could probably supply much needed brains in his racket, but dope is one thing I don't touch, not even the racket angle of it.

Apparently the girl hadn't heard much about me, either. The kid figured I needed cash and would take anything she offered, gladly. Now when I asked for her name she snapped her purse shut and started to get up.

"Sit still," I told her gently. "There's nothing to get excited about. You've done your part, and you can't help it if I refuse the offer you've made. So now, just as one woman to another, let's have a little talk. Smoke?"

When we had cigarettes going she seemed to forget her nervousness. But she still watched me with sort of a sidewise glance as though she expected a couple of guns to appear around the corners of the rug and begin shooting. Perhaps she had heard something about me.

"Tell me your name," I went on presently.

"Kate Travers," she said softly.

"All right, Kate," I continued. "You know who I am, and now that we're acquainted I'm going to tell you something. You look like a nice sort of girl to be mixed up in this dope business. Just how—"

"Oh, I don't use it myself," she broke in quickly.

"I didn't think so," I responded, smiling faintly. "You're just playing along with Suds for what you can get out of it. That right?"

Kate Travers nodded and dragged at her cigarette. I framed my next speech carefully.

"I'm going to tell you something, Kate. Maybe you know it already, and maybe you don't. It doesn't matter much. I just want you to know that I'm not the least bit interested in Suds Garland, personally or financially. Feel better now?"

"But you—"

"Sure," I broke in swiftly. "Suds and I teamed up against Buzz Mallon. That was business, but I didn't take a cent from Suds. Partners in a business arrangement aren't necessarily friends. Suds and I worked together to protect ourselves. But that's all over now."

"Then you won't consider my proposition at all?"

I pitied the kid. She asked that question out of sheer ignorance. She was in the middle of something she didn't know a thing about, just acting as the cat's paw for Garland.

"No," I answered, moving my head

slowly from left to right. "The proposition doesn't interest me. We're talking as friends now."

"But what will I tell—"

She stopped suddenly and stared at the cigarette in her hand with frightened eyes. She knew she had said too much, but it was too late to take back her words.

"You've got an out, Kate," I explained. "A good out. Suds can't blame you if I won't agree to throw in with him. I'll put it in writing if you want me to. I don't want to get you into trouble."

"Kind of you," she murmured.

I PAUSED a moment and during the brief silence I wondered why I was being so lenient with the kid. I should have tossed her out the minute she tried to bribe me to join Suds Garland's mob. But I didn't.

Perhaps I saw in her a vision of myself a few years ago—young, slightly innocent of certain phases of gang life, and a little fearful of everybody and everything. Well, I was still young, but no longer innocent. And I was entirely without fear of physical forces. I'd managed to take care of myself, had fought my way up to the top of a big mob, and had seen it crumble under me.

Now I was lone-wolfing it, freelancing in crime for what I could get out of it. But I wasn't taking part in a dope racket, and anything Suds Garland had to offer was connected with dope. I had the Club Bijou, and was making money. For the moment that was all I wanted.

Later, perhaps, I would start building another mob. If I could find the right men to work with I'd do that. But it was all in the future. The loss of Dan Reilly, Biff Brons and Blimp Sampson, who had died in my fight with the cops, was still too recent to raise my hopes of ever finding men who could take their places.

So while I looked at the pathetic, frightened figure of Kate Travers I felt sorry for her. I did the best I could, but it wasn't much. Her troubles were not mine. She was sitting in with Suds Garland and there was nothing I could do about it. But I told her something I thought she should know.

"I'll be frank with you, Kate," I said finally. "You've probably heard that Queen Sue, Sue Carlton, was the toughest mob leader that ever pulled a rod. Well, I am hard sometimes. You've got to be in this life. But there's a time and place for everything. So you've got nothing to worry about now. How long have you been with Suds?"

"Two weeks, but I've known him—"

"No matter about that, Kate," I interrupted. I didn't want her life history. "He expecting you back right away?"

"I'm seeing him tonight to give him your answer."

"Fine. Now, I'll tell you what you do. Got a boy friend?"

Kate looked up, then nodded slowly. I went on.

"Well, run around and see him for awhile. I'll get in touch with Suds myself and deliver my message in person. Then when you see him tonight there won't be a chance for him to get sore at you. Okay?"

"That's awfully kind of you, Queen," the girl said tremulously, "but Suds said I'd have to arrange things with you or—"

"Don't worry about that. Suds won't have anything to say, won't do anything to you." I smiled my assurance and she brightened. I honestly believed at that moment I was telling the truth. "So just run along now. It's not quite three o'clock. Have dinner with the boy friend and I'll fix everything with Suds."

After again thanking me, the kid moved to the door. I saw her to the elevator and then went back to my apartment and watched her leave the front entrance of the building a few minutes later. Suds should have known better than to pick a kid like her to talk to me about joining a racket.

When the kid passed out of sight along the street I turned away from the window, went over to the telephone, and called Suds Garland's number. There was no answer, so I made a mental note to call him later and dismissed the frightened little Kate Travers from my mind.

I had other work to do, what with managing a night club, arranging for liquor deliveries, entertainment, and a lot of other details and it wasn't until almost an hour later that I remembered I had to call Garland and arrange for a meeting with him.

I'd just lifted the receiver when the door-bell rang. I got up, moved across the room, opened the door and got a real surprise.

STANDING in the doorway, his soft felt hat pushed back off his brow, was Sid Lang, the big detective from the District Attorney's office who had broken me as a mob leader. I hadn't seen him since that night in Cincinnati when I had trapped him in my room and had purchased my freedom by sparing his life.

Since then the indictments against me had been quashed. So I put a big smile on my face, knowing full well there was nothing to fear.

"Come in, Sid," I said, not stopping to wonder why he was calling on me. "Certainly is nice to see you again. How's the D. A. and all your flat-footed playmates?"

The broad face of Sid Lang didn't relax in a smile. His cold eyes held mine steadily as he stepped into the room. He kept his hands in plain sight so I didn't make any moves toward the gun on my right leg.

"'Lo, Queen," he said laconically when the door was closed. "Heard the news?"

"The D. A. after me again?" I laughed.

"No. I'm not with the District Attorney's office any more. I'm working for an agency now—private dick."

"Trying to drum up business with me?"

"Cut it, Queen!" he said sharply. "I just heard something I thought you ought to know."

"Nice of you, Sid," I nodded, wiping the smile from my face. "When did you start playing on my side of the fence?"

"Don't be funny," he continued. "A kid by the name of Kate Travers was gunned out awhile ago, a half dozen blocks from here."

My heart stopped.

"I got it straight," Sid Lang went on slowly, his voice sounding strangely hollow, "that she left you a few minutes before she got it. She was running with Suds Garland's mob. I happen to know that he wants you to join up with him."

Lang paused. I wasn't telling him anything, so I merely said, "Yes?" and waited. A moment later Lang added:

"The cops found fifteen thousand in marked bills in her purse. I'm interested because Kate Travers was— my girl friend!"

CHAPTER II

CLEVER—BUT NOT ENOUGH

RED RAGE gripped me as I heard Sid Lang's words. For a moment I didn't think about him or his feelings. I saw only the clever plot that Suds Garland had tried to trap me with.

It was all plain enough now. Perhaps Garland had really wanted me to join his mob at first, but my refusal had angered him. So when I wouldn't change my mind he wanted me out of the way. Perhaps it wasn't just business that was on his mind, and in turning down his business proposition I had unconsciously insulted his amorous intentions.

Well, it was too late to worry about what had brought on all the trouble. Kate Travers was dead. But I saw his whole plan.

Not for a minute had Garland expected me to refuse the money that Kate had offered. He had taken it for granted that I had taken the money. Then he had the girl killed so I would get into a pile of trouble.

And trouble it would have been. The cops would have swarmed all over me, for Suds Garland would have tipped them quietly that I'd taken money from the kid and then had had her killed so it wouldn't become known that Queen Sue could be bought.

Yes, it might have worked out that way. Suds Garland had planned carefully. The only hitch in his plans had been the fact that Queen Sue is her own boss. I never sell out to the side with the most money.

In the midst of my thoughts I was suddenly brought back to the present. Sid Lang stepped in close to me and gripped me hard with a big hand on either shoulder.

"What d'you know about the kill, Queen?" he demanded, icy points of cold rage appearing in his blue eyes.

"Better talk fast because I'm going—"

"You're going to do—nothing!" I snapped.

"I'm going to kill you just as sure as I'm standing here! You put Kate on the spot and—"

My harsh laugh brought back his common sense. Looking him in the eye, every muscle in my small body steeled against the pain of that iron grip on my shoulders, I gave him glare for glare. Physically I didn't have a chance against him, but I won that silent clash of wills.

"Sorry, Queen," he muttered brokenly a moment later, taking his hands from my shoulders and flopping into a chair. "I guess I—lost my head."

"Forget it, Sid," I said quietly. "We all think we're pretty tough until something comes along that hits right at our hearts."

He nodded slowly. "Kate meant a lot to me. You wouldn't know how much."

A BITTER smile curled my lips. In a low voice I said:

"I know exactly how you feel. Remember Chick Wilson and Dan Reilly? Well, you can't tell me a thing about sorrow. I've been there myself. You're just getting a dose of what I felt when you helped gun out Dan and Blimp and—"

"But I had to do—"

"Sure," I broke in quickly. "There was nothing personal in it. I know that. You just happened to be on the side of the law. I wasn't. If it would have done me any good I'd have killed you long before this. But that wouldn't bring Dan or Chick back. Neither will killing me give Kate a new lease on life. How did she happen to tie up with Suds?"

"Don't know—unless it was the money in it. We were going to be married as soon as I got enough money saved. But you don't put aside much in my work and—"

"Yes, she was just the type that would try to help her man. I'd have done the same myself. She probably thought she could step out of it after she'd made a couple of thousand. What did you let her do it for?"

"I couldn't stop her, Queen. She was in with Suds before I knew it. Then when I found out about it I didn't know how to go about telling her that she was making a mistake. You see—"

"Of course I see," I answered in a tired voice. "You men are all the same; great big strong brutes who can lick their weight in wildcats, but you're afraid of a little woman who might get angry with you. Kate didn't know what it was all about—didn't realize what she was doing. Listen."

I told Sid Lang how the kid had tried to buy me. That part of it I told quickly so he wouldn't get another idea that I'd had anything to do with the killing. Then I explained what had been behind her murder.

When I finished, Sid Lang took off his hat, ran broad fingers through his thin blonde hair, and looked at me with bleak eyes.

"God only knows why, Queen, but I believe you. See you later."

He got up and moved quickly toward the door. But I was quicker. "Calm down, bright guy," I ordered, turning the key in the lock and slipping the piece of metal down the neck of my dress. "You're not leaving here until you cool off."

"Give me that key before—"

He never finished that sentence. As his big hands reached for me again I sidestepped away from in front of the door. At the same instant my right hand shot under the hem of my dress and came out with my gun in my fingers.

"Back up, Sid!" I snapped. "You're not such a bad guy for being a dick, and you're not going to make a

damned fool of yourself. Sit down—before I send you to the hospital with a slug in your leg. You'll be safe there."

For a moment I thought my argument wasn't going to work. I've never seen a guy with more nerve than Sid Lang has, but he knew I meant every word I said. He'd learned by experience that Queen Sue doesn't bluff.

WHEN he was seated in the chair again I gave him some advice.

"I didn't want to do this, Sid, but I had to. You don't mean a thing in my young life, but listen anyway. If anything happens to Suds Garland now, the cops will come looking for you. You aren't on the force now. You're just an agency man—a private dick. And you might end up in the electric chair. Get it?"

He got it all right, but he didn't nod immediately. Behind his cold eyes I could see that his brain was working again.

"That's fine," I continued. "Perhaps in a way I was partly responsible for what happened to Kate, but you can't go around shooting a guy just because you know he's guilty of a dirty trick. You've got to have proof."

"I'll get it, and then I'll—"

"You listen to me! Get yourself a good alibi and sit tight. Remember, the cops will look you up if anything happens to Suds Garland."

"You mean you are going to—" Lang half rose to his feet in his eagerness.

"Sit down, Sid. That's better. I'm saying nothing about what I'm going to do or not going to do. I'm just giving you some good pointers. You happen to be a dick and I happen to be—well, a gang girl. We've always been enemies, but we're calling a truce for the next few days or weeks."

"I guess we are," nodded Lang resignedly. "But I'm not letting you

SNOWBOUND

fight my battles. I see the point in what you've been talking about, and I'll take it easy. Think I'll go now."

There was no use of talking to him any longer, so I went over, unlocked the door, and then stepped aside as I put my gun back on my leg. Sid Lang paused at the threshold and looked down at me with a faint smile.

"Thanks, Queen, for not letting me go off half-cocked," he said quietly. "I'll remember that."

Yes, he would remember that I'd done him a favor, but he didn't fool me. I knew as well as though he'd told me in so many words that he was going to kill Suds Garland, regardless of what I had said. And after I'd closed the door behind him I did some fast brain work.

Then a few minutes later I stepped to the telephone and called Suds Garland's number again. This time I got him on the wire. After that I didn't waste time.

"Don't ask who's calling," I said quickly. "This is just a friendly tip. You're on the spot!"

Before Suds could say a word I hung up. He had been clever in trying to frame me for the killing of Kate Travers, but not clever enough to outwit Queen Sue. My telephone message would give him something to worry about.

CHAPTER III

STRAIGHT TALK

DON'T get the idea I was playing stoolie for anybody. No, nothing like that. I just didn't like the way things were shaping up.

There was a lot more to this whole business than surface indications showed. In the first place, Sid Lang's explanation of how Kate Travers happened to be in with Suds Garland's mob was very weak. But right at the moment I wasn't arguing the point.

My best bet was to play a waiting game, and I did just that. With Sid Lang thinking that I believed his story I figured something would break. Of course, I was taking a big chance that I wouldn't get in a jam, but I can usually take care of myself.

So far as Lang wanting to kill Suds Garland was concerned, I knew it was true. Garland had gunned out the girl and ought to pay for it. But for no reason at all both Garland and Sid Lang were trying to get me into the fight.

That's why I tipped Garland that he was on the spot. I didn't want anything happening to him until I found out just why and how I figured in his plans. I knew something would happen if I let things run their course. And it happened, but not as I'd expected.

I was sitting in my private office at the Club Bijou two nights later when there was the sound of scuffling outside my door. It was long past midnight and with a big crowd in the dining room I thought it was just a couple of drunks who'd found their way back into the corridor that led past my office.

A moment later I discovered what it was all about. The door opened and Francis, my head waiter, and one of the bouncers dragged in a small man who was sniveling and begging for mercy. I took one look at the three of them, then got up and closed the door behind them, locking it.

"What's up, Francis?" I demanded, frowning at the little man who suddenly became silent when he saw me.

Francis was nothing like his name sounded. He was more than two hundred pounds of bone and muscle packed into six feet of height. In the dining room, bowing and smiling to the patrons of the club, he looked and spoke like a gentleman. Out of character, he was the best muscle man I had.

So when I asked that question

Francis scowled, jerked the little man around in front of him and snapped:

"Caught this guy peddling dope—snowbird himself."

I TOOK a moment to think that over. The Club Bijou is on the lower East Side and in that district nobody but Suds Garland sells the stuff that makes old men out of young men quicker than anything else in the world. So I figured this was another of Garland's bright ideas.

"What's your name, buddy?" I asked.

The little man cringed and looked up at Francis and the bouncer like a whipped dog. Then he babbled:

"I ain't done nothing! These birds just framed me—"

"Search him," I ordered, not wanting to hear his sob story.

"Already did it, Queen," replied Francis. "Here's what he had left."

He took a number of small folded papers from a side pocket of his tuxedo jacket and tossed them on my desk. I gave them only a glance and then looked back at the little man.

"So they framed you, eh?" I said quietly.

The little man nodded vigorously.

"Like to sniff a deck? Fix you up—steady your nerves," I continued, and almost smiled at the little man's reaction.

He looked at the folded papers on the desk, licked his lips with a nervous tongue, and frowned with indecision. He didn't know whether I was kidding him or not. I didn't wait for him to make up his mind.

"Sock him once, Francis," I instructed, "and toss the rat out into the alley. He won't come back."

Francis and the bouncer dragged the little guy out before he could squeal. A few minutes later I picked up the bindles of coke, went into the ladies' room, and washed them down a toilet. Then I went out to the main room and looked over the crowd.

Had the guy really been peddling the stuff in the club, or was he just trying to hide it? I didn't know, but I wouldn't have been surprised if Suds Garland had made a plant and then tipped the narcotic agents to raid me.

But there was nothing to gain by trying to figure things out by mere headwork. Francis had spotted the fellow before he could do any harm. So I dismissed the incident from my mind and sat down at one of the tables with some friends.

An hour later I was still there, laughing and chatting after the floor show had played its last turn of the night, when Francis gave me the high sign from the side of the room. I excused myself and went over to him.

"Suds Garland just went back to your office," he whispered rapidly. "I couldn't stop him without raising a row and that would have been bad for business."

"Anybody with him?" I inquired. Things were beginning to move faster. I like speed.

"Two bodyguards. What'll I do?"

"Get a couple of the boys and hang around the corridor. No gunplay unless I give the word. Don't want to ruin business. See?"

Francis nodded and I started to move toward the corridor that led to my office in the rear of the building. I'd taken two steps when Francis caught me by the arm.

"Where you going?"

"To my office," I answered quietly. "Any objections?"

"No—but I don't want you to get hurt."

I smiled. "Thanks, Francis. Save your sympathy for Suds."

With that I moved on. It seemed like old times again to have somebody worrying about my safety. But it wasn't unusual. I pride myself on picking men who are loyal to me through thick and thin. And Francis was proving me right.

Once out of sight of the crowd in the main room I got the gun from the holster on my leg. Then with the comforting feel of steel in my palm I moved quickly down the corridor.

AT THE door of my office I paused for a moment and listened. Little sounds of movement came from the room, but there was no talking. Suds was apparently looking over the place before he settled down to wait for me. I didn't give him time to get impatient.

Turning the knob with my left hand, I opened the door a few inches, and slipped silently into the room. The next moment I had the door closed again, my gun up at my hip, and my back to the wall.

"Looking for me, Suds?"

The three men whirled at the sound of my voice. At the moment I had entered the room they had been crowded around my desk with their backs to the door.

None of them had their guns out. But as I spoke one of the bodyguards, a young fellow with a smooth, beardless face, raised his right hand toward an armpit holster.

"I wouldn't!" I snapped, and the youngster froze.

"What's the meaning of this?" demanded Suds.

I narrowed my eyes slightly while I smiled at his weak attempt to bluff my play. His tall, thin body was stooped in a half-crouch as though he was going to leap across the room at me. His black eyes were expressionless, but the sight of my gun had caused the blood to drain from his ruddy face, leaving his skin the color of dirty milk.

"Sit down, all of you," I ordered. "You, Garland, squat at the desk, hands on the glass where I can see them. Snap into it!"

Suds Garland didn't argue. He seated himself in the chair in front of the desk and flattened his hands, palm downward, on the top like I'd ordered. The two bodyguards flopped into a couple of chairs along the wall at the right of the desk.

"Hands on your knees—and keep them there!" I continued.

They didn't need to be told twice. My smile broadened as I looked at each of the three men for a moment in silence. Then abruptly I wiped the smile from my face, bent slightly, replaced my gun in the holster on my leg, and then straightened.

"Think you're pretty tough, eh?" I sneered as the three held their poses. "Dealing with a woman is usually soft pickings for hard guys like you. Well, here's your chance to prove how tough you are. Reach for your gats!"

For perhaps all of ten seconds none of the three men moved a muscle. Maybe they knew I wasn't bluffing when I put my gat back on my leg. I knew I could beat them to the draw and none of them wanted to take the chance. Where I only had inches to move my hand they had feet, and covering distance in split seconds counts on the draw.

Finally Suds Garland shifted his eyes to the men along the wall and shook his head slightly. I laughed harshly.

"Bright guy, Suds," I snorted. "Telling the boys not to draw when they've already made up their minds to be good. I guess my reputation isn't so bad!"

Suds spread his lips in a sickly smile. "We're just making a friendly call, Queen. You beat up Johnny's brother and—"

"Who's Johnny?" I wanted to know.

Garland nodded toward the beardless fellow who looked like a kid alongside the other muscle man who had a scarred lip and a broken nose.

"Okay," I said. "Go on with your song and dance."

"Well, you beat up Johnny's brother and—well, I just wanted to know what the idea was," Suds finished lamely.

"And I'll tell you," I returned in a harsh voice. "Dope peddling—or planting—is out at the Club Bijou. Get that straight! The next time I catch one of your punks around here you pick him up at the morgue. See?"

"But, Queen, I thought we were friends?" whined Garland.

FOR a moment I didn't know whether to laugh or call Francis and the boys and have the three of them thrown out. But I did neither. I just nodded slowly.

"I'm going to talk straight," I said quietly. "I think I was right when I guessed that you thought you were going to have an easy time fighting a woman. Now, I'm going to tell you something, Suds, and your two trained seals can listen in for future reference."

I paused a moment, but Garland had nothing to say. So I went on.

"A month ago when we were both fighting Buzz Mallon we played ball together. But if you got the idea we were friends you were mistaken. I told you then I didn't like dope and wouldn't join your racket. You, Suds, came into power after the cops wrecked my old mob and I had to leave town. You only know Queen Sue from what you've heard about her. If you were bright, you'd have learned something from what I did to Mallon."

"Didn't I help you get rid of Mallon?" Suds asked in a thin voice.

"You did, but I also helped you and that squared our account," I shot back quickly. "And from now on you'd better watch your step, or you'll think Mallon had an easy time of it. Maybe I'm not running a big mob like I used to, but I'm still Queen Sue. That's not boasting. That's a fact. Remember it."

"Ah, you're just nervous about something, Queen," shrugged Garland.

"Not half as nervous as you," I pointed out, smiling at the way Suds and his henchmen were holding the pose I'd given them. "You're walking out of here like good little boys, unless you want a skinful of lead. Move!"

The three of them got slowly to their feet. Keeping their arms at the sides they moved slowly towards the door. I backed off to one side, kept my back to the wall, ready for anything. But nothing happened that time.

Suds paused at the door and the other two crowded around him.

"Sorry we can't be friends, Queen," he said.

"I'm not," I replied. "Just because you had an easy time of rubbing out one woman you don't have to think all of them are that easy. And don't try to plant any more kills on me."

Suds arched thin eyebrows in feigned surprise. "Me—tried to plant a kill?"

I laughed again. "Forget it, Suds. It didn't work. But don't make the same mistake twice. By the way, better get a couple of guys with nerve. Bodyguards that let a woman bluff them don't amount to much."

Garland didn't reply to my taunt. He swung open the door and ran smack into Francis in the corridor. The other two crowded out after him and I smiled at my head waiter who looked at me for instructions.

"Take them out the front way," I said. "Just a little friendly call, but give them the works if there's any funny business. Scram."

Suds gave me a parting glare. My little talk hadn't accomplished much, but I knew it would serve to bring matters to a head. And it did, even sooner than I expected.

CHAPTER IV

FOOLISH BUSINESS

DAWN was breaking when I finally left the night club. I hadn't given Suds Garland and his mob a second thought since I'd seen him go down the corridor with Francis and the boys.

There had been no trouble at all about their leaving. But the moment I stepped out of the Club Bijou into the first faint light of a new day I had the uneasy feeling that something was going to happen. Perhaps it was just the eery half-light between night and day that affected me that way, but I was taking no chances.

A slight fog had settled over the city and now hung in shifting ribbons that swirled along the street like ghosts hurrying to escape the rising sun. I noticed those little details unconsciously because I wasn't interested in the beauties of a new day at the moment.

Across the pavement from the entrance of the club a cab waited. There was nothing unusual in that because the doorman or Francis always ordered a cab for me when I left in the mornings, and any cab they ordered was safe.

So with scarcely a glance to either side I walked across the sidewalk and stepped into the cab. Then just as I seated myself I caught a glimpse of moving figures in the fog beyond the entrance of the club.

Before I could say a word the doorman, who was on duty late that morning, slammed the door and the driver let in the clutch. The figures in the fog grew plainer as they approached the cab, heads down, hands sunk deep in the side pockets of their coats.

I didn't wait to see more. The cab started to move as I opened the door on the far side and stepped out into the street. Shielded by the slowly moving cab from the figures on the sidewalk, I slipped across the street and was partly concealed by the fog.

I hadn't acted too soon, for as I reached the opposite curb guns crashed across the street. A man cursed, and the cab stopped with a sudden squeal of brakes. I counted five quick shots. Then the slap of running feet on pavement came to me.

Straining my ears to keep the running men within earshot, I started along the street after them. A moment later the fog parted and I got a brief view of two men. Instantly my gun was in my hand, but even as I raised it the fog closed in again and the men were lost in the half-light.

Then as I started to cross the street again I heard the low purr of a powerful motor behind me. At the same time there was a chorus of shouts from the Club Bijou as Francis and some of the late diners and drinkers piled out on the street.

Almost before I knew it a long sedan slid past me in the fog and swung in toward the curb. The sound of running stopped.

Thinking fast, I sprinted across the few yards that separated me from the big car and swung up on the trunk rack that jutted out over the gas tank in the rear as the car gathered speed.

Minutes passed while the car swung around several corners, putting plenty of distance between it and the Club Bijou. I had all I could do to keep my balance on my precarious perch during the first few moments of that ride, but finally the car settled down to a steady run.

A few minutes later the protecting wisps of fog became thinner and finally vanished. But the hour was early and the few persons that were on the street didn't give me a look.

THEN after about ten minutes of fast riding the car slowed down and slid in alongside the curb on one of the side streets uptown. I watched my chance and slipped off the trunk rack just before the car stopped.

I'd just gained the shelter of the doorway of a small apartment house when a rear door of the car opened and two men hit the sidewalk, moving fast. I raised my gun, then changed my mind.

They thought they'd got me in the taxicab. It wouldn't hurt anything to let them continue to think that for awhile.

The house before which the car had stopped was a two story brick structure. The first floor was vacant, so I figured the boys were to meet Suds Garland on the second floor. He had lost no time in repaying the courtesy I'd shown him at the Club Bijou.

But I couldn't tip my hand in broad daylight with no means for a getaway. So I put my gun back on my leg and watched the men go into the house. A moment later the car pulled away from the curb and disappeared around the next corner.

Five minutes later I was walking fast across town. I'd recognized one of the men who had tried to get me as the young fellow who'd been with Garland, but after being up all night I needed sleep more than anything else. I was going to have a lot of work to do that night.

Presently I caught a cab and twenty minutes later I was at my apartment. I had the driver wait for me while I packed a bag, and then went up to a hotel in the theatrical district.

It was almost three o'clock in the afternoon when I got up, bathed, dressed, and had breakfast sent up to my room. Then I phoned Francis at his apartment.

"God, Queen!" he exclaimed when he heard my voice. "I thought they'd taken you for a ride."

"Almost did," I admitted, "but I'm still alive and kicking. Get a couple of the boys and meet me at the club at five-thirty sharp. I've got work for you."

Well, that was that, I thought while I ate breakfast and then took a cab across town to Simon Grundish's office. I was going to need some airtight protection, and perhaps an alibi, and Grundish was the man who could fix it for me.

The political power behind the throne at City Hall didn't keep me waiting. He met me at the door of his private office right after I'd sent in my name. His wizened face and pale eyes seemed almost joyful when I greeted him and closed the door.

"What have you been up to now?" he asked quietly, knowing that I didn't waste time with social visits during business hours.

"Nothing much," I smiled. "Suds Garland tried to gun me out this morning. That was foolish business on his part. Understand?"

"I think I do," returned the little old man who had been instrumental in seeing that the old indictments against me had been dismissed. "Remember what I told you about Garland a month ago? Well, I still think he's bad company. It won't be any great loss if he—"

"Think you can fix it for me if there's a flareback after I get done with him?"

Grundish frowned for a moment, then nodded.

"Good," I smiled. "Seems like a lady can't even run a night club around this city any more without having some guy think he owns her. I don't like it. I think I'll have to branch out into something bigger just to keep the small timers away from me."

"Suds Garland isn't a small timer."

"No, and he's not so big, either. He thinks he's tough just because he makes a lot of money out of the racket. Maybe he was tough once, but money and good living have made him soft. It's ruined more than one good man, and dope doesn't draw good men."

"Well, Queen," Grundish shrugged, "you branch out any way you want to. I'd be careful of Garland, though."

"From now on I'm going to be," I admitted. "Just pass the word along to the cops that I know nothing about the dope business. See?"

GRUNDISH smiled his thin smile which was as near as he ever came to genuine mirth. I left him a few minutes after that, knowing that even if some bright cop did want to ask questions he wouldn't get far. Grundish would see to that.

It was almost five-thirty when I reached the Club Bijou. Francis and four of the bouncers at the club were already there, waiting for me to give them the office. I did, starting first with the address of the house where the two men from the car had holed up.

"Drop out there after it gets dark," I ordered, "and smoke the boys out. It's a fairly quiet neighborhood so don't make too much noise."

"Leave it to us, Queen," promised Francis. "Anything else?"

"I think that will be enough for one night," I replied, and didn't smile when I said it. That business wasn't any joking matter, but I knew those two punks would never squeeze another trigger.

And they didn't. Francis and the boys returned to the club around ten o'clock that night. I listened quietly while Francis told me how they'd trapped the pair in the upper apartment. Maxim-silenced guns had done the rest.

I figured that incident would make Suds Garland think twice before he tried any more funny stuff with me. The killing of Kate Travers had ceased to be of importance in my mind, because to me the quarrel with Suds Garland was nothing but a personal grudge fight.

So I paid off on that job and when the club opened for business at midnight Francis and the boys were on deck as usual.

Everything went along quietly that night for the first hour or so, and then in the midst of the floor show, shortly after one-thirty, Suds Garland pulled the most foolish stunt of his career.

I was standing at the doorway of the corridor that led back to my office when it happened. The orchestra was playing a snappy little number and the chorus was cavorting across the floor when suddenly there was a stunning roar of an explosion.

Instantly the lights went out. Glass crashed at the front of the club and was lost in the crescendo of splintered wood, hurtling bricks and falling plaster. One guess was enough to know what had happened.

Suds Garland's mob had tossed a pineapple into the entrance hall!

CHAPTER V

THE QUEEN ACTS

FIGHTING my way blindly through the darkness and the crush of the mob that tried to rush the front entrance, I finally gained the main door. By that time tiny flames were crackling in the wreckage of what had been a hall, and were gaining headway fast.

The crowd of diners and dancers didn't get far. The whole front corridor was a shambles. Then over the shouts of the crowd sounded the bellowing voice of Francis, directing them to the rear corridor which led to an alley in the back.

With one accord the crowd rushed the narrow hall. It didn't take five minutes for them to jam themselves out of the main room. By that time I'd found a fire extinguisher in the darkness and was trying vainly to stem the tide of the flames.

Francis and some of the boys were lighting the place as best they could with flashlights. Other waiters were working more fire extinguishers and making no progress. Then suddenly in the distance I heard the clang of fire bells and the wail of police sirens.

"No talking, boys," I ordered, shouting to make myself heard. "I'll deal with the cops."

A chorus of agreement came to me out of the semi-darkness of what a few minutes before had been a brilliantly lighted spot of night life. I thought of the checkroom girl and wondered whether any guests had been caught by the blast.

For the first few minutes the battalion chief and the sergeant in charge of the emergency squad of cops had their hands full with the fire and the crowds that gathered in the street. Then when the flames were under control both the chief and the sergeant looked me up.

"Well, young lady," began the grizzled fire fighter, "What have you got to say for yourself?"

"Who tossed the bomb?" shot in the sergeant, another veteran of bulldozing tactics which were usually effective.

"One at a time," I said quietly. "Suppose we go back to my office. It's still in one piece."

When I had a cigarette going in the back room and had rubbed most of the sweat and grime from my face and hands, I looked the two men in the eyes. They'd been firing questions at me continually, but they hadn't been able to break down my pose of ignorance.

"Listen," I said finally. "If I knew who did this, I'd tell you. Right at the moment this night club happens to be my only means of making a living. It's going to cost money to make repairs, but that's my worry. That's all I know. The blast get anybody?"

The two men exchanged a quick glance. Then the sergeant cleared his throat and said:

"Killed the checkroom girl and injured a man. That's all we've found so far."

"Who was the man?"

Why I asked that question, I don't know. Right at the minute I really wasn't interested in who the man might be, but the question popped out before I could stop it. A moment later I was glad I'd asked.

"The man was a private detective," said the sergeant. "Name of Sid Lang."

I didn't move a muscle as I heard those words, but my brain was working hard. What had Sid Lang been doing at the Club Bijou? Had he suspected that I'd had the two men, Suds Garland's bodyguards, rubbed out? I didn't know.

So I kept my face expressionless while I said:

"That's tough. Tell the guy I'll stand good for his hospital expenses and those of anybody else who was hurt. I don't want to have it said that Queen Sue doesn't take care of her friends. Tough about the checkroom girl. She was a nice kid."

"And you don't have any idea of who might have tossed that bomb?" persisted the battalion chief.

"None at all. You might scout around and see whether any of the neighbors saw anybody they'd

Swaying in the doorway, his head swathed in bloody bandages, was Sid Lang!

recognize just before it happened. I wasn't paying anybody protection and wasn't asked to. I just don't know who might have wanted to ruin my business."

"That's a lie, Queen Sue!"

I OPENED my mouth to deny that accusation, but I didn't speak. The voice had sounded strangely familiar, but had not come from the sergeant or the fire chief. Suddenly

I caught my breath as I looked past them.

Swaying in the doorway, big hands braced doggedly against the jambs, his head swathed in bloody bandages, was Sid Lang!

"What are you doing here?" demanded the sergeant. "You ought to be—"

"That's—all right," gasped Lang, waving the sergeant's objections down while he crossed the room unsteadily and stopped in front of me.

For a moment none of us spoke. Hovering outside the door, I could see the dim form of Francis. Then I looked up and met Sid Lang's boring gaze.

"Get out, you," mumbled Lang. "I want to talk—to the girl—alone."

Slowly the two older men moved to the door and closed it after them. In the light of the flash that was propped up on one corner of the desk Lang's blood-streaked face was ghastly. I expected him to collapse any moment, but when I placed a chair for him he merely shook his head and remained standing.

"Sorry, Queen," he said slowly with a great effort, his voice nothing but a hollow whisper. "Didn't mean —to spoil your play."

"You didn't," I assured him. "You ought to be in the hospital."

"Going there—soon." He paused, laboring for breath. Finally he went on. "Listen, Queen. I'm out of this— for awhile. I'm going to tell you something. I didn't give it to you straight—on Kate Travers."

"I know you didn't," I responded. "Come clean this time."

"Yes, do that. Kate was an under-cover agent. Wasn't working for the agency—just for me. She thought she could get more than I could. I told you straight about—what she meant to me. I'm hired to bust Suds for some rich guy. Garland made a snow-bird out of his son. And so far Suds has made a bum—out of you. Get it?"

"Better rest up in the hospital," I said quietly. "You're off your head."

"Want me to—tip your play to the cops?"

"Spill and be damned!" I snapped. "I'm taking orders from no dick— not even a private flattie! Beat it!"

My heart stopped as Sid Lang turned slowly, laboriously toward the door. I wasn't fighting his battles, and he knew it. He had hoped to en-list my aid against Garland by giv-ing me the straight story on Kate Travers.

Perhaps under ordinary circum-stances I might have been impressed. As it was, I was fighting my own battles. I had a lot to settle with Suds Garland and his dope racket, but I wasn't giving Sid Lang any definite indication of what I was go-ing to do to Garland. After all, Sid Lang was on the side of the law. I wasn't.

I'd played a lone hand this far, but as Lang started towards the door I thought sure he was going to spoil my play. Then I sighed with relief as he opened the door and said:

"I was wrong, sarge. The girl's okay. God—I'm tired!"

As he finished speaking in a hoarse whisper, Sid Lang stumbled. Only the strong arms of the sergeant and the battalion chief kept him from crashing to the floor. Instantly I was at his side.

He opened his eyes for a moment. A faint smile wreathed his pallid lips as he looked up at me. Then he re-laxed and lay still.

"Just fainted," grunted the ser-geant. "Hey, somebody! Give us a light!"

I CAUGHT up the flash from the desk and led the way down the corridor to the alley. Silently I paid tribute to the sheer nerve that had kept Sid Lang on his feet until he had set me straight on the Kate Travers business. Perhaps that was what he had come to the club to do in the first place. It didn't make much difference now.

When Lang had been carted away in an ambulance the sergeant turned to me.

"A real man, that one," he said with genuine admiration. "He did great work while he was with the D. A.'s office."

"I know it," I said softly, and let it go at that.

SNOWBOUND

The sergeant looked at me hard for a moment. Then he nodded.

"I guess you do," he agreed, remembering how Sid Lang had smashed my old mob. Then he added, "Well, I'll leave a police guard here, young lady, till morning. If you hear anything about who did this, let us know."

Thanking him quickly, I made my way back into the club and found Francis. By some strange means he had managed to avoid ruffling even a hair of his shiny head, and his dinner clothes were still as immaculate as though he had just come on duty. That suited me fine.

I'd been doing a lot of headwork in the spare moments I'd had between arguing with the sergeant and the battalion chief. I meant to pay my debt to Suds Garland in no uncertain way, but first I was going to play havoc with certain parts of his racket. So I gave Francis his instructions quickly.

"Get four or five of the boys who are still presentable. I'll meet you a couple of blocks away, corner of Severn and Leistner, in twenty minutes. We've got a lot to do, so make it fast."

Watching my chance, I slipped out the back way again. A few minutes later I was at an all night garage, renting a sedan. I drove the car myself and picked up Francis and the boys right on schedule.

During the time Suds and I had been fighting Buzz Mallon, Suds had made the mistake of showing me what he called "spots of gold." In reality they were nothing but high-class apartments in the swankier districts of town where those who could afford to pay plenty were privileged to indulge their dope habits unmolested.

Suds furnished protection for the places and maintained them for his high class clientele. I meant to smash at least three of the places that I knew existed.

Perhaps this bit of sabotage sounds like a childish prank, but it wasn't. Suds had struck at my pocketbook through bombing the Club Bijou. I meant to cut into his bankroll by smashing his expensive joints. Loss of money in a racket hurts worse than having a couple of punk gunmen killed.

SO WHEN I picked up Francis and the boys I explained the situation to them rapidly. They were all for the idea immediately and were in high spirits as I started uptown.

For my part, I wasn't exactly lighthearted. Anything can happen when you start out on a job like that, and right at the moment I didn't want anything to happen to me before I got to see Suds Garland personally.

He had a lot to answer for, and I meant to make him do it. Still, I've never been able to send my men into a place that was too tight for me to go myself. And I always lead the way when there's work to be done.

This time was no exception. When I pulled up at the corner above a tall apartment house twenty minutes later I cautioned the boys to go easy with the gats, and then piled out of the car.

Francis had a gun equipped with a silencer so I had him follow close behind me while we walked down to the entrance of the building, a half block away. The four other men paired off behind us.

Only one mug was on duty in the lobby. I gave him a bright smile as I walked towards the elevators, and then as I passed him I turned quickly, slipped out my gun, and jammed it against his back.

"Quiet!" I warned, and the guy wilted. Suds didn't seem to have luck in picking gunmen.

Francis pushed the signal bell at the elevator and a moment later the car stopped at the ground floor. It was one of those automatic affairs and it crowded us considerably as we all piled into it. I didn't take my gun from the mug's back for a moment.

On the way up to the tenth floor Francis relieved the guy of his rod and turned him over to the boys. Then as the elevator stopped, Francis and I stepped out while the rest of the boys held back. So long as the door was open the elevator couldn't be called to any other floor.

Walking towards the rear of the building, we didn't see anybody in the corridor. When I came to the door of apartment 1014 I pushed a bell button.

Almost immediately the door opened. Francis jammed his foot in the opening and followed it with a massive shoulder as he dug his gun into the belly of a guy with a long, thin face. After that there was no trouble at all.

I signaled the boys in the elevator and they came trooping back to the apartment. Half a dozen couples and two unattached men were lounging around the lavishly furnished rooms in various stages of helplessness. There had been a larger crowd earlier in the evening, I knew, because of the heavy reek of opium smoke that was still in the air.

We had a little trouble herding the people into one of the back rooms with the guards. Two of the women had to be carried, but after that the boys had the place to themselves. In less than ten minutes it was one sweet wreck. Then we left.

We visited the other two places before we called it a night. At the third one Francis had to put a bullet through one guard's belly before he'd listen to reason, but there was no other trouble. Then I felt better.

Back in the car again, I told the boys to call at my hotel the next day for their pay, and then promised them a vacation while the Club Bijou

was being remodeled. I let them out at one of the better hot spots, and then returned the car to the garage.

It was only a few minutes past three when I left the garage. I had intended to return to the hotel and catch up on some sleep, but after I'd caught a cab I decided to drop around to my apartment and get another dress. Crawling through that wreckage hadn't helped the looks of my evening gown much.

After that bit of work I figured Suds Garland would be plenty busy for a few hours, listening to the stories his guards would tell. I didn't know then that he still had another card up his sleeve.

I'd been dragging on a cigarette, very much pleased with myself, but when the cab came in sight of my apartment house I got a shock. Several cars were parked along the curb and a large crowd was gathered around the entrance of the building.

A crowd at that time of the night meant just one thing. The cops were staging a raid, and something told me they were looking for me.

CHAPTER VI

IN THE BAG

QUICKLY I leaned forward in the seat, rapped on the glass partition, and told the driver to swing around the next corner and stop. While he followed those instructions I did some fast headwork.

By the time the cab halted alongside the curb I'd decided to see for myself what all the excitement was about. So I paid the driver and let him go. Then I started down the street towards the crowd.

If the cops were looking for me, I knew it wouldn't be a bad idea to find out what I was wanted for before they found me. There was enough of a crowd in the street to give me a chance to look around and ask some questions without being too conspicuous. And that's just what I did.

At first I tried to piece together the comments of the spectators that I overheard, but except for a lot of excited chatter about nothing in particular nobody was volunteering real information. Finally I moved in beside a man at the edge of the crowd.

"What happened, buddy?" I inquired, smiling my sweetest. "Raid a disorderly house?"

The man smiled at my sally. Then he became very blasé.

"Maybe that's what it is," he answered. "There's nothing to see here. I'm going home and get some sleep."

I was all set to crack wise at him when suddenly I felt a hand close over my left arm. Turning my head, I looked into the pale eyes of Simon Grundish. So I didn't say a word, just responded to the pressure on my arm and followed him down the street, away from the crowd.

When we were alone he took his hand from my arm. Grundish wasn't much of a night owl, and at his age when he was on the street at that hour I knew it was serious. But I waited for him to open the conversation.

"I just heard about it, Queen," he said a moment later, "and came right down to see what I could do. Lucky I found you."

"Yes, it is lucky," I admitted, "but I don't know what it's all about. What do the cops want me for now?"

"You don't know?"

"I don't. I just arrived before you found me."

"Well, Queen, this is pretty serious. The men who raided your place were Federal narcotic agents."

"What!" I stopped and looked hard at Grundish.

"That's right, Queen," he continued. "They found a large quantity of dope—cocaine, I think it was —in your apartment. We're going to have a devil of a time beating the

rap on that charge. I'll do what I can, but I can't promise—"

"Jeeze, what a lousy break that is!" I interrupted. "Snowbound, and no way of explaining that dope in my apartment!"

"No way at all that I know of. Looks like Suds Garland has played his ace."

"Yeah, but I'll beat the rap." I said that impulsively, not having the faintest idea of how I was going to do it. Then I got an idea. "Let's walk."

WE WALKED, and I did some hard thinking. Presently I thought I had things doped out enough to give Grundish my idea.

"Listen," I began, speaking slowly in a low voice, "remember Sid Lang, the big detective who used to work for the district attorney? You know, the guy who smashed my liquor mob."

"Yes, I know who you mean. I don't think I ever met him, but—"

"Well, you're going to meet him. He's in the Mercy Hospital with a cracked head. That blast at the club caught him—killed my checkroom girl at the same time. He's a private dick now and has been working quietly on breaking Suds Garland's racket."

"Did he put the Federal agents on you?"

I shook my head. "No, nothing like that. Suds thinks he's clever, but he isn't. He planted that dope in my place—not Lang—and then passed along the tip for the raid. Remember the girl who was killed several days ago shortly after leaving my place?"

Grundish nodded.

"Well," I continued, "she was Sid Lang's sweetheart. That's something he's got to settle with Suds himself. So I want you to see Lang as early as you can. Explain the situation to him. Tell him I'm going to do him a favor and expect one in return."

"But what can he do that I can't, Queen?"

"Just this. He's been on the prod against this dope racket. He knows who's at the head of it and probably was all set to make the pinch when he got smacked by that blast. I could use his testimony if the Feds get me and bring me to trial. See?"

"Bright idea, Queen," said Grundish admiringly. "I could probably fix the case, but it would take time and might cause a lot of questions to be asked. It isn't as though it were merely a liquor charge."

"Okay, then. You do that for me. Also see my lawyer and send him around to the hotel later today. You might drop around yourself and tell me what Sid Lang says. I think he'll come through. He's a pretty white guy for a dick. And thanks a lot for showing up when I needed you most. See you later."

"Where are you going now?"

"Me?" I put on a good act of being surprised. Then I smiled slightly and added, "I'm getting under cover where it's safe."

"Do that," said Grundish in parting.

My smile became bigger while I turned and watched Grundish walk off down the street, his short, thin body looking very frail in the darkness. And I had good reason to smile.

I wasn't going under cover just yet. I was going to settle the score with Suds Garland in the only way he seemed to be able to understand—with guns.

It was still more than an hour before daylight, and I figured I had time enough to call upon Garland in person that night. The weight of the gun on my leg gave me added confidence as I hailed a cab a few minutes after Grundish left me.

Giving the driver an address that would bring me within a block of Suds Garland's place, I lighted a butt and settled back to enjoy the ride.

Fifteen minutes later I left the cab and waited until the car moved away again getting down to the business at hand.

THE apartment house where Garland was living was a six story structure, situated on a corner. Along one side ran an alley that showed the faint outline of fire escapes up the side of the building in the darkness. The other side of the building was adjoined by a small brownstone front.

I didn't waste any time trying to climb up the fire escape. Suds lived on the fourth floor and that was too much of a climb for the time I had to spare. I went right to the main entrance and looked over the array of bell buttons and name cards, among which was one plainly labeled Garland.

But I didn't push the bell under that card. I selected two apartments on the sixth floor and held down the buttons for a full minute of steady ringing.

The street door was one of those safety latch things that can be opened from any apartment in the building. Somebody in one of the two apartments I was ringing would almost certainly release the latch, late though it was. And they did.

With the first click of the latch I was in the building. The main corridor was dimly lighted by widely spaced bulbs. I found the stairs and climbed fast, ignoring the automatic electric elevator opposite the steps. Too much noise might warn Suds of my visit.

At the fourth floor landing I paused. Not a sound came to me. As yet the people on the top floor didn't suspect they were receiving no visitors and had not opened their doors to investigate.

Silently I moved along the corridor until I stopped at the door of Suds Garland's apartment. Then after a final glance along the hall I got my gun in my right hand and pressed the doorbell with my left forefinger.

. I was taking a big chance, and I knew it. I wasn't certain that Garland was home, and if he was I wanted to be ready for anything. I was.

After a couple of minutes there was the sound of a key turning in the lock. Then several bolts were shot back. Keeping off to one side of the door, my back flattened against the wall so that I was out of sight, I waited.

I felt rather than saw the door swing open on silent hinges. For a long breathless moment I thought my plan wasn't going to work. Then, curiosity aroused, Suds Garland himself put one foot over the threshold and looked out along the corridor.

My gun hit his belly and stayed there.

"Inside!" I breathed, increasing the pressure of the gun as Garland recoiled from its touch. "Keep your hands high!"

His eyes went wide with sudden terror, but he raised his hands without a murmur. The next moment I was on the other side of the door and had kicked it shut and locked it.

"Got company?" I asked.

Suds shook his head. I didn't believe him.

"You lead the way. I want to talk to you, but if you're lying I'll give you the business pronto. Move!"

He walked steadily enough into the living room. There I found a couple of softly shaded lights burning. Garland was in his shirt sleeves, and had apparently come in only a few minutes before I arrived. His hat and coat were lying on a chair as though he had just taken them off.

So far as I could see he hadn't been lying after all about not having company. From the living room I could see into a small dining room.

Beyond that I knew was a bedroom, and both rooms were in darkness.

BUT I didn't take any chances with Garland. The boy was tricky, and before I faced him again I relieved him of a snub-nosed .38 revolver that bulged plainly in his hip pocket. Then with a gun in each hand I backed around in front of him and made him sit down on a divan. I remained standing.

"Suppose we cut the talk short," I opened, noticing that Suds had regained his composure. If I hadn't been so mad I might have known that his confidence spelled trouble.

"Just as you say, Queen," he answered evenly. "You didn't have to come busting in here like that. I'd have let you in."

"Yes, you *would!" I jeered. "I'm finished with playing nice with you, Suds. I'm going to show you how tough a lady can be."

"You and who else?"

"We won't argue the point," I went on. "I want a signed confession from you that you planted that snow in my apartment."

"What snow?"

His pose of innocence was funny. But I didn't laugh.

"You've got a pencil in your vest pocket," I continued. "Get that newspaper off the floor in front of you. Write the confession on the margin. I'll dictate it."

"I'm a hard man to deal with, Queen," he stated with a great show of nerve. "A hard man. You just think I'm soft because I've been easy with you. Now I'm going to show you just how tough I am."

"Can the chatter!" I snapped. "Get that pencil in your hand!"

I gestured with the gun in my left hand. Suds Garland laughed softly, derisively.

"You little fool!" he blazed, leaning forward while he looked up at me with flashing black eyes. "You've been covered ever since I sat down. Give it to her, Gus, if she moves a muscle!"

For a moment I didn't know whether he was merely bluffing or really meant that speech. The business of getting you to look behind you for an attack from the rear was old stuff. So I hefted the guns in my hands and watched Garland closely.

Suddenly I froze.

"Right," drawled a voice behind me.

Suds Garland had not been bluffing. The single word told me that a gunman was concealed in the darkness of the dining room. Just when I thought I had Garland in the bag I had been trapped myself!

CHAPTER VII

NOT SO TOUGH

FOR a full minute I remained perfectly motionless. Not a sound could be heard, save the hoarse breathing of Suds Garland and the man behind me.

The strain was terrific, but I've been in a lot of tight places and my nerves can stand plenty. This time was no exception. If I could prolong the suspense either Garland or the fellow called Gus would break under the nervous torture. But I wasn't doing nothing while I waited.

I was thinking—hard!

Finally as Suds moistened his lips with the darting point of his tongue I raised my left thumb and slowly pulled back the hammer of the .38. There was a sharp click as the hammer settled into the full cock position.

That slight sound only served to increase the tension. Garland's black eyes narrowed to slits. The muscles of his lean face became rigid as he sought to control his features. I might be in a tight place, but he certainly wasn't having a picnic.

"Well?" I said softly, and in that intense silence it sounded as though I had shouted at the top of my voice.

I wasn't making a grandstand play. Pulling back the hammer of the .38 had been straight business. I figured that if it came to a showdown with the man behind me I could get in at least one shot that would keep Garland with me when I went down under a bullet.

But I really didn't want to kill Suds Garland—yet. I wanted him to live long enough to write that confession and sign it. After that I would kill him with his own gun and make it look like suicide. That would give him the best out he could get.

When there was no answer to my single question I knew Garland and the guy behind me were uncertain about their next move. They had expected me to drop my guns and be a good girl, but they didn't know Queen Sue.

After another minute or so of silence I got tired of waiting. It was evident enough that both men knew what would happen if the guy in the dark took a shot at me. But waiting was getting me nothing. I wanted action.

"Take plenty of time to think it over, Suds," I advised in a sneering voice. "If you're the hard mug you think you are, tell your buddy to squeeze lead or drop the gun."

"You—you don't have a chance, Queen," he stammered after a moment. Little beads of sweat oozed from his face and formed bigger drops that ran down his cheeks and the sides of his nose unheeded. "You can't get out of here alive."

"Speaking for yourself?" I threw back coolly.

But I wasn't as cool as I sounded. I'm only human after all and with a guy like Garland I couldn't tell how this battle of wills was going to turn out.

My last crack floored Garland for a moment. Then he looked past me and did things with his eyes.

I guessed what he meant, and raised the gun in my right hand slightly. Then I shifted the .38 slightly to the left where it would be handier for a quick shot without interfering with the movement of my right arm.

Suds' work with his eyes had meant only one thing. The man behind me was to close in and overpower me without risking the chance of Garland getting shot.

THE next moment soft-soled shoes slithered over the floor behind me. But I didn't turn immediately. I waited until I figured the man behind me was almost within reach. Then I went into action.

Raising my right hand swiftly, I brought the nose of my automatic down hard on Suds Garland's mouth. Simultaneously I whirled towards the left, brought the .38 in the open away from my body, and squeezed the trigger once.

I hadn't been a moment too soon. The guy behind me had raised the gun in his right hand to club me down. The bullet from Garland's gun caught him in the center of the throat under the chin, passed upward through his head, and knocked plaster from the ceiling.

The impact of the bullet lifted him up on his toes. Then while the roar of the shot still seemed to fill the room he started to fall.

I shot a quick glance at Garland. The guy who claimed he was so tough was groveling on the divan from the blow on the mouth that had brought blood spurting to his smashed lips. I started to talk fast, but something that wasn't on the schedule took the words out of my mouth.

The guy who'd tried to slug me hit the floor with his face. At the same instant his gun exploded as his right hand thumped the rug, throwing the muzzle of the gun upward.

He wasn't six feet from the divan when he fell. The bullet plucked at the skirt of my dress and slammed into Suds Garland's chest. The guy called Gus must have used hollow-nosed slugs, for that hunk of lead made a gaping hole as it tore through flesh and bone.

I didn't wait to see more.

Slipping my automatic back into the holster on my leg, I quickly wiped the butt of the .38 with a corner of my dress and tossed the gun down beside Suds. I didn't try to remove all traces of fingerprints. It would look more natural if they were only smeared so they couldn't be recognized.

One look was enough to know that trying to get a confession from Garland was useless. He was still alive, but that slug had ripped a lung wide open. Already bloody froth bubbled to his lips.

I didn't wait to see the end. Less than a minute had passed since I'd fired that first shot, but voices in the corridor told me that I didn't have a moment to spare.

Moving swiftly, I passed through the dining room and into the bedroom. Another moment and I had the window up, and stepped out on the fire escape. A police siren moaned plainly as my feet touched pavement again, and I was a block away when the cops rushed into the building.

Yes, Suds Garland thought he was pretty tough. Maybe he was. But all men—and women, for that matter— look alike to a hunk of lead.

The cops put Suds Garland's death and that of Gus down as a duel over gang affairs, and I didn't tell them any different. On the advice of my lawyer I gave myself up and stood trial on the dope charge.

But I didn't stay snowbound long. Sid Lang's testimony about the dope ring resulted in my acquittal, and I wondered what Suds thought of me beating the rap with the aid of a dick.

VIVIAN LEGRAND

Espionage attracted feminine participants in the pulps. Myra Reldon was an agent in The Shadow's adventures. Sally Vane was the G-woman in the *G-Man Detective* pulp. Two attractive women, Mary Michelson and Louise Curran, vied for the affection of Max Brand's "Spy" (Anthony Hamilton), whose adventures were serialized in *Detective Fiction Weekly*.

Eugene Thomas (b. 1894) used a real woman as the basis for his Vivian Legrand series in *DFW*. The stories proved so popular, they were continued without pretense to truthfulness long after he had exhausted his facts.

An editorial in the January 12, 1935, *DFW* gives some background: "Eugene Thomas is a newspaper man, war correspondent, and soldier whose adventures have taken him all over the world, from New York to South America, Mexico, California, and the Far East. It was in Shanghai that he first picked up the trail of Vivian Legrand, 'The Lady from Hell,' whose amazing true story begins in the next issue. . . . In his travels through the Orient he met and talked with many people who had known, or had been victimized, by Vivian Legrand. She used many names—but her flaming red hair, the exotic beauty that hypnotized men, and her cold audacity marked her trail plainly and enabled Mr. Thomas to follow her amazing career. He also struck up a friendship with Adrian Wylie—a fictitious name, since the real 'Adrian Wylie' is still alive and provided much of the material for these stories. Wylie has reformed completely, and is living quietly, though with vivid memories of the exciting years when he was known and wanted by the police of three continents.

"From the Far East Eugene Thomas went to Mexico, where he joined Felix Diaz in the Vera Cruz revolution. When the revolt fizzled, he went on a walking trip through Europe. Here he struck the trail of Vivian Legrand again. Thomas was in Fiume when the World War broke out. He managed to escape to Italy, walked from Venice to Genoa, and shoveled coal on a tramp steamer to get back to the States. He joined the artillery when the United States entered the war, and was wounded at Verdun three days before the Armistice.

"After the war he returned to newspaper work and writing. A play by Eugene Thomas will be produced on Broadway next year. . . ."

Reprinted here is "The Lady from Hell: The Episode of the Secret Service Blackmail," from the February 9, 1935, issue of *Detective Fiction Weekly*.

The LADY from HELL

The Episode of the Secret Service Blackmail

A True Story

By
Eugene Thomas

The steel door behind the painting swung open

From the Fortress of the Bald Doctor with the Yellow Eyes Vivian Legrand Snatches a Letter Worth Three Thousand Pounds

COL. SIR MARK CAYWOOD, Chief of the British Secret Service in the Far East, was an exceedingly worried man on two counts this June night.

The first worry rose from a cablegram in code received that morning from the Viceroy of India giving him to understand, in no uncertain terms, that the Viceroy expected results in the matter that was just then occupying the undivided attention of the secret service as well as causing new wrinkles and gray hair among the higher members of British India officialdom.

The second worry rose from a note

received an hour or so before, signed Mrs. Legrand, and stating that the writer would call at his office at eight that night for an interview of importance. No answer had been requested, and, apparently, none had been expected, the writer taking it for granted that the interview would be granted her.

In his files were several reports on Vivian Legrand, who was wanted in Shanghai in connection with the murder of her father, the notorious Duke Donellan. Under ordinary conditions, Sir Mark would have simply ordered the lady held for the Shanghai police. The matter was not so simple, however. As a matter of fact, Sir Mark did not dare arrest her, for she was present in Rangoon as the guest of a native potentate, the ruling Rajah of Salingar. To arrest his guest would be an offense to the rajah that Sir Mark did not care to commit.

So, as the clock approached eight, he sat alone in his study beneath a madly whirring fan and sweltered and swore. Not once did Sir Mark suspect that there might be a most important connection between that note and the cablegram.

A houseboy appeared like a white wraith. Sir Mark looked up.

"A lady who says that you desire an appointment with her, O Presence."

The colonel stared. The effrontery of the woman, making it appear that the appointment was of his seeking! He did not realize—nor did many another of her victims in later years realize—that Vivian Legrand almost invariably and at once placed the other person on the defensive. It gave her the advantage. The colonel bit his lip, then said slowly, "Show the lady in."

He watched the doorway and presently a figure materialized. He rose—

and came out of the shell. His official reports on Vivian Legrand had not prepared him for what he saw. No man could question her beauty. Her red hair caught the shaded light on the colonel's study table and became a quivering flame above the exquisitely modeled, exotic face. The clinging black gown she wore seemed molded to her shapely form.

"You are Mrs. Legrand?"

"I am Mrs. Legrand," Vi responded in the husky contralto that was one of her charms. The smile she bestowed upon him was completely disarming.

"Since I received your note," the colonel told her, settling behind the desk, "I have, if you will pardon me, been more than a little puzzled. I cannot imagine anything that cannot be taken up with my secretary."

"I told you that I wanted to see you regarding a matter of importance."

S HE paused and smiled. Had Sir Mark known what was in her mind at the moment the smile might not have pleased him as much as it did. Vivian Legrand lay back in silence in the long rattan chair, quite at ease, her hands clasped in her lap, chin tilted, eyes looking upon him as a cat's eyes look upon the mouse it is about to play with.

"What happened on the night of June 14th?" she flung at him.

He glared at her, consternation written on his features.

"You don't mean—"

"But I do," she assured him.

He drummed upon the desk.

"You have not answered me," she reminded him after a moment. "Shall I tell you what happened that night, and what the consequences are likely to be?"

He raised a hand swiftly. "Please.

These things are best not discussed."

She went on relentlessly. "On the night of June 14th a paper was stolen from your safe . . . a letter that had been written to you by a man named Ivan Stavinsky, a prisoner who had been sentenced for life to the penal colony on the Andaman Islands. If that letter falls into the hands of a certain power to the north of India, it might precipitate a war."

The colonel leaned forward tensely. "You know the contents of that letter?"

"What I know is locked away safely until the time is ripe to bring it forth. Meanwhile, I will say this much. That letter has not left Rangoon."

For a moment Sir Mark sat motionless and expressionless. Then he said briefly:

"Unless you are willing to answer my question truthfully, there is no need to continue the interview further."

She dismissed the implication with a shrug. "Frankly, I do not know the contents," she said. "But I do know where it is."

Instantly he was on his feet. "You do?"

She nodded. "How much is it worth to you if I recover that document, Sir Mark?"

He stared at her in amazement.

"You—recover it? But that is impossible!" He stopped, struck by a sudden thought, and she laughed.

"Wrong, Sir Mark. I am not the person who stole that letter. But I repeat that I know who did—know where it is—and if it is worth—shall we say three thousand pounds to you— you may have it back again."

It was with difficulty that Sir Mark suppressed an impulse to smile. He said soberly:

"I'll confess that I do not know how

you learned of this matter. But since you do, won't you be more explicit? To—ah—propose to blackmail the British Secret Service seems rather incredible."

In her turn, Vivian Legrand suppressed an impulse to smile. She wondered what Sir Mark would say were

VIVIAN LEGRAND

she to tell him that the secret service of the Mandarin Hoang Fi Tu, underworld leader of Manila, was fully as good as that of the British; and when it came to gathering information among the underworld occupants of the Far East, much better than the British.

She said swiftly, stabbing each word at him as if it were a weapon.

"I mean, quite simply, Sir Mark, that I can and will do—for the sum of three thousand pounds—what your entire police and secret service have failed to do."

He chewed his lip. "Really, won't

you throw a little more light on the subject?"

"No," she replied curtly. "Either you accept my offer, or you don't."

Sir Mark's forehead wrinkled in an official frown.

"This is most extraordinary. Is that a—er—threat?"

It seemed impossible that a girl as superbly beautiful as this one should be sitting across the desk from him calmly blackmailing him, and through him, the British Empire!

Vivian Legrand laughed, that laugh that rippled low in her throat.

"Dare one threaten the British Secret Service?" she purred.

Sir Mark drummed upon the surface of the desk again. His thoughts at that moment were none too pleasant.

"Well, what are your terms?" came at length from him.

She was aware that she was mistress of the situation and she enjoyed the position.

"I wish, first of all, an invitation for myself and Mr. Adrian Wylie to the Official Ball to be held next Wednesday. I want you to have at that ball three thousand pounds in bank notes, and be prepared to pay them to me that night upon delivery of the letter. And lastly, I wish you to arrange with the municipal police of Shanghai that any charges against me in connection with the death of my father be dropped."

Sir Mark stared at her in amazement.

"You ask the impossible."

She made an impatient gesture.

"You are not dealing with a fool or a child, Sir Mark." I know that the municipal police in Shanghai, upon your request, will wipe out all record of any charge against me."

Their eyes met and there followed a quick duel. The man's smile was a signal of defeat.

"You are a very resourceful woman," he said.

"I have to be," she said. "You accept?"

"I accept," he said. "The charge will be quashed. You shall have your invitations tomorrow. And I shall be prepared to carry out my part of the bargain on the night of the ball. The cash will be ready."

She smiled her approval, gave him her hand and moved to the door; melted into the dusky hallway, leaving Sir Mark seated at his desk with a feeling of bafflement.

II

FOR six weeks Vivian Legrand and her companion in crime had been the guests of the Rajah of Salinger, following her rescue by the rajah from his own brother in the depths of the Malayan jungle. Vivian Legrand and Adrian Wylie had plotted with the Mandarin Hoang Fi Tu to topple the rajah from his throne. Yet when their plot failed Vivian and Wylie had made the rajah believe that they were motion picture people, making pictures in the jungle, Wylie being the director and Vivian Legrand the actress.

The rajah had offered the two of them his hospitality as recompense, in some part, for the injuries she had suffered at the hands of his brother, and Vivian Legrand, still thinking of a ruby mine which the rajah owned, had accepted.

When she returned from her meeting with Colonel Sir Mark Caywood she found Wylie waiting for her on the after deck of the rajah's yacht.

She dropped down into a chair beside him.

"Well," she said briefly, "we are to deliver the letter to him next Wednesday night in return for the payment of three thousand pounds—cash on the nail."

"Very nice," Wylie reflected, a touch of sarcasm in his manner. "Now all we have to do is the thing that the whole British Secret Service in the Far East has failed to do—discover who has the letter, get it away from them, and deliver it. Of course we'll find that quite simple."

Doc Wylie had not yet discovered what would be quite plain to him in later years of their partnership in crime—namely, that Vivian Legrand never took a step in one of their schemes without the next step being clear before her.

"I know who has it, and know how to get it," she assured him.

Wylie sat up, astonishment written on his face.

"You do?" he said incredulously. "I received the mandarin's cablegram only this morning. In less than twelve hours, in a strange port, you've discovered what the British Secret Service failed completely to find a trace of?"

Vivian Legrand bent closer and lowered her voice.

"I reasoned," she said, "that because Russia was involved the secret service would be looking for a Russian angle. And I reasoned that the man clever enough to steal that letter would also be clever enough to make sure that there was no visible thread connecting him with Russia—that it would be someone on whom the breath of suspicion would never fall.

"And I reasoned also that a document containing as much political dynamite as that letter would never be entrusted to a subordinate. It would be delivered by the principal himself to the Russian authorities—to make sure of getting the credit.

"The first thing I did was to check the steamship sailings. There has been no boat sailing from here for a Russian port, or a port where connections could be made for Russia, since June 14th. The first boat is next Saturday. I discovered that three persons had

DOC WYLIE

booked passage through to Harbin, where connections can be made on the Chinese Eastern Railroad for Siberia and St. Petersburg. Two of them were obviously impossible suspects. The third seemed impossible, and yet if my line of reasoning was correct, it had to be he. I went down into the Chinese quarter, managed to get hold of a discharged Chinese servant—and I was right."

"Who is it?" Wylie asked.

"Dr. Basil Orbison," Vivian Legrand responded.

Wylie thought a moment. " Never heard of him."

"HE is a doctor, half Greek, half English who is making an exhaustive study of tropical diseases," she told him. " He lives some seven miles out from the town. He is an exceedingly peculiar individual, yet well liked by the English. A friend of the Governor's, who is often called in by the hospitals here when something beyond their medical experience comes up. Not the slightest breath of suspicion that he might be connected with Russia, and yet his house is surrounded by a high wall and guarded like a fortress. And unless I'm a fool the letter we want is in that house."

Wylie looked at her seriously. " Where it's likely to stay if that house is as well guarded as you say."

" That's why I asked for—and got —invitations to the Official Ball on Wednesday night."

Then she made a swift gesture to Wylie as the tall form of the Rajah of Salingar loomed in the shadows of the deck. The rajah was their anchor to windward, their safeguard. As guests on his yacht they could go almost anywhere, move in circles that otherwise they could not enter. He must not be permitted to suspect, even for a moment, that they were not motion picture people. And then, too, there was the matter of the ruby mine that was a part of the royal properties of Salingar.

Educated at Oxford, the rajah's English was practically flawless, as he stopped beside them in the shadows and greeted his guests warmly. Vivian Legrand leaned back a trifle, so that the glow from a lantern at the companionway made highlights in the red of her hair and etched her exotic face in soft relief. Then she patted a cushion beside her and the rajah sank down upon it.

Wylie watched the absorbed face of the Malay ruler for a moment as the man talked with Vivian, and then with a grim smile of satisfaction got to his feet and went below to his cabin.

III

THE orchestra was playing a slow waltz when Vivian Legrand came up the steps of Government House on the arm of the Prince of Salingar, with Doc Wylie following discreetly behind.

A cap of cloth of silver hid her flaming hair, and a flame-like spray of egrets swayed above her head. Gown and hands and throat were shimmering with jewels—some of them given her by the rajah, others that he had loaned her. Pendants dangled beside cheeks that were pale as if all the blood had been drained out of them, but her lips were blood red.

The Governor and his wife greeted them courteously, and if their eyes widened a trifle at the sight of a white woman attending the Official Ball on the arm of a native rajah, it was not noticeable.

Vivian Legrand's greenish eyes, shadowed with lids as purple as grapes, flitted here and there about the long room. She was searching for someone, and presently she caught sight of the man she sought—Basil Orbison.

He was talking to a woman, and for the first time Vivian had a good look at him. His gaunt face was as pale as anything that lives in darkness. A bony, fleshless sort of face, plastered over with lifeless skin; ugly and interesting. The eyes glittered in bony sockets. Dark hair flowed back from a high forehead.

The woman with him claimed Vivian Legrand's close attention, for she was the key to her plan. Without her, Vivian was helpless. By a coincidence that was no coincidence on Vivian's part the two women wore the same type of headdress—silver cap fitting over the hair, from which rose the flame-like spray of egrets. It had cost Vivian Legrand fifty dollars to find what kind of head dress the woman would wear, and to have the Chinese dressmaker make a duplicate of it for her.

Wylie, walking down the room beside her, was the only one who caught the whisper that came from her lips.

"That's the woman—talking to Orbison—you know what you've got to do—be ready when I get Orbison out on the veranda."

The next moment Vivian Legrand was smiling up into the eyes of the Rajah of Salingar.

With the rajah at her side she moved slowly about the room. Several times she stood close enough to the woman with Orbison, who was addressed as Madame Carpenter, to hear her voice. It was a low-pitched, well-modulated voice, and Vivian Legrand fixed its tones firmly in her mind.

Within an hour she had contrived to meet Dr. Basil Orbison and had steered him deftly to a corner of the veranda. His back was to the clustered shrubbery which bordered the veranda, and even if he had heard a faint rustling in the shrubbery he would have put it down to the passage of a night bird.

They stood there talking for a few minutes. There was not the slightest change in Vivian Legrand's manner or voice to indicate that she saw the stealthy shape that loomed up in the shrubbery behind the doctor. So cleverly did she hold his attention that he never knew what hit him.

His limp form slumped to the floor, and almost instantly Wylie had vaulted over the railing, still holding the blackjack.

"Get him over the railing, quick," Vivian Legrand said tensely.

Together they raised him and lowered him. While Vivian Legrand stood on the balcony above, Wylie swiftly went through the man's pockets and found the thing for which he was looking—a key ring.

"How long will he be out?" Vivian Legrand asked as he passed the keys up to her.

"Fifteen minutes—maybe twenty," Wylie said.

"It will have to do," she said tersely. She moved swiftly down the veranda and descended the steps to the garden. Wylie met her where the sanded path passed beneath the overhanging branches of a Yiang-ylang tree. She took a silken wrap that he carried and flung it over her dress. She turned up the collar, hiding her face from view.

Side by side they passed through the garden gate and approached the spot where Orbison's powerful car was parked. As they came opposite the spot where the chauffeur sat, Wylie paused and extended his hand.

"So sorry you're not feeling well, Madame Carpenter," he said with just the right touch of concern in his voice. "You're sure you don't want me to go with you?"

"Quite sure," Vivian Legrand answered, making her tones as like that of the woman who was Orbison's companion as she could. It was not the last time that her gift for mimicry would stand her in good stead. " I shall be quite all right. I am so sorry to leave so early, but Dr. Orbison understands. Good night."

Then, before the chauffeur could get out of the car, she opened the door and slipped into the rear.

" Home," she said quietly. Then, as the big car slid smoothly from the curb she leaned back with a sigh of relief. So far her scheme had worked without a hitch. If only she had a little more luck she would win.

FROM Government House to Orbison's fortress-like home was seven miles, but the car did it in fifteen minutes. The chauffeur let his passenger out of the Rolls and inquired :

" Shall I wait for madame ?"

Vivian Legrand gestured a negative, crossed the porch and rang the bell.

The butler opened the door, saw what he deemed to be the woman who had left the house with the doctor standing on the threshold, and flung the door open.

Quite unsuspiciously he closed the door behind him, shot the bolt—found a revolver jammed into his ribs.

" Don't move. And don't speak," Vivian Legrand whispered.

The butler stood with his fingers jammed against the wall, utterly unable to comprehend the turn of events. His face went pale, not so much from fear of the gun as fear of what his master might do when he found that entry had been effected so easily into a house that was guarded like a fortress.

" Now," whispered Vivian Legrand, " where are the other servants ?"

" In their quarters," came the surly answer.

" Where does your master keep his safe ?" she demanded.

" I don't know," he spat back at her.

" At three I shoot," Vivian Legrand said curtly. " One—two—"

" Upstairs in his study," the man cut in hurriedly. " Take that gun further away. I don't like it so damn close."

" Lead me to the study. And don't try any funny stuff. I'll shoot first and ask questions afterwards. And don't figure that because I'm a woman I won't shoot. I will."

The man started forward, then stopped abruptly. From the rear of the house the sound of voices and the blare of a phonograph had come suddenly as a door was opened. The servants were making merry in their master's absence. Then the door was closed again and the noise cut off as abruptly as it had begun. There were tiny beads of perspiration on the butler's forehead.

" That was lucky for you," Vivian Legrand said grimly. " You'll be the first to get hurt. Go ahead."

Surrendering to the menace behind him, the butler moved forward across the red-tiled floor and slowly ascended the carpeted stairs. At the head of the stairs he indicated a door at the right of the hallway.

" That's the study," he said sullenly. " You won't be able to get in. He keeps it locked all the time."

Vivian Legrand's answer was to take the bunch of keys from her hand bag.

" Unlock the door," she said curtly to the butler. Under the muzzle of the menacing revolver the man tried the keys. The second fitted. The door swung open.

" Inside," she told him curtly. Once the man was inside she touched the light switch on the wall, and then closed the door with her foot. The butler turned and peered at her, again endeavoring to see her face. She checked him.

"No tricks, unless you want to commit suicide," she warned him curtly. "Here!" She touched a big chair with her foot. "Sit here."

Whipping a scarf from the table in the center of the room she effectively blindfolded the man. No sense in leaving a trail that could be followed, she felt—and that was to become one of the cardinal principles of the Legrand ring of blackmailers in later years, one of the things that baffled the police of three continents. There was rarely a trail that led to one of the gang.

Slowly her eyes went from object to object in the room, measuring, identifying. It was unlikely that Dr. Orbison would have a letter as important as was this one lying around loose. It was undoubtedly well hidden. She discarded the big writing desk with one cursory glance. That would be the first place that a searcher would look, and the doctor would realize that.

There was no safe in sight, but a large painting on the far side of the room caught her eye. It was out of harmony with the rest of the room. No reason for it to be there. And no reason either for it to be set into the wall, instead of hanging as a painting normally would.

A quick search and she found a spot on the wall beside it where the wall paper was smudged, as though fingers had been often pressed there. She pressed with her thumb. A click and the painting swung outward, disclosing the steel door of a safe behind it.

Again the key ring that she had taken from Orbison's pocket went into play and the steel door swung open.

There was nothing in it, however, except a small box with a few bills, a package of letters, and a thin rod of steel with a cross piece at one end. A hasty inspection showed that the letter she sought was not among the bundle lying in the safe.

Glancing at the butler, who was sitting taut in his chair, listening to every movement, Vivian Legrand picked up the T-shaped rod of steel and inserted it in a round opening in the back of the safe. There was a faint click and the door of a hidden compartment swung outward. Lying in the compartment was a long envelope. She opened it swiftly. It held the letter for which she was in search.

IV

VIVIAN LEGRAND knew enough of the political background of the Far East to grasp at the first reading the tremendous import of that document. She knew the importance to England of the Khyber Pass, the only practicable route from the north into India, the route through which every invader of India from the time of Alexander the Great has come, the pass through the mountains that has been so heavily fortified by England that it would be impossible for an invading army to force it.

And here was a letter to the British Secret Service from a Russian agent offering to barter to the English knowledge of a hitherto unknown pass through the mountains for his freedom.

The writer went on to say that he had discovered this pass, and had been mixed up with a riot in the Calcutta bazaars, arrested and sentenced to life in the Andaman Islands before he could report his discovery to his superiors in St. Petersburg.

Vivian Legrand's greenish eyes narrowed thoughtfully as the full import of the thing flashed over her. No wonder Sir Mark Caywood had been willing to pay three thousand pounds for the return of this letter. Knowledge of this unguarded pass into India from the north, in the hands of Russia, was a constant threat to the security of the British rule in India. And Russia? What would the knowledge be worth to her? Not a single implication of the potential possibilities that the situation held was escaping Vivian Legrand's mind.

So engrossed was she in the contents of the letter that she did not notice the butler's right hand groping for the cord of a bell pull that hung quite near. When she looked up from the letter the man's arms were again resting on the arms of the chair.

She was in the act of folding the letter when the room door flung open, and four of Orbison's men hurled themselves in. For a split second they stared in amazement at finding a woman in jewels and plumes in that place. Vivian Legrand's arm reached the alabaster globe above her head. She turned the lights out.

She was through the group like an eel as they sprang for her. She was down the stairs, across the hall, with the front door open, inserting the key in the outside, before the first of her pursuers reached the bottom of the staircase. And then she stopped short in consternation. Just walking up to the front door was Dr. Basil Orbison.

He looked at Vivian Legrand, and his thin mouth moved in a slow smile. He bowed in exaggerated courtesy.

"So, it is the lovely lady of the Official Ball who honors me with a visit —in my absence. So fortunate that I returned in time! I would have regretted missing you."

His eyes flickered from Vivian Legrand to the armed men who stood in the hallway behind her. Then he took her arm and urged her gently back into the house and into a room on the right.

The butler followed them, a gun poised in readiness.

Vivian Legrand halted just inside the door. She stood beside one of a pair of tall vases of blue pottery, wide of neck and bellying out as they curved toward rounded bases. The vases stood on each side of the doorway.

Dr. Orbison dropped into a chair and peered up at her like an expectant vulture.

"I congratulate the British Secret Service. I really did not credit them with sufficient intelligence to trace this little affair to me."

Vivian Legrand did not move.

"She was looking for a paper of some sort," the butler burst out. "And she got it!"

"Your handbag," demanded Orbison.

Vivian Legrand extended the bag. He went through it rapidly, dropping the small revolver it contained on the table. Then he returned it to her and shot a string of sibilant words that Vivian Legrand took to be Russian to the butler. The latter went to the door and a moment later a Chinese woman appeared at the doorway.

"Chu-Chi will search you," Orbison announced. "I have called her, not from motives of delicacy, but because a woman is more likely to find a woman's hiding place than a man."

He watched in silence as the Chinese woman searched Vivian Legrand swiftly and expertly, overlooking no possible place where a letter could be hidden. She reported in Chinese that there was nothing hidden upon the red-headed woman.

ORBISON'S thin mouth curled up; the vulture's hairless head bobbed up and down as he waved the Chinese woman impatiently out of the room. His long fingers curved slightly, as if, filled with desire, they tensed to leap at Vivian Legrand's throat. There was strength in those fingers, she knew—enormous strength. Meeting the cold eyes she knew that this man would murder her without a qualm. But she did not flinch from his gaze. Instead she smiled quite calmly. The letter was safe. He did not suspect where it was—would probably never find it unless she revealed its hiding place. And she knew that she held the trump card.

"Where is the letter you took from my safe," he demanded.

"I took no letter," Vivian Legrand answered steadily. "Your butler summoned help before I could find it."

Orbison laughed, a sudden little laugh. Vivian Legrand realized where she had heard the counterpart of that laugh before—the same little laugh over sudden silence that may be heard just before the Chinese executioner raises his sword for the stroke that will sever his victim's head from his shoulders.

"I know that you lie," Orbison said. He stroked the curve of his mouth with his tongue's tip, very much as if tasting blood and liking it. "It would be wise to tell me now where it is. You will eventually."

"I didn't find it," Vivian told him. She put the right trace of impatience into her manner. "Can't you see that for yourself? Your men came while I was searching. I had to run for it. You caught me just as I was about to leave the house. Common sense should tell you that I am not lying."

As she talked a great satisfaction came into her heart. Orbison had made one fatal error. All she needed now was time and luck to win clear.

"I think we can refresh her mem-ory," Orbison went on, speaking to the butler. He made Vivian Legrand a little bow. "You will excuse me a moment, I am sure."

Opening a door on the further side of the room he disappeared. Vivian Legrand could see that it was a room of gleaming white enamel, with strange instruments and tubes on white tables. Taking her eyes from the door she glided sidewise, crabwise, toward the table in the center of the room. Her movements were almost imperceptible. Her eyes flickered for a second over the safety catch of the butler's gun. It was still locked. Did the man know it? Upon the answer to that question hung life or death.

Then Orbison entered the room again, carrying in one hand a small test tube and in the other a hypodermic syringe.

"You really are an utter fool," Vivian Legrand told the doctor.

"So?" he mummured softly. He filled the hypodermic. "And what leads you to that conclusion?"

"Because," Vivian Legrand said with superb indifference. "You haven't the ability to distinguish the truth from a lie. I came here to get that letter—yes. But I had no connection with the British Secret Service. My scheme was to steal the letter to show you that I was a better woman to have as an ally than an enemy—and once I had blackmailed you into obtaining me a post in the Russian Secret Serivce, to return the letter to you."

The doctor laid the hypodermic down carefully; took out a cigarette. His case fell to the floor. Vivian Legrand took a step, picked it up and returned it. Orbison was clever. But even he saw nothing in the movement that brought her a step closer to the table.

"A man of real cleverness would be able to see the advantage of having me as an ally," she went on. "Also, he would realize that I wouldn't come here without c e r t a i n—er—precautions. There will be inquiries if I do not return."

"There will be no inquiries," the doctor returned indifferently.

Again Vivian Legrand took a sidewise step. Again her eyes flickered to the safety catch. It was still down.

The doctor picked up the hypodermic. "Now we will make the injection," he murmured. "It would really be useless to resist."

Vivian Legrand did not reply. She was within reaching distance of the library table now—and on the table lay her own gun, dropped there by Orbison when he searched her bag.

She made a careless step toward the table—and whirled, gun in hand, facing the two men. The butler pulled the trigger of his gun. There was no explosion.

"Hands up! snapped Vivian. Orbison's head turned like that of a startled vulture at the crisp command. "Drop that gun, you!"

V

THE two men stood as if frozen. Then the butler's gun dropped to the floor, and his hands followed Orbison's above his head. Now it was that Vivian Legrand's greenish eyes bit into the vulture features of Orbison. She moved backwards toward the door to the hall. So engrossed was she by the men's upraised hands, and the gun on the floor, that she failed to see the sudden grimness that darkened the face of the doctor.

She felt the high heels of her evening slippers touch the door sill. Her free hand reached out and down into one of the blue vases, where she had dropped the letter. Then, with the precious document in her hand, she reached for the door knob.

Without warning the doctor's upraised hands darted for a weapon.

Vivian Legrand whipped about with the swiftness of a striking serpent. With a half turn of her body, she shot. Orbison dropped, face down.

Through narrow green eyes she glared at the butler. He glanced once at his dead master. Then his hands reached higher, trembling.

Vivian Legrand opened the front door. A moment later the roar of an automobile told that she was escaping in safety.

TWO hours later Vivian entered the salon of the rajah's yacht and dropped a package of Bank of England notes in front of Wylie.

"Three thousand pounds," she said curtly. "It was worth five."

"You delivered the letter?" Wylie asked.

"I delivered the letter," she said. "But I read it first. And we must sail in an hour."

Wylie sat up alertly. "What's up? Danger?"

She shook her head.

"No. Money. There is a prisoner on the Andaman Islands worth a fortune to whoever reaches him first. And if we can outsail and outwit the Russian and the British secret services, we'll have something they'll pawn their souls to ransom."

"But the ruby mine," Wylie protested.

"That can wait," Vivian Legrand said firmly. "When we have no further use for the rajah as a blind—then will come the time for securing his ruby mine."

ROSITA STOREY

Argosy, the grandfather of all pulps, was launched in 1882 by Frank Munsey as "The Golden Argosy." It was a weekly juvenile story paper. In 1888 he shortened the title and converted it to an adult fiction magazine that carried a variety of stories, mystery, action, war, and Western.

"There's scarcely another magazine in the field that touches this one for variety," notes *Writer's Digest* in its March 1938 issue. In 1943, Argosy was converted into a slick-paper magazine.

Canadian-born Hulbert Footner (1879–1944) brought his Rosita Storey series to *Argosy.* The character also appeared in six hardcover books. Footner was a newspaperman, actor, and playwright. He wrote fifty-nine mystery novels and short-story collections.

Madame Storey appears in "Wolves of Monte Carlo" from the August 5, 1933, issue of *Argosy.*

Wolves of Monte Carlo

By HULBERT FOOTNER
Author of "The Death Notice," "Easy to Kill," etc.

Novelette—Complete

With Monte Carlo police powerless, it took Mme. Storey, famous woman detective, to outwit the band preying on helpless visitors

The disguised "Lady Wedderminster" had won a thousand francs

CHAPTER I.

WEARY OF CRIME.

WHEN Mme. Storey and I arrived at Monte Carlo she registered us at the Hotel de Paris as Mrs. Renfrew and Miss Renfrew. I was to pass as her sister-in-law, instead of her secretary, for the time being. She wanted to avoid the attentions of society and the press.

But the world's most famous woman detective couldn't get away with it. I noticed that the clerk looked at her hard and consulted a photograph under his desk. Presently an elegant gentleman came bustling up and introduced himself as *le directeur*. Bowing like a jackknife he ushered us with his own magnificent presence to a beautiful suite on the second floor. I am sure they were the best rooms in the house.

"Ah, *très belle!*" said Mme. Storey, looking around her. "But much too grand for me, *monsieur*. I can't afford it."

"*Non! Non!*" he protested, waving

his hands. "You misunderstand, *madame*. Your privacy will be respected, but we know who you are. You shall be the guest of the principality of Monaco as long as you will honor us. His Highness the Prince has commanded it!"

"Nice of him," said Mme. Storey.

When the little man had vanished in a cloud of compliments, she said to me dryly, "Something tells me there's

gentleman arrived in our salon. He was less showy than the first one, but better style. Prominent Executive was written all over him—or whatever the French equivalent may be. This was the President of the Society of the Baths of the Sea, the concern, I may say, which runs Monte Carlo lock, stock and barrel—under the amiable eye of the Prince, of course, who is the principal stockholder. I shall re-

They were a strangely assorted group of players

a nigger in this elegant woodpile, my Bella!"

However, the rooms were lovely; a corner suite with windows on one side looking out on the Casino and the gardens, and on the other the ineffable blue sea. Whatever they may say, the old Hotel de Paris is still one of *the* hotels of the world, and they went all out for us. Bellboys arrived in a procession, bringing baskets of flowers and fruit, and boxes of chocolates.

Presently, as if to give point to Mme. Storey's words, another elegant

fer to our caller merely as Monsieur B. He kissed our hands, and came right down to business. "This lady—" he asked politely, looking at me. "May I speak before her?"

"My secretary, Miss Brickley," said Mme. Storey. "She is present at all interviews."

"Nothing could be more opportune than your visit to Monte Carlo at this time," said Monsieur B., enthusiastically. "I have read so much of your successes in solving intricate crimes. Of all people in the world, you are the one I most wish to consult with. Professionally, I mean."

" But I'm on my vacation!" objected Mme. Storey.

" No matter—no matter! You can deal with this affair without in the least interfering with your pleasures."

"What is it?" she asked.

His face turned grave. " There is a gang of young men operating here," he said, " preying upon the wealthy women who come to Monte Carlo. Every day ladies are being blackmailed, and in some cases robbed. Last week it all culminated in the suicide of a lady of title, here in one of our hotels."

" I hadn't heard of it," said Mme. Storey.

"We kept it out of the papers," he said, " but of course it's a matter of common gossip. People say, naturally, that she lost all she possessed at the gaming tables. But that is not so. She was robbed and blackmailed by this band of thieves, blackmailers and gigolos. The unfortunate lady could not face her family."

MME. STOREY was not attracted by the case. " Gigolos?" she said, running up her eyebrows. "Surely that's a matter for your police."

" They are helpless," said Monsieur B., spreading out his hands. " When we make an arrest, there is never any evidence because the victim will not testify. Whenever these young men become known to us we can put them on the train. But soon they return—or others take their places. We can forbid them to enter the Casino, the Sporting Club or the hotels under our management, but they pick up their victims outside. And if they suspect that the eye of the police is on them, they tempt or trick their intended victims

into going to Menton, or Nice, or Cannes, where they are out of our jurisdiction."

Mme. Storey sent a droll glance in my direction. Evidently Monte Carlo was losing business; that was the real rub.

" These men, in themselves they are nothing," Monsieur B. went on, dismissing them with a gesture. " What makes them dangerous is the fact that they are organized and directed by a subtle intelligence here in Monte Carlo. —Find that man or that woman for us, *madame*. Break up this ring, and you can ask what you will of us!"

She shook her head. " I am here on my vacation," she said. " I am weary of crime. Better order me changed to a more modest suite, *monsieur*, and forget about me."

" Never! Never!" he protested. " In any case, you remain our guest, *madame*."

He brought up all the arguments he could muster. Would she not, as a woman, undertake to rescue her fellow-women from these birds of prey? Many of the victims had been American ladies. Did she not feel it her duty to—? And so on.

Mme. Storey continued to smile, but she shook her head quite firmly. And being an experienced man, he soon saw that it was useless. He left us.

———

CHAPTER II.

ONE SIDE OF THE RING.

A FEW minutes later Mme. Storey and I, having changed our dresses, were seated on the terrace behind the Casino. It was in the middle of the afternoon. After the fogs and frosts of northern France, the hot and brilliant sunshine was like paradise. Below us the calm sea was bluer than ultramarine. The fantastic architecture of the Casino; the gay clothes of the women; the profusion of flowers; the band playing a Strauss waltz—everything contributed to the holiday spirit. We dissolved in satisfaction.

"Let's do something foolish," said Mme. Storey.

Presently a young man came strolling by—one of the handsomest young men I have ever seen. He looked like a Spaniard or a South American; smooth olive face, glowing dark eyes, slim and graceful as Mercury. He looked at Mme. Storey out of the corners of his fine eyes, walked on a little way, and came back again.

"Here's one of them," she murmured.

"Surely not!" I protested. "That boy looks like one of the young angels painted by the Italian masters."

"Quite!" she said dryly. "But you never can tell about young men. They don't begin to show their real character until they pass thirty."

When he passed the second time he looked directly at Mme. Storey with his compelling eyes. She smiled frankly, and he stopped.

"Charming afternoon," he said, raising his hat. His English was as good as mine.

"Charming!" said Mme. Storey.

She glanced at the vacant seat beside her, and he dropped into it. He looked about twenty-four, but might have been older. Dressed with the plainness that the most fashionable young men affect, everything about him was just right.

"You have just come?" he said.

"How did you guess it?"

"The terrace has a brightness it never had before," he said seriously.

She laughed delightedly. "Well! You're what we call a fast worker in America!"

He did not smile. He wasn't looking at me, but I could feel the almost hypnotic effect of his eyes. "I mean it," he said. "I have never seen anybody like you."

"Compliments are so nice!" murmured Mme. Storey, trying not to laugh. "You see, they've gone out of fashion in my country."

He glanced at me significantly, and then back at her as much as to say that if she would get rid of me he would really tell her something. But Mme. Storey made believe not to get it.

"A woman like you is wasted in a country of businessmen," he said.

"Well, one can always get on a ship," she said. "Here I am!"

"I had a feeling when I got up this morning that something wonderful was going to happen to-day," he murmured thrillingly.

MME. STOREY could no longer hold in her laughter. It rang out delightedly. The young man turned angry.

When she was able to speak she said —still rippling with laughter:

"I'm so sorry! I like you, really. You're so easy to look at. But I can't play up to you. Surely it must be a strain on you, too, to be so romantic. Be yourself, and let's enjoy the lovely weather."

There was a visible struggle in his handsome face. He scowled, and rubbed his upper lip. Then suddenly he joined in her laughter. That changed the whole character of his face; made him look like one of our nice American boys. He had beautiful white teeth, and I began to like him.

"You're right," he said, "it *is* a

strain. But ..." He finished with an expressive shrug.

Mme. Storey finished his sentence for him. "You mean it's your job to be romantic? I know. And I ought to tell you that I am a very poor prospect. You'd better toddle along and look for some lady who is older and who is starving for romance."

His head went down, and a spasm of pain crossed his face. "You see too much," he murmured. "You despise me."

She shook her head. "I never despise anybody."

He raised his head. He was quite humble now. "I'd like to take a holiday from my job," he murmured, "if you would let me stay with you."

"Why not?" she said. "I'm sure you're the handsomest young man in Monte Carlo. What shall we do?"

"Do you like dancing?" he asked eagerly.

"I adore it!"

"There's a *gala* at the Sporting Club this afternoon."

"Let's go ... But we must introduce ourselves. I am Mrs. Renfrew, and this is Miss Renfrew, my sister-in-law."

"I am Raoul d'Aymara," he said, as simply as if he had been a marquis. Perhaps he was. Spanish marquises have fallen on evil days, just now.

"We must have another man," he went on. "There are several fellows I know along the terrace.—There's Nickol Copenhaver, the Dane. He's dumb, but he can dance."

Raoul signalled to an elegant young fellow who was loafing by the balustrade of the terrace, and the latter started towards us. Raoul said hurriedly, half ashamed:

"You understand, I shall have to pretend to be romantic, when Nickol

is in hearing. He wouldn't understand anything else."

The new young man came up and was introduced. He fell to my share. Tall and blond, he seemed to be slightly "in the gauze" the whole time. I kept wondering if he had a real man's feelings inside his handsome shell.

IT began to grow chilly on the terrace, and we adjourned to the Sporting Club. The old Casino having begun to grow out of date, the management has provided this gorgeous new palace of amusement to keep up the tone of Monte Carlo. There is nothing like it in our country. The ceiling of the restaurant must be forty feet high. One has a grand feeling of spaciousness. And what a floor! What music! What food!

The dumb Nickol danced like another Maurice. It was heavenly.—But all the time I wondered if I was in the arms of a blackmailer and a robber. Well, danger added a spice to my pleasure. I envied the other couple a little. Raoul could not only dance, he could also talk. He seemed to be filled with a kind of desperate gaiety.

When the four of us were together at the table, it was funny to see him start making love to Mme. Storey, with a perfectly serious face. I suppose the boys spied on each other. However, as there were two orchestras, there was not much pause between dances.

Once or twice Raoul asked me to dance, just for appearance's sake. And when he was out of Nickol's hearing, the poor lad seemed to have a yen to be frank and open. I liked him better and better. In his fun, however, there was a bitter, reckless note that made me want to mother him. But always I was conscious of danger.

Most of the time he talked about Mme. Storey. " Isn't she wonderful? I wouldn't have believed it possible that a woman of brains could be so—so—well, you know what I mean—so lovable !"

" Then you know who she is?" I said.

" Of course I know—Rosika Storey. Such a thing can't be hidden.—I would be willing to bet that everybody here knows who she is. I can hear them murmuring when we dance around together."

We danced for awhile. Raoul's style was bolder and faster than Nickol's. He guided me as smoothly and surely through the crowding couples as a bird slips through the branches of a tree. Presently he said with a laugh that didn't hide the feeling in his voice:

" Meeting a woman like that has pulled me right up by the roots! I'll never be the same man again. What is it you say in America? I'm a gone coon !"

I didn't like him any the less for saying that.

When the dance was over, we strolled out into the beautifully lighted gardens. I saw that Mme. Storey and Raoul had some sort of an understanding. They dropped Nickol politely at the foot of the hotel steps, but Raoul came up to our suite with us. In the face of the young Dane as he turned away there was a sharp, mean look that I didn't like. Raoul didn't seem to care.

UP in our salon, all Raoul's pumped-up gaiety dropped away. His smooth young face looked drawn and haggard.

" I can't stay," he muttered. " This place is about as healthy for me as Fascist headquarters to a communist."

He moved around the room in a halting way, his head down, stroking the backs of the chairs.

" You said that you had something to say to me?" said Mme. Storey gravely.

" Yes. I'd better say it and go ..." It wasn't so easy for him to get it out. He made a couple of false starts. " Something has happened to me this afternoon. I—I— Oh, well, never mind me! I don't mean anything in your life."

" If you're up against it, you do," she said quickly. " If you're sick of your crooked job here."

He laughed. " Sick of my job! Oh, God! Believe me, I've been sick of my job for a long time. But I kidded myself. Now I can't kid myself any longer.—No !" he cried out sharply. " But leave me out of it! This is what I want to say: you must get out of Monte Carlo—at once! By the first train !"

" But why?" asked Mme. Storey.

" I can't tell you that. I can only say that you're in danger—horrible danger! You can't fight this thing; it's too well covered. They'll get you if you stay here !"

It was obvious that he thought Mme. Storey had accepted the job of breaking the ring of blackmailers. She didn't undeceive him.

She said, " If I were to leave now, it would be suspected that you had warned me."

He laughed a bitter note. " I expect they know it already."

" What will you do? You can't go on with your present life."

" Never mind that. Only do what I say. You see that I'm in earnest. It's true I'm taking a risk in warning you, but let that go. It's the first decent act of my life. Let me feel that I've done some good. Will you do what I say? Will you go?"

"I don't know. I'll have to consider it," said Mme. Storey.

He turned to me in a kind of desperation. "You persuade her!" he said. "I can see that you're fond of her. Don't let her soil her hands with this pitch.—Go away from here. There are plenty of places where you can amuse yourselves. If she stays here they'll get her!"

I could only spread out my hands helplessly. It was not for me to say anything.

"Raoul," said Mme. Storey frankly, "come in with us. You're in wrong. Join up with us and get a fresh deal. With your aid I could smash these scoundrels!"

He shook his head. "No," he said gloomily, "I couldn't betray my mob. —That's the right word, isn't it?—I've done pretty nearly everything in my short life, but I've never been a traitor."

"Then get out of Monte Carlo yourself," she said, "and keep on going until you are out of reach of the ring. Go to America if necessary. I'll stake you—because I think you're worth saving."

He stared at her, and a wonderful light broke in his face. He seemed to be dazed by her offer. "A fresh deal?" he stammered. "Could I?—Could I?"

Mme. Storey unlocked her writing case. "You'd better get away in a hurry," she said.

He pulled himself together. "Yes! I'll be followed from the moment I leave here. But I think I can shake them off. I'll walk out of town. The railway station will be watched. I'll pick up the bus for Nice, somewhere along the road, and take the train from there."

Mme. Storey had taken a packet of banknotes from her case, and was writing a card. "Give this to my agent in Paris," she said. "And let me hear from you through him."

Raoul thrust the notes and the card in his breast pocket. His face was working strangely. "I can't say anything," he muttered.

"Don't try," said Mme. Storey.

He seized her hand and was about to kiss it, but she drew it away. "You may kiss my lips," she said smiling.

He did so, and immediately ran out of the room, staggering slightly.

When he had gone I dropped in a chair. I felt as if all the strength had oozed out of my legs. "What will you do?" I faltered. "When he disappears they will suppose that he has confessed everything to you."

"I reckon they will," said Mme. Storey coolly. She considered for a moment. "I don't know what I shall do," she said slowly. "But certainly I'm not going to let anybody run me out of Monte Carlo."

I knew she was going to say it, but a little groan escaped me.

"But you don't have to stay here, Bella," she added, with quick kindness. "After all, this is a holiday. There is no need for you to be frightened to death."

"I stay where you are," I said grimly.

CHAPTER III.

THE OTHER SIDE.

AFTER Raoul had gone, Mme. Storey looked over some mail that had arrived during the afternoon. Amongst it was a note which had been delivered by hand. It was signed by one Amos Rudd.

"Bless my fathers! Amos Rudd!" she exclaimed. "He used to be a great man in New York—president of the Madison National. Sold out when his bank was merged. I thought he had passed out years ago; and here he is, risen like Lazarus, in Monte Carlo. He must be about a hundred."

Mr. Rudd had written to ask her to dinner at his villa. He apologized for the shortness of the notice, saying that he had just heard of her arrival; and as he was entertaining some of his friends that night, he hoped she would dispense with ceremony and join them. He would be very glad to have her traveling companion also, he said.

"Let's go, Bella," said Mme. Storey. "If he's a resident here, we may pick up some valuable information."

I agreed of course, but I had an uncomfortable feeling that she was about to be drawn into the ugly case of the gigolos in spite of herself.

So a telephone message was sent to Mr. Rudd to say that we were coming, and we proceeded to get dressed.

Our host, we found, lived in almost feudal fashion in a sort of castle on the Cap Martin side. We were welcomed in a salon big enough for kings, with a loggia opening on the moonlit sea. Rudd was a tiny man, like a fledgling bird all beak and eyes, with no feathers to speak of. Thus age returns to the semblance of youth. He had hardly a fledgling's innocence, though. There was a fixed, malicious grin in his little withered face.

I disliked his wife at sight. She was not the same wife he had left New York with, Mme. Storey remarked later. A tall, luscious blonde with drooping lips and weary eyes; a woman of the highest fashion strung with jewels; she looked, to put it bluntly, capable of any crime.

Mr. Rudd squeaked, "Rosika! You were only a little girl when I saw you last! You've grown older and I've grown younger.—He! He! He!"

His wife drawled with infinite fatigue, "Chawmed, Mme. Storey. I hope you won't find Monte *too* boring."

The company was a small one. There was a Prince Grimaldi, a tottering old *beau* with his hair plastered down. Several American women hung around him simply because the taste of his title —which they pronounced "Prance"— was like honey on their lips. There was a count who was a little younger but worse favored; and there was a bundle of wraps and veils enclosing an aged lady who was related to the late Sultan of Turkey. All we could see of her was a long and inquisitive nose.

Amongst the Americans there was a bloated couple who were always spoken of in hushed voices as the James Wentworth Hawkinses. What they had done to deserve it I couldn't find out. The male Hawkins resembled a bulldog, except that no dog could look so brutal. Something happens to Americans when they forsake their own country for good. They hit the skids morally.

Mme. Storey and I were much the youngest persons present. Amongst that crew, my tall friend stood out like a lady in a museum. They all felt the contrast I think; and they lavished compliments on her—and cordially disliked her.

DINNER was kept waiting by the non-arrival of somebody called Turner Moale. From the conversation I gathered that no affair in Monte Carlo was complete without Turner Moale. He was president of the golf club and chairman of the carnival committee; his name headed every subscription list; he gave the most delightful entertainments at his villa on the rock of Monaco. His Highness the Prince himself had lately honored him by coming to dinner.

Turner Moale—Turner Moale—the name rang through my head like some old rhyme. Suddenly it came to me that my mother used to talk about Turner Moale. When she was a girl, he was the Number One matinée idol of New York. Women used to mob the stage door in order to touch him as he passed. Presumably he had been forced off the stage by age; and here he was, established as the social arbiter of Monte Carlo. I wanted to change the ancient wheeze to run: When Americans die, they rise up in Monte Carlo. I felt as if I was in a company of ghosts.

Presently he arrived; a very old man but marvelously well preserved. I expect he had been in the hands of his valet for hours before the gathering. Looking rosy and dignified, beautifully turned-out, he was certainly a personage. Everybody had to look when he came in. With his cool airs and his affability, he was like a little Highness himself.

He made directly for my employer, and kissed her hand as if he were conferring an order upon her. "Rosika Storey!" he exclaimed. "The desire of my life is granted!" He drew her hand under his arm. "I shall take you into dinner. I don't care what anybody says. I shall fight for the privilege!"

Everybody laughed.

When we sat down at the table there was a burst of animation, as if a large tap had been turned on. Everybody was smirking, ogling, flirting, while they picked at the different courses which were whisked on and off. But while their lips smiled, their eyes were ghastly. Mme. Storey has taught me something about eyes. Every one of those dapper men and bejeweled women was frantic with boredom. They hated each other; they hated themselves. People in that state are ripe for anything.

Excepting Turner Moale perhaps. He appeared to be serene. But perhaps it was only because he had a more perfect control over his eyes. He was no better than the others, but he had a better style. He was like the popular ruler of some little country a long time ago, who had nothing to fear. There are no rulers like that nowadays.

"I haven't been to America for years," he said. "I can't endure their barbarous customs! In America, I am told, men wear dinner jackets when there are ladies present.—I shall never go there!"

MME. STOREY led up to what she had in mind by telling of our encounter with the good-looking young man on the terrace—just the beginning of it. They listened with smiles, but one could see that they disliked the subject. Mme. Storey said with an innocent air:

"I suppose terrible things may happen to a woman who falls for those handsome rascals."

Silence around the table.

She went on. "In fact, I have heard various references to women being robbed and blackmailed at Monte Carlo."

Not a word. Mrs. Hawkins tried to create a diversion by asking the prince if he liked *sauce bearnaise* with his *entrecôte*.

Mme. Storey kept on. "Mr. Rudd, have you ever heard of these things?"

"Not I! I'm the wrong sex."

His feeble joke produced a great laugh. Mme. Storey, undiscouraged, blandly addressed Turner Moale, at her side. "What do you think, Mr. Moale? Are these pleasant young fellows that one sees on the terrace dangerous criminals?"

"I hope so!" he said maliciously.

There were loud cries of protest from his admirers.

"It adds zest to life," he said. "We are too far sunk in our creature comforts. Nothing like a good crime or two to rouse us!"

"I like to read about crimes in Chicago," drawled Mrs. Rudd, "but not at my own front door."

"The nearer, the more exciting!" said Turner Moale.

"By himself, no young man is especially dangerous," said Mme. Storey. "But suppose they combine to stand or fall together. Suppose they are only tools in the hands of a master who uses them for his own ends. That would be a dangerous racket. The boys, you see, would be comparatively innocent. And all they would have to do would be to allow the women to make fools of themselves. Then the master would apply the screws."

"Superb!" cried Turner Moale, with his noiseless old man's laugh. "You are wasted as an upholder of the law, Rosika. If you were a criminal you would go down in history!"

"Of course it's only the women in hotels who are victimized," said Mrs. Rudd languidly. "It doesn't affect those of us who are residents here."

The old Turkish woman shook with laughter inside her wrappings, as if she knew some devilish joke.

"Blackmail will soon become a lost art," lisped the old prince, "because people are proud of being bad nowadays."

"Then you can blackmail them for being found in church!" retorted Turner Moale.

"If you've got a good balance at the bank, you don't need to care what anybody says about you," put in Amos Rudd, grinning like a death's head.

His wife flashed a spontaneous look of hatred down the table.

"About these women who are blackmailed," said Hawkins brutally. "If they make fools of themselves, I say they deserve no better than they get."

Mme. Storey took no further part in the discussion. She let them thrash it out amongst themselves, as if she had learned what she wished to know.

After dinner we all drove into town to take a whirl at the tables of the Sporting Club—a super gambling house; quiet, elegant, spacious. They never allow it to become crowded; and after all, plenty of room is the greatest of all luxuries.

With mask-like faces, all the members of our party put up large sums at roulette. The Turkish lady stretched forth a claw from her wrappings, but it trembled violently. I saw old Amos Rudd staking the dilapidated prince on the sly. I wondered if they paid him for coming to dinner. Turner Moale played at another table, and kept his back to us.

Later we descended to the night club for more dancing. It was not exactly exhilarating to be pushed around by tottering noblemen or resuscitated Americans.—I thought of the handsome Raoul longingly.

WHEN the party broke up we were besieged with invitations. These people did nothing in the world but give each other dinners every night. However, Mme. Storey evaded them politely.

"I may be obliged to leave Monte Carlo to-morrow," she said. "I dare not accept anything."

How thankful I was to get back to our own quiet rooms!

"Pretty awful, wasn't it?" said Mme. Storey, smiling. "However, the evening was not entirely wasted."

I looked at her inquiringly.

"Mrs. Rudd possesses a photograph of Raoul," she said, lighting a cigarette. "Along with pictures of many other handsome young men."

"What does that mean?" I said.

"I don't know. It's only a beginning."

"Then you are going to take this case!" I exclaimed, with a long face.

"I may be forced to," she said.

I opened the casements and we stepped out on the balcony and looked down at the sea, powdered with the shadowy radiance of the moon. The moon itself was over our shoulders. It was very late, and the town had fallen quiet. The fantastic Casino over the way was dark. Silence and moonlight, the unchanging things, held the frivolous city in a spell.

Out of the silence we heard a far-off cry.

"What was that?" I said, startled.

"Some poor soul in trouble," murmured Mme. Storey.

It had nothing to do with us, so far as we knew, but I found myself trembling all over. "Let's go in," I said.

CHAPTER IV.

THE MURDERED.

I SPENT a bad night and got up ready to hate that gay and beautiful place. Mme. Storey was a little pale, too. In silence, we ate our *petit déjeuner* by the open window.

As we sat lingering over our cigarettes, an envelope was brought to her which bore the imprint of a café in Monte Carlo. No name was written on it; only the number of our room. She read it, and handed it over to me without comment.

Dear R. S.:

I know that it is foolish of me to write to you, but it eases me so! They have me on the run, though so far I have been able to keep a jump or two ahead of them. I am waiting here for a friend who has promised to bring me a disguise. If I could only say some of the things that I feel! But I must not. I have no right. I can say this, though. Through you I have found myself. Whatever may happen to me now . . .

There was a break at this point, and the letter was carried on in a different hand, an uneducated hand, and in French. Translated it ran:

The gentleman told me who this was for. He had to leave in a hurry. I let him out through a back window.
Pierre,
Waiter at Café des Arcades.

Mme. Storey and I exchanged an anxious glance. "Let's go and see the grand vizier," she said.

She was referring to *M. le President* of the Society of the Baths of the Sea. I nodded, and we got ready.

There was nothing frivolous about that official's suite. Very handsome and austere. As soon as we entered we perceived that something unusual was up. Excited looking clerks were passing in and out, and we had to wait until a couple of gaudy policemen made a report to Monsieur B. A presentiment of evil struck a slow chill through my veins.

When we were shown into his private office, Monsieur B. still looked disturbed.

In her forthright way Mme. Storey said, "What has happened, *monsieur?*"

"Why, nothing—nothing at all," he replied quickly—too quickly.

Mme. Storey merely looked at him in the way that draws people out.

"Well, a distressing accident," he said. "An unfortunate young man killed himself last night by jumping over the cliffs of La Turbie."

In spite of myself a little cry was forced from me.

"What's the matter with *mademoiselle?*" he asked, staring.

"She doubts that it was suicide," said Mme. Storey gravely.

"What else could it be?" he said irritably, throwing up his hands. "Some poor fool who has lost all at the gaming tables! Anyway, he killed himself outside our borders, though the French authorities seem to think we are responsible."

"Who is he?"

"I do not know, *madame.* All marks of identification had been destroyed. An investigation is in progress."

"Where is he?"

"At a mortuary in Beausoleil."

Mme. Storey's face was like marble. "Is he—recognizable?"

"Yes. I am told that his face escaped mutilation, though almost every bone in his body was broken."

"I wish to see him."

He jumped up waving his hands in distress. "No—no! It is too horrible! Isn't there somebody who could act for you? Some man?"

"I am accustomed to acting for myself," she said.

A MOMENT or two later, we were in Monsieur B.'s car, climbing through the narrow winding streets that lead to Beausoleil, the upper town. All Monte Carlo is built like a flight of steps up the side of a mountain. Beausoleil is in French territory.

The mortuary was a private one attached to an undertaking establishment. There is a stark, nightmare quality about such places in France.

At the door of the inner room, Mme. Storey said kindly, "You don't have to come in, Bella."

I shook my head, and followed at her heels like a shadow. It would have been worse to wait outside for her.

A small, bare room with whitewashed walls and cement floors. A smell of iodoform. In the middle a slab with a sheeted form upon it; a table at the side, with the dead man's clothes under another sheet.

An attendant standing beside the slab pulled down the sheet a little way and we saw—what we expected to see—Raoul's handsome head. He was no longer glad nor sorry; neither proud nor shamefaced. Death had shaped a perfect classical mask. The brown, wavy hair; the clear olive skin; the sensitive mouth. And so young—so pitifully young!

I began to shake inside; the tears were running down my face without my knowing it.

Mme. Storey, as always when under strong emotion, was pale and cold. She said, "This man was murdered!"

"How do you know?" gasped Monsieur B.

"His lips were sealed with surgeon's tape. If you look closely you can see traces of the gum ... I wish to see his hands."

The sheet was pulled down further, and I turned away. I could not bear any more. I heard her say:

"Observe those marks on his wrists, *monsieur.* He was bound and gagged when he was carried to La Turbie."

Monsieur B. made incoherent sounds of distress.

When we had returned to his car, Mme. Storey told him what we knew about the dead man. The name he had given us was no doubt assumed.

Mme. Storey said, " I am now ready, *monsieur,* to undertake the work you offered me yesterday."

Now that murder had come into it, he was not so eager. " There must be no ugly publicity," he muttered.

She looked at him coldly. " It suits me to have as little publicity as possible," she said. " But in advance, I won't consent to conceal anything."

" An ugly murder—just at the beginning of the season! Ruinous! Ruinous!" he cried.

" You can't clean up a mess without making a bad smell," said Mme. Storey. " Ruinous! Ruinous!"

" Very well," she said crisply, " if you wish to withdraw your offer, that is quite all right. But in that case I must warn you that I shall go ahead on my own. Whatever happens, I am going to see that the murderer of this man—I mean the *real* murderer—is brought to justice."

That brought him down on the run. " No! No!—*Madame!*—Of course not! Don't speak of such a thing, I beg. Certainly my offer of yesterday stands. I am anxious to coöperate with you in every way possible. No expense must be spared!"

CHAPTER V.

THE DICTIONARY.

WE went right on to La Turbie in the car. Monsieur B. said we should find his chief of detectives on the spot. The road zig-zagged endlessly back and forth across the face of the almost perpendicular mountain back of Monte Carlo. Though La Turbie almost overhangs the resort, it is a half-hour's drive around those hairpin curves.

Like all the ancient villages thereabouts, La Turbie resembles a solid block of masonry tucked in the folds of the mountains. It is dominated by a huge ruined tower built by the Romans. Below the ancient part, is a modern esplanade ending in a sort of round bastion at the very edge of the cliffs. It was from this bastion that the body had been flung.

Mme. Storey had the car stopped some distance short of the end of the road, hoping to find the tracks of the car that had preceded us some eight hours before. But the pavement was hard, and so many people had shuffled back and forth that all marks of tires were obliterated.

Within the circular parapet at the end, a knot of people were gathered, peering over, discussing the affair.

The chief of detectives joined us. Mme. Storey looked at him and then looked at me ruefully. A worthy man! When Monsieur B. asked him what had developed, he shrugged and spread his palms. Every soul in La Turbie had been asleep when it happened. Some, perhaps, had been wakened by the young man's cry; but they didn't know what had wakened them.

The village people drew back wonderingly at the sight of Mme. Storey. They suspected a tragic romance. We looked over—not at the glorious panorama of mountain and sea, with the red-roofed town two thousand feet below, but straight down to where we could see a dark strain on the rocks at the foot of the cliff. I shivered. I can't say how far down it was—hundreds of feet.

They told us that the spot where the body had fallen was inaccessible from below; consequently men had been lowered from the parapet to fetch it up. Indeed, the ropes were still there, and the men who had gone down were now telling the story to their neighbors, over and over.

Mme. Storey said, " I will go down." There was a chorus of remonstrances from the Frenchmen. She merely waited with a cold smile until they had talked themselves out.

" I shall go for you," offered the detective.

She shook her head. " I must use my own eyes."

In the end, of course, she had her way. The men who manipulated the ropes constructed a sort of sling for her. They helped her over the parapet; and presently I saw her swinging between rocks and sky, seated in the sling, clinging to the rope above her head with one hand and holding a cigarette in the other. It made me giddy, and I drew back. The village people were staring as at a marvel.

There was no accident. In half an hour they helped her over the parapet and she stood beside us, safe and sound.

" Did you find anything?" asked the detective excitedly.

" No," she said coolly.

WHEN we drove away in the car, she opened her hand and showed us a brown button. Clinging to it was a scrap of frayed woolen cloth of the same color.

" When they took off his bonds, there was a brief struggle," she said. " He caught hold of a button on the coat of one of his assailants, and it came away in his hand. Observe that the cloth is of the finest quality, and that the button is sewed on with silk thread."

The French detective struck his fist into his palm. " I will find the wearer of that coat, *madame!* You may leave it to me!"

" Quite!" she said, dryly.

Back in the town, we parted from our companions. The detective went off to set the usual machinery of the police in motion, while Mme. Storey and I went in search of the Café des Arcades. There was none of the Monte Carlo glitter about this place. It was the sort of shabby, inviting little resort in a side street where French people love to sit by the hour, talking, playing dominoes, writing letters. At this time of day it was almost empty. When we sat down, a waiter assiduously wiped the marble table in front of us. He was a young man with a friendly smile, but all the stored-up wisdom of the café waiter was in his wary eyes.

" Are you Pierre?" asked Mme. Storey.

" But yes, *madame*," he said startled. " How do you know my name?"

" You signed it to a letter that you sent to me last night."

" Yes—yes!" he said. " And you are the lady? Ah-h!"

" What do you know about the young man who gave you that letter?"

Pierre spread out his hands expressively. " I know nothing, *madame*. He is a customer. He is generous. I do not know his name."

From behind the bar the proprietor was looking at us curiously Mme. Storey ordered *apéritifs*. Pierre flew to get them.

When he returned she asked, " What made the young man leave so quickly last night?"

" I do not know," said Pierre. " He show me a fifty-franc note. He say quiet, ' Is there a way out at the back?' I say, ' Follow me.'—I take him into the storeroom. He go out through the window like a bird, shove the letter in my hand, say, 'Send it to Suite A, Hotel de Paris.'"

"He was waiting here for a friend. Did his friend come?"

"Ah yes! The *mademoiselle.* She often meet him here. Very pretty. She come, and I say, 'Your gentleman is gone.'—I didn't want to frighten her."

He gave us a good description of the girl.

"You must have some idea of the danger that threatened him," said Mme. Storey.

Pierre shrugged. "Well, there were four men waiting in the street," he said. "Afterwards they went away."

"Could you identify them if you saw them again?"

An expression of prudence came over the waiter's face. "Ah no, *madame,*" he said quickly. "It is impossible. It was dark in the street. Their hats were pulled over their eyes."

"Pierre," said Mme. Storey gravely, "they got him!"

"*Mon Dieu!*" he said softly. "Is he dead?"

"He is dead!"

Pierre bustled away toward a table at a little distance, where he fussed among a pile of magazines that lay upon it. He came back bringing one of them with his professional smile. This was for the benefit of the watching proprietor. Pierre's eyes were full of tears, I saw.

"*Violà!—L'Illustration, madame,*" he said briskly. He leaned over and gave the table a swipe with his cloth. His back was turned toward his boss. "I have something else for you," he whispered.

Digging into a pocket under his apron, he produced a tiny book in a pretty white binding. Mme. Storey quickly slipped it out of sight.

"He give me that with the letter," whispered Pierre. "He say, 'If they get me you will hear of it, Pierre. If they get me, I want the lady at the Hotel de Paris to have this. If you hear nothing, throw it into the sea. It would be dangerous to have it on you.'"

Somebody called to Pierre, and he hustled away. He could give us no further help.

UNDER cover of the magazine, we examined the little book. To our astonishment it was—a dictionary! The slip cover was a handsome affair of vellum, decorated with gold, green and red bands, but it held just a common little five-franc English-French dictionary. Every traveler knows the sort.

Mme. Storey ran over the pages hastily. They showed no marks.

"Just an ordinary dictionary!" I said, disappointed.

"No," she said thoughtfully. "He had some special reason for sending it."

After a moment or two the explanation came to her. "This is the code book used by the gang in exchanging messages. It is not the first time that a dictionary has been used for that purpose. It will be useful."

We returned to the hotel. On the way, Mme. Storey telegraphed to Philippe Grandet in Paris, asking him to come to Monte Carlo. He was a clever man who had worked for her on several former occasions. I had an uncomfortable feeling that we were being followed through the streets, but I couldn't spot anybody. When I suggested to Mme. Storey that we ought to have protection, she merely shrugged.

"They would never dare murder us, Bella," she said lightly. "That would cause a sensation big enough to drive them out of business.—Though it would be one way of winning our case."

A busy day followed. Mme. Storey was in hourly consultation with the police. They were efficient enough, as police go, but lacking in originality. I needn't put down everything we did, because in a case of this sort you have to start a hundred lines of investigation of which ninety-nine come to nothing. The chief of detectives did *not* find the coat from which the button had been torn; neither did he locate Raoul's little friend. Perhaps it was she who had betrayed Raoul.

During the afternoon, Mr. James Wentworth Hawkins called up. He wished to know if Mme. Storey was still in Monte Carlo, and if she was available for dinner that night. The sound of his thick, cruel voice over the wire made me shiver.

Mme. Storey declined. Awfully sorry, she said, but she had a business engagement she couldn't get out of.

"Business in Monte Carlo!" he said with an unpleasant laugh. "That *is* uncommon!"

While the band was playing, we sat down on the terrace for a breather; and there we had an odd experience. No handsome young man made eyes at us to-day, but one such did sit down in a chair perhaps a hundred feet away. My eyes almost popped out of my head when I saw him take out a little white book with gold, green and red bands on the cover, and start reading it.

In a minute or two, another young man approached him, showed him something in his hand—I had a glimpse of the red and green on white—and the first man made a somewhat lengthy communication. If only we could have heard it! The second man strolled on then, while the first remained sitting. Ten minutes later a third young man appeared, and the same performance was gone through with.

"The little book increases in importance," said Mme. Storey dryly. "It is their code, and also the badge by which they know each other!"

She had not said anything to the police about this book. "Do you intend to point out these men to the police?" I asked.

She shook her head. "The police will accomplish nothing. And it is up to you and me to complete a case before we strike."

When we returned to the hotel, she looked at the little book thoughtfully. "It would be unlucky if they discovered that we possessed this," she said. "It is possible that they have spies in the hotel, and our rooms may be searched while we are out."

She sealed it up, therefore, and posted it to herself in care of *poste restante*, Nice, where we could pick it up at any time.

CHAPTER VI.

BY WAY OF WARNING.

WE worked very late that night. The *commissaire de police* sent Mme. Storey a batch of reports from the various men who had been at work on the case during the day, and after studying them, she dictated suggestions for the work of the following day.

All was sealed up and sent off by a waiting messenger, and then we sat in the salon of our suite, smoking, talking idly, letting ourselves relax in preparation for sleep. It was about half-past one, I suppose. A great silence had fallen on Monte Carlo, broken only by the occasional dull roar of a car on the main road, far away. The southern French, like their neighbors the Italians, have a great fondness for roaring through the small hours with their cutouts open.

Suddenly there was a discreet tap on the door. We had heard no one approach.

"Who is it?" asked Mme. Storey, coolly.

A low voice answered, "A letter from the *commissaire de police, madame.*"

There was something not quite right about that voice, and Mme. Storey's face turned grim. I was thankful that the door was a stout one, and securely bolted.

"Shove it under the door," she said.

There was a silence. No letter appeared. Then the voice whined:

"It is too thick to go under the door, *madame.*"

"Then it must wait until morning," she said coolly. "I have retired."

Another pause. Though I put my head to the door, I could not hear a sound from the other side. But I had the feeling that there was more than one man in the corridor, conferring. Then we heard retreating footsteps.

I looked at Mme. Storey questioningly. My heart was beating like a motor. Still, the incident appeared to be over.

She lit a fresh cigarette, saying, "They must think we are downy birds!"

There was another tap on the door.

"Well?" said Mme. Storey.

"If you please, *madame,*" said the whining voice, "the *commissaire* says it is very important."

Mme. Storey's lip curled in contempt. "Go away!" she said. "If you bother me again, I shall telephone to the office."

We were both facing the door, listening for the sound of his footsteps. One of those mysterious intimations caused me to turn my head. I saw four masked men. They had entered through the balcony windows. One of them, I saw almost immediately, was wearing a brown suit with a button missing. That was the thing which struck me most forcibly.

Before I could scream, a soft mass was thrown over my head and drawn tight; a down coverlet. A bent arm was flung around my head, drawing it back until I thought my neck would break, stifling any cries. I was held thus while a rope was cast round and round my body, binding my arms and legs fast. I guessed that Mme. Storey was being treated in the same way, but I could hear nothing.

I struggled with all my might. I did my utmost to cry out. But it was no good. The men who had hold of me knew just what they had to do. I was like an infant in their hands. They worked with terrifying swiftness. Before I had recovered from the shock of being seized, I was hoisted over the shoulder of one of them and run out through the door.

All this time something hard—a towel I suppose—was pressing the coverlet into my face and I was at the point of suffocation. Fiery spots danced before my eyes, and my ears rang. My senses wavered. Down the corridor, through another door, and down a flight of steps. I could hear no sounds, however. They must have been in their stocking feet.

Endless corridors, scraping against first one side then the other. My senses weren't registering properly.

We stopped, and I heard a voice say as from an immense distance, " Open the door and look out."

Another answered, " All clear."

I was shot into the open air, and immediately flung into a car which started, with the exhaust wide open. Then I passed out.

BUT only for a moment. When consciousness came back, the exhaust was still roaring. I could breathe more freely now. The pressure had been removed from my face, but there was a rope drawing the coverlet into my mouth so that I could not cry out. I groaned, but that feeble sound was swallowed in the noise of the engine. Suddenly the exhaust was shut off, and I judged that we had passed out of town.

We slowed down for a sharp turn, passed it, and increased speed again. We almost stopped, crawled around a complete half-turn, and speeded up again. Another turn, and I knew where we were. Climbing to La Turbie!

I hope I may never know such another moment. Up to that moment I had been blindly resisting, like an animal. Now I knew fear, and it drained all the blood from my heart. I pictured the hideous cliff I had looked over that morning, with the stain of blood on the rocks below. A phrase rang through my head—" Broke every bone in his body!" The prospect of such a death was worse than death. I died a thousand deaths on that mountain road. I fairly went mad because I could not scream and struggle.

I had no sense that Mme. Storey was anywhere near me. So far as I could tell, I was planted on the back seat of a closed car, with a man on either side of me. They spoke not a word. Silent on each side of me, they afflicted me with an unspeakable terror, like two death's heads conducting me to my own funeral!

As we crawled around one of the close turns, I heard a speeding car above us, and then I knew why Mme. Storey was not beside me. For awhile I forgot myself in the horror of her death.—A life like hers to be cut off!

When the car stopped, I went mad with fear again. I was all fear. In my imagination I was screaming at the top of my voice: " No!—No!—No!" But in actuality I could make no sound.

There was a pause while the two parties conferred together. A voice said:

" Send the little one first."

Another answered, " No, both together."

Suddenly all fear left me. I suppose it is like that with men in battle, when faced with inevitable death. The thought comes to one: well, what's the difference?

One man took me by the shoulders, another by the ankles. They gave me a little shake, as if to make sure of their grip.

From the other party came the cold voice:

" Swing them well out. Three times. —Let go when I say three."

At that moment my whole life seemed to spread out before me. Every loved face that I had ever known passed before my eyes.

They began to swing me. One!— Two! — Three! — They let go ... I knew nothing more ...

AFTER awhile, as it seemed to me, I began to dream. A delicious dream of running water; a swift little river in the American countryside, with alders and willows growing overhead, the sunlight striking through and dappling the water. A drowsy June afternoon, with the hum of bees. Blue sky, white clouds, grass rippled by the wind.

Suddenly I realized that it was faintly light, and that Rosika was bending over me with a face of concern. She was bathing my temples with a wet handkerchief. For a moment I thought I had wakened in another world.

"Where are we?" I asked.

She smiled. "In the same old wicked world, my dear!"

I was filled with a grinding confusion. "But—but—" I stammered.

"Look around you!" she said.

Raising myself on my elbow, I saw that I was lying in grass at the foot of a low stone wall. We *were* at La Turbie, because I saw the ruined Roman tower against the pale morning sky. But it was *not* the hideous bastion on the edge of the cliffs. Below me were ghostly olive trees on their terraces.

"Look!" said Mme. Storey. "When I got clear of my bonds I found this pinned to my sleeve."

She held up a piece of paper on which some words had been roughly printed. I read:

This is just to show you what we can do when we want to. We don't like killing women, but if you don't take warning from this, we won't stop next time with giving you a fright.

Then the reaction set in.

"We're all right! We're all right!" I screamed, laughing and crying together. Then I was sick.

When I felt better, Mme. Storey helped me to my feet, and we climbed over the wall. The road lay on the other side of it.

I was still pretty groggy.

"I'm sorry, we have a long walk before us," said Mme. Storey. "Fortunately, it's down hill. Our abductors were wonderfully considerate. They brought our coats along, and flung them over the wall after us."

I looked down at Monte Carlo, just beginning to show through the mist.

"Horrible, horrible place!" I said with a shiver. "The hotel management must have been a party to what happened last night.—To be kidnaped out of our own rooms!"

"Not at all!" said Mme. Storey coolly. "You've lost your sense of proportion, Bella. We are up against a gang of clever and adventurous rogues, that's all. No doubt they hired the room over ours, and dropped down to our balcony with ropes.—They were perfectly acquainted with the interior of the hotel. They carried us down the service stairs and through the service passages. At that hour of the night they would be deserted. If there was a watchman, he was bribed."

"And what are we going to do now?" I asked.

"We are going to act just as our enemies want us to act, like a pair of frightened women. We are going to take the first train out of Monte Carlo. It leaves at quarter to seven."

CHAPTER VII.

"LADY WEDDERMINSTER."

A WEEK later, Mme. Storey and I returned to Monte Carlo. Those seven days had been filled with busy preparations, and our dearest friends would not have recognized us in our new rôles. Philippe Grandet had been recalled to Paris because he was too old for the particular work in hand, but we had a new emissary who had been sent on five days in advance.

Mme. Storey and I had fled all the way to London. Satisfied that we had left our spies in France, we then returned to Paris on an unfashionable train, and put up at a small hotel on the left bank. On our first day there we were walking through the Luxembourg Gardens when we came upon a handsome young man seated on a bench in an attitude of complete dejection.

"There's our man!" said Mme. Storey instantly.

He was blond and well-built, and there was a special attractiveness about him, compounded of good humor with a spice of the devil. Furthermore, he was an American, God bless him! and he was out of luck. His long legs were stretched in front of him, his hands thrust in his pockets, his chin resting on his breast.

Mme. Storey stopped. "You seem to be in bad, George?" she said with a cool and friendly smile.

"In bad!" he cried. Then he got a good look at her and sprang to his feet. "Lady," he said solemnly, "I'm so deep in bad it would take a hundred-foot ladder to fetch me above ground! ... My name is Charlie, if it's just the same to you."

We took to him instantly.

"Well, Charlie," said Mme. Storey, "perhaps I can give you a job. Come along and have lunch with us at the Medici Grill, and we'll talk it over."

Charlie was the lad for us, all right. His other name was Raines, and his story was a simple one. The son of a rich man, he had been sent on a tour of Europe to complete his education, and he had liked Paris so well that he had refused to leave it. This had resulted in a break with the old man. Charlie thought that he could make his own way, but he had soon discovered that while Paris is paradise for a young American with money, it is hell for him who hath none. So here he was, chucked out of his hotel, and too proud to cable home.

Mme. Storey's intuition had not deceived her. Charlie looked upon the affair as a big lark. She told him about Raoul, and warned him that if he were found out it would cost him his life. He waved it aside.

"All my life I've longed to have a real adventure!" he said.

He left for Monte Carlo that same night, with a replenished wardrobe and a pocketbook stuffed with notes. He traveled under his own name, with his own passport. His instructions were:

To put up at the Hotel de Paris and start playing at the Casino or the Sporting Club. He was to plunge until he had lost or appeared to have lost all his money. Then he was to get into a row with the hotel over his bill, and to move into a cheap lodging. He was to continue to wager a few francs daily at the Casino, as if the madness had got him, and he must sell off his belongings and eat at the cheapest *estaminets*. After that, he was to let things take their course. If a crooked proposition was put up to him, he was to receive it indulgently.

"The lady in Monte Carlo who picks out the young men for this game is a connoisseur of manly good looks," said Mme. Storey dryly. "I think I have gauged her taste correctly. Blonds are always in demand."

"Spare my blushes, Lady!" said Charlie, grinning.

"When I get to Monte Carlo, I shall be known as Lady Wedderminster," Mme. Storey went on. "My arrival will be announced, and you can communicate with me at the Hotel de Paris. But don't put anything compromising in a letter. We will arrange a safer means of communicating."

SO Charlie had gone on, and five days later Mme. Storey and I followed him. During every spare moment of that time, and all the way down in the train, we rehearsed our new parts. Mme. Storey is a past mistress of the art of disguise, but she never loses sight of the fact that acting is more important than disguise.

Lady Wedderminster is a real person, and a friend of Mme. Storey's. It is one of the historic names of England, but its present bearer is a retiring person who goes very little into society. She had never been down to the French Riviera. English passports had been secured for us through influence.

Mme. Storey was turned out as one of those incredibly dowdy English women of high position. I don't know where they have their clothes made; perhaps by the village dressmaker. Such women care nothing for the styles of the moment, and they are hung all over with the strangest trimmings. And such hats! Such feather boas! Such shoes—miles too big, and turning up at the toes!

Her face was in character. She was too wise to make up as if she was old. That will never pass muster in the sunlight. But any woman can make herself look like a fright. Mme. Storey's hair was bleached to a nondescript mousy color, and she had applied a wash to her complexion that made her look sallow and haggard. Her eyes were hollowed, to give her a hungry and discontented look. I ought to say that this make-up was a cruel libel on the gracious lady who had given permission for her name to be used; but it was typical of hundreds of Englishwomen that one sees on the Riviera.

Such a woman nearly always has an unfortunate " companion," just to have somebody to order around, and I was that companion. My red locks were dyed an uninteresting brown; I wore a pair of owlish glasses; and my nose was reddened a trifle. As for my clothes and hats—Ye Gods! All I need say is that they were supposed to be Lady Wedderminster's cast-offs, and they looked it.

Such extraordinary looking women are very often wealthy. We telegraphed from Paris for a suite at the Hotel de Paris, and went down on the Blue Train. In the hotel, Mme. Storey was superb; she complained about everything, sending the servants scurrying in a dozen directions. The English are not loved in foreign hotels, but they get excellent service.

As for myself, I am not a very good actress, but my part was a simple one. All I had to do was to look frightened, something I could very well get away with on returning to Monte Carlo.

WE played a waiting game at first, while Mme. Storey's agent fed items to the Paris *Herald* concerning the arrival of Lady Wedderminster on the Riviera—the great wealth of the family—the part it had played in history, and so on. As the *Herald* is the newspaper of the English-speaking contingent, we knew that this stuff would be read in the right quarters. Meanwhile, Lady Wedderminster was playing heavily at the Casino, and for the most part winning. She was then invited to join the Sporting Club.

There had not been a word in the newspapers about the murder of Raoul d'Aymara or the activities of the police. As a matter of fact, after Mme. Storey's disappearance, the case gradually petered out. There was never any inquiry for the poor lad. Like a trim yacht at sea, he had appeared for a brief space out of the fog, and had been swallowed up in it again.

We were bothered about Charlie Raines. No communication was received from him. If he failed us, our whole elaborate plan would collapse. Moreover, we felt a very human anxiety as to the fate of that engaging young man.

Finally we saw him on the terrace, all decked out in his new clothes. He was one of a quartette which included a dark, wicked-looking young man, an admirable foil for the gay Charlie, and two handsome, fashionably-dressed women. All eyes followed them as they strolled along, laughing. A charming picture—if you didn't know the dark undercurrents at Monte Carlo!

This suggested that Charlie had at least got a toe-hold in the blackmailing ring, and we were relieved of a part of our anxiety.

During the afternoon of that day, as Mme. Storey and I were sitting on the terrace listening to the band, the same dark young man dropped in a chair alongside us. There was something vaguely familiar about him. My intuition told me that he was one of those who had entered our room that night, and the skin on the back of my neck crawled. But of course I could not have identified him.

He was a different type from the others; older and harder, with a wicked roll to his dark eyes. Well, many women are thrilled by that sort of thing. He said to Mme. Storey in French:

"What trashy music they play!"

She did not answer him; but at the same time she contrived to look as if she wanted to. A nice piece of acting.

The timid woman who is longing for an adventure.

"I beg your pardon," he said. "I spoke without thinking."

"That's all right," stammered Mme. Storey. "I—I don't mind."

He allowed a little more warmth to come into his voice. "If they would only play good music! One gets so tired of the glitter and frivolity here."

"You must excuse me," she murmured. "My French is not very good."

"So! Then I will talk English! ... I felt at once that you were musical. One cannot be mistaken. The women one meets are so soulless! It is only once or twice in one's lifetime that one sees a woman with soul. You feel the mysterious currents of sympathy passing back and forth—and then—*voilà!* you forget the conventions. Again, I must ask you to forgive me!"

So that was the line they took with a plain woman!

I realized that my presence was only obstructing the free development of this comedy, so I got up and strolled away along the terrace.

WHEN I got back, half an hour later, he had progressed from sympathy to the subject of dancing.

"I do not dance," Mme. Storey was saying in the awkward, wistful manner which she had assumed.

"You *could* dance," he murmured. "A woman full of music like you!"

"I never had a chance," she said, looking down at her hands.

"I understand," he said sympathetically. "And of course you do not like to begin on a public floor ... But you could dance with me," he went on, lowering his voice, "without any of the trouble of learning. Because we are in sympathy!"

Mme. Storey said nothing.

"I have a friend who has a little studio of the dance on Avenue de Joffre," he went on. "Such a charming place! Would you like to come and see it?"

She shook her head.

"I am not a dancing teacher," he said, as if his feelings were wounded. "My father is the director-general of the Sûreté de France, and he allows me a sufficient income. I ask this solely for my own pleasure."

She was obdurate in her refusal. "I would like to dance," she said, "but I am not at my ease with foreigners. If I could find an English teacher—or an American ..."

The young man appeared to be crushed with disappointment. "I am sorry!" he murmured. "Very, very sorry that I have not had the happiness to please you."

Mme. Storey was giving an imitation of a woman to whom no one has ever made love before. "I — I like you," she murmured, "but you are strange to me."

Soon after that he rose to go. "If we meet again on the terrace, may I have the pleasure of talking with you?" he asked.

"If you wish," she said, looking away. She would have blushed if she could, but that was impossible.

"I shall watch for you every afternoon!" he said eagerly. He placed his heels together and bowed. "Permit me to introduce myself—I am Marcel Durocher."

He handed her his card.

"I am Mrs. Bradford," said Mme. Storey in confusion. "I'm sorry I haven't a card with me."

"And this lady?" he said.

"Oh—Miss Toller, my companion!" she answered carelessly.

He left us. When he was out of hearing, Mme. Storey murmured:

"Well, I planted a seed in his mind. Let us pray that it will sprout."

CHAPTER VIII.

THE DANCING LESSON.

ON the following afternoon we were seated on the terrace when Mme. Storey said suddenly, "It *has* sprouted!"

Following the direction of her glance, I saw Durocher coming along with Charlie Raines in tow. My heart began to pound against my ribs. Fortunately, Mme. Storey's scared, red-nosed companion was not forced to take any part in the scene that followed.

Charlie had learned his lesson well. He never batted an eye when he was introduced. It was only by a slight subcutaneous flush in his pale cheeks that I knew he had been told that "Mrs. Bradford" was Lady Wedderminster. His manners were perfect.

They talked about all sorts of things. Lady Wedderminster appeared to warm towards the handsome young American. Marcel made believe to be jealous, but his wicked eyes were full of satisfaction. It was not necessary for anybody to steer the talk around to the subject of dancing. After awhile it got there by itself.

"Charlie is a wonderful dancer," said Marcel, jealously.

Lady Wedderminster looked at Charlie eagerly.

"Marcel mentioned that you would like to learn to dance," said Charlie. "I'd be tickled to death to teach you, if you'll let me. There's a little dance studio on the Avenue de Joffre where we can practice. But I'll bet you anything you like that inside an hour you'll be ready to take the floor at the Sporting Club."

"I should like it," murmured Lady Wedderminster, uncertainly, letting a world of meaning appear in her hungry, hollow eyes.

"You go with him!" grumbled Marcel jealously. But his pleased eyes were saying, "She's hooked!" ... It was good comedy.

"Well, come on, let's go!" said Charlie.

We climbed the steps to the street, and Marcel hailed a taxicab. Lady Wedderminster said with that insulting indifference that she assumed toward her "companion":

"Cora, you run off to the Café de Paris. Buy yourself a drink on the terrace, and wait until I come back."

This was about three o'clock.

SHORTLY before five they returned. I was sitting with my drink before me, when they got out of a taxi at the pavement. Marcel raised his hat and walked off; Mme. Storey and Charlie came to my table. Charlie was saying:

"Thank God! he's left us. At the studio, I didn't dare come out of my part for a moment. That guy has eyes like a lynx, and ears like nothing human!"

They sat down. "What wonderful disguises!" Charlie went on. "Both you and Bella.—Marvelous! Even now, I can't believe that you are really you."

"Restrain your enthusiasm," said Mme. Storey in the dull manner of Lady Wedderminster. "Marcel has gone, but there are other spies. Act toward me as if I was a difficult prospect that you were working on, and you can say whatever you like."

Charlie passed a hand over his mouth. "I can't help grinning when you and Bella and I are together," he said, apologetically.

"Why didn't you let me hear from you?" she asked.

"I couldn't. Until now, I've been watched night and day. This is the first time Marcel has left me on my own."

"Good! That means you have passed.—What has happened?"

"Well," said Charlie, "after I had been thrown up on the beach for a couple of days, this guy Marcel picked me up. Offered to share his room with me. Made out it was pure friendship. He has a swell room, in a villa on the main street, a little way out. We always ride in and out on the bus, though it isn't far.

"I haven't got any of the dope on the gang yet. Marcel admits, of course, that he's a gigolo, but he makes out that he's on his own. He's training me as his side partner. He feeds me a line of cynical philosophy that would have corrupted the Angel Gabriel when young. I appear to lap it up like milk. —One thing struck me as funny: he had me get my photograph taken in a photomat one day. Just for a joke, he made out."

"He wanted to show it to his bosses," said Mme. Storey. "Go on."

"I haven't been told anything," said Charlie, "but I have put two and two together. There are a lot of these bozos in Monte Carlo. They live around in different places, and they don't associate with each other except when they need help. For an identification badge, each one has a little white book to show, but I haven't been given one."

"I know the book," said Mme. Storey dryly. "What about the boss?"

"Haven't heard a whisper about him," said Charlie. "But I know there is a boss, because Marcel gets orders from him in writing that he translates with the aid of the little white book. He makes reports to his boss, too. But how he gets his orders or sends his reports I don't know."

We sipped our *thé au rhum*, the gypsy orchestra played a *czardas*, and the people went hurrying along the pavement to the Casino. They always hurry when they go in.

"Now that you and I have joined up," Mme. Storey said to Charlie, "we must pull off our trick swiftly. If there is any delay, we are certain to be found out and then—good night! ... Have you any idea of what their intentions are toward Lady Wedderminster?"

Charlie shook his head. "Blackmail, I reckon."

"That's what I think," she said. "But blackmail is too complicated and too slow an operation. We must try to tempt them to rob me outright."

"Robbery!—Good Lord!" muttered Charlie, changing color.

"When you make your report to Marcel about me," Mme. Storey went on, "tell him that I confided to you that I had brought a large sum in cash to Monte Carlo, because I didn't want my husband or my bankers to know that I was going to gamble. Tell him that I have almost doubled it since I came, and that I am carrying half a million francs around with me because I'm afraid to leave it in my room."

"But—but—" stammered Charlie, "they will attack you!"

"You are coming out of your part," she warned. "We will take care of that.—If I figure correctly," she went on, "as soon as Marcel gets this information he will report it to his boss, and then he will receive instructions

how to act.—Ah! If you could get me a copy of Marcel's instructions, we would have them dead to rights!"

"I'll do my damnedest," he said.

CHAPTER IX.

BEGINNER'S LUCK.

THE time that followed was hard on the nerves. Charlie reported to Marcel that Lady Wedderminster was carrying around half a million francs on her person. Marcel reported the fact to his boss, and received instructions from him what to do. But Charlie was unable to find out what those orders were.

Charlie said to us at the next opportunity, "While Marcel was decoding his letter from the boss he caught me looking at it. He didn't say anything, but his face turned ugly. When he had digested the contents he lit a match and burned it up."

"Hm!" said Mme. Storey grimly. "Never allow yourself to look at one of the boss's letters again. Make no attempt to get hold of them. We don't want to lose you. I'll put out another line."

"They write to each other on small pieces of paper," said Charlie, "and enclose their letters in little envelopes about two inches by three in size. There is no address on these envelopes. How they come to Marcel, or how he sends them, I can't guess. They don't go through the mail, and no messengers come to the house. Marcel goes out by himself about nine o'clock every morning, but I reckon it wouldn't be healthy for me to try to follow him."

"It would not," said Mme. Storey. "But you can bring me one of the envelopes they use, if Marcel does not burn them."

Thus we were in the position of expecting to be robbed at any moment, without knowing either when or where the blow would fall. Mme. Storey did, as a matter of fact, carry around the half million francs with her. The bills were marked. What made the strain harder on me was that she took to going out by herself at all hours. That perpendicular line appeared between her brows which always warns me that the situation is serious.

Marcel's instructions to Charlie were merely to "Keep the old girl going." Sometimes, when Charlie met us, Marcel would be with him; sometimes Charlie came alone.

Meanwhile, smart society in Monte Carlo, having been impressed by the social items in the Paris *Herald,* began to take notice of Lady Wedderminster. Amos Rudd sent her one of his characteristic notes, asking her to dinner. She answered it in the third person, with that superb nonchalance of which only the English are capable.

Lady Wedderminster presents her compliments to Mr. Rudd, and begs to thank him for his invitation. Lady Wedderminster never accepts invitations from those whom she has not had the pleasure of meeting.

So much for Amos!

Mr. and Mrs. James Wentworth Hawkins came to call. Their names were announced over the telephone.

"Why are they so famous?" I said.

"For no reason," said Mme. Storey, "except that their names appear so often in the Paris *Herald.* That's what they live for."

WE went down to the hotel drawing room to receive them. I didn't like them any better at a second view. Like so many married couples, they bore a strong resemblance to each other. Fat and brutalized by rich living, they were two of the most useless cumberers of the earth I have ever encountered.

Mme. Storey, alias Lady Wedderminster, was polite and a little bored. She forced them to make the running. They stumbled through it somewhat confusedly, but were determined to see the visit to a finish. When they got up to go, Mrs. Hawkins said effusively:

"I hope you'll set a night when we may have the pleasure of having you to dinner!"

"So kind of you," drawled Lady Wedderminster, playing with her bracelet. "But I've come to Monte Carlo for a rest. I'm not accepting any invitations. I'm sure you'll understand."

"Oh!" said Mrs. Hawkins.

When they had gone, Mme. Storey said dryly: "They won't be any the less anxious to have me, just because they were turned down once."

One afternoon, when Mme. Storey had sat down at a roulette table in the Sporting Club, she found herself almost directly opposite Turner Moale. I was standing meekly behind several others grouped about the table to watch the play.

Mr. Moale paid no attention to us. The man's distinction was remarkable. Even in the hurly-burly around the table he seemed set apart like a little Highness. He was beautifully dressed, and he could gamble without losing his dignity. In his eyes showed that intensely withdrawn look that denotes the born gambler. Well, if you require excitement, there is nothing like roulette. I have enough excitement in my job.

The supposed Lady Wedderminster put a thousand francs on number 33, and won. An excited murmur went around the table. Turner Moale took notice of her. Presently she won again, and refused to play any more for the moment.

"It is so tiresome when everybody follows one's play!" she said casually as we left the table.

WE went into the café and ordered *apéritifs*. Presently Turner Moale came strolling through the rooms, putting on his royal show whether anybody was watching him or not. He stopped by our table.

"May I introduce myself?" he said with engaging affability. "I am Turner Moale."

Lady Wedderminster could afford to unbend with him because his style was so much better than that of the other Americans. "I have heard of you," she said. "Won't you sit down? I am Lady Wedderminster."

"Yes, I know," he said, seating himself.

"How did you know?"

"I asked at the roulette table where we were both playing just now. Everybody around the table knew you. Everybody was talking of your luck."

She frowned. "How annoying!"

"Why?" he asked.

"Somebody may carry the news back to England."

"What of it?" he said.

"I do not come of a gambling family," she said dryly.

"Thank God I have no family!" he said with calm assurance. "And so I can say it openly—I love to gamble! When I gamble, I am twenty-one again!"

Lady Wedderminster s m i l e d. "Sometimes life is dull in England," she said, looking down at her hands.

"You like it here?" he asked.

She shrugged in a manner that allowed him to suppose anything he wished.

"How long shall you remain in Monte Carlo?"

"As long as my luck holds."

"Ah, I wish I could catch a little luck from you, Lady Wedderminster! I always lose!" He said it with a wave of his hand.

"I don't always win," she said.

"But according to the gossip of the tables, you are thousands and thousands ahead," he said, laughing. "Do you know what they call you? The Golden Milady."

Lady Wedderminster smiled.

Charlie came searching for us through the rooms, and she rose like a woman transformed.

"Charlie!" she murmured, slipping her hand under his arm. "I was so afraid you weren't coming!"

Charlie was wise. He realized that a show was being put on for somebody, and he played up to her. "I am a bit late," he said, patting her hand. "So sorry!"

"Come!" she said. "I have so much to tell you. I won a hundred thousand francs to-day."

Suddenly she appeared to recollect Mr. Moale, and became the reserved Englishwoman again. "Oh! Pardon! ... *Au revoir*, Mr. Moale. I hope we may meet soon again."

She moved away, leaning on Charlie's arm.

CHAPTER X.

IN AT THE KILL.

ON the following night, Charlie turned up at the hotel resplendent in evening dress. My heart warmed to him, he was so handsome and droll, so essentially decent. He was very much upset. I could see the faint flush under his pale skin. He came alone, and we received him in the parlor of our suite.

"Rosika," he said in a voice that shook a little, "I'm supposed to persuade you to dine with me to-night at a little place up in the mountains."

"Well, I am persuaded," she said smiling.

"But in the mountains!" he cried in distress. "And in a place chosen by themselves.—I don't know what will happen. How can I go through with it?"

"But I wish to be robbed," said Mme. Storey. "I am counting on it!"

"Don't joke about it! Suppose they were to hurt you!"

"They won't hurt me, because I'm going to squawk and give right up."

"I'm to persuade you to leave Bella at home," he said.

"Oh, no!" I exclaimed involuntarily.

"What! Are you so anxious to be robbed?" asked Mme. Storey teasingly.

"No! But it would be worse to be left here alone, and not to know what was happening. I couldn't bear it."

She considered for a moment. "I believe I'll take Bella in spite of them," she said. "After all, it would be natural for the Englishwoman to have a spasm of propriety at the last moment, and to insist on taking her companion."

"I don't even know where the place is," Charlie went on, pacing the room in his agitation. "Only the chauffeur knows. You see, they don't trust me completely. It's supposed to be called Bruno's, and I was told to describe it to you as a very plain little place, though the last word in smartness. Only a few people know of it. All this is just a stall, I reckon."

"No matter," said Mme. Storey.

"Just as I was leaving," said Charlie, "Marcel caught up my hand to compare my wrist watch with his. He said with a grin, 'Dinner will be served at seven-thirty. When you hear the canary sing, I suggest that you excuse yourself from the room for a moment. It will help to save your face later.' "

"Good!" said Mme. Storey. "That is exactly what you must do."

"I would feel like a cur if I walked out and left you to the mercy of those scoundrels!" cried poor Charlie.

"Your feelings do you credit," she said, "but you must suppress them and use your head."

"All right," he muttered. "But it's not going to be easy!"

WE set off at seven. The car we picked up at the hotel door appeared to be an ordinary taxi, but of course it had been planted there for Charlie. We climbed rapidly through the narrow, twisting streets to the upper town. When we came out on the well-remembered road with the hairpin curves, I turned a little sick with apprehension. La Turbie again!

However, a mile short of that village we turned sharply to the right and sped around the side of the mountain in the opposite direction. The lights of Monte Carlo sparkled fifteen hundred feet below.

"This is the Grand Corniche Road," remarked Mme. Storey. "I have been looking at the map."

After traveling for a mile or two and putting a shoulder of the mountain between us and the friendly lights of town, we drew up before an ordinary little house on the outside of the road; a narrow one-story house clinging to the steep mountainside like a limpet. The windows were shuttered tight.

"Is this the place?" asked Mme. Storey, loud enough to carry to the chauffeur's ear.

"Oui, madame. C'est chez Bruno," he answered. "Un bon restaurant!"

Charlie whispered, "Do you want to turn back? It would be natural."

"No," she said, "I'm supposed to be an infatuated woman. Such a one would be blind."

Certainly a more suitable place for the commission of a crime could scarcely have been found. The little house crouched alone under the stars, surrounded by dark mountain masses.

We got out, and the chauffeur drove on out of sight. The road was too narrow for him to turn around. He was supposed to return for us at eleven.

Charlie rapped at the door, and we were admitted directly into a big kitchen where a white-clad chef presided over the stove, an assistant and a waiter. All had a self-conscious look, as if they had been listening for us. There were no women visible.—But the smell of the cooking was real.

"Anyhow they're going to feed us," murmured Mme. Storey, sniffing.

The men lined up, bowing as the custom is.

There was a look of animal greed in the chef's little eyes. He expressed surprise at the sight of me. "Dinner was ordered for two persons," he said respectfully.

"I brought my companion," said Mme. Storey, in the cold, English voice. "Does it matter?"

"Mais non, madame! There is sufficient. Descend, if you please."

Owing to the manner of the house's construction, the dining room was below. We passed through a narrow hall to the stairs. Opposite the kitchen was a door which stood open just an inch. The room beyond was dark. My skin prickled as I passed that door. Instinct told me there were men in the darkness, listening.

Downstairs, a small, plain room with a table set for two, a sideboard and a sofa. The waiter followed us in and set a third place. He kept his eyes down the whole time, and I was unable to read his expression. At the end of the room there was a glass door leading to a tiny terrace. From the terrace, steps rose to the kitchen above. The windows of the room looked down into a black abyss.

I cannot remember what we ate. Mme. Storey said it was excellent. I shoved the food down my throat merely because I thought it would look suspicious if I sent it back untouched. Charlie's was the hardest part to play, because he was supposed to make a noise as if he was having a good time. He drank a lot of wine.

IN the beginning, there was a good deal of running about, and the sound of voices as if there were parties dining in other rooms. Just stage business I assumed. All this died away, and silence filled the house, except for what noise we made ourselves.

With the coffee and a liqueur the waiter brought the bill. When Charlie had paid it, the man left the room with a furtive look. It was the first time I had seen his eyes.

Presently we heard the main door of the house close, and a bar fall across it. Just for an experiment, Mme. Storey rang the bell. Nobody came.

"The staff has walked out on us," she murmured.

Charlie had the liqueur glass at his lips when the bird whistle was softly sounded upstairs. It was quite obviously one of those lead whistles with a pea in it to imitate a trill.

A cold perspiration broke out on me. Charlie turned pale and put his glass down.

"Must I go?" he murmured.

"Go!" said Mme. Storey. "There is no danger if only you will keep quiet."

"Excuse me a minute," he said, raising his voice; and dragged himself out of the room, starting up the stairs.

He had no more than reached the upper floor when all the lights went out. It was so unexpected that a little cry broke from me. Hysteria gripped my throat. I clung to Mme. Storey.

"Steady!" she whispered. "There is no danger!"

That was all very well for a brave person; but my nerves were fluttering like aspen leaves I almost hate her at such moments.

We heard the door from the terrace open. A flash light was switched on and cast in our eyes. In its light we clung together like any two frightened women. In the light reflected from the walls I could see that two dim shapes had entered. Their faces were indistinguishable. One was a powerful figure.

"Don't scream," said the smaller man, hoarsely.

"What do you want?" asked Mme. Storey, letting a quaver come into her voice.

"The bundle of thousand-franc notes you have on your person," he said. "If you give them up, you won't be harmed." The voice was disguised, but I recognized it.

Mme. Storey hesitated.

"Quick!" the man said, "or I'll take them from you!"

Hastily, she unfastened the notes, which she carried inside her dress, and threw them on the table. He put the light on them.

"All right," he said, thrusting them in his pocket.

Up to that moment, everything had gone exactly as Mme. Storey had foreseen. We would have been allowed to go, and there would have been no trouble, had it not been for one of those accidents that one can never provide against.

I was wearing a string of common crystal beads around my neck. They were of no value, but they were clear and small, and I suppose in the flash of the electric torch they glittered like diamonds. The big man was a common fellow, and he yielded to temptation. Slyly moving close to me, he put his two hands around my neck and jerked the string apart.

When his hands touched me I could not help myself—I screamed with all my might. The sound was too much for Charlie. There was the sound of a blow and a fall from above, and Charlie came leaping down the stairs shouting thickly:

"Keep your hands off them! Keep your hands off them!"

A SCENE of insane confusion followed. The smaller robber shouted: "Silence that fool!"

I had an impression of the big man drawing a gun. Mme. Storey leaped forward and struck the flash light out of the first man's hand. It went out and rolled away on the floor, and we were left in complete darkness.

I heard the man scrabbling on the floor for his torch. The other kept shouting: "Light! Light!"

Somebody grabbed my wrist and pulled me violently toward the door at the foot of the stairs. There we met another man, cascading down the stairs. There was a brief struggle. Somebody was thrown down with a groan, and I was dragged on up the stairs. All this in the dark.

The kitchen was lighted with a candle. Just inside the door stood a fourth man, with a chair raised over his head, prepared to smash the first one who entered. Somehow, we banged through the door across the landing, and got it shut behind us. It had both a bolt and a key. We leaned against it breathing heavily, Mme. Storey, Charlie and I.

"You spoiled everything by your outbreak," said Mme. Storey sternly.

"How could I help it?" groaned Charlie.

"Never mind now. Listen!"

There was a furious pounding at the door, and we backed away from it. Marcel cried out—no longer taking any care to disguise his voice:

"Give us that fellow and we won't hurt you. He brought you here, didn't he? He betrayed you into our hands. Now he has betrayed us. Give him up to us, and we'll let you go."

No answer from our side of the door.

Marcel flung himself against it, cursing horribly. Luckily, it was a heavy door. Several of the men put their shoulders against it. It creaked dangerously, but held. Finally Marcel screamed in a voice breaking with rage:

"The ax! The ax!"

There was a pause. I felt like a rat in a trap. But Mme. Storey actually lit a cigarette. When the light flared up I saw that her face was calm. Inexplicable woman!

Charlie went to a window which opened on the road.

"Don't open the shutters!" she said sharply.

"Can't we do something—something?" I groaned.

"Wait!" she said.

Marcel aimed a blow at the door that split one of the panels but did not shatter it. Before he could strike another, there was a crash from the kitchen and a rush of feet. An appalling struggle took place out there. Not a cry was raised; only the sound of blows and stamping feet, and one crash after another as the tables were overthrown, the crockery broken, the cooking utensils flung together.

"Let me get into this!" said Charlie thickly.

"There is no need," said Mme. Storey, barring the way.

Suddenly it was over, and we heard a low voice issuing commands. Then the voice was raised, calling:

"Lady Wedderminster! Lady Wedderminster!"

"Here!" cried Mme. Storey, unlocking the door.

We followed her into the kitchen. They had got the lights turned on. It was like a battlefield. Against the far wall stood four sullen, beaten men, handcuffed together. Six *gendarmes* took off their *képis* and wiped their moist foreheads. Our old acquaintance, the chief of detectives, was in command.

"*Voilà, madame!*" he said. "You see we have them. You are a brave lady!"

Marcel, frantic with rage, spat out a stream of curses at the sight of Charlie. "Traitor!—Traitor! I'll get you yet!"

"Oh, I reckon you'll be put away for quite a spell," drawled Charlie.

MARCEL was wearing a brown suit. All the buttons were on it to-night.

Mme. Storey walked to him and examined it attentively. "Chief," she said, turning, "one of the murderers of Raoul d'Aymara wore a suit of this material. You have the button that was pulled off his coat. It was the middle button on this coat. You can see where the hole in the cloth has been stopped. And the present button has been sewed on with cotton thread, not silk like the others. This is your man!"

The chief's face was a study. "But, madame," he stammered, "how did you—how did you know about that affair?"

"All will be explained later," she said.

He knew her then, and his eyes almost started from his head. "Incredible!—Incredible!" he whispered.

Marcel knew her, too. A wild terror came into his face. He had no more to say.

"Chief," said Mme. Storey, "I beg that you will take these men into town and lock them up quietly and secretly. If the news of their arrest should get about, their master will escape us."

"I understand, *madame,*" he answered, bowing. "It shall be done."

Charlie could no longer hold himself in. "How did the police get here?" he demanded.

"I gave them a tip," said Mme. Storey, carelessly.

"How did you know where the place was? I didn't know."

"I intercepted Marcel's instructions from his boss this morning."

"Good heavens!" muttered Charlie. "You might have let me know," he added in a grumbling voice. "It would have saved me a lot of mental agony."

"Exactly," she said smiling. "That's why I didn't tell you. You were watched every minute. This was your first job, and if you had not appeared to be nervous their suspicions would have been aroused ... But I admit I

ought not to have brought Bella along," she added teasingly. "That was an error of judgment."

I hung my head. "Well, if you had felt that man's fingers around your throat ..."

She laughed.

MME. STOREY accompanied the chief of detectives back to town, in order to be present when he compared the button and its torn piece of cloth with Marcel's coat. She sent me directly to the hotel with Charlie, and I did not see her again that night.

Next morning when I got up she had already gone out. Shortly before ten, she returned wearing an inscrutable smile. "Get your hat, Bella, if you want to be in at the death," she said.

The chief of detectives was waiting for us in the lobby of the hotel. The three of us crossed the street and entered the Casino, which had not yet opened its doors for the day. Our companion concealed himself in the room on the left, where one presents his credentials and obtains cards for the gaming rooms, while we took up a position in the middle of the entrance hall. Through the glass we could see the most determined gamblers waiting on the steps for the doors to open.

"What are we here for?" I asked. I was still nervous.

"To nab the big boss," she said, smiling.

"How will we know him?"

"He will come out of the cloakroom, the *vestiaire*—if he comes at all—carrying a very swanky overnight bag of brown seal."

At that moment the doors were opened and the waiting people swarmed through. First, they all made their way to the cloakroom to leave their wraps.

Along with the intending gamblers there was a large personally-conducted party of tourists, and all this made a great deal of confusion. I could not possibly distinguish everybody.

"Never mind their faces," said Mme. Storey. "Watch for the bag. I checked it here myself half an hour ago."

She took pity on the torment of curiosity that my face must have expressed, and in a low voice she explained what had happened, without ever ceasing to use her keen, busy eyes on the people who passed to and fro in front of us.

"Their method of corresponding was as simple as it was ingenious. It was Marcel's habit to board a bus every morning at nine o'clock. That gave me the lead. I noticed that he always took the same bus—number sixty-three. He occupied the last seat in the left-hand corner, where he would slip his little envelope in the crack of the cushioned seat and leave it there. He always got out at the Casino Gardens. Somewhere further along the route, the boss would get on and find his letter or leave one.

"Bus sixty-three was their post-office. On its return trip, Marcel would board it to see if anything had been left for him. As soon as I got on to this, I waited for the bus after Marcel got off, copied the note, enclosed it in a fresh envelope, replaced it, and got off again. If I had continued to the end of the line, I might have been able to spot the boss, but the risk was too great. You see, it would have been entirely out of character for Lady Wedderminster to be found riding on ordinary street busses."

"How could you read their letters?" I asked.

"With the dictionary it was easy. Without the dictionary, their code would have baffled the greatest expert of them all. For any word beginning with A they would put down the first word that followed it in the dictionary. For a word beginning with B the second word that followed it, and so on through the alphabet. The language used was English, and to make detection more difficult, all the little words, such as pronouns, prepositions and articles, were written in correctly."

"Where does the brown seal bag come in?"

"In the boss's final instructions to Marcel yesterday, he told him to put the half million francs in the bag, check it at the *vestiaire* of the Casino, and send him the check in the usual manner. I found the bag in Marcel's room, and I obeyed instructions."

TIME passed. The gamblers hurried past us with their curiously intent expressions, as if they were bound on errands of life and death. The tourist party, having been taken for a tour of the rooms, streamed out of the building gaping. A ceaseless procession of motorcars rolled up to the door and discharged their aristocratic freight. Beyond, the sun was glorious on a bed of pink cyclamens.

The suspense was horrible. I was looking for something I had never seen. Suppose our man had had a warning and failed to turn up? One of the most difficult things in the world is to keep your attention focused on individuals in a moving crowd. Scores of faces, passing one after another, have a hypnotic effect. In spite of yourself they begin to blur; they all look alike.

I had a dread that I might fail. I couldn't take things in quick enough. People passed with the lower part of their bodies hidden. "Stop! Stop!" I cried in my mind. But they were already gone.

In the end, I was staring at the brown bag for a full second, I suppose, before I realized with a terrific shock that *that* was what I was waiting for. My heart began to pound; my eyes flew to the face of the man who carried it ... It was Turner Moale. I experienced a curiously gone feeling, as if the earth had dropped away under me.

Turner Moale walking out of the *vestiaire* as if he owned all Monte Carlo! He was clad in a springtime symphony of grays; hat, tie, suit, spats; with yellow gloves and a yellow carnation in his buttonhole. Mme. Storey dropped her umbrella on the floor with a clatter, and the chief of detectives appeared from his place of concealment.

"Lady Wedderminster!" c r i e d Moale gaily. "You *are* astir early! And going to play at the Casino, too?"

"Chief!" said Mme. Storey a little grimly. "There is your man."

That unhappy official turned as pale as paper. "But, *madame*," he protested, "surely there is a mistake. Monsieur Turner Moale is one of our most prominent residents!"

"Oh, quite!" said Mme. Storey. "But in that bag you will find the half million francs that was stolen from me last night."

The man's aplomb was perfect. He never turned a hair.

"Why, Lady Wedderminster, what is the matter?" he asked, laughing. "You appear to be making a charge against me. How odd!"

"*Monsieur,* this lady is Madame Rosika Storey," said the shaken chief.

This was a facer for Moale. The moment he was told who she was, he recognized her.

He took it on the chin.

"So it is!" he cried, almost gayly. "But what has that to do with me, *monsieur?*"

"Look in the bag," suggested Mme. Storey to the chief. "Here is a key. I found it in Marcel's room."

"In Marcel's room!" repeated Moale sharply. His dark eyes rolled like those of an ugly horse.

"Marcel Durocher and the shock troops were arrested at Bruno's last night," she said dryly.

The chief took a look in the bag, and his hesitation vanished.

He placed a hand on Turner Moale's shoulder.

"Remove your hand!" said Moale like an offended Highness—and the policeman obeyed.

Moale instantly recovered his affability. "Let us not make a public scene," he said. "My car is here. Come to my house and we'll talk it over."

"I suggest the police station," said Mme. Storey.

Driving away in the car, Moale suddenly dropped his pretense of innocence. "Lady, I salute you!" he said in his gay manner. "How did you come to pick on me?"

Mme. Storey loves a good loser. "Have a cigarette," she said. "I suspected you because I couldn't figure out where a retired actor had found the money to entertain on such a princely scale."

"You are marvelous!" he cried—but all the steam had gone out of it. Suddenly he looked shrunken and old, and I couldn't help feeling a kind of regret.

It was like witnessing the destruction of a unique work of art.

MEANWHILE, Charlie had been sent to sit on the terrace, where he was told to read the little white book. It was the agreed signal between the wolves. One by one, they approached the reader. He sent them to Marcel's room on the pretext that they were to receive instructions there, and each one was arrested as he came. Thus the whole bunch was rounded up in the course of the day.

There was no evidence against these handsome good-for-nothings, and they were merely sent out of the principality with a warning not to return; an exile that would pretty well ruin them all.

Mrs. Rudd likewise escaped punishment, though she was certainly an accomplice of Moale's. It seemed that her wealthy husband had always kept too tight a hand on the purse strings, and Moale had paid her well for her help. She presently ran away with a more open-handed man, and old Amos married again.

When the trial came on, Marcel Durocher gave evidence against his associates. The three men who were arrested with him at Bruno's were the same three who had assisted at the murder of Raoul d'Aymara. Marcel related his dealings with Turner Moale in detail. He swore that until the moment when he was brought face to face with Moale in court he had never laid eyes on him, and didn't know who he was.

Moale was sent to prison for life—not a long term in his case. Marcel got twenty years. And the three others received lesser sentences.

As for Charlie Raines, having had the adventure of his life, he was perfectly content to sail for home and take a job in the old man's stove factory. From Cherbourg he sent me a postcard with a spirited sketch of himself balancing a kitchen stove on the tip of his nose. Underneath he had written: "Ex-gigolo juggling junk!"

THE END.

ʊ   ʊ   ʊ

Strangest Forest Fire

IN the Angeles National Forest, California, a fire was started recently by an odd assortment of incidents which sound like a Rube Goldberg cartoon.

A gopher hustling through the grass crossed the path of an extremely vicious snake which instantly sank its fangs into the small animal. The struggle between the rodent and the reptile stirred the curiosity, or appetite, of a hawk lurking overhead. Down swooped the bird and it in turn seized the snake in his powerful claws.

However, none of the combatants reckoned on the nearness of a high tension wire, for when the bird rose they struck the line and became entwined about it. Shorted, the wire crackled and fell to the ground, setting fire to some dry brush.

The only ones left to relate the tale were the fire fighters who, after some slight damage had been caused, extinguished the blaze.

Edward J. Wilkinson.

"Murder by Mail" by Frederick Nebel, *Dime Detective Magazine,* June 1936. Copyright © 1936 Blazing Publications Inc. (*) All rights reserved. Used with permission Dorothy B. Nebel.

"The Domino Lady Doubles Back" by Lars Anderson, *Saucy Romantic Adventures,* June 1936. Copyright © 1936 Fiction Magazines Inc. Certified search shows no notice of renewal.

"Fingers of Fear" by Frederick C. Davis, *Ten Detective Aces,* September 1934. Copyright © 1934 Magazine Publishers Inc. Certified search shows no notice of renewal.

"The Duchess Pulls a Fast One" by Whitman Chambers, *Detective Fiction Weekly,* September 19, 1936. Copyright © Blazing Publications Inc. (*) All rights reserved. Reprinted by special arrangement with Mystery Writers of America Inc.

"Double Trouble" by Richard Sale, *Detective Fiction Weekly,* October 31, 1936. Copyright © 1936 Blazing Publications Inc. (*) All rights reserved. Used with permission Richard Sale.

"Death to the Hunter" by Judson Philips, *Detective Fiction Weekly,* February 18, 1933. Copyright © 1933 Blazing Publications Inc. (*) All rights reserved. Reprinted with permission Brandt & Brandt Literary Agency Inc. and Judson Philips.

"The Jane from Hell's Kitchen" by Perry Paul, *Gun Molls Magazine,* October 1930. A certified search shows no notice of copyright.

"Snowbound" by C. B. Yorke, *Gangster Stories,* October 1931. Copyright © 1931 Good Story Magazine Co. A certified search shows no notice of renewal.

"The Lady from Hell: The Episode of the Secret Service Blackmail" by Eugene Thomas, *Detective Fiction Weekly,* February 9, 1935. Copyright © 1935 Blazing Publications Inc. (*) All rights reserved. Reprinted by special arrangement with Mystery Writers of America Inc.

"Wolves of Monte Carlo" by Hulbert Footner, *Argosy,* August 5, 1933. Copyright © 1933 Blazing Publications Inc. (*) All rights reserved. Reprinted by special arrangement with Mystery Writers of America Inc.

(*) Blazing Publications Inc. is the successor-in-interest to Popular Publications Inc., The Frank A. Munsey Company, and The Red Star News Company.

Attempts to reach certain of the authors or their heirs have been unsuccessful.

BGSU LIBRARY

DISCARD

POP CULT PS 648 .D4 H37 1986

Hard-boiled dames

A113 0923257 4